W9-CDA-732

Don Green —

ALSO BY ADAM SMITH

The Money Game
Supermoney
Powers of Mind

PAPER

SUMMIT
BOOKS
NEW YORK

MONEY

BY
ADAM SMITH

Copyright © 1981 by George J. W. Goodman
All rights reserved
including the right of reproduction
in whole or in part in any form
Published by SUMMIT BOOKS
A Simon & Schuster Division of Gulf & Western Corporation
Simon & Schuster Building
1230 Avenue of the Americas
New York, New York 10020
SUMMIT BOOKS and colophon are trademarks of Simon & Schuster
Designed by Irving Perkins Associates
Manufactured in the United States of America
Printed and Bound by the Haddon Craftsmen, Inc.
First edition

Library of Congress Cataloging in Publication Data

S, Adam, 1930-
Paper money.
Bibliography: p.
1. Inflation (Finance)   2. International finance.
3. Economic history-- 1945-.   4. Organization of
Petroleum Exporting Countries.   I. Title.
HG229.S62   332   80-29184

ISBN 0-671-44825-0

Some of the material in this book has
previously appeared in different
form in *The Atlantic Monthly* and *Esquire*.

Contents

Acknowledgments

This book has many debts. I would like to thank particularly those who read the manuscript and commented on it. Naturally, the responsibility for it is my own. I owe thanks to the Department of Economics of Princeton University, on whose Advisory Council I have served for thirteen years, and to its chairman, Professor Burton W. Malkiel, for facilities made available to me.

Professor Dwight Jaffee of Princeton not only read the chapter on housing but assisted in preparing the charts for that chapter. Roger Starr of the Editorial Board of *The New York Times,* a former housing commissioner, also commented on the housing chapter.

The chapters on the dollar, the impact of oil prices, and the recycling of the dollar were read by Ralph A. Dungan, United States Director of the Inter-American Bank; John G. Heimann, Comptroller of the Currency of the United States; Charles Morris of the Chase Manhattan Bank; and Peter B. Kenen, Walker Professor of Economics and International Finance at Princeton University. I am thankful for all of their comments.

Professor Geoffrey Watson of Princeton gave me useful comments on the problems of modeling and quantitative techniques

9

and on the economists, as did Professor Robert Lekachman of the City University of New York, in the material on Keynes in the same chapter.

I am particularly grateful to Dr. Thomas McHale, former Senior Adviser to the Kingdom of Saudi Arabia, and to Wanda Jablonski, publisher of *Petroleum Intelligence Weekly,* for giving me their comments on the development of OPEC and the role of the Saudis; and I thank Dr. McHale also for his hospitality in the Middle East.

In connection with the same material, I am grateful to Dr. Juan Pablo Perez Castillo, the director for Venezuela of the Inter-American Bank, for material concerning his father's role in the history of OPEC.

I wish to thank Professor J. C. Hurewitz of the Middle East Institute of Columbia University for inviting me into the continuing seminar of experts on Middle East problems.

I thank Daniel Yergin, director of the Energy Project of the Kennedy School at Harvard and co-editor of the Harvard Business School energy report, for his thoughtful comments throughout the manuscript, particularly on energy and recycling. I would like to thank also Professor Robert Stobaugh of the Harvard Business School, the other co-editor of the Harvard energy report, for early assistance in dealing with this topic. Professors Hendrik Houthakker and A. J. Meyer of Harvard were also helpful in an early stage.

For giving me comments on the material on the stock market, I am thankful to Warren Buffett of Omaha, Nebraska, Martin Sosnoff, chairman of Atalanta Corporation, New York, and Burton Malkiel of Princeton.

I am grateful to Professor Lester Thurow of MIT and Robert M. Solow, Institute Professor of Economics at MIT, for their time, their comments, and the use of some unpublished material.

I wish to acknowledge also former Undersecretary Robert V. Roosa, Assistant Secretary C. Fred Bergsten, former Secretary W. Michael Blumenthal, and especially former Undersecretary George W. Ball.

Also John Lichtblau of the American Petroleum Institute, Stephen Stamas of Exxon, Pierre Wack of Royal Dutch/Shell, Jack

Sunderland of Coroil, and Charles Maxwell of Cyrus J. Lawrence, Inc.

Also Professor Dankwart A. Rustow of New York University, Professor Robert Triffin of the University of Louvain, Geoffrey Bell of J. Henry Schroder International, Ltd., Walter Levy of W. J. Levy and Associates, Professor Charles Issawi of Princeton University, Professor Richard Quandt of Princeton University, Professor Bernard Lewis of the Institute for Advanced Study at Princeton, and Alan Greenspan of Townsend-Greenspan and Co., Inc.

For assistance in statistics appropriate to their fields, I am grateful to David Armour of the International Monetary Fund, David Foster of Salomon Brothers, and Lawrence Goldstein of Drexel, Burnham and Co.

Melvina al-Izmirli of the Embassy of Saudi Arabia in Washington provided patient help with the checking on that country. Kevin Lippert's assistance was of great help in the research.

Finally, I wish to thank three journalists who have written so well in these fields. They were generous with their notes, their sources, and their insights. They are Anthony Sampson in London, and Martin Mayer and Chris Welles in New York.

1

IF TIMES HAVE BEEN SO GOOD, WHY DO WE FEEL SO BAD?

Dr. Burns

Every once in a while, almost a decade ago, I would get a skidding feeling. You know the feeling. You are in your car, listening to the radio or just thinking, and very momentarily, the wheels are not solidly on the road, which is wet from rain or snow. Subliminally you sense that slide, you snap back to awareness, you react. I was getting this feeling, not in a car, but sitting at a desk, reading about prices and money rates. Sometimes I got the feeling in the supermarket when the clerk gave me the change—very little change. I made an appointment to see Dr. Burns.

There was nothing wrong with me physically, and Dr. Burns was not a medical doctor. He was an economist, and at that time he was chairman of the Board of Governors of the Federal Reserve, the government's bank. Naturally I did not want to say, "I have this skidding feeling about inflation," as if it were a stomachache, so I framed some questions that I hoped were intelligent, and I rehearsed them in the taxi on the way to the Federal Reserve Board building in Washington. Then, as it turned out, halfway through our talk I said, "I have this skidding feeling."

I was known to Dr. Burns because, two years before, I had noticed a dangerous situation which the Federal Reserve averted. I wrote a brief account of the panic that did not happen, "The Day the Music Almost Died," in *Supermoney*. The Penn Central Company had gone bankrupt on a Sunday morning, leaving $200 million in commercial paper worthless, as well as other debts, and it was feared that on the following Monday and Tuesday the markets would be so frightened that they would not renew the existing short-term debt of other shaky borrowers. The next names on the list were Lockheed, Chrysler, and Pan American. If those large borrowers couldn't find money somewhere, they could not pay their bills, and then their creditors wouldn't be able to pay *their* bills, and a financial avalanche would start. The Federal Reserve called up its member banks and said they should come and get the money needed to weather the crunch and to put that money out. It was like having a huge overload in the network of electric utilities which would black out the country, and then having a master engineer pull all the reserve power into the system. Actually, that is what the Federal Reserve is supposed to do, and why it is called the "Lender of Last Resort." The big marginal borrowers still had their problems—even now they do—but the *system* went right on functioning, and nobody noticed, just as nobody notices a power blackout that doesn't happen.

When you enter the government's bank, the Federal Reserve, the uniformed guard at the desk asks you your name and purpose, writes those items in his ledger, phones for your escort, and clips a pass to your lapel. Wide marble stairs, left and right, allow the center space of the atrium to rise three stories. The floors are Italian and Belgian travertine marble, as befits a bank. Your footsteps echo as you walk. On the second-floor balcony you see a curious phenomenon: six huge dark-brown doors, spaced out along each balcony, facing another six huge dark-brown doors on the opposite balcony, the atrium in between. One door for each of the twelve regional Federal Reserve banks. They are a stage setting, perhaps for a Hitchcock movie. You would expect to find, beyond each of them, a baronial, cavernous boardroom, with high ceilings and oversized furniture. The doors do open, but into quite ordinary offices, with metal desks and metal filing cabinets and electric typewriters. There is no particular relationship of any of the doors to any of the offices.

There are no tellers, no grilles, and not much in the way of human traffic. The French architect Paul Philippe Cret worked in symbols other than the twelve great doors: the nature goddess Cybele in relief over the fireplace in the long room in which the governors meet, and the Great Seal of the Federal Reserve in the floor. With the height of the ceilings, and the chandeliers, and the indirect lighting, he gave the building the feeling of a temple, if not a cathedral—hushed, majestic, appropriate for a great bank.

When this building was constructed, in 1937, it was the first in Washington to have central air conditioning. Like a proper small cathedral, it has some works of art, part of a collection donated by an industrialist, but the subjects of the art are not the theme of the bank. The collection travels to museums, and the bank borrows their paintings in turn, so that the art on the walls of the bank changes.

The framers of the law that created this Bank were literally panic-stricken. Schoolchildren once learned the dates of bank panics in history as if they were battles: the

Panic of 1837, the Panic of 1873, the Panic of 1893, the
Panic of 1907. Boom, bust, the agitated lines of depositors
stretching out into the street, people anxious to get their
money out while it was possible; then collapse, and depression. When Congress established this Reserve system in
1913, it contemplated that the Reserve could stop a run on
the country's banks with money that was not gold, not
silver, not anything in the vaults. By a series of mecha-
nisms, the Federal Reserve could add money to the government's own bank account. Stricken banks would have a
senior friend, and the Federal Reserve, the central bank,
would regulate the country's supply of money. This office
has great financial power.

In his book-lined office, Arthur Burns is smoking his
pipe. That is no surprise. He is almost never without it; he
takes it to the House, the Senate, the White House; he can
orchestrate the lighting of it between sentences like an
actor. He wears rimless glasses, and his white hair is parted
in the middle. He is a former Columbia University professor, an authority on business cycles. After we have talked
for a while, I bring up my question.

"What," I say, "is an acceptable rate of inflation?"

A cloud of pipe smoke rolls across the coffee table.

"An acceptable rate of inflation? An acceptable rate?
Why, zero. Zero!"

That was not the number I had been expecting. It was,
quite probably, the last time anyone set *zero* as an inflation
rate. It was a good answer, very Burnsian, the kind of
answer that had made him a symbol of probity throughout
the world. But I don't quite believe him. I have this feeling . . .

"Skidding?" says Arthur Burns. "Skidding?" He relights
his pipe and considers the symptom. Like a sympathetic
internist, he nods.

"Something has happened to our system of responses,"

he says. "This long and unhappy war, the American people are troubled, busing, urban race riots, women marching in the streets . . .

"If only life would quiet down for a while," says Arthur Burns.

Life did not, needless to say. The war ended and the campuses quieted down, but gas lines appeared. OPEC became a familiar acronym. "Energy crisis" produced a glaze in the eyes of listeners. Unconsciously, instinctively, Americans began to feel disorder, change, a sense of entropy about their economic future. They no longer had the warm postwar feeling that this is the American century and we control our destiny; instead, there was a visceral malaise, like a dark shadow in a half-remembered dream.

In the spring of 1980, Arthur Burns went to testify before the Senate Banking Committee. He was no longer the chairman of the Federal Reserve, he was a scholar at an institute; but his views were sought, and he no longer said anything about a zero rate of inflation. He had, himself, that skidding feeling. He brought with him his own favorite three causes of inflation, and nine causes that other people had mentioned (see Notes in the back of this book). He said that the feeling of security produced by the social legislation of the 1930s was disappearing, with "ominous consequences," and he worried about the "social glue" that held the society together.

In the 1970s there were two ways to notice that the behavior of Americans was changing. The first was to read the statistics that said that Americans were no longer saving as much and were borrowing as much as they could. The second was to listen to the talk, almost obsessive talk, about prices, *things,* real estate, houses—especially houses. How much is your house worth? What did you pay for it? How much is that apartment? The unarticulated theme of these conversations was this: How do I get out of the currency and into something that will hold its value, or increase? Where is the store of value? The assumption, quite correctly, was that simply to hold dollars was to lose.

Winston Churchill once said, "We shape our houses, and then they shape us." He was referring to the architecture of the House of Commons, but his remark is marvelously apt. We shape our institutions, and then they shape us. The currency is an institution. (By currency, I mean the broadest definition, that which is used as the medium of exchange, the store of value.) When people believe in the currency, they save it and lend it for long periods of time, and those long periods permit still other institutions to take hold. In the nineteenth century the British government sold bonds that were perpetual. A generation ago the United States government could easily sell bonds due in thirty years. In the 1920s, in their hyperinflation, the Germans would not hold their currency for an hour. They felt they were in the hands of dark and alien forces. The "social glue," in Arthur Burns's phrase, dissolved, and in the confusion, that previously well-ordered society listened to the voices in the microphones that offered easy villains and simple solutions.

This book is an account of how we got to where we are and a sketch of some events that may lie ahead. You have a powerful advantage in understanding these events, because you are reading a book. I mean this quite seriously. Most of your countrymen get their information now from images. Television is wonderful for drama, for personality, for games confined by time and space. But this is not a story that lends itself particularly well to images, because it contains some abstractions. Some people, including me, have tried to broaden the story into images, but not with much success. Even in this account, numbers must sometimes be the characters, leaving the human actors to be described only by brief Homeric epithets.

Yet, following one trail and then another, I have found the relationships between events and people and behavior to be fascinating, as compelling as any television drama. For example: We are familiar with the shock of oil prices and the strains it has placed on the economy. Although OPEC began officially in Baghdad, it really began in the bedside notebook of a South American lawyer who was an admirer of one of our own institutions, the Texas Railroad Commission. The cartel that so aroused this man was formed by some grouse shooters at a castle in Achnacarry, Scotland. The action that triggered the formation of OPEC took place on the twenty-ninth floor of a Manhattan skyscraper. The banking system that received the vast flow of funds from the oil producers grew from the actions of a Russian bureaucrat in London. The grouse shooters, the lawyer, and the Russian all have something to do with the worth of a bank account and the price of a house.

This is only one part of the story. But detailing these connections has a purpose other than sketching some little-known history.

It is not only the warm, comfortable postwar feeling of being in control of destiny that is gone; it is the warm, comfortable margin for error. We may muddle through the world's financial problems, but there are some dangerous flash points ahead.

If difficult times arrive, will people understand what has happened? Or will they seek easy villains and simple solutions? After seven years of an oil crisis, four Americans in ten don't know we import any oil. Think of all those supertankers wallowing into the oil ports; think of $90 billion a year going out for the oil in those tankers; think of gas lines, odd and even days, the "moral equivalent of war"; still, nearly half the people don't get the idea that we take in the oil and send out the money.

Gallup polls like that give me the same skidding feeling

I had when I read all the numbers and went to see Arthur Burns.

How We Got to Where We Are: The Old Days

We have gotten so used to inflation now that we have forgotten what it was like to operate in an environment in which prices did not leap and sellers did not build in an extra piece for inflation. The inflation rate in the United States in the first half of the 1960s was between 1 percent and 2 percent.

So, while some elements of this story go back to 1928, and 1717, and 1913, 1965 makes a very good starting point. The economy was running at full capacity then, and the United States was escalating its presence in Vietnam. The planes and the jet fuel and the combat boots were going to cost something, and the bill had to be paid. But Lyndon Johnson chose to duck the explicit way, which would have been to raise the money in taxes.

President Johnson, as quoted by David Halberstam, said: "I don't know much about economics, but I do know the Congress. And I can get the Great Society through right now—this is a golden time. We've got a good Congress and I'm the right President and I can do it. But if I talk about the cost of the war, the Great Society won't go through. Old Wilbur Mills will sit down there and he'll thank me kindly and send me back my Great Society, and then he'll tell me that they'll be glad to spend whatever we need for the war."

When the Council of Economic Advisers began to press him for a tax increase, Johnson summoned key members of the House Ways and Means Committee to ask their advice. But the figures he gave them for Vietnam were deliberately low, and with those figures the Ways and Means Committee let him go back to the council and say that he had gone to Congress and discussed it but could not get the votes.

With the civilian economy already operating at capacity, military needs competed with civilian needs, army boots with civilian shoes, military industries with civilian industries, producing a classic excess-demand inflation: not enough goods. All wars must be paid for; in this case the tax was not explicit, a special tax, but implicit: inflation. So we began with the unpaid bill of the Vietnam War.

The inflation that President Nixon faced was modest by current standards, but at roughly 5 percent it was still double its pre-Vietnam standard. Classic medicine was spooned out: tighter credit, higher taxes. The economy slowed down, but the inflation didn't. It had more momentum than the medicine spooners figured. By August 1971 Nixon had to face a decision, just as Johnson had. The polls showed that Nixon was running behind Edmund Muskie in a potential reelection fight. So Nixon adopted a twofold approach: he ordered wage and price controls, and at the same time his fiscal policies stimulated the economy. Arthur Burns, who had picked zero as a good rate of inflation, was at the helm when the money supply ballooned, which led his critics to say that his goal was all pipe smoke. Nixon's tactic worked in its timing; at election time the economy was rosy and prices, by law, relatively stable. But once the election was over, the controls had to come off. The suppressed inflation burst forth again; all the businesses that had frozen their prices marked them up as soon as they were legally able to, and demand was high because of all the excess money around.

To the political moves of Presidents Johnson and Nixon you could also add the weather and the missing anchovies. The weather helped to produce a bad wheat crop in Russia, and the Nixon administration saw an opportunity to win some points from the farmers in the election. But it sold too much wheat. Once the Russians took their purchased wheat away, Americans scrambled to buy their own grain.

There is always some out-of-place variable like the anchovies. In this case the anchovies swam away from the coast of Peru, no one knows where to, and the fish that ate the anchovies followed them, and the fishermen came back without the fish, and the European cattle feeders who normally used fish meal as feed switched to grain, and flew to Minneapolis and occupied the hotel rooms the Russians were just checking out of. The result was an explosion in grain prices.

So our overture has political decisions and industrial inflation and agricultural inflation—a nice running head start, but so far, all very classic kinds of inflation, not enough goods for the money.

And while the hotels of Minneapolis were filling with grain traders, and the money was flowing and business was good, OPEC was yawning and stretching its muscles like an aroused leopard, and that is such a major change we will come back to it in a while.

If Inflation Hasn't Been So Bad, Why Do We Complain So Much?

Inflation is complex, as you can see, and all the simple stories about it are too simple.

There are two simple factors involved, though, which you already know.

The first is that when you pay more dollars for something, one of your fellow citizens gets those extra dollars. Obviously. Our economy is already "indexed" to some degree. If it were perfectly indexed, everything would go up at exactly the same rate—wages and prices and dividends. So one problem is that some things go up more than others, leaving unhappy those who lag in the escalation.

The second point you already know is that things used

to go up and down, and they don't do that anymore. They go up and up. Or they go up, pause, look around, and go up again.

The way economists put this is to say that wages and prices have lost their sensitivity to changes in business. Automobile sales may fall apart, but the price of automobiles doesn't go down, nor do the wages of auto workers. What do you think is going to get cheaper? Do you put off buying anything until the price comes down? Some things do get cheaper: electronic calculators, home computers, items whose technology is leapfrogging. Some things we don't notice much and don't complain about: toasters, electric alarm clocks.

Everything else seems to go up: houses, shoes, doctor bills, tuition, cars, food, haircuts, lipstick, chewing gum. In a period of slack, prices are, the economists say, "sticky downward." When business improves, the prices unstick and go upward.

We don't really know why prices are sticky downward, but one probable reason is that this is the price we have paid for the prosperity and stability we have had since the Great Depression. If recessions are short and contained, sellers stand pat and wait for the upturn, to cover their costs. Unemployed workers draw their benefits; they usually don't go out and take any job at any price. But most businesses don't fire people when their sales slack off, because they think sales will pick up again and they don't want to lose good people to their competitors.

If businesses were as frightened as they were in the 1930s, they would sell at a loss and let their workers go, and workers would take any job. But we don't have that kind of fear as a motivation, and we certainly wouldn't want to have it.

In the past decade we developed not only inflation but the *expectation* of inflation, and that psychological force is easily the equal of all the technical economic forces.

Economists will also tell you, just looking at the numbers, that things have not been so bad. We only think they've been bad.

For example, the 1960s were a period of optimism, and the 1970s of pessimism, so the 1960s were booming and not the 1970s, right?

The 1960s were indeed booming. Real income, corrected for inflation, went up 30 percent. And the 1970s? Real income went up 28 percent, almost the same. And those gains were spread out among white and black, farm and urban, male and female. Some groups do fare worse than others: academic salaries haven't kept pace, nor have those of newspaper reporters, for example. But the culprit isn't just inflation; the number of students in universities is dropping off, so university faculties are shrinking, not expanding as they did in the 1960s. And there have recently been as many students in journalism schools as there are reporters and editors in the whole profession, perhaps a fallout from the drama of Watergate. Inflation gets blamed sometimes when it is not the cause, and if we ever get inflation back to zero, it may surprise us to find we still have some problems left. But on the average, the gains are spread out.

Then why do we feel so bad? Lester Thurow, a cherubic former Rhodes scholar, an MIT economist, suggests two reasons. One is "money illusion." Wages went up 134 percent in the 1970s, but "real wages," adjusted for inflation, went up only 28 percent. That's like getting a raise of $134, but having $106 immediately taken away. You feel robbed. You don't consider that much of your raise was inflation. The second related element is our puritanism. We think we earn what we get, so we deserve the whole $134. Some hidden force is taking the money away when we deserve it all.

Robert Solow, a cheerful, ebullient MIT economics professor, suggests still another reason why we feel bad: we have to work harder for the same goods. In the thirty years after World War II, productivity went up and up, and so did the standard of living. It took less and less labor per hour to turn out the same goods. But recently productivity has flattened out. Is that because nobody wants to work hard anymore? Or because Yankee ingenuity has disappeared? Or because so much money goes into government regulation, which doesn't turn out more goods per hour?

Professor Solow grants that yes, we have more regulation; yes, we allocate more to the environment; and yes, maybe technological change has slowed a bit. But what the numbers really tell us is that the work force has expanded, particularly with young workers—the baby boom, grown up—and with wives going to work. It takes a while for newer workers to be productive. That bulge in the labor force hasn't been matched by spending on new equipment, and new equipment makes each worker more productive.

This is cheerful news, because those workers are going to get more productive with experience. And we could devise tax incentives for businesses to speed up the ordering of new equipment. The tax laws may get better. So if we realize our illusions, if we improve our productivity, our national mood will improve.

We have touched, very briefly, on some elements in the story of paper money we won't be coming back to again: wages, prices, "sticky downward," and "money illusion," the last being that empty feeling we get from having more money and less satisfaction.

There are two other elements in the story of paper money that sometimes carry the whole blame for inflation. Unless you're used to the terms, they can sound very abstract. The first such element is deficits in the federal budget: the government spends more than it takes in. There is one obvious way this adds to inflation. When the government doesn't take in as much money as it spends, it has to go to the marketplace and borrow the rest. In the marketplace it meets private borrowers, who might be borrowing to build new plants or new houses. When the government competes heavily with those borrowers, that competition forces interest rates up, and interest is one of the costs of doing business.

But some folks say more than that; they say *all* our problems would be solved if only the government balanced its budget. Before we agree to that, though, we have to see what the federal government does with its money. What if the federal government gave the money it borrowed to the cities and states? Sometimes the states are in surplus when the federal government is in deficit. So we have to take all the governments together, federal, state, and local; and when we do, we see that the deficits don't necessarily match the inflation rate. Governments obviously ought not to be in deficit all the time, because then they are attempting to be the first beneficiaries of inflation: they borrow from savers and repay with cheaper dollars. If the government does not believe in the currency, who will? Lenders get more and more reluctant to lend to governments that borrow more and more. The government and its budget are indeed a problem, but not the only problem.

The second element that some folks assign all the blame to is another part of the government: the Federal Reserve. "Some folks" in this case are the monetarists, who can play many tunes on one fiddle string. They say, for example, that if the Federal Reserve kept the supply of money to a low, predictable rate, all else would follow. There's no question that a supply of money growing faster than the output of goods and services contributes to inflation. The Federal Reserve says it is committed to slowing down growth in the supply of money. Yet, in the Notes of this book, you will find a simple table of two measures of the money supply; in the past five years, inflation increases even as the money supply begins to contract. So the money supply alone is not the cause of inflation. The money supply, like energy, is a subject for arguments of theological intensity, and you can find a great deal already published if you wish to pursue this.

Taking for granted that we live in an interdependent world, all of these elements are at least theoretically under our control as a nation: wages, prices, productivity, "sticky downward," federal budgets, and the money supply. Having said that all simple stories about inflation are too simple, and having mentioned these elements from the domestic "track," we are going to follow the "outside" track on the trail of the money. That is a story that ranges out of economics and into politics and international affairs and all over the world. In it the elements are much harder to control; many of them can't be. So it's urgent that we understand OPEC and the financial implications of energy, and the recycling of petrodollars, because we can't just call Washington and say, "Fix it." The lead time is longer on these "outside" problems, and we've already lost a lot of time.

Note one element of technique: we measured one way we feel—terrible—against the data, which tells us that things aren't so bad. That's one enormously useful attribute of economics: it tests "anecdotal evidence," or "what everybody knows." Is the spending of big government the cause of our inflation? West Germany's government takes a larger percentage of national output than ours, but its inflation rate is less. Is the money supply the cause of inflation? The money supply in Switzerland and West Germany has been increasing at a faster rate than ours, but they have lower rates of inflation than we do. It all goes back to the complexity; all the simple stories are too simple. We are unconsciously conditioned to the thirty-second story with a solution, even if we resist it. Would you like more romance? Brush your teeth with _____ and make them whiter; romance appears in thirty seconds. Aging, family respect, love, security—all dramatized and solved in thirty seconds, called a commercial. And we know those simple stories are too simple.

Having said that economics is wonderful, and having used the arguments of two very smart and personable economists, Professors Thurow and Solow, I am now about to step to the other side and say that the economists aren't solving our problems. We look to them, as we look to the doctors in the white coats. What's happening to prices? What do we do about inflation? Are the labor unions out of line? What should we do about energy?

Then the answers come back all over the place. I never met an economist who didn't have an answer. Many economists have been generous to me with their time; they have given me unpublished papers to read; they have read drafts of this book and commented on them; they have spent unpaid hours in conversation about them, all out of generosity and in the interests of goodness and truth—and I am about to take a gentle, loving nip at the hands that have fed me, also in the interests of goodness and truth. I am doing this precisely because we *do* call up the economists; presidents and prime ministers and newsmagazines call them; they have become authority figures. We need them, but they are not as certain as they were only ten or fifteen years ago.

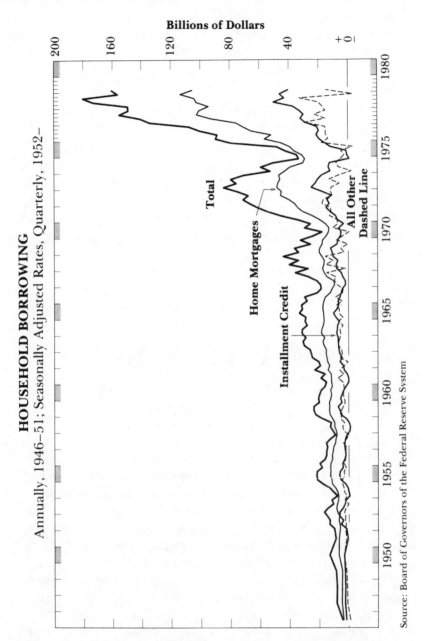

HOUSEHOLD BORROWING
Annually, 1946–51; Seasonally Adjusted Rates, Quarterly, 1952–

Billions of Dollars

Source: Board of Governors of the Federal Reserve System

Here is a graphic representation of the change in American behavior in the 1970s. You'll have to turn the page sideways to get the right perspective on this chart from the Federal Reserve. It shows how debt exploded compared to previous decades. The American people didn't lead this trend, they followed it, but everybody got the word: grandfather's virtues are gone; don't save, *borrow*. The implications of this startling picture reappear in a later chapter.

2

WHY NOT CALL UP THE ECONOMISTS?

Will Rogers

The word *economics* derives from two Greek words: *oikos,* "household," and *nomia,* "management, arrangement, control." Thus economics is household management. I like that better than the dictionary definition, which says that economics is the science relating to the creation and distribution of wealth and the consumption of goods and services. I like it better because economics isn't quite a science, no matter what the dictionary says. If economics were a perfect science, we could call up the economists, give them the problems, and ask them to have the solutions back on Wednesday.

Experimental science, said James Bryant Conant in the marvelous little book *On Understanding Science,* is based on observations, then on an experiment that uses those observations; and anyone, anywhere, anytime, should be able to repeat the experiment if its basis is true. A "conceptual scheme" holds the related experiments together, produces further experiments, and science marches on. Time doesn't matter. A magnet pulls today, and the same magnet pulls tomorrow. Alas, economics isn't so neat. A tax today might work differently from a tax next year. And the observations themselves are more suspect than watching a magnet pick up a tack.

The pure scientist has an advantage over the economist: he works in a laboratory, where he can control the factors he starts with. The economist has to use the actions of people, and people do not behave as consistently as magnets or laboratory mice. Nor do economists go out among the people, like the disguised prince in the fairy tale, to see what's going on; they call up government agencies and get the data from them.

"There are very few economic facts which we know with precision," wrote Sir John Hicks, an Oxford University Nobel Prize winner, in *Causality in Economics*. ". . . most of the 'macro' magnitudes which figure so largely in economic discussions are subject to errors and ambiguities which are far in excess of those which in most natural sciences would be regarded as tolerable. There are few economic 'laws' which can be regarded as at all firmly based."

It's natural for us to call up the economists and ask for the answers, and it's confusing when the answers come back all over the place.

"An economist," said Will Rogers, "is a man that can tell you anything about . . . well, he will tell you what can happen under any given condition, and his guess is liable to be as good as anybody else's, too."

There are two points to be made here. The second is strategic and has to do with the waning of a great theory.

The first is tactical and can perhaps be illustrated by this little story.

"You Keep Bringing Up Exogenous Variables"

I have a friend called Arthur, who has a pleasant smile, a wife, two children, two sets of skis, and who has, in economics, what is called an ideal quantitative background. Practically from second grade, Arthur loved math. It was a mystery to him why some people had to chew their pencils in math exams; to him, math was as easy as watching television was to some of his contemporaries. And although excellent marks came showering upon him all through school, he was never a serious, innovative mathematician. Great mathematicians, like competitive swimmers, mature early. At sixteen they have solved Fermat's Last Theorem, and at twenty-six they had better be teaching somewhere, because they are burned out. Arthur knew, at eighteen, that he was not that kind of scholar-mathematician, so he looked around at college and found a congenial home in economics. Arthur's hardest course came in his freshman year; it was English, and he had to write a paper on two Joseph Conrad stories, *Heart of Darkness* and *The Secret Agent.* He had a ghastly time with it. When he finished the Conrad paper, he says, he was very glad that he would never again have to do anything like that.

The graduate students who taught sections of the economics courses were very strong in econometrics, which is a mathematical and statistical form of economics, and Arthur was marvelously adept at that. After he got his Ph.D., Arthur thought about teaching. But one of his professors was a consultant to a commercial firm I will call Economics, Inc., which had built a computer model of the whole economy and which sold this service to various businesses. Eco-

nomics, Inc., offered Arthur such a high starting salary
that he went right to work there and has been very happy
ever since.

At various times I visited Arthur, and we would sit at his
computer console. His cuffs would shoot out of his sport
jacket, and his fingers would be poised over the computer
keyboard like those of E. Power Biggs at the organ. The
computer keyboard was like a typewriter keyboard, *q-w-e-
r-t-y-u-i-o-p*, except that it had a lot of extra keys you had
to press before you could ask it questions. Once, I had just
come back from the Middle East and I was worried that
the price of oil might go to $15 a barrel, or even $20 a
barrel.

"Ask it what the inflation rate will be if oil goes to fifteen
dollars a barrel," I would say, and Arthur would go tapety-
tapety-tap on the keyboard. The answer—when the computer did not ask us for more information, or tell us to
start over—would appear on the CRT screen. "Wow," said
Arthur. "Inflation of nine percent, all other things being
equal."

"Ask it what the mortgage rate will be with oil at fifteen
dollars a barrel," I said. Tapety-tapety-tap. "Ten percent?"
Arthur said. "That's awfully high. It can't be right. Maybe
we have to have an assumption about housing starts, too."
Tapety-tapety-tapety-tapety-*tap*.

I have called Arthur, periodically, over the years, but I
have never had to act specifically on his information. In
1973, for example, Economics, Inc., missed the inflation
rate by a wide margin. "Well, we did better than the Council of Economic Advisers," Arthur said, referring to the
group appointed by the President, which sits in Washington. "They predicted inflation would be down to two and
a half percent." Indeed they had, and Economics, Inc.,
had done better.

In order to have something as neat and symmetrical as
an equation, you have to have assumptions, even if the

assumption is very basic—let × equal the unknown, let $\sum$ mean "the sum of." There is an old joke, used by economists at departmental dinners, in which three men are stranded on a desert island and all they have is one huge can of tuna, but the tuna is inside the can and they are starving. The first man, a physicist, suggests a way to make a fire hot enough to melt the can. The second is an engineer, who is thinking up a complicated slingshot that will hurl the can against a rock with enough force to puncture it. The third is an economist. He has the answer. He says, "Assume a can opener." Then he proceeds with a theory.

Economics, Inc., had all kinds of assumptions and all kinds of assessments.

None of this, by the way, hurt Economics, Inc. Businessmen and institutions quested for certainty, and the computer at Economics, Inc., was very certain, even if it was not always right. The CRT screen would say ERROR if the processing was inconsistent, but not if the conclusions didn't match the brawling world outside.

As I said, I was worried about the Middle East. If the price of oil went high enough fast enough, we would have a depression because all that money for imports would get taken out of our economy, unless the oil countries reinvested the money productively, unless the Federal Reserve loosened the money to make up for the oil, unless the new price of oil brought up more oil . . . you see the process. So I was talking to Arthur about Saudi Arabia, and the health of King Khalid, and the Shiites of the eastern province who worked in the oil fields, and I could tell it all sounded to Arthur like Conrad's Congo in *Heart of Darkness*—unfathomable. Revolutionary Iran had thrown out the Shah, the price of oil was doubling, gold was going to new highs, and I had been saying how far off the great Economics, Inc., model was; it wasn't telling me what I so urgently needed to know. Arthur lost his temper.

"You keep bringing up exogenous variables!" he shouted.

Like *economist, exogenous* is another Greek-rooted word, from *exo*, "outside, coming from outside."

"Who the hell knew there was an ayatollah?" Arthur said. "Who knew the Russian wheat crop was going to bomb? Who cares about whoever it is in the eastern province?"

"But *life* is exogenous variables," I said. All I wanted was the answers. I was worried that if *one* ayatollah could, in a short time, cause oil to go up, the truckers then to go on strike, the airlines to flirt with bankruptcy, the defense budget to gather momentum, the Japanese to replace us as the buyers of Iranian oil—what if there was *another* fanatic Islamic cleric somewhere dictating into cassettes? What if there was a sorehead colonel in an oil country deciding that Allah wished the prime minister to meet with a nine-millimeter bullet?

But Arthur had hung up. And suddenly I knew one of the problems with economics. Arthur was brilliant. He had never sold a can of shoe polish, or bought a carload of lumber, or hired anybody, or fired anybody, or even worried about his checking account; in fact, he had never done anything but economics. In his own shop he could make lemmas dance around stochastic equilibria, he could rip off multiple regressions, he could make equations whistle "Dixie." The trouble came from that joke, "Assume a can opener." For deep, deep in the Economics, Inc., computer was a very tiny person upon whom the assumptions were based. Would the tiny person spend? Would the tiny person save? If you tapped the tiny person on the knee, his leg would jerk; if you tickled him, he would laugh. But the tiny, tiny person, upon whom all the vast panoply of computer modeling had been done, *was an economist.* If you asked him something, he would take a tiny sheet of yellow paper and ask, "What are the costs, and what are the benefits?" With a column for each, very coolly and rationally. He never threw an ashtray at his tiny wife, breaking a window and raising the gross national product by the price of the new window. Fear and greed and panic and emotion and nationalism and religious fervor, ayatollahs and Shiites and sinister Middle Eastern colonels were not part of his world.

This is *not* meant to be a trivial complaint about the limits of models. That is of interest to the people who use them, who naturally want to do the best possible job, and the subject has been well debated by such respected figures as Harvard's Hendrik Houthakker, an expert on econometric models and the varying relationships known as elasticities. I have another friend, Princeton's Geoffrey Watson, who, many years ago, with James Durbin, derived an equation that made them both famous in the field. The Durbin-Watson equation is one test for the mathematical work upon which the complex computer models are based. "Mathematics has so much prestige," Geoffrey says, "that people sometimes back away from their own intuitive judgments. What used to be called 'political economy' at Oxford and Cambridge has been overshadowed. I had a distinguished economics professor at Cambridge, Richard Stern, whose background was in classics."

There were once two kinds of economists, one might argue: the Smiths and the Ricardos. The Smith is the 1723 Adam Smith, and the Ricardo is David Ricardo, his immediate successor. Both the Smiths and the Ricardos were concerned with human activity and with the institutions that produce, preserve, and distribute wealth. The Smiths observed; the Ricardos sought the universal and logical principles, using algebra and its succeeding languages. The Smiths looked for what is to be explained, the Ricardos for the principles that did the explaining. Until comparatively recently, economists could write in both languages; that is, they could describe human activity in some detail, using the detail in written analysis, and they could reason mathematically and abstractly about the governing principles.

Today the Ricardos are fashionable and the Smiths are not. Economists who write well in English—there may be eight of them—run the risk of being labeled with the pejorative term "literary." The Ricardos admire the elegance of perfect equations; the highest terms of their praise are "rigorous" and "scientific."

When the problem was contained enough, when the numbers were discrete enough, the mathematical descriptions of the Ricardos worked. Government economists who favored deregulation of the airline industry found that scenario unfolding much as they had planned. But too often the real world did not match the movements of that tiny economist inside the computer. All through the 1970s, the economists missed the impact of OPEC because, when they described it mathematically, they treated it as if it were a rational, profit-maximizing convention of economists. They did not know about *asibaya,* the Arab sense of community, nor could they quantify Third World indignation at past histories, or Middle East rivalries, or Western myopia, all of which became more important than the more easily quantified data. Some years ago the sociologist and pollster Daniel Yankelovich described a process he called the McNamara fallacy, after the Secretary of Defense who had so carefully quantified the Vietnam War.

"The first step," he said, "is to measure what can easily be measured. The second is to disregard what can't be measured, or give it an arbitrary quantitative value. This is artificial and misleading. The third step is to presume that what can't be measured easily isn't very important. This is blindness. The fourth step is to say that what can't be easily measured really doesn't exist." The philosopher A. N. Whitehead called this tendency, in another form, "the fallacy of misplaced concreteness."

The Hopi language, an American Indian language, contains no words, grammatical forms, constructions, or expressions that refer to what we call "time," or to past, present, or future. The whole structure we base on "time"

—wages, rent, credit, interest, depreciation, insurance—cannot be expressed in Hopi and is not part of that world view. The main Eskimo language has twenty-seven different words for snow, each connoting another nuance of texture, utility, and consistency, so the Eskimo's ability to communicate about snow is far greater than ours. The picture of the universe, of "reality," shifts from language to language. The economists whose counsel we seek—as do presidents and prime ministers—speak from a world within the world, just as the Hopi spoke from a world without time, credit, wages, and rent. That cold, neat, elegant world of mathematics views a different reality than blunt, ambiguous English.

Poets know they must use the slippery sibilances and jagged edges of language, as well as the meanings of the words, to communicate. Poets know that life throws up exogenous variables. I made a note that at the next meeting of the Advisory Council of the university Department of Economics on which I serve I would propose that we recruit some poets. I am sure the council will treat the suggestion as merely amusing, and I'm not totally sure it's a great idea; but I know it's aimed in the right direction. I sent Arthur the classic *Language, Thought, and Reality* by Benjamin Whorf, from which I took the example of the Hopi, but I haven't heard back. Maybe it reminds him of *Heart of Darkness,* and maybe he's just too busy.

The Waning of the Great Doctrine

The rise of the Ricardos came from the publication of a powerful work by a man who could be counted as both a Smith and a Ricardo. That work was John Maynard Keynes's *The General Theory of Employment, Interest and Money.* After Freud, we looked at dreams and the unconscious differently; after Keynes, we had another view of economics. That book changed not only the way we see the world, but the way the world is governed.

Keynes could write English very well. Some of the polemic letters he wrote to the London newspapers in the 1920s are superb. A Cambridge professor himself, he circulated the drafts of his *General Theory* among a group of Cambridge economists. One of these was R. F. Kahn, who had won a degree of fame within the profession for developing the concept of the multiplier, which we needn't stop the story for. The multiplier was important to the *General Theory* because it gave Keynes an analytical tool for his argument. Kahn did more than supply the multiplier; he supplied a lot of algebra. The letters between Keynes and Kahn reveal Kahn urging more complex proof in his attack on the automatic nature of markets.

Some of the *General Theory* is felicitously styled, but much more of it is extremely complex, dense, and comprehensible only to skilled technicians. The equations demonstrated what changes in government policy are necessary to produce the maximum level of output. If we give some paragraphs to the Smiths, we must give the bulk of the work to the Ricardos, and that became the style of academic economics.

Keynes was an extraordinarily versatile man. Born to solid Victorian comfort, he became an editor, a journalist, a farmer, a civil servant, an entrepreneur, a corporate director, and a teacher, as well as the greatest economist of the century. He married a ballet dancer and managed a ballet company. He was a successful financial speculator and the chairman of an insurance company, as well as a director of other companies. When, at his death, he was asked what he regretted, he said he wished he had drunk more champagne.

Keynes grew up amid Victorian optimism, and he was convinced that reason could solve the problems of the human condition, especially the reason of those educated at Eton and Cambridge. "Nothing is required and nothing will avail," he wrote, at the depths of the Depression, "except a little, a very little, clear thinking." It was not reasonable that men should be desperate, idle, and hungry when the problem was not famine or earthquake or war or the lack of material resources, but "some failure in the immaterial devices of the mind, in the working of the motives which should lead to the decisions and acts of will, necessary to put in movement the resources and technical means we already have."

The *General Theory* thus offered faith and hope. Depressions were not like famines, natural events to be fatalistically endured. Public policy could do something. A stalled economy was a car without a "magneto"; we might say spark plug or ignition. A government that could end depression, by whatever means, had the obligation to do so.

It is hard to convey now the despair that was brought by the Great Depression. But even before the publication of *The General Theory* in 1936, governments were spending. In Germany rearmament produced full employment; in the United States Franklin D. Roosevelt was improvising. (Roosevelt did not read Keynes, though some of his advisers did. When the President met the economist, he said later to Frances Perkins, "I saw your friend Keynes. He left a whole rigamarole of figures. He must be a mathematician rather than a political economist.")

Keynes created tremendous excitement. "We were the forerunners of a new dispensation," he said of his elite group, in another context, "and we were not afraid of anything."

The triumph of the Keynesians gave the academic economists all the ingredients necessary for a priesthood. They had a holy book, a doctrine. Although the holy book offered redemption, it could not easily be read or interpreted by laymen, thus necessitating the existence of a priestly class. Harvard professors hurried from their classes to catch the afternoon congressional express to Washington to advise the government. During the 1950s and early 1960s, the prosperity was the greatest in half a century, perhaps the greatest in Western industrial history. The doctrine led to expectations; government could move against the business cycle, flatten out its perilous peaks and dreadful valleys, bring prosperity back when that prosperity departed. Then the expectations grew even greater: government could do not only what *worked;* it could do what was *fair,* at least what was considered fair by legislators. If the risks of farming were too great, society could underwrite those risks. If proper housing was a social consensus, society could underwrite housing.

Only a generation before, the business cycle had been thought to be as untamable as drought, flood, and fire; now it was expected that it was not only tamed, but tunable, to a fine degree. In the early 1960s the inflation rate was negligible, unemployment minimal, and output set new records.

By 1966 Walter Heller, one of Kennedy's economic advisers, could be permitted a crow of triumph. In his Godkin lectures at Harvard that year, he proclaimed the success of the "new economics": "Two Presidents [Kennedy and Johnson] have recognized and drawn on modern economics as a source of national strength," he said, "using, for the first time, the full range of economic tools."

That was the high point. The dragons of inflation and unemployment began to snort in their caves, and "stagflation," an awkward beast, a hybrid of inflation and stagnation, roamed without serious natural enemies. Cynics said there were two sure signs that the Keynesian era was waning. One was that *Time* magazine put Keynes on its cover, thirty-four years after his death. And Richard Nixon said, "I am a Keynesian. We are all Keynesians now."

Paul Samuelson's textbook, first published in 1948, educated a whole generation of students in Keynesian economics and sold 10 million copies. Personally, Samuelson has been as beloved a teacher as ever there was, and he became the first American to win the Nobel Prize in economics. Under "The Composition and Pricing of National Output," in *Readings in Economics,* he reprinted the second Adam Smith's "The Cocoa Caper," after which we held periodic conversations over the years, most recently on the mysterious national malaise: if the numbers are good, why don't we feel good?

We were sitting, on one occasion, in his river-view office at MIT. Crews warmed up on the Charles River outside; Samuelson was wearing sneakers after his 7:00 A.M. tennis game. Is Keynes really dead?

"The fact is that what we've got, a Keynesian economy, is economically stable. It's just politically unstable. The self-interest that the early economists counted on as a balance leads, in a modern economy, to collusion among the self-interested groups."

We have an economic system that works, except for the people in it? But the people *are* in it. If the mixed economy doesn't work so well, what next?

"We have no breakthrough on stagflation. But is there another system that works better? More government? Wage and price controls? They work well in the short run, but prices go up when the controls come off. There are two thousand radical economists in this country, and they haven't produced any real ideas.

"The other direction? Go back to the nineteenth century? It's hard to dismantle a mixed economy. Milton Friedman doesn't really successfully address himself to a mixed economy. Some younger economists are paying attention to the old Austrian school, to economists such as Friedrich August von Hayek, who believed the free market would do the job. But in the Depression, von Hayek said there was nothing to be done; we were just paying for our sins. Nobody wants to go back to *that.*"

And why the malaise?

"The malaise just isn't in the figures. Something else must be going on."

"The profession has lost its confidence." The speaker is a younger economist, Stanley Fischer, coauthor of a new best-selling textbook, *Macroeconomics*. Younger economists have been pulling back from the Keynesian faith. "We still believe," says Fischer, "that the government should use its monetary and fiscal policy in the face of major disturbances. But you have to proceed with caution. The policy itself may be destabilizing."

The policy destabilizing! The government is iatrogenic —stay away from the doctor; the cure is worse than the disease.

"Even carefully calculated policies have consequences you don't anticipate. We're not going back to the thirties, but now we think that the period from 1948 to 1973 was quite extraordinary, a unique time. Economists got some of the credit. Now the scenery is such that you have to be much more careful. There is much less scope for policy errors. Almost all the young economists I know are more right-wing than the older generation. There's a feeling that there's not a lot you can do to move the economy in the direction you want."

Not a lot you can do?

The General Theory offered certainty. What could offer the same certainty?

"I don't think there is the same certainty," Fischer says. "Students want small problems. Economists want to move cautiously. There is no big picture."

No big picture! The old faith has waned; the new has not yet arrived. No new star has risen in the east. The old conceptual scheme that bound the observations together has frayed, with no successor. Keynesians, neo-

Keynesians, post-Keynesians, and anti-Keynesians all squabble with Marxists, libertarians, and various shades in between. Once again the problems seem bigger than men's abilities to solve them. The optimistic credo, the vision of men as responsible and capable, acting in benign self-interest, has faded, to be replaced by a smaller, less confident, more flinty-eyed world view.

"During the long period of sustained innocence in the 50s and 60s," wrote George Ball, in a wicked, witty column, "we basked in the happy conviction that economics was a developed science, roughly equivalent to the age of sulfanilamide in medicine. We were shocked to find that the state of economic science more nearly paralleled Dr. Harvey's discovery of the circulation of the blood. Honest practitioners no longer try to hide their dubiety; many are quite frankly resorting to leeches and poultices. I have faith that our economy is sufficiently robust to survive, yet I cannot forget the infant Louis XV, who, after contracting smallpox, was saved from death only because his nurse hid him from the ministrations of the doctors whose vigorous attentions killed his father and his brother."

Such jibes would not have been possible two decades ago. If you consider some of its stupendous intellectual achievements, economics is a long way from the discovery of the circulation of the blood. Wassily Leontief, for example, designed an input-output analysis for a whole economy, and won a Nobel Prize for his work. Now there are input-output models for a hundred countries, for a whole planet—breathtaking! Leontief himself said, "When I introduced mathematics to the Harvard economics department in 1931, I did not know it would become *gymnastics*." But the constitution upon which one body of economic law was written is now suspect. The people do not behave as they should.

We forget that by historical standards, these are still very good times. We see problems—rich countries and poor countries, industry and the environment, energy and food, inflation and unemployment—and we expect so much, because that Keynesian élan was so great. Even if the economists could speak both English and Hopi, they would be hard pressed to meet our expectations.

Don't shoot the piano player; the poor fellow's doing his best. The people who pay the economists want answers right away. We have to remember that the economist frequently says, "Assume a can opener." We have to keep in mind that inside that giant computer is the easily tickled, tiny little fellow who walks and talks like an economist, and the computer, being just a machine, takes its clues from him.

Why is this even relevant? Having been part of the solution, economics has become part of the problem. There's one atmosphere when a powerful king is on the throne, and another after the king is dead and his little son is six years old and the dukes are all battling for position.

We have this curious malaise, and when we turn to the profession for reassurance, we sense its members are not so sure themselves. That lack of certainty leaves an opening. The opening gets filled by those who sound *very* certain and say the world is going to hell in a hand basket. The doomsters don't have to be as careful as the mainstream economists, but their very intensity wins audiences, and then *that* bit of behavior has to be taken into consideration.

Let's try a bit of doomstering ourselves—bears in the night. It's fun to compose. What follows is Apocalyptic Fiction, set in the future. A young Japanese student in the United States is writing home. There is one trick involved; see if you can pick it up.

3

APOCALYPTIC FICTION

New York
May 34, 198—

Professor Noritake Watanabe
Faculty of Economics and Sociology
Saiwai-cho, Takamatsu 760
Kagawa University
Kagawa, Japan

My Dear Professor:

I am writing this to you on the computer terminal in the Nippon Club, so I know that you will have it tomorrow. I tried to telephone you, but as you told me, the American telephone system is so unreliable it is "down" much of the time. One must wait three days for an overseas call, and then there is so much static and interference I prefer the old reliable Hitachi terminal. If only the Americans would permit our new equipment in! I find it hard to believe that it was the Americans who invented the transistor and the whole technology of semiconductors! It is we who have showed them how to use it.

I want to thank you again for the grant that has enabled me to come here. I will do my best to fulfill your expectations of me.

Upon my arrival at the airport I noticed a long line of Americans opposite me, waiting to trade their shabby currency for External Dollars, or to fill out the forms for Petrofrancs. When I say "shabby currency," I mean that it gets ragged very quickly and falls apart in your hand. I imagine they will be very glad to have the issue of New Dollars at the ratio of one hundred to one. The Americans seemed in good spirits but threadbare. I remember your comparison of them to the Britons who, as you noted in your paper in the year 1980, spent only $4.75 in 1980 dollars in dry cleaning per annum per person, and looked it.

Getting into New York City was quite an adventure. The Arabs on our aircraft seemed to whisk through customs, were greeted by their American business servants, and stepped into waiting limousines. With Hisae Robata, student of Professor Shimetsu Tokagawa of Kyoto, I negotiated an old yellow taxi for the trip into the city. We offered $27,000, which may have been too much, but we were tired and wanted to get to the hotel. Of course, $27,000 is only 3 Petrofrancs, but no one at the airport taxi line would change a Petrofranc, except into dollars.

The road into the city contained many potholes. The driver said the road had not been repaired since the city went bankrupt at the beginning of the Great Inflation. There was such a jam-up of cars that our driver took a shortcut. He slowed down at a curve, and we were stopped by bandits! Three black men and two white men, bearded, in combat fatigues and sunglasses, carrying carbines and the small handgun sold so universally in America as the Saturday Night Special.

"Aw, not again. You guys hit me on the way to the airport," our driver said.

"You got an RP pass, man?" said the apparent leader.

"My cousin has the RP pass; it's his taxi," said our driver. The leader hit him in the stomach with the butt of his carbine.

"Nobody travels the roads without an RP pass," said the leader. Our driver doubled up in pain. "Next time, bring it."

So the bandits were not true bandits, but some of the Revolutionary party marauders one hears about. Otherwise we would have been shaken down for our Petros and our cameras, and who knows, maybe even the gold in our teeth. We were frightened, I can tell you!

I appreciate your efforts in putting me up at the Plaza. While it is not as clean and efficient as the Japanese hotels in New York, it does provide a quick introduction to the society.

Across the street from the hotel, in the park, are literally hundreds of beggars. Young black women carrying children in their arms come right up to your taxi and try to put their upturned hands through the window. But the crisply dressed Disney Guards keep them away. The Disney Guards are a welcome sight everywhere, with their polite if somewhat mechanical manners and their neat, gray white-belted uniforms. I understand they began as guides in the popular tourist attraction before they were in such demand as a private security force.

One is surprised, of course, at the roulette wheels and gambling machines in what was formerly the Palm Court at the Plaza, where once, I am told, tea was served to wealthy dowagers. But of course the gambling fever is evident everywhere.

On the way up to our room—we had to wait over an

hour for the room to be cleared—the elevator operator stopped the elevator between floors. We were frightened again!

"Change money?" he said. "Petrofrancs?"

We said we were simple students, and we did not want to change money.

"Give you fifteen thousand dollars for a Petrofranc," he said.

We said we simply wished to get to our rooms. He offered us a line of cocaine, some marijuana, and women. Of course, with the penalties for changing currency posted everywhere, we were not about to try that, even though the hotel man's offer was generous.

Once we had showered, we took a walk. Hisae watched part of the Trial of the Oil Company Presidents on television, and I watched it briefly. Of course, it has gone on so long that most of the Americans are bored with it, but the characters have become familiar, like those in a television series. One knows right away that the Texaco president will whine and say that he only carried out orders. The scrappy little one, from Mobil, will protest his innocence, repeating the same legal phrases. The bald, dignified one will view it as a scene in history of which he is not really a part.

We missed a skirmish right outside the hotel, between the Disney Guards and the RP. The Disney Guards had caught two young black men looting a store. Under these circumstances they were going to have a Street Corner Trial, which they are allowed to do under the Emergency Law. A Street Corner Judge arrived in a police car, but the television cameras could not be set up in time. The idea is that if people see thieves being efficiently tried, and even sometimes executed, right on the spot, and on television, that will be a great deterrent. Actually, it is rarely done. Apparently an RP car drove up; the RPs inside threw a gasoline bomb and then tried to get the looters into the car. But their own car was blown up instead. A police car took the looters away. Hisae and I missed the whole thing.

Two of the Disney Guards were still there. They were very flushed and happy. They looked about our age. Some Texans or rich farmers came up and slapped the Disney Guards on the back and wanted to buy them a drink. The Disney Guards are always neat and polite, almost apple-cheeked. They refused the drink.

Fifth Avenue was like a country fair, thronged. There were Latin Americans and Arabs, and the women the hotel clerk called "Gulfies," dressed completely in black, with frightening-looking plastic masks, used instead of veils. These are the wives of the businessmen from the Gulf states of Abu Dhabi, Qatar, Bahrain, and so on, who dress still in the orthodox fashion on the streets. The shops glitter with luxury merchandise.

We looked at the display in Brooks Brothers, which as you remember once had a store in Japan. A man's suit, on sale, marked down from $54,000 to $43,000. Shoes, $22,000 a pair! You were right to tell me to wait and buy my clothes here. What bargains! Of course, as you say, the workmanship is shoddy, and if you buy a suit, you must not get caught in the rain because it will shrink, or fall apart.

One hears, as one walks around, what seems to be distant gunfire—sharp cracks, like a car backfiring, and an occasional boom. That is from the Northern Sector. The crack, crack, crack, boom blends right in. After a while it is no worse than Tokyo traffic. Of course, in the Northern Sector the gunfire is very real! The violence is political now, with the RP and the bandits, but as you often said, that long predated the inflation and was ascribed to the nonintegration of agricultural people into urban settings. I remember when you were on the Lexington Avenue bus and someone was knifed; everyone else jumped off the

bus, and you were the only passenger who would help the
bus driver take the victim to a hospital! At any rate, there
are in our hotel some Arab students, our own age, who say
that New York is not much worse than Beirut in the late
1970s. You have to know the right people to travel from
sector to sector, that's all; and you have to know which
streets are all right on which day.

The electricity in the hotel went off intermittently, once
for as long as two hours. The sign in our room says that
water is turned on from 6:00 to 10:00 P.M., and from 7:00
A.M. to 10:00 A.M., but something must have gone wrong
this morning because there was no water. Perhaps it is the
strikes of the utility workers.

This morning Hisae and I went to a market, Gristede's,
which is part of the chain controlled by Tegemann of Germany and owned by the Kuwaitis. Bread was only $195 a
loaf. Orange juice was but $88 a can. These items must be
subsidized. So, if one asks how the Americans can afford
to live, without barter or illegal dealings, there is part of
the answer. Just enough items are subsidized. No American could afford to eat fish, except the local fish, in season,
which are bartered and come in outside the Food Controls.

However, Hisae and I were able to get some very nice
sashimi in one of the charming Japanese restaurants, and
we were even able to pay in Japanese currency when we
did not have proper change.

Hisae then went to arrange this trip to Washington, and
he was uncertain as to how to do it. The train to Washington is very, very cheap, only $1,100; since it was a govern-
ment-owned company, Amtrak, and since the government
denies much of the inflation, it has raised the fares very
slowly. But the train is always very crowded, with people
packed in as in the Tokyo subway at rush hour. It may
take six or seven hours, and it is a very uncomfortable
ride, with a breakdown almost every day. And with every

breakdown there is the possibility of train robbers. However, the train would leave Hisae a lot of money in his travel allowance. The Eastern Shuttle runs from time to time, for $66,000, and there is the elegant turbo plane, which takes no longer than the shuttle, but it is available only for Petros and is nicknamed the Arabian Express. Indeed, it is operated by Saudia Airlines. But Hisae does not want to spend all his Petros at the beginning of his year here.

On the West Side we saw the barricades and the barbed wire, which are so familiar from television. Beyond them we could see the boarded-up stores and quiet streets, and beyond that what seemed to be many acres of rubble and burned-out buildings. At the barricades we saw the water trucks with their high-pressure hoses, the concrete blockhouse, and a pickup truck with a twenty-millimeter aircraft cannon mounted on the rear.

We went to the Washington Square area, which we had been told was safe this week. Hisae was trying to find a friend of his who is a student at New York University, but he was not in his room.

So we sat in a café. A middle-aged man went from table to table, singing ballads. He accompanied himself on the guitar. He had dark eyebrows and sang us "My Love Has Flown like the Crane" very sweetly, with only a slight American accent. He is a professor who once spent an exchange year at Kyoto. Now he must supplement his income, because of the inflation. We gave him a generous tip, and he went on to the next table and sang another song.

On the television screen we could see Senator Burr at his rally. I believe it was at a football stadium in Texas. The audience at the rally could see close-ups of the senator's face on the huge screens within the stadium. He has a large head and even white teeth. There were Disney Guards everywhere, smiling and friendly. The music was stirring and got the crowd in a good mood. Then Senator Burr held up his hands. The crowd got very hushed.

"I love you," he said.

The crowd was waiting for that, and it cheered and cheered and began to chant.

The senator held up his hands again. Then he said, very slowly, that he cares about the people, that they have worked hard, they have been robbed of their savings, their children have no chance, their schools are falling down, their country was once great and is sick, it must be cleansed and restored to its greatness.

Then he got angry. He said the Oil Company Presidents are not the real traitors; they are only puppets. He knows the names of the real traitors.

He told about the bureaucrats who ride in their shiny limousines when no one else can keep a car repaired. He told about the people who have gotten rich while everyone else has suffered. The traitors must be brought to justice, he said, and the foreigners who are in league with them must be kicked out.

This made Hisae and me feel uncomfortable, even though we are here on authorized scholarships. The rally crowd was on its feet, shaking its fists—even the Disney Guards. The Disney Guards are usually friendly, but when there are so many of them, the friendliness disappears.

Then the senator got very soothing, and the crowd very quiet.

"You and I are one," he said. At this point, apparently, he always says the same things, and the crowd waits for it, knowing the cadences, as if in a religious ceremony. "Your heart is my heart," he said. "Your justice is my command. Your anger is my strength. Your will is my peace."

Then the crowd cheered.

The English phrase "your will is my peace" does not make good sense to us. After a few months here, our English will improve, and we will understand.

It was a relief to reach the cool atrium of the Nippon Club, which has been much expanded since you were last here.

My honored teacher, I would appreciate it if you would call my parents and tell them I am safe. Their fears were needless. You know how parents are.

I am very excited about my project. Tell my mother not to worry.

Your most devoted
Shigetsu

4

THE CHILLING SYMBOL: A WHEELBARROW FULL OF MONEY

That's apocalyptic fiction, set in a future time.

I said there was a trick in this little chapter, and it is this: *everything in it has already happened.* George Orwell did not write *1984* only about Russia; he did have Yevgeni Zamyatin's *We* as a model, which was about Russia, but the bureaucracy in *1984* was that of the BBC, where he worked.

Everything in that chapter has already happened, but not all at the same place at the same time. The stabbing on the Lexington Avenue bus was reported in *The New York Times* on June 8, 1970; all the passengers scrambled off, except one visiting Japanese professor, who helped the bus driver take the victim to the hospital. It was a tiny story; we take that level of violence for granted. The sight

of military trucks parked at intersections—trucks with
high-pressure hoses or twenty-millimeter aircraft cannon
—has been unhappily familiar in quite a few cities around
the world. So have the uniformed private guards. I have
already been to the rally of the charismatic leader, only he
was not a senator and the rally wasn't political.

Those high prices—the hyperinflation—have turned
up in Latin America, in Asia, in the Middle East, in countries where events and the economy have slipped out of
control. We have had such hyperinflation in the United
States, but "not worth a Continental" and "Confederate
money" are out of our vocabulary now.

The New York Times printed a letter from a lawyer, once
a sixties activist, who wrote this: "I don't understand what's
going on. I make a good salary, but the prices of houses
and apartments seem outrageous. Money doesn't mean
anything. Your income goes up, but taxes go up and ex-
penses go up and the rest goes right out of your wallet. I
don't think anybody's in control; it feels like things are out
of control."

This lament is common. There is an archetypal fear at
work here, just beyond the realm of consciousness. The
fear is of losing what you have. For Americans of previous
generations, "losing what you have" meant losing a job
and not being able to get another, or losing the family
farm to drought, dust, and the bankers. There is probably
a group of cells somewhere in the cerebral cortex that
resonates to the fear of the unknown, of the enemy tribe
over the horizon, of strange men on horseback burning
farms. The current form of this fear is relatively new to
Americans now alive: it is that the currency is losing its
value, becoming meaningless. We are told that Americans
have changed their economic behavior in the past five
years; they have stopped saving, and they spend even
when there is no immediate necessity to spend. Europeans
know the symbol of meaningless currency: it is the wheel-

barrow full of money, the image of the Great Inflation in Germany in the 1920s. The Great Inflation not only helped bring Hitler to power; the memory of it has an effect even today, and it has some lessons for us.

Before World War I Germany was a prosperous country, with a gold-backed currency, expanding industry, and world leadership in optics, chemicals, and machinery. The German mark, the British shilling, the French franc, and the Italian lira all had about equal value, and all were exchanged four or five to the dollar. That was in 1914. In 1923, at the most fevered moment of the German hyperinflation, the exchange rate between the dollar and the mark was one trillion marks to one dollar, and a wheelbarrow full of money would not even buy a newspaper. Most Germans were taken by surprise by the financial tornado.

"My father was a lawyer," says Walter Levy, an internationally known German-born oil consultant in New York, "and he had taken out an insurance policy in 1903, and every month he had made the payments faithfully. It was a twenty-year policy, and when it came due, he cashed it in and bought *a single loaf of bread.*" The Berlin publisher Leopold Ullstein wrote that an American visitor tipped their cook one dollar. The family convened, and it was decided that a trust fund should be set up in a Berlin bank with the cook as beneficiary, the bank to administer and invest the dollar.

In retrospect, you can trace the steps to hyperinflation, but some of the reasons remain cloudy. Germany abandoned the gold backing of its currency in 1914. The war was expected to be short, so it was financed by government borrowing, not by savings and taxation. Fifty years later, the United States did not finance the Vietnam War by savings and taxation because its leaders thought that Vietnam was only a limited involvement and would be over quickly. In Germany prices doubled between 1914 and 1919, just as they have here in the past ten years.

The parallels are limited. Germany had lost a war. Under the Treaty of Versailles it had already made a reparations payment in gold-backed marks, and it was due to lose part of the production of the Ruhr and of the province of Upper Silesia. The Weimar Republic was politically fragile.

But the bourgeois habits were very strong. Ordinary citizens worked at their jobs, sent their children to school and worried about their grades, maneuvered for promotions and rejoiced when they got them, and generally expected things to get better. The prices that had doubled from 1914 to 1919 were doubling again during just five months in 1922. Milk went from 7 marks per liter to 16; beer from 5.6 to 18. There were complaints about the high cost of living. Professors and civil servants complained of getting squeezed. Factory workers pressed for wage increases. An underground economy developed, aided by a desire to beat the tax collector.

On June 24, 1922, right-wing fanatics assassinated Walter Rathenau, the moderate, able foreign minister. Rathenau was a charismatic figure, and the idea that a popular, wealthy, and glamorous government minister could be shot in a law-abiding society shattered the faith of the Germans, who wanted to believe that things were going to be all right. Rathenau's state funeral was a national trauma. The nervous citizens of the Ruhr were already getting their money out of the currency and into real goods— diamonds, works of art, safe real estate. Now ordinary Germans began to get out of marks and into real goods. Pianos, wrote the British historian Adam Fergusson, were bought even by unmusical families. Sellers held back because the mark was worth less every day. As prices went up, the amounts of currency demanded were greater, and the German central bank responded to the demands. Yet the ruling authorities did not see anything wrong. A leading financial newspaper said that the amounts of money in

circulation were not excessively high. Dr. Rudolf Havenstein, the president of the Reichsbank—equivalent to the
Federal Reserve—told an economics professor that he
needed a new suit but wasn't going to buy one until prices
came down.

Why did the German government not act to halt the
inflation? It was a shaky, fragile government, especially
after the assassination. The vengeful French sent their
army into the Ruhr to enforce their demands for reparations, and the Germans were powerless to resist. More
than inflation, the Germans feared unemployment. In
1919 Communists had tried to take over, and severe unemployment might give the Communists another chance.
The great German industrial combines—Krupp, Thyssen,
Farben, Stinnes—condoned the inflation and survived it
well. A cheaper mark, they reasoned, would make German
goods cheap and easy to export, and they needed the export earnings to buy raw materials abroad. Inflation kept
everyone working.

So the printing presses ran, and once they began to run,
they were hard to stop. The price increases began to be
dizzying. Menus in cafés could not be revised quickly
enough. A student at Freiburg University ordered a cup
of coffee at a café. The price on the menu was 5,000
marks. He had two cups. When the bill came, it was for
14,000 marks.

"If you want to save money," he was told, "and you want
two cups of coffee, you should order them both at the
same time."

The presses of the Reichsbank could not keep up,
though they ran through the night. Individual cities and
states began to issue their own money. Dr. Havenstein, the
president of the Reichsbank, did not get his new suit. A
factory worker described payday, which was every day at
11:00 A.M.: "At eleven o'clock in the morning a siren
sounded and everybody gathered in the factory forecourt

where a five-ton lorry was drawn up loaded brimful with paper money. The chief cashier and his assistants climbed up on top. They read out names and just threw out bundles of notes. As soon as you had caught one you made a dash for the nearest shop and bought just anything that was going." Teachers, paid at 10:00 A.M., brought their money to the playground, where relatives took the bundles and hurried off with them. Banks closed at 11:00 A.M.; the harried clerks went on strike.

Dentists and doctors stopped charging in currency and demanded butter or eggs, but the farmers were holding back their produce. "We don't want any Jew-confetti from Berlin," a chronicler quotes a Bavarian farmer. The flight from currency that had begun with the buying of diamonds, gold, country houses, and antiques now extended to minor and almost useless items—bric-a-brac, soap, hairpins. The law-abiding country crumbled into petty thievery. Copper pipes and brass armatures weren't safe. Gasoline was siphoned from cars. People bought things they didn't need and used them to barter—a pair of shoes for a shirt, some crockery for coffee. Berlin had a "witches' Sabbath" atmosphere. Prostitutes of both sexes roamed the streets. Cocaine was the fashionable drug. In the cabarets the newly rich and their foreign friends could dance and spend money. Other reports noted that not all the young people had a bad time. Their parents had taught them to work and save, and that was clearly wrong, so they could spend money, enjoy themselves, and flout the old.

The publisher Leopold Ullstein wrote: "People just didn't understand what was happening. All the economic theory they had been taught didn't provide for the phenomenon. There was a feeling of utter dependence on anonymous powers—almost as a primitive people believed in magic—that somebody must be in the know, and that this small group of 'somebodies' must be a conspiracy."

When the one-thousand-billion-mark note came out,

few bothered to collect the change when they spent it. By November 1923, with one dollar equal to one trillion marks, the breakdown was complete. The currency had lost meaning.

What happened immediately afterward is as fascinating as the Great Inflation itself. The tornado of the mark inflation was succeeded by the "miracle of the Rentenmark." A new president took over the Reichsbank, Horace Greeley Hjalmar Schacht, who came by his first two names because of his father's admiration for an editor of the *New York Tribune*. The Rentenmark was not Schacht's idea, but he executed it, and as the Reichsbank president, he got the credit for it. For decades afterward he was able to maintain a reputation for financial wizardry. He became the architect of the financial prosperity brought by the Nazi party.

Obviously, though the currency was worthless, Germany was still a rich country—with mines, farms, factories, forests. The backing for the Rentenmark was mortgages on the land and bonds on the factories, but that backing was a fiction; the factories and land couldn't be turned into cash or used abroad. Nine zeros were struck from the currency; that is, one Rentenmark was equal to one billion old marks. The Germans wanted desperately to believe in the Rentenmark, and so they did. "I remember," said one Frau Barten of East Prussia, "the feeling of having just one Rentenmark to spend. I bought a small tin bread bin. Just to buy something that had a price tag for *one* mark was so exciting."

All money is a matter of belief. *Credit* derives from Latin, *credere,* "to believe." Belief was there, the factories functioned, the farmers delivered their produce. The central bank kept the belief alive when it would not let even the government borrow further.

But although the country functioned again, the savings were never restored, nor were the values of hard work and decency that had accompanied the savings. There was a different temper in the country, a temper that Hitler would later exploit with diabolical talent. Thomas Mann wrote: "The market woman who without batting an eyelash demanded a hundred million for an egg lost the capacity for surprise. And nothing that has happened since has been insane or cruel enough to surprise her."

With the currency went many of the lifetime plans of average citizens. It was the custom for the bride to bring some money to a marriage; many marriages were called off. Widows dependent on insurance found themselves destitute. People who had worked a lifetime found that their pensions would not buy one cup of coffee.

Pearl Buck, the American writer who became famous for her novels of China, was in Germany in 1923. She wrote later: "The cities were still there, the houses not yet bombed and in ruins, but the victims were millions of people. They had lost their fortunes, their savings; they were dazed and inflation-shocked and did not understand how it had happened to them and who the foe was who had defeated them. Yet they had lost their self-assurance, their feeling that they themselves could be the masters of their own lives if only they worked hard enough; and lost, too, were the old values of morals, of ethics, of decency."

The fledgling Nazi party, whose attempted coup had failed in 1923, won 32 seats legally in the next election. The right-wing Nationalist party won 106 seats, having promised 100-percent compensation to the victims of inflation and vengeance on the conspirators who had brought it. A British economist who had been in his country's delegation at the peace treaty had written a polemic called *The Economic Consequences of the Peace*. Fired from the Treasury, John Maynard Keynes wrote brilliant, quick-tempered articles to London papers, recalling his foresight.

Since our own time of economic nightmare was not

when a currency lost its meaning but when men lost jobs
—the Depression—we have not had the German fear of
losing what you have because of explosion of the currency.
We are far more likely to have a soggy British-style inflation than a frenzied German-style hyperinflation featuring
wheelbarrows full of money. But the lessons of the Great
Inflation go beyond the simple formula of the monetarists
—that if the money supply is limited, all will be well. The
lessons have to do with belief and instinct. When Americans create a mania for housing—not building houses, but
bidding up housing at the rate of $100 billion a year, as
they have done in the past five years—they are losing belief in their currency as a store of value.

Why does everyone talk so obsessively about houses?
What can be so interesting about bricks and mortar and
plumbing and wiring? It isn't the houses themselves, the
architecture, the layout, the traffic patterns, the kitchens,
how we shape the houses and how they shape us, that is
the obsessive topic. It's the prices. The reason there is so
much talk about condos and co-ops and houses is that
there is a new twist to the old adage "A house is not a
home." When is a house not just a home? When it is a way
to flee the currency.

5

WHY HOUSES BECAME MORE THAN HOUSES

"The Government Wants You to Buy a House"

"I'll tell you what people are talking about," said a Chicago editor. "Not politics, not sex, not sports. Real estate. Who paid how much for what, what they're asking for it now, do you know any good deals."

"I bought my house for fifty thousand dollars seven years ago," said another editor. "I could sell it today for one hundred thirty-five thousand. Houses are the only way to keep up with inflation."

This is the conventional wisdom, repeated all over the country. Prices in some areas went up so fast that some observers thought the housing scene was dangerous, that housing was a "bubble" that, if burst, could hurl the country into depression and cause universal damage. There was no doubt that housing had become expensive: the median price of a house was heading toward $100,000. The enthusiastic citizens discussing housing believe housing can only go up. What they do not see is that it is not really housing that is going up, but the currency going down. Housing offers a way to borrow now and pay later, and the housing debt, the mortgage, leverages the ownership in a period of rising inflation. It has been the one hedge open to almost everyone, a way, in financial jargon, to "go short" the dollar. The housing numbers tell us where much of our money has gone, what social choices we have made, and what we have come to believe.

Let's go to the videotape, as the sportscasters say. We're going back ten years, to a 1971 conversation between Adam Smith and the articulate television talk-show host Dick Cavett. Smith doesn't get the most important idea across.

> CAVETT: We've gotten this far and I've understood absolutely everything you've said.
>
> SMITH: I'm not sure what I've said.
>
> CAVETT: Well, we were talking about the best investment you can make, and you seemed to be hedging—
>
> SMITH: Oh, no, the best investment you can make is a house. That one is easy.
>
> CAVETT: A house? We were talking about the stock market. Investments—
>
> SMITH: You asked me the best investment. There are always individual stocks that will go up more, but you don't want to give tips on a television show. For most people, the best investment is a house.
>
> CAVETT: All right, why a house?
>
> SMITH: The government wants you to buy a house. It will give you a quadruple subsidy if you buy a house. It doesn't care if you own stocks; in fact, it will tax you more. You should do what the government wants.

CAVETT: [*Smiles*] I already have a house. I'm glad I've
made the government happy.

SMITH: Can I tell you—

CAVETT: —how I've made the government happy? Yes.

SMITH: Yes, four subsidies, or benefits, anyway. First, if
you buy a house, you can deduct the interest on the
mortgage. Second, you can deduct the real estate
taxes you pay. Third, if you ever sell the house at a
profit, and you buy another house, you don't have to
pay a tax on the profit. And finally, and most important—the system of credit built up over the years that
we have doesn't exist in a lot of other countries.
That's four. The system—all the intermediate credit
agencies that support the lending system—is a form
of subsidy.

[Cavett flinches almost imperceptibly at the words
intermediate credit agencies. He looks intelligent and in-
terested, but this is very abstract. Good television
guests are not abstract; they talk with passion about
passion, love, courage under pressure, sex, the habits
of other celebrities. They do not say words like *intermediate credit agencies.* Explain it? No, go on.]

CAVETT: I already have a house. Now what?

SMITH: Buy another house. Rent it to somebody—rent
it to your brother-in-law, or anybody.

CAVETT: [*Smiling*] I don't know about that; then he's
going to call me up and say the roof leaks—

SMITH: That's true—

CAVETT: [*Warming to the idea*]—the kitchen sink is
plugged up, crabgrass is running wild across the
lawn—and the government isn't going to help me, I
bet. Is it?

SMITH: No, the government only wants you to buy it.
Although the government wants you to own a house
so badly I wouldn't be surprised if there weren't a
part of some agency that would help you unplug the
kitchen sink.

CAVETT: I think I've done enough for the government.
Let's go back . . .

The switchboard did not light up. It was 1971, and people did not hoard houses. They owned their houses, whenever possible, and sometimes they owned a vacation house. Owning a house that you rented to someone else was for the middle-middle, lower-middle classes, the two-family city house with the stoop, the owners living in one, with the husband-landlord in shirt-sleeves and suspenders who could fix the plumbing, if you could find him. Neighborhood stuff. Not a national speculative medium.

Smith only scratched at the fourth subsidy. Let's have a replay in which Smith is allowed to do a better job on it.

> SMITH: The government wants you to buy a house. I've told you the first three ways it will subsidize you. The fourth is the most important, much bigger than the other three. The best thing about buying a house is that you can get a long-term, fixed-rate mortgage. If we have inflation, you pay back with cheaper dollars. And there's no risk. With a house, you can go into a savings and loan and borrow money for thirty years. Only the biggest corporations can borrow money for such a long period. Now leave the house itself, whether it's red or green, brick or wood, aside for a moment. Houses are wonderful because society—the government—has given you a way to owe money for a long period. What are the risks? Let's say you get a mortgage at seven and a half or eight percent. What if the rates go down, back to five percent? Then, in almost every case, you can go in, pay off the mortgage, and get another one at the lower rate. If your mortgage is brand-new, you'll have a penalty, depending on what your state law allows; but that fades away quickly after a year or two, and usually a one-percent drop in the interest rate makes up for any penalty. If rates go *up*, the bank can't raise them, but if they go down, you can lower them. The mortgage rate isn't much higher than the inflation rate, and since you can deduct the interest, the use of the

money is almost free. If inflation brings higher interest rates, the money really will be free. It's a one-way
street, in your direction, one of the great free rides.
CAVETT: I'm going to run out and buy another house
now, and I'll split the profits with you when I sell it.

Fish don't know they're in water; we're not usually conscious of the social consensus in which we operate. The
social consensus that says you should have your own house
is very powerful. It was not always so. Each generation
takes its environment for granted. It does not want to hear
that Mom and Pop trudged four miles through the snow
to school. It might want to hear Grandpa's tales of the
Great Depression, or the Great War, because they happened so long ago they have a certain charm; but Grandpa
doesn't live with the family these days; in fact, he is living
in a quadruply subsidized condo in Florida.

Once, in this country, people did not own the dwellings
they lived in. Farmers might, and rich people might, but
most people did not, because in order to buy a house, you
had to save up at least half the price of the house. The
other half was a mortgage, but it was due in five years,
which made the monthly payments relatively large. Sometimes the mortgage was for only one year and had to be
renegotiated every year. Furthermore, the mortgage was
a burden, an element for melodrama.

In the melodramas just beyond memory—maybe a frag-
ment of a Chaplin film, or an old play done as a burlesque
—the landlord is a wicked fellow with black mustaches
who comes demanding the payment and chases the beautiful Anabelle Lee around the dining-room table. When
she resists his advances, he says, "Out! All of you! By Friday noon!"

No wonder it was the objective of every family to be free
of debt. To pay off the mortgage was the goal of the family
—or the church, or the company; and when the mortgage

was paid off, there was a party, a mortgage burning, with cheers as the match was struck and touched to the hateful deed, and drinks all around.

In Arthur Miller's great play *Death of a Salesman,* Willy Loman has literally driven himself to his death. In the final scene his wife, Linda, speaks at his grave. She says she does not understand what he has done. "Willy, I made the final payment on the mortgage today. We're free and clear . . . we're free . . . we're free."

We have come a long way. Today, no one wants to be free of the mortgage.

Mortgage. *Gage* is derived from a French word meaning "hand." A hand, in Saxon and Norman times, was laid upon the land, to secure a debt of the landholder. Under the common law there were two types of gages. If the lender took control of the property, collecting its rents and produce until the debt was paid, that was a "live" gage. The creditor kept the land long enough to collect the rents and profits sufficient for his debt, then returned it.

The second gage was known as a "dead" gage. The debtor kept control of his land and made payments from its income. *Mort* being the French word for "dead," the instrument was known as the *mort-gage.* If the borrower did not meet the payments agreed to, the lender could seize the property under the *mort-gage.* But if he made the payments, the borrower always retained control.

In the nineteenth century, in this country and in some countries in Western Europe, "building and loan" associations were formed to hold the savings of working people and to lend those savings for home building. The building and loan, or savings and loan, might give a mortgage for three to five years. But as late as 1920, 60 percent of all homes occupied by the owner had no mortgage at all.

In the Great Depression unemployment reached 25 percent of the work force. Families agonized as they got one

month, two months, three months behind on the mortgage payments. Farmers could not sell their produce and
lost their farms. Depositors withdrew their money from
the savings banks, and the lending institutions had little
choice but to foreclose on the defaulted loans. Even families that had some income found that when the mortgage
came due, the savings bank would not renew it; it could
not afford to. The savings bank directors saw the lines of
depositors on the sidewalk, waiting to get their money out.
They did not want to have mortgage money tied up for
three years. In statistical terms there never were massive
and wholesale evictions, but newspaper pictures from the
early days of the Depression show families with their furniture on the sidewalk, the children crying, bird cages,
toys, household goods all stacked on a sofa or a table, and
nowhere to go. The fixed terms of the mortgage seemed a
relentless burden. (In deflation, with *falling* prices, fixed
terms are worse every year.) The breadwinner of the family might be out of work, or at best on a reduced salary.
Wives did not work, and the pennies earned by teenagers
carrying groceries and delivering newspapers did not contribute significantly. *Nowhere to go,* the picture in the papers, was a lurking fear.

Herbert Hoover actually began the First Wave of social
legislation. There was no intent, in the waning days of his
administration, to encourage everyone to buy a house; the
intent was to help the foundering and dying savings banks.
Hoover established the Federal Home Loan Bank Board,
with twelve regional banks, patterned after the Federal
Reserve. The banks were to get money from the Treasury
and lend it to the gasping savings banks, using their mortgages as security. Then Franklin D. Roosevelt took over
and acted with bolder strokes. His administration formed
the Home Owners Loan Corporation, which allowed the
individual homeowner to stretch out the payments as long
as fifteen years, rather than three or five. Naturally, that
made the monthly payments much easier.

The centerpiece of Roosevelt's housing legislation was the National Housing Act of 1934, which established the Federal Housing Administration, the FHA. Like the Home Owners Loan Corporation, the FHA was there to try to keep a system alive. When you read this act, the word *insure* must catch your eye. The FHA will *insure* mortgages up to twenty years. It will *insure* mortgages on low-income housing built by state and local governments. It will *insure* a savings and loan that makes a loan for repairing or improving residential real estate. In other words, the frightened savings bankers need not be afraid to put money out; something was behind them. If the homeowner lost his job or could not keep up the payments, FHA insurance would help the lender; the FHA would take over the mortgage.

Even so, the traumatized loan officers were slow to act. Some said that each Congress could not insure anything beyond its own term, like a city council. Even in 1939 FHA-insured mortgages were only 10 percent of the total. Savings banks thought the government wanted to bolster their rival full-service commercial banks.

The FHA made mortgage lending a national activity. Because the FHA stretched out the term of the mortgage, and because it thus made the monthly payments and the down payment so much lower, it produced an environment in which, for the first time in American history, you could buy—in terms of monthly payments—as cheaply as you could rent. It is almost inconceivable today to think of a government agency as costing nothing, but the FHA had that virtue. It charged a very small premium on each mortgage as an insurance fee, and for the first thirty-six years of its existence, its books show that as an agency it actually made a profit.

By the end of World War II, the banks were full of money, money from the savings of workers who couldn't find goods to spend it on. The returning veterans deserved rewards; one of the rewards they got was a Veterans Administration guarantee that protected the lender against loss (to a certain limit) on a loan to a veteran. Housing tracts sprang up with signs and banners: "Vets—No Money Down." The banks had money to lend, and now they were protected from stupidity, bad loans, and depression trauma by government guarantee. (Depression trauma was hard to shake off. Of the first $8,000 houses in Levittown—$8,000 was the full price of the house— Eric Larrabee wrote in *Harper's,* in 1948: "Nearly everyone is agreed that today's housing values are inflated, and that the collapse will have to come some day.")

In 1920 somewhere around 50 percent of Americans lived in what the 1948 Housing Act would call "decent housing": "having indoor plumbing and no dilapidation." By 1960, 82 percent of the population lived in "decent housing" and 62 percent owned their own homes.

Those statistics represent a legislative and social triumph. The First Wave of social legislation saved a bankrupt system, turned it around, and created, over a generation, owner-occupied housing nationwide. Savers put their money in the banks, the banks lent the money to house buyers, the house buyers paid off the loans, and the government agencies behind the process cost the taxpayer almost nothing.

Franklin D. Roosevelt had seen one-third of a nation ill housed and ill fed. Lyndon Johnson could not say that; the children of the beneficiaries of the First Wave of housing legislation, by the mid-1960s, had houses of their own. Still, there was a gap, and a vast and rich country, Johnson urged Congress, should have housing for all its people. Johnson's staff told him the Great Society needed 26 million housing units over the next ten years, and the institutions of the First Wave of legislation were good for only about 1½ million housing starts a year. Johnson was mindful, too, that there was a powerful construction industry: not only the builders, who were politically sensitive and who generally knew their local congressmen well, but building-materials suppliers and bankers. A generation of bankers had grown up with the security of government agencies standing behind their mortgage loans. In a good year the building industry could be 10 percent of the gross national product.

The problem was that there was still housing to be built —the incremental 1 million units a year—and in the mid-1960s housing was having trouble getting funds, largely because the boom conditions created by the Vietnam War diverted the funds of the lenders to investments that would bring more immediate returns.

The Great Society produced a Second Wave of housing legislation, more agencies, more acronyms, this time with some endearing nicknames. FNMA, or "Fannie Mae," the Federal National Mortgage Association, was already in existence. Fannie Mae could go to the market and borrow, almost as easily as the government itself, and use the money to buy mortgages. Now Fannie Mae had a little sister, "Ginnie Mae," GNMA, the Government National Mortgage Association. Ginnie Mae could buy mortgages that Fannie Mae couldn't, because Ginnie Mae's were for subsidized housing. And there was a little brother, "Freddie Mac," the Federal Home Loan Mortgage Corporation. Like his sisters, Freddie could raise money by selling bonds in the public marketplace; unlike his sisters, who would keep the mortgages, Freddie Mac bought mortgages from savings and loans when they needed cash and sold them back when they were flush.

From 1968 to 1980, after the Housing Act of 1968, the Federally Sponsored Credit Agencies, Fannie and Ginnie and Freddie and their farm cousins, sold $361 billion in government-guaranteed bonds and put that money out. In the same period outstanding mortgages rose from $265 billion to $760 billion. Fannie and Freddie and Ginnie were very busy, and sometimes they met the rest of the government borrowing at the same marketplace, which sent the rates up; and sometimes, as in 1974 and 1975, they were even borrowing when the government was trying to restrict borrowing. Some of the people left behind by the First Wave and the years of prosperity did get housing. All the new mortgage money produced an 11-percent rise in the construction of new houses. The critics said that much of the money available from that family of Federally Sponsored Credit Agencies went out into the market and chased the *existing* supply of housing. If mortgage credit was available, savings institutions and banks would lend it. The more money there is around, the more there is to be spent, and the more borrowers pay for houses, which encourages other people to borrow because when prices accelerate, there is always that feeling of buy now because tomorrow may be too late.

California Dreamin'—4BR, 2 bth, $1,000,000

California is supposed to be a glimpse of tomorrow. In the 1970s the price of California housing became breathtaking.

To be fair, it was not only all the money available from Fannie and Freddie and Ginnie. These phenomena are self-fueling after a while. The California population was growing, and the cost of land went up. Environmental restrictions proliferated. It might take approval of twenty-five separate agencies to begin a housing development. California savings and loans were aggressive in putting money out. Several of them were publicly held savings and loans, companies with common stock listed on stock exchanges, which wanted to have good earnings to report. Good earnings come from lending money.

Californians were the first to realize that Linda Loman should not have paid off the mortgage, that the debt that

Grandfather feared could be, in the new scheme of things, the path to riches. In the old, sober days, you might go into a savings and loan, and the gentleman in the starched collar would want to know what your income was, how you were going to keep up the payments. Then an appraiser would go out to look at the house and say, "Well, let's see, this house is selling for thirty thousand, but it's ten years old, it's depreciating, the paint is peeling, say twenty-five thousand . . ."

In the 1970s the idea of a California house depreciating was as foreign as Mars. The smell of Boom was everywhere. It caught even those who were not particularly attracted by it. A former president of Freddie Mac, William Popejoy, arrived to head up a large savings and loan, American Savings. He had moved from the suburbs of Washington, D.C., "and we bought a four-bedroom house in Benedict Canyon for a hundred and sixty-five thousand dollars. We'd get over six hundred thousand for it now, in just five years." If you could do that, without trying, what could you do if you were trying, if you were refinancing the first house and buying a second? "I own ten million dollars' worth of houses," said a thirty-year-old actor who had once been in a Jack Webb television series. Boom! Like Midland, Texas, in 1957; like Wall Street in 1968; like Riyadh, Saudi Arabia, in 1976. Money everywhere. The California dinner parties were all full of talk of overnight fortunes.

I went to see Harleigh Sandler at his office in Beverly Hills. I suspected he was not going to make me feel good. Harleigh has a pointed beard and wears pointed Western boots. He has been in the real estate business in Beverly Hills since 1955. Once, I lived in Los Angeles, off Benedict Canyon. "That house," Harleigh said, "sold for maybe eighty, thirteen years ago. Today, half a million. More." That did not make me feel good.

But, I told Harleigh, in those days, when you moved,

you sold your house so that you could buy another one.
People did not hoard houses.

"We sell ten million dollars' worth of houses a week now,
five hundred million dollars a year," Harleigh said. "We
have a whole division that sells houses with a minimum
asking price of one million dollars."

We talked about a house I had once thought of buying,
on Hazen Drive. It had been empty at the time. A nice
house, nice view, paneled library, high ceilings, a roomy
kitchen, a pantry. The asking price had been $104,000.
There was a $90,000, 6-percent first mortgage on it.

"I think that house sold within the last six months," Harleigh said, reaching for the Los Angeles multiple-listing
guide. "Yes. A million two. You could have had it for
fourteen thousand cash and taken out more than a million
one in thirteen years. That's better than Wall Street."

"It sure is. Who could afford that house?"

"Somebody who just sold another house. See, California
is always ahead of the rest of the country, and California
is on to what's real. Money isn't worth anything. Real estate
will always go up. You can't get a secretary for a thousand
dollars a month, because nobody can live on a thousand
dollars a month. The condos at Century City were listed at
four hundred twenty-five thousand dollars when they
were being built. Before they were finished, the owners
could resell them for two hundred fifty thousand dollars
higher."

"Nice condos?" I asked.

"Nice enough—you can walk to shops—but not really
nice, not like the ones on the water or anything."

Harleigh's office is on the second floor of the building
at 420 North Camden Drive. On the first floor—cubicles,
phones ringing, women shouting across the partitions—
the back wall was covered with posters in the shape of a
diamond. That is the Honor Roll—agents who have sold
more than $1 million worth of houses during the year. I
asked what a blue diamond meant. That is for agents who

have sold more than $3 million worth of houses. There were more than a hundred names on the million-dollar list.

I made a date for the next day to look at houses with two of Harleigh's agents. Then I went to see Stuart Davis.

Stuart swiveled comfortably at his desk in his tenth-floor suite. Stuart has silver hair and looks like a chairman of the board. He is the chairman of Great Western, one of the biggest savings and loan associations in California, with $9.75 billion in assets. From his window you can see the dun-colored hills covered with houses whose market value bubbles up like oil. I wanted Stuart to tell me that this is all temporary, that it's going to start over, so that the rest of us can get in on it, so that the world will make sense again. Stuart has been a savings banker for forty years.

"No, it's not a bubble," Stuart said. "If this was a troubled time, we'd be seeing delinquencies, late payments; but our delinquency rate is only fifteen-hundredths of one percent. In California we need two hundred seventy thousand new units of housing a year. We're only building two hundred thousand. In apartments vacancies don't exist. Demographically, we're just seeing the home-buying age group get started. That's young couples in their late twenties and early thirties. In the eighties that age group will increase by ten million nationally.

"People have seen what inflation does. They're afraid of stocks and bonds, but everybody's an expert on a house. I think housing will go up faster than inflation. You might find a leveling off in the high-priced houses—a million and up—and there's no limit on demand for the middle-priced house, three or four hundred thousand."

Middle-priced? Will Great Western make loans on these middle-priced houses? How will the young couples buy them?

"Well, we don't like to go above two hundred fifty thousand dollars on a loan, and now we ask twenty percent down or higher. So maybe you have a working wife and some help from the parents. And you're talking about the West Side."

Two of Harleigh's agents, Irma and Lee (as I'll call them), took me to look at houses. Irma, who had been selling for seven years, had a blond beehive hairdo. Lee was younger and had just come from San Francisco. We looked first at a small Spanish-style house south of Wilshire Boulevard. South of Wilshire is less fashionable.

"But it is Beverly Hills," they said, "so the schools are good, and it's flat, so kids can ride their bikes. Now this house is what we call a fixer-upper or a starter. It's a fixer-upper because it needs some work and a starter because it's the kind of house you start out with—a young couple with small children."

The house was on perhaps a third of an acre. It was about forty years old, and the original builder had attempted to give it some distinction with a high-ceilinged living room and arched doorways. A tricycle sat in the living room. The paint was peeling. Upstairs there was a master bedroom with bath and two children's rooms with a bathroom between them. "3BR, 2bth, charm."

"The asking on this is five hundred ninety-five," said Irma, "but I think it would go foy five hundred seventy-five. It needs some work."

"That's five hundred ninety-five thousand," I said. "Young couple, starting out. What would a bank lend? Where would they get the down payment?"

"You might get two hundred fifty from the bank on this," Lee said. "I would think maybe that both husband and wife work or that they get some help from their parents."

"It can't be like this all over southern California," I said. "Six hundred thousand dollars for a small three-bedroom house?"

"Oh, no," Lee said. "In the Valley you could get a house like this for one-third as much. And maybe east, like Pasadena, it would be cheaper, but it's smoggier. This is Beverly Hills. Good schools."

"If the struggling young couple did buy this house," I said, "and if they did get a loan, the interest alone would be more than three thousand a month. With taxes, the payments might be over six thousand a month."

"Like I said, they probably both work."

"At what?" I asked.

We went to look at a house six or eight blocks away, north of Wilshire, north of Santa Monica, in a more fashionable area. It was an English-style house, tightly shuttered, on perhaps half an acre, with other houses adjacent and an alley in the back. We couldn't get in. No one had left a key, and there was no one home.

"This is your tear-downer," Irma said.

"Tear-downer?"

"You wouldn't want it. It has a bad floor plan, and it needs some work," she explained.

"Somebody will buy this and tear it down? How much is it?"

"The asking price is a million, but it would go for nine fifty."

We looked at another house, an empty house a block away. A builder had bought it, remodeled the kitchen, installed an intercom, and converted a small bedroom into a walk-in closet.

"This closet has eighty feet of pole," Irma said. Pole is wood. It is what runs across the closet, what you hang your clothes on. Pole ran around the room on two levels.

The master bedroom opened onto a deck, upon which sat a Jacuzzi.

"The builder thinks this Jacuzzi is great," Lee said. "But it's out in the open, so the houses on each side can see you, and also the houses across the valley. So I don't think it's such a great idea, because unless you're an exhibitionist you'd have to wear a swimsuit in your own hot tub."

The backyard was pleasant. There was a tennis court.

"There are two problems with this tennis court," Irma said. I could see one: the tennis court had been squeezed in, so that there were perhaps only five feet in back of each baseline instead of twenty. No serious tennis player would consider it.

"The court is east-west," Irma said. "Your north-south court goes for a lot more."

"I think he should tear down the court and make it north-south," Lee said, "and maybe he could get the room in beyond the baseline."

The asking price was $1.85 million. "I happen to know he paid eight ninety for it and fixed up," Irma said, "with the tub and all that pole and a raised tub in the bathroom and everything."

The master bedroom had an elaborate bath, off the closet with all the pole. The two smaller bedrooms shared a bath. I asked what would happen if the builder didn't get his $1.85 million. "It'll be two million, because by that time more time will have gone by," Irma said.

"Maybe an Iranian will buy it," Lee said.

"No," Irma said, "the downstairs is dark. Your Iranian likes bright contemporary stuff—no arches and maybe marble."

"Do you get lots of Iranians?" I asked.

"Lots," Irma said. "And Mexicans. Now, your Mexican might like this house. We had a Mexican the other day, came with his daughter, his daughter liked a house, he brought a suitcase with a million one in cash. And the president of Gabon bought a house the other day for two million when the asking price was only a million seven. But he wanted it in a hurry. It closed in three days."

I didn't remember anything about a coup in Gabon.

"Gabon is in Africa," Lee said. "That one was in the paper."

"Is this boom based entirely on flight capital?" I asked. We can, after all, disregard its effect on the rest of us if it

is. I had to explain the term: money fleeing some disagreeable political situation.

"I had a very young, attractive couple from South Africa
who wanted to pay for a house completely with diamonds," Irma said.

"That would be flight capital, I suspect," I said.

"But we get a lot of people from Toledo and Chicago,
too," Lee said, "because it snowed so much there last year."

That didn't quite count as flight capital.

"What's the single most valuable asset in selling a
house?" I asked.

"If you can put 'tennis court property' in the ad," Irma
said.

"How much would that add to the value of the property?"

"In Beverly Hills, half a million," Irma said. "That's if
the court is actually there."

"But you can't say it's there if it's not, can you?" I asked.

"You can say 'tennis court property' if there's room for
a court, but you wouldn't get a half a million more, only a
couple of hundred."

"Some of these prices are crazy," Lee volunteered.

The houses that Irma and Lee had in their listings were
in six areas of West Los Angeles. There was Beverly Hills
proper, where your house on the 500 block would go for
$800,000 and your house on the 800 block, just three
blocks away, for $1.8 million. Then there were the hills
and canyons that had a Beverly Hills post office address
but were actually in Los Angeles. Then the Sunset Strip
and West Hollywood, with older, smaller houses. Then
Westwood, the area around UCLA. And finally, Brent-
wood and Pacific Palisades.

Irma is doing very well. If she sells half a dozen million-
dollar houses, her commissions come to $360,000, and
even when she splits that with Harleigh, that is a good

wage for showing people houses. Lee is just starting out, but she has high ambitions. She lives in a small apartment. Last year she made only $31,000, but that was her first year, and it wasn't a full year.

"I want to be a star," Lee said.

A movie star? A television star?

"No, you know, a salesperson."

"You mean a real estate star."

"Yes. Like Joyce. And Marcia. Joyce got her license in 1973. She was a schoolteacher, and I think a part-time stewardess, before."

"How long does it take to get a real estate license?"

"The course is six weeks."

"Then there must be more real estate salespersons all the time."

"There are. You have to work hard at it. You have to get the seller to list with you, and you have to hustle the buyers. But I know some of the women on that diamond chart in the office who buy real diamonds every time they make a sale."

"Is that what you'll do when you make your first big sales?"

"No, I think I'll buy a fixer-upper and fix it up."

"For half a million?"

"All you have to do is sell a couple of houses and get a big mortgage."

We went back to the office. The phones were ringing.

I sat leafing through the listing directory that covered all of Los Angeles. Each house is listed with a description; many have pictures. The lowest listing I found was for $197,000.

A woman with blond streaks in her hair and a purple blouse leaned over the partition to talk to Lee.

"The Roxbury house just went on at two point eight," she said.

"Oh, wow," Lee said. "Who got it?"

"Marcia," said the woman.

Lee looked at me significantly.

"I know," I said, "you want to be a star."

A colleague of mine went to a one-day extension course at UCLA, the University of California, Los Angeles, on real estate.

"There will be no real estate recession in California," he and his classmates were told, "because so much money wants in. The best thing that can happen to you is high construction costs and increased inflation." Sanford Goodkin, president of a national company that provides financing help to real estate investors, had organized the lectures. "Prices will go up," Goodkin said. "There's just a limited amount of land in California. We really want inflation. The problem is that while it's kind to real estate people, it destroys the rest of the country."

The California real estate boom is not limited to West Los Angeles. A friend of mine was offered a job as director of long-range planning for a major utility in northern California. He lived in a New Jersey suburb, in a house with four bedrooms that had gone up from a purchase price of $90,000 to $255,000. But when his wife went house hunting in the San Francisco suburbs, she found that a similar house would cost $700,000. The hiring company had to help him finance the new house and make arrangements. The cost of California housing is such that it is contributing to the revival of pockets of New England. The computer and semiconductor industries have prospered on the peninsula south of San Francisco, and they continue to grow at a rapid rate. But they lose engineers to the computer plants of New England, where housing is not so expensive.

Does what goes up come down? When you first encounter the four-bedroom, million-dollar house, you might say, this is a bubble, a fad, like when the seventeenth-century Dutch tulip growers bid up the price of a single tulip to half the price of a good ship. Everyone whose house has tripled in price feels very smart. If the house has tripled in its potential asking price, the equity in the house may be up ten times. Real estate brokers have confounded the doubters, and they have put energy into renting office space and hiring people and competing for sales, and they feel duly and only properly rewarded by doing a half a billion dollars a year in volume with gross commissions of $30 million. One of my old maxims runs: *Financial genius is a rising market.* Booms create heroes. Someone who can flip a coin to come up heads ten times in a row will be asked not only about his technique of flipping nickels but about his opinions on events in Washington.

The conventional wisdom was certainly that housing was—to use the recurring metaphor—a "bubble" about to burst. "Bubble," said *The Wall Street Journal, Business Week, Forbes, Barron's, Financial World,* and *Money.* "All such obsessions have ended in crashes," said *Business Week.* "No boom lasts forever," said *Forbes.* "Why should this one be different?" *Barron's* excerpted a study that predicted that the break in housing prices could be as great as the 1929 crash in the stock market.

California was not the only place that was bubbly. In Aspen, Colorado, a three-bedroom ski condominium that sold in 1974 for $150,000 was $675,000 five years later. Chicago, Washington, D.C., and Florida reported the same phenomenon. Fashionable suburbs in other areas, New Canaan and Rumson and River Oaks, all carried real estate listings with some houses at $1 million. "These prices are crazy," said the people who had once thought of themselves as middle-class. At the same time they felt smart in their ownership, even with a more modest house. Two-bedroom houses in these areas will soon go for their 1980 California price of $200,000, and $200,000 still buys a lot of lamb chops. If inflation continues at 10 percent, the million-dollar house will not be so uncommon, because prices will double every seven years.

Do they say, of land, "They ain't making any more of it"? True. But even in the most densely populated areas of the country, there is still room for vast populations. If you drive from Philadelphia to New York through the most densely populated state in the country, New Jersey, you are in almost continuous suburb; if you drive on the other axis, from the northeast to the southwest, you can go thirty minutes at a time without seeing a house. Why should bricks and mortar, wood and paint, increase in price even faster than inflation? It is because not only is the currency diminishing in its worth relative to fixed objects, but *belief* in the currency is diminishing even faster, at a geometric rate. Thus the conventional wisdom, that what goes up must come down, may be false physics.

When this has happened in other countries, some have knocked zeroes off the currency. One hundred Old Francs become one New Franc. If the million-dollar house is too embarrassing for a national standard, then let it sell for only $100,000. That, of course, is only cosmetic, unless other actions are taken.

Could there be a real estate crash, as there was a stock market crash in 1929?

Obviously, if there is a speculator in Orange County, California, who has bought fifteen condos and pyramided them, using the unrealized price appreciation from one to buy the next one, that speculator can easily be shaken out. If the rents do not cover the mortgages, if taxes go up faster than rents, if the whole game does not continue at the same rate, the speculator is vulnerable and so is the condo situation in Orange County, California. A speculator who finds there are five bidders when there are no available condos can find that the bidders pull back when there are suddenly a couple of condos free and for sale.

But Orange County is not the country, and in most places speculators do not own fifteen condos. In Buffalo, New York, they still think a million dollars is a lot of money. It takes relatively few Middle Eastern folk to have an impact on the flatlands of Beverly Hills and only a slightly larger number of flush Latin Americans to take the prices in south Florida to a titillating fever pitch.

What does history tell us about housing prices?

Ancient history: the Census Bureau tells us that housing prices were not affected by the Panics of 1893 and 1907, nor the mini-depressions of 1913–14 and 1920–21. But that was before Fannie and Freddie and Ginnie and the social consensus that everyone ought to have a house and that it was the responsibility of government to help provide what everyone ought to have. Prices did indeed fall during the Great Depression of the thirties, but most of the fall occurred from 1930 to 1933, when the thrift institutions were closing their doors. House prices stabilized with the National Housing Act of 1934 and remained stable through the thirties. The prices began to move up through the forties, and they have never stopped since.

Modern history: housing prices chugged right along, through the stock market breaks of 1966 and 1970 and 1974, all of which were associated with credit crunches, when interest rates went up and credit became hard to get. In 1974 the stock market dropped 49 percent, interest rates reached a peak, and housing starts declined 65 percent. Yet the national indices for single-family houses kept bumping right along. Here is the average selling price of existing homes, from the National Association of Realtors:

1972	$30,000
1973	32,900
1974	35,800
1975	39,000
1976	42,200

1977	47,900
1978	55,500
1979	64,200

Why do houses—historically—resist the storms around them?

In all markets, psychology is an important factor. A pension-fund manager may switch from IBM to Treasury bills and back to IBM. All it takes is a phone call, or three phone calls. There is a less efficient market in art, and postage stamps, and Chinese vases, but you do not *need* the art or the Chinese vase. You *do* need to live somewhere.

It seems utterly obvious, but frequently, in economic analyses, sometimes the utterly obvious is "anecdotal evidence" and is left out.

You paid $60,000 for your house. Now, your neighbors tell you, it is worth $150,000. Why don't you sell it? You don't sell it because of a very simple four-word question.

Where would I move?

All the other houses have gone up, too, and so have apartment rents, and with so little apartment building, apartments are not so easy to find. But you could do it, if you were willing to find the apartment, call the real estate broker, and entertain the prospective buyers who come tromping through, fingering the drapes and slamming the closet doors.

In other markets, price declines trigger selling, because people will sell something they believe is going still lower. The current generation of householders is not likely to sell, even if houses begin to decline in price; they are more likely to wait out the bad times.

In the stock market, or the commodities market, if your stock or your commodity declines, you may get a margin call—be asked to put up more money. But your bank does not care if your neighbor sells his house for less than he paid. You just keep up the mortgage payments. And even if you have trouble with your payments, the bank is not going to twirl its black mustaches and chase your pretty daughter around the dining-room table. For the bank to say, "Everybody out! Friday noon!" it has to go to a legal expense, and make a bad mark in its own books, and then resell the house, assigning someone else to show it and say, "Don't finger the drapes." The bank doesn't want to do that.

There is still one more factor, again so utterly obvious it must be expressed. The numbers on the New York Stock Exchange can be read by everybody everywhere, all across the country. The same for commodities. You can walk into a brokerage office, make a phone call, read your morning paper. But if you live in Dothan, Alabama, you may not ever hear about the bust in Orange County. If you live in Lexington, Kentucky, or Cape Girardeau, Missouri, all the Iranians in Beverly Hills can sell out and move back to Iran, and you will only know about it if Johnny Carson makes a joke of it.

Which is not to say that Dothan and Lexington and Beverly Hills are not all in the same country. They were more separate before Fannie and Freddie and Ginnie, but now the mortgages are pooled nationally, and the price and availability of money are going to be national in scope.

Now let us look at a very interesting table, on pages 90 and 91, which comes from Alan Greenspan, who was on President Ford's Council of Economic Advisers. The numbers on this table are very large. In fact, nine digits have been left off each number after the decimal point. Nine zeroes. In other words, everything is in billions.

Look first at line fifteen. That is total mortgage debt, going from $223.6 billion in 1970 to $654 billion in 1979. That represents all the money being lent by the savings and loans and the banks, with the help of Fannie and Freddie and Ginnie.

Now look at line fourteen. The total market value of all
the houses in the country goes from $645.6 billion to
$2,253.7 billion; that is, more than $2.2 trillion:
$2,253,700,000,000. An abstraction. A very large number.

And if you subtract line fifteen from line fourteen, you
get $1.6 trillion. That is how much we all own of our
houses, net of the mortgages.

Compare that with $961 billion, which is the value of all
the stocks listed on the New York Stock Exchange, and
$460 billion, which is the value of all the bonds, and you
come to this conclusion: *The savings of America have gone
into houses.* And some of the speculation has gone into
houses, but there is $1.6 trillion of house out there which
the citizens own.

You can debate how much, more or less, of this is true,
if you are a housing economist. Alan Greenspan says
maybe the savings rate is not a lowly 4 percent; maybe it is
8 percent, because the savings have gone into house payments, not into the bank. For the moment let the housing
economists argue that one.

My second conclusion, based on the first conclusion, is:
You can't have a crash that looks like a crash in housing.

If there are 86 million houses out there, 56 million of
them owned by the people who live in them, that is a very
powerful political force. In 1929 there were only 1.37 million brokerage accounts available to be wiped out.

Any government that was around when the Crash came
would not be there very much longer. Fifty-six million
owner-owned houses, each with Mom and Dad and Buddy
and Sis, or some variation, is an enormous constituency.
Eighty-four percent of families making more than $20,000
a year own their own homes. Government-backed tax-
exempt bond issues subsidize even the prosperous. Home
ownership is more widespread than churchgoing.

If you were a stock market investor in 1974, you might
have said, "I used to own Avon Products at ninety, and

This chart looks a bit formidable, but the key figures are indicated by arrows. We have $2.2 trillion worth of houses, and $654 billion of debt against them.

OWNER OCCUPIED SINGLE-FAMILY HOMES
$ BILLIONS (Add nine zeros)

	1970	1971
Increase in market value—total	51.4	96.1
Less—purchase of new homes	19.6	26.0
= Incr. in market value exist. homes	31.7	70.0
Less—realized capital gains	8.5	13.7
= Additions to unrealized gains	23.2	56.3
Mortgage debt extensions—new homes	10.6	17.2
Less—scheduled amortization	13.4	14.3
= Incr. mtg. debt ex net ext. exist. homes	−2.8	2.9
Increase in total mortgage debt	11.1	21.4
Net extensions on existing homes	13.9	18.4
Increase in home equity—total	40.3	74.7
Attributable to—capital gains	17.9	51.6
other	22.4	23.1
Total market value (end of period)	645.6	741.6
Total mortgage debt (end of period)	223.6	245.0
Debt/market value	0.346	0.330
Memo—Disposable personal income	685.9	742.8
+ Net ext. of debt on exist. homes	13.9	18.4
= Disp. personal income + debt	699.8	761.2
Less—personal outlays	635.4	685.5
= Personal savings (adjusted)	64.4	75.7
Savings rate (adjusted)	9.2	9.9
Savings rate (official)	7.4	7.7

Source: Townsend-Greenspan & Co., Inc.

1972	1973	1974	1975	1976	1977	1978	1979
90.0	155.2	109.8	121.0	156.4	226.7	353.1	299.9
32.7	35.3	31.4	35.4	49.8	66.9	80.1	81.8
57.3	119.9	78.5	85.6	106.6	159.8	273.0	218.1
18.3	25.2	29.2	36.1	49.2	69.8	77.3	90.4
39.0	94.7	49.3	49.5	57.4	90.0	195.7	127.7
21.8	23.6	20.3	20.8	26.4	39.0	48.3	51.3
15.8	17.8	19.6	21.3	23.6	27.2	31.9	37.2
5.9	5.8	0.7	−0.5	2.8	11.8	16.4	14.1
29.8	31.0	26.0	31.8	49.7	71.8	82.1	86.7
23.9	25.1	25.3	32.3	46.9	60.1	65.7	72.6
60.2	124.2	83.8	89.2	106.7	154.8	271.0	213.1
33.4	94.7	53.2	53.3	59.7	99.7	207.3	145.5
26.8	29.5	30.7	35.9	47.0	55.1	63.7	67.7
831.6	986.8	1096.6	1217.7	1374.1	1600.7	1953.8	2253.7 ←
274.8	305.7	331.7	363.6	413.3	485.1	567.3	654.0 ←
0.330	0.310	0.303	0.299	0.301	0.303	0.290	0.290
801.3	901.7	984.6	1086.7	1184.5	1305.1	1458.4	1623.2
23.9	25.1	25.3	32.3	46.9	60.1	65.7	72.6
825.2	926.8	1009.9	1119.0	1231.4	1365.2	1524.1	1695.8
751.9	831.3	913.0	1003.0	1115.9	1240.2	1386.4	1550.4
73.3	95.5	96.9	116.0	115.5	125.0	137.7	145.4
8.9	10.3	9.6	10.4	9.4	9.2	9.0	8.6
6.2	7.8	7.3	7.7	5.8	5.0	4.9	4.5

now it's sixteen." Can you see dinner parties where everybody who once said, "I paid sixty thousand for this house,
and now it's worth one hundred fifty thousand," says instead "I paid one hundred fifty thousand for this house,
and now it's only worth thirty thousand"? Or worse: "I've
owned this house seven years, I can't keep it up, the bank
is coming to take it away on Friday"?

Not to mention that all the banks and savings and loans
would be pretty well wiped out. I suppose it could happen,
but that wouldn't be capitalism, or modified capitalism,
anymore, and under that scheme no student could go to
college whose parents had ever owned a house, because he
would be part of the old bourgeois privileged class.

Certainly you can have a crash in housing; it is thinkable
but unthinkable, like nuclear war. If we get to the day
when the $1.6 trillion in savings-in-housing is gone, no
one is going to be on the side of the banks, no bankers will
twirl their black mustaches and say everybody out by Friday, because there will not be any banks. There will be one
bank. In the Soviet Union there is only one bank, one real
bank, called the Gosbank. It is the biggest bank in the
world, and it is all the banks in Russia. Let housing crash,
1929-style, and you will have television commercials with
little jingles telling you about the savings rate at the American Gosbank.

But your wary eye has caught the edge in that firm
prediction about housing. You can't have a crash that
looks like a crash. What could you have?

You could have the end of the house as the wonderful
inflation hedge. The numbers on the sales prices of houses
would still go up, and whether the house value went up
faster or slower than the inflation rate would depend on
the area of the country and the size and location and at-
tractiveness of the particular house.

The housing industry, when it looks at the chart on the
next page, feels cheery. This is a chart about household

THE BABY BOOM AND THE DEMAND
FOR HOUSING

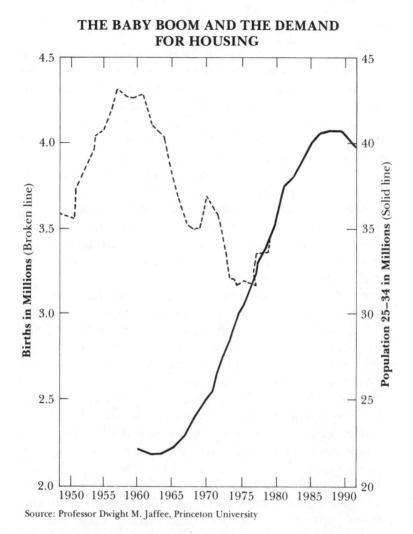

Source: Professor Dwight M. Jaffee, Princeton University

We had a computer draw this chart. The dotted line shows the curve of
the post-World War II baby boom, which peaked in the late 1950s. The
baby-boom children naturally, a generation later, turned into Household Formations, the handholding 25- to 34-year-olds, represented by
the solid line. What the chart tells us is that household formations
inspired by the baby boom of the 1950s climb through the early 1980s,
then flatten out and turn down. Behind the baby boom is, naturally, a
baby bust—the household formations from the children of the 1970s.
So the incremental demand for first-time housing will diminish.

formation, a little exercise in demography. It shows the postwar baby boom, which is now mature enough to be having a baby boom of its own—not that it is quite so enthusiastic as its parents. The housing industry figures you can go to college or not, you can live with your girl friend in a loft if you want to, but sooner or later the old genes and primordial urges are going to get to you, and you are going to be twenty-five to thirty-four years old, and you are going to become a household formation. And household formation translates into buying a house.

There are already 86 million houses in place, and on the other side of the household formations is a decided downturn in household formations, and markets anticipate the future—or are supposed to.

Leave aside, for the moment, the eventual fall in household formations; by that time the cost of energy and the cost of everything else may have changed the whole pattern of living. For a good while the primordial urges will perk, and households will form, and houses will be built.

What else do we need? Money.

In the 1970s house prices actually outdistanced the ability of the traditional buyers to carry the mortgage. What brought houses within range again was the addition of a new element in the work force: the working wife, the two-income family. Lenders began to accept the second income when considering a loan, just as—with some encouragement from government agencies—they also accepted the incomes of minorities, women, and single people.

The next chart has quite a complex title. It is called "Mortgage and Installment Debt, Scheduled Repayments, and Interest As a Percentage of Cash Disposable Personal Income." That translates into: Can you meet the payments? Let's call this item payments, for short. We can see that payments have risen gradually over thirty years from a little more than 12 percent of cash disposable personal income to almost 30 percent. This is a gross statistic; since

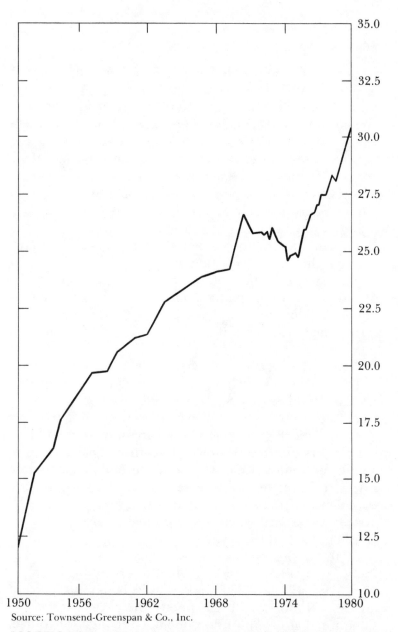

Source: Townsend-Greenspan & Co., Inc.

MORTGAGE AND INSTALLMENT DEBT, SCHEDULED REPAYMENTS, AND INTEREST AS PERCENTAGE OF CASH DISPOSABLE PERSONAL INCOME

The question is: can people meet the payments on their houses? This chart tells us it's getting harder and harder because, even though incomes go up, the payments go up more, and take an increasing percentage of income.

20 percent of the people have no debt, the proportion of payments for those who do is even higher.

Fannie and Ginnie and Freddie have made the payments easier, and the working wives have kept them going; but somewhere north of 40 percent there is going to be real resistance. People will not likely use half their incomes for housing when other prices are going up as well. The costs of housing are not going to decrease. The plumbers are unlikely to cut their prices, since they are trying to buy houses, too, and so are the masons and the electricians and the roofers and the surveyors and the lawyers and the clerks at the title companies.

With each notch that interest rates go up, another group of buyers has to drop away. The National Association of Home Builders reports that 70 percent more buyers can afford the payments at 9-percent interest rates than at 13 percent.

What is the conclusion? *The free ride in housing is over.*

The free ride is the long-term fixed-rate mortgage, that no-loss situation that Smith should have spelled out on "The Dick Cavett Show." The lenders are getting wise.

Fannie and Freddie and Ginnie are only there to bring the lenders and the borrowers together. That family inspired the confidence of the public to put its money into savings institutions, just as its earlier members inspired the confidence of the shaken bankers to go on lending. The system works well when inflation doesn't erode the purchasing power of the savings.

In the 1960s borrowers were able to get thirty-year money at 6 percent and less. The Bowery Savings Bank in New York still has $500 million on its books at 6 percent and less. No matter what happens, the payments stay the same for that group of householders, though, of course, the loans are gradually getting paid off. In the 1970s borrowers got their money for thirty years at 7 and 8 percent.

The money for those loans came largely from passbook

savers. Christmas Clubs, Chanukah Clubs, children saving for ice skates and stereos—there is $1,176,000,000,000 still outstanding in passbook savings, and those lenders have sponsored the California house millionaires and the Chicago condo buyers and all the other house buyers.

Some of the passbook savers got wise and transferred their funds to savings certificates in the very same banks at higher rates, 10 percent and 12 percent and more. Still others bought money-market funds and Treasury bills and other instruments. The smartest went out one door of the bank and came in the other as borrowers.

When the small saver's passbook becomes a symbol of foolishness, that is unhealthy. Even if we say that the savings have gone into houses, the percentage of income we save is nowhere near that of the other industrial powers. The Germans and the Japanese save far more of their incomes, and those savings can thus be used for more modern equipment and for new ventures, and before you know it, just to get simple, Toyotas and Datsuns and Volkswagens are everywhere, and all the workers at Chrysler and their families and their cousins and the dealers are feeling uneasy.

So the holders of the passbooks, the foolish children, were one sponsor of the free ride.

Who else pays the bill?

The savings banks themselves pay some of the bill. If we can't control inflation any other way, we cut back on credit, other borrowers crowd out the housing industry, mortgage rates go so high they scare the borrowers, and the savings banks' profits melt away. That's a cyclical disease of savings banks. But they don't go broke.

And the new borrowers pay the bill. The old borrowers are safe at their 6 percent, and 8 percent, and 9 percent, and the savings bank isn't going broke, and you can only con the children with the passbook savings for so long. Where else do you get the money? From the young people who want to buy a house, from those hand-holding formations. They have to pay a higher rate to help carry the old 7-percenters. Fewer and fewer young people will be able to enter an inflated housing market.

Finally, we all pay the bill, because we are all subject to the inflation that helped produce the free ride, and shoes and lamb chops and tuitions go up for everybody. If you have a 7-percent mortgage and your house is worth half a million dollars, you may gripe about shoes and lamb chops and tuitions like everybody else, but your heart isn't in it.

Let's look at another chart.

Before 1970 the increases in mortgage debt rarely exceed $15 billion a year.

By the late 1970s the increases in mortgage debt roared along at $100 billion a year.

What is fueling that is an absolute frenzy of house buying and mortgaging, a thrashing shark pool. It is that frenzy that makes the house-buying market seem like a bubble. How does the mortgage debt get to go up so much? The capital gains on the existing houses also go up $100 billion. Four million houses get sold a year, with an average capital gain of $25,000, and the new owner takes out the biggest mortgage he can get, and the old owner buys another house and takes out the biggest mortgage *he* can get.

That's one reason some economists kept forecasting a recession in the late seventies, long before a recession ever arrived. They would look at all the numbers and say, "Well, the folks are about out of money, now we have a recession." But the recession didn't come when it was supposed to, because conventionally you don't count capital gains as income and you don't count debt as income, so the economists didn't count them. The figures said folks were out of money, but the figures didn't count the ballooning house prices, the 4 million houses a year sold with an average capital gain of $25,000.

INCREASE IN MORTGAGE DEBT

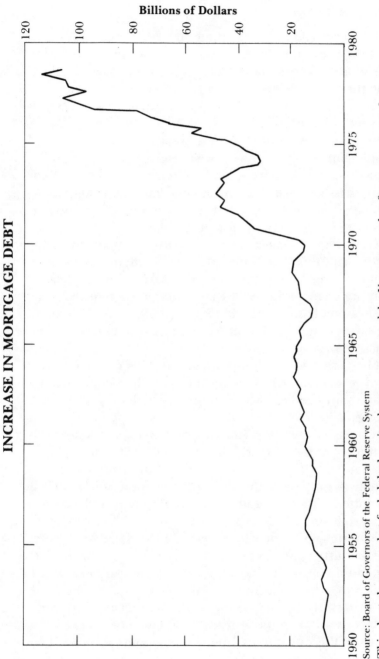

Billions of Dollars

Source: Board of Governors of the Federal Reserve System

This chart shows us what fueled the housing boom: mortgage debt. You can see that for twenty years, from 1950 to 1970, houses were places to live. Then they became something more: the way to borrow. Mortgage debt has been growing by hundreds of billions of dollars each year.

The year 1980 marked the end of the free ride, or at least the beginning of the end of the free ride.

The savings banks could look at their own books and see that the sixties borrowers had tied up money for thirty years at 6 percent, and the seventies borrowers at 7 and 8 percent. In the great crunch of 1980, the savings banks were out of money anyway and breathing hard. Their deposits could waltz right out overnight, and they did; to keep them, the savings banks had to pay, not the 5 percent in the passbooks of the foolish children, but as high as 16 percent. They were irritated that borrowers and speculators were tying up funds for thirty years.

Every night, when the savings banks scanned the computer printouts that replaced the old ledger sheets, they could see this house still there at 6 percent, that one at 7. Nothing to be done about that. And always that threat of "disintermediation," the deposits melting away. A bind. So the savings banks did what has become common corporate practice: they cried.

They cried in Washington, where tears frequently pay off, if accompanied by political clout. The Federal Home Loan Bank Board, which regulates federally chartered savings and loans, took notice—not that it hadn't been noticing anyway. "We cannot possibly expect lenders to guarantee the cost of credit over the next thirty years," said Jay Janis, the chairman. "Try getting your corner gas station to guarantee the price of gasoline." So the FHLB permitted all its federally chartered savings and loans to issue rollover mortgages, which it called "renegotiated-rate mortgages." You can still get the mortgage for twenty-five or thirty years, but every three years (or four, or five, depending on what kind of mortgage the bank writes) the bank can adjust the rate of interest you pay. The bank can't mark up the mortgage to the market level immediately, but at the end of three years, say, it can increase or decrease the rate one-half percentage point per year. You have ninety days to shop around for a better deal if it decides to move the rate.

Almost as it was back in the twenties. But there is a critical difference. In 1931 the bank could say, "Your mortgage is due, and we don't want it anymore. Pay it off." Now the bank has to renew it; you just may not like the terms.

In some states, in recent years, savings and loans had already instituted variable-rate mortgages. So some consumers have already felt a jump in the payments. The renegotiated-rate mortgage is one way the lender has of keeping up. The lenders also devised other ways: the graduated-payment mortgage, in which the payments get bigger as they go on; and the reverse-annuity mortgage. One recent innovation is "appreciation-participation loans," in which the lender gives you the money, but he wants one-third of the profit on your house when you sell it. All of these devices will make home purchasing possible, but they will also make borrowing more expensive than it was in the decades of the long-term, fixed-rate mortgage.

The Internal Revenue Service deserves a note here. The social consensus—that everybody ought to have a house —led to rules of taxation that favored the homeowner, the quadruple subsidy. The Revenue Service is now chipping away where it can most easily—in the second house, the extra house, by limiting the deductibility of interest, and in the depreciation schedules. Such rulings don't affect the primary consensus, every man in his own home, but they do affect the speculative edge of housing. If the Internal Revenue Service has its way, it will chip further as time goes by.

If the lending institutions finally adapt to inflation, and if 56 million households already own their houses, and if the IRS is beginning to frown on the house that isn't lived in by the owner, and if the payments are going north as a percentage of income, you would have to conclude that the free ride is over, and the sure thing is not quite so inevitable and sure.

But the cooling off of a boom doesn't mean that what goes up must nominally come down. No one is going to restore the purchasing power of the foolish children with the passbooks, and the new citizens of California and Texas aren't ready to move.

The experts look at household formations and see booming years for housing. The demand will be there for a while. Environmental restrictions will not disappear; they have become as much a part of the social consensus as housing itself. Land will not get any cheaper, and local agencies, which govern how builders can build, will not put themselves out of business. Houses will become, like cars, smaller and more energy-efficient. The areas of the country in which people want to live will have more money than housing, and the house prices will go up. The areas of the country from which people depart may actually have more houses than money to buy them, and it will be hard to sell those houses.

The bulge in household formations comes a generation after a baby boom, but we can, beyond the twenty-five-to-thirty-four-year-old hand-holding household formations, see declining college applications, empty dormitory rooms, and boarded-up primary schools, from the baby bust that succeeded the baby boom. That baby bust will show up in the housing market in the next decade.

The National Association of Home Builders ran some numbers through its econometric model, which said that the median house, priced at $63,300 in 1979, could cost $156,500 in 1989; but that is not quite the bonanza that it seems. There are several can openers among the assumptions. One is that the lenders will keep lending to the borrowers, that money will appear from savers in savings banks and life insurance policies. We can agree that all of the subsidies for housing will still be in place, and that there will still be a social consensus that everyone should own a house. When measured against the currency, houses will seem to go up in price, because there is nothing to hold the currency to a standard, to keep it from going down.

But a decade hence we will have 100 million houses, some new and handsome, some old and wearing down. They will not be financial vehicles; they will not be the common way to flee the currency. They will just be places to live. Whenever a borrower finds a lender to lend at a long-term fixed rate, the borrower prospers if inflation increases.

When Herbert Hoover looked out the White House window at the mounted policemen and the bonus marchers, he was not trying to set into motion a vast and far-reaching change in the country's financial structure. Franklin D. Roosevelt had no particular design; he, too, was trying to save the banks, and he compared himself to a quarterback who had to see how one play turned out before he called the next one. But the financial structure did change, little by little.

Lee and Irma, trying to get onto the diamond chart in southern California, do not think of their efforts in relation to a social revolution, any more than do the frenzied condo buyers in Chicago and Orange County and south Florida. The thirties pictures of families with their furniture on the sidewalks are yellowed and forgotten.

When the flight from the currency began, there was a place for the refugees—the housing market, supported by that invisible fourth subsidy. In the 1970s houses became not just a place to live, but an investment medium, and then a speculative one. Now we are reaching the point at which medical offices and corner stores become condos, so that the occupiers can become borrowers. This is stretch-

ing the social revolution past the point of what was intended, past what is fair, to the point, somewhere, where
the process will not work. We ought to be able to have
reasonable rental housing as well. Housing is a cumbersome place to have the national savings; it immobilizes
them and accelerates the accumulation of debt that began
as a logical response to the era of paper money. Carried
on long enough, that accumulation is going to defeat the
consensus image that we started with, a family in its own
affordable house.

It was logical for a mortgage debt to balloon and for
housing to become such a speculative medium. Logical,
but not healthy. But for houses to become simply places to
live, we need a more stable financial climate. And that
depends on some other variables—exogenous variables, as
the digital scholars say. Meanwhile, housing is not the only
way to flee the dollar.

6

THE PROLIFERATING DOLLAR: HOW THE KEY CURRENCY GOT DEBASED

My Darling Swissies

Several years ago a very successful Boston lawyer of my acquaintance decided he no longer wanted to have any dollars. He sold his house and rented another one. He sold his securities. He put the proceeds into gold and silver and foreign currencies. He began to travel to Switzerland with some regularity and to lunch with foreign-exchange experts.

I used to argue with him. My friends in the Treasury told me the dollar was cheap, and I was not ready to abandon America. It was beyond the limits of imagination then to think of gold going from $150 to $850 or to think that the United States would send $100 billion a year abroad for a product it burned into the air.

My Boston lawyer was so successful that his currencies became little friends. He crooned to them like a witch to her cats. "My Swissies," he would call his Swiss francs. "My Swissies were thirty-five cents when I bought them. My Swissies are backed by gold, and the inflation rate in Switzerland is lower than anywhere else. Then my Swissies were forty-five cents, and then fifty-five, and then sixty, all the time everyone else was holding ugly old dollars. Come, little darlings, seventy cents is easy; you can do it, my pets, you can do a dollar by year's end."

He had a little more trouble with his deutsche marks; that is, he had trouble getting on an intimate basis with them. Deutschers? Deutschies? He was never quite as comfortable with the diminutive there as he was with the Swissies; sometimes he had to call them "DM." But the DM were good to him, too. His Netherlands guilders were more like cousins, but against the dollar even they looked good.

My Boston lawyer became the living example of the economic man in Gresham's Law. Sir Thomas Gresham was the founder of the Royal Exchange in London in 1566, and you will recall his law—"Bad money drives out good" —which always sounds funny, because why wouldn't the good, like the Seventh Cavalry, drive out the bad? But if you have two currencies, say, dollars and Swiss francs, and one is going to lose half its value (bad) and the other is going to hold its value (good), which would you spend right away? Which would you save? Thus the bad currency goes out and circulates, and the good gets put away and saved. So said Thomas Gresham. My Boston lawyer sent away his depreciating dollars and stocked up with his darling Swissies.

If you have dollars and you want to trade them, it is not difficult. You can go to a bank and buy virtually any currency in the world. Americans take this for granted, though there have been times when the citizens of most countries could not easily get out of their own currencies because of exchange controls. British travelers within memory learned to be charming spongers abroad, because they could not leave England with more than £50.

You can, in addition to buying currency, buy traveler's checks denominated in marks or yen or sterling. The problem with buying currencies or traveler's checks is that you lose the interest on the money, and you do have to put the pieces of paper somewhere, which might be inconvenient.

You could open a savings account in a foreign "hard" currency, but you might get less interest than in a dollar savings account. In the case of the Swissie, Swiss banks will actually sometimes charge you for leaving the money there. They do not want those dollars bidding up the price of the Swiss franc, because then, when they want to sell chocolate bars and watches and electrical equipment, the price to the dollar holders like us will be still higher, and they will lose their share of, say, the watch market. (In fact, they already have.) And the Germans do not want the mark to be overly popular, because if the mark goes up against the dollar, a Volkswagen will cost $15,000, and even Detroit will undercut it.

Nonetheless, you can buy bonds, Swissie bonds, DM bonds, and yen bonds, and you will get some interest; if the dollar continues to suffer, you can sell your DM bond at some future date and get even more dollars for it. That's the theory.

And if you really want to gamble, you can buy not just a currency, but a contract for the future delivery of that currency. If you think the Swissie is going to go up 10 cents, you can buy a Swissie contract on any of several exchanges and borrow most of your purchase. In six months you collect your Swissies, turn them back into dol-

lars, and you have made a lot of money. Of course, if the
Swissie goes down, you lose your stake.

By fleeing the dollar, my Boston lawyer relieved himself
of the home-team blues. Everything that was bad news for
me became good news for him. I worried about our energy profligacy because I could see us sending out the
dollars every month by the billion; the same news was
cheering to him. "Did you see," he would say, "what our
deficit was last month? Oh, my. Did you see, the Saudis
are going along with the latest oil hike? The spot price for
oil is up to forty dollars. Those guys out in the desert are
going to pile up a hundred billion dollars this year—you
think they're going to keep them all in dollars? They've
already got dollars coming out the kazoo. No, they've got
to keep diversifying. Otmar Emminger, the last head of
the Bundesbank, said that even if the Arabs didn't pull
their dollars out, more of this year's new money would go
to other currencies. My Swissie is going to one to one. One
dollar, one Swissie."

"A three-dollar Swiss chocolate bar," I said.

"So what?" he said. "They'll make so much money banking, they'll buy the rest of the world's chocolate."

When President Carter ordered Iranian assets seized,
my Boston lawyer was exultant. "Oh, my," he said, "im-
pounding the bank deposits. That has to send a shiver
through all our desert friends. They must think, Hey,
we've got a lot stashed there. What if they seize ours?
Good-bye, Wall Street; hello, Frankfurt. The Swiss won't
be able to fend them off, and the spillover will be into the
deutsche mark and the guilder. Easy money."

I was despairing of the home team. The Europeans
were angry at that time because their energy use had gone
down while ours went up, and the dollar bled painlessly,
like slit wrists in a bathtub. Our citizens did not comprehend. If I were sitting in Jidda or Kuwait or Abu Dhabi, I
figured, where would I put this year's hundred billion?

The Swissie was really too small, there weren't enough of them in circulation for big buyers, and there was that negative interest rate. The next currency was the mark—there were plenty of marks, and the German inflation rate was still relatively low. I assembled a portfolio—on paper—of DM bonds. I looked forward to a meeting with my Boston lawyer's currency coach, a Swiss banker called Edgar.

We will come back, in a moment, to the Boston lawyer, Edgar the Swiss banker, and the Swissies. My Boston lawyer is a nice example of microeconomic behavior, as well as a living example of Gresham's Law. His behavior—moving from currency to currency, not necessarily into Swissies—is duplicated on a much larger scale by institutions, worldwide banks, international companies, by the treasurers of British Petroleum and Volkswagen and IBM and Shell. My Boston lawyer can play with his Swissies so easily because there is a functioning international monetary system through which currencies are exchanged, orders given in different languages, oil and coffee and computers financed, delivered, and paid for. The System —we will now capitalize it—has given us, since World War II, one of the greatest periods of prosperity in all of history.

The System is in some trouble. One of its most respected figures is H. Johannes Witteveen, a balding, bespectacled Dutchman with a thin mouth and a lapel full of honorific ribbons. Witteveen is the former managing director of the International Monetary Fund, former finance minister of the Netherlands. "There have been so many changes, and they come so fast," he said, "and nobody really understands the international monetary system. I believe the long-run stability of the system is in question."

I heard this opinion expressed even more eloquently at one of the meetings of a year-long colloquium on the System. Nonprofit sponsorship, distinguished participants,

paneled walls, portraits of the learned gentlemen of by-
gone years, a long U-shaped table, yellow pads and neatly
sharpened pencils at each place, a glass of water precisely
at the upper right-hand edge of the yellow pad, working
paper mailed beforehand. Across the U of the table I
could see Henry Kaufman, the interest-rate guru from
Salomon Brothers, and three places down, Albert Wolji-
nower, the First Boston economist known as "Dr. Death"
for his gloomy but accurate predictions about the economy. The discussion was getting quite heated; the non-
bankers were attacking the bankers for making such loans
abroad that they risked the future. One of the silver-
haired bankers answered an exchange—I wrote on my
yellow pad—"but then the System would not survive! This
wonderful, delicate mechanism we have built since the
war, this world System of flowing trade and flowing
money, that worked so well, would die! And we would
have the most serious depression! The System must survive!"

The assembled company got very quiet; it was unused
to such emotion, such poetic cadences; it was not quite
sure whether the cadences were from Lincoln's second
inaugural, or Shakespeare's this-sceptered-isle, or even
Star Wars; but everybody agreed, the System must survive.
I think that was the last point on which everybody agreed.

Discussions about the System tend to use very abstract
phrases such as "balance-of-payments deficit," "trade balance," "current account," "J-curve," and "liquidity." When
I was an active member of the Editorial Board of *The New
York Times,* and agitated about the problems of the System,
there was a copy editor who would always sigh deeply
when my grave opinion arrived, and he would say, "What's
liquidity? Nobody knows what liquidity is." I would say,
"The ability to turn assets into cash, and from that, an
ample supply of money, the degree of money and near-
money around," to which the reply would be, "What's a

one-word synonym for *liquidity?*" I never found a one-word synonym; if any reader has it I would be grateful for it; and the word *liquidity* itself never made it through.

I am used to such terms, but I noticed that my use of them brought to the meetings of that august board, even though its members were sophisticated and concerned, a certain amount of finger drumming, foot tapping, and industrious doodling on notepads. They were eager to get on with advising the President on his foreign policy, the Congress on its domestic policy, and the people on their behavior. I also noticed that my opinions, whether delivered on Monday, Tuesday, Wednesday, or Thursday, always ran on Saturday, which is the day of the *Times*'s smallest circulation. "Why am I Saturday's child?" I asked. "The Government will read you on Monday morning, when it is fresh," I was told. But I knew. Trade balance, current account, J-curve, and balance-of-payments deficit are not easy breakfast fare. In what follows I am going to risk a degree of flippancy and a tone that may seem primerlike to the System's practitioners, so that I don't always have to be Saturday's child.

The Key-Currency Country Gets a Privilege

The key currency is what the world uses as its denominator. The world has been used to saying, "How much is that in dollars?" When we talk about the dollar, we have an emotional involvement that goes beyond the denominator of the System, because this key currency is our currency, what we walk around with in our purses and wallets.

Let's start with an easy example. The Saudis have sold a lot of oil. They want to build an industrial plant at Jubail, so they ask for bids. The South Koreans come in with the low bid. They send a whole army of workers to Saudi Arabia, who live in dormitories and work like beavers.

They bring steel and valves and instruments and piping and plastics, and they put up the plant. Japanese ships bring the goods. The Saudi currency is the riyal. The Korean currency is the won. The Japanese currency is the yen. What do the Koreans get paid in?

The answer is none of the above. The Koreans get paid in dollars. The world trades in dollars. The dollar is the key currency. The deal may be between the Saudis and the Koreans—and this happens to be a real example—and the transfer may take place between the Saudi banks and the Korean banks—or it might go through London or Tokyo—but it is denominated in dollars. Everybody knows what a dollar is, though they argue about what it is going to be worth. And because the transaction is in dollars, sooner or later it has to end up on a ledger in New York.

That's one problem. We have a sign up in all the airports saying that it's a federal offense to take more than $5,000 out of the country unless you fill out a form; but there is a whole world out there trading in dollars, banking dollars, investing dollars; and those dollars could ultimately be a claim upon us. Not only could they be used to whisk away the apples and computers and textiles we are about to reach for ourselves, but they allow the holders of those dollars to voice irritation about the state of the dollar. And not just irritation. OPEC says, "You let the dollar go downhill, we have a lot of dollars in our savings account, we're going to raise the price of oil, just to stay even." Then everybody who buys oil gets mad, not just at OPEC, but at us. Because with the oil price up, we have a bit more inflation as the cost is passed through, and the dollar goes down some more, and the price of oil goes up again—a disagreeable cycle.

C. Fred Bergsten, in *The Dilemmas of the Dollar*, says there are three stages in the life of a key currency. In the first stage everybody's happy with it, and nobody wants to cash it in. In Stage Two there is a lot of key currency out there, an "overhang" as it's called, a nice ominous word that precedes Bergsten's use of it. Stage Three: everybody's afraid to cash in the key currency because the system will collapse. The private dollar holders cash in first; then the official holders start to worry.

I'd say we're certainly in Stage Three. The "overhang" is there, getting bigger. There is an entire dollar trading system all outside the United States, and outside the regulatory province of the United States. And nobody wants to see a line start at the teller's window that stretches out into the street, because there's nowhere else to go, especially for the big, official dollar holders.

A key-currency country, in a way, has some of the attributes of a bank.

What are such attributes?

When you put your money in the bank, you want to be able to get it back. That's first. If you think you might not get it back, you'll keep it under the mattress. That's why American banks advertise, "Accounts insured to $100,000." Call this factor *safety*.

When you put your money in the bank, you want to be able to get it back when you want it. You don't want to be told, "Fill out this form and wait sixty days." In other words, you want the bank to have the resources on hand so that you're not tied up. Call this factor *liquidity*.

And the use of the money is worth something, so you want interest, rent on the money. Call this factor *yield*.

Now let's see what this means in terms of a country's currency. *Safety* means the bank still has to be there. The country has to be politically stable. A big bank account in Havana in 1958 doesn't mean a damn thing in 1960. So the country has to have solid institutions, a respect for law so that the buyers of the key currency don't find the rules changed. Life being what it is, the country's institutions must be protected by military power and political influence.

And the country has to protect the value of its currency,

both at home and abroad. The money has to stay worth what it's worth. For that it needs a healthy economy, with economic growth and price stability. That will give it *liquidity.*

The *yield* will be taken care of by the supply of, and demand for, the currency. A higher rate of interest might make up for some decline in the currency. Supply and demand in the contemporary world come not only from the marketplace but from the government's bank, the central bank, and that bank must inspire trust.

I do not know what prompted Sir Isaac Newton, that irascible genius of science, to peg the pound to gold during his tenure as Master of the Mint. Maybe an apple fell near his head. When we think of Isaac Newton, we think of calculus, optics, mechanics, the laws of motion, the *Principia,* gravity, and a whole breathtaking array of scientific achievement. We do not think of Isaac Newton, Master of the Mint; but in 1717 the Master of the Mint said that one guinea, that is, 21 shillings, would be worth 129.4 grams of gold, and thereby he said, *We intend this currency to hold its value,* and thereby he created a key currency. Almost.

Sir Isaac, at this point in his career, was Master of the Mint because it was a sinecure. He dominated not only British science but world science. He had had his nervous breakdowns; his great friend Fatio de Duillier, the Swiss mathematician, had died, leaving him heartbroken, and he was in the right political party. He was made Master of the Mint as a reward for his loyalty and achievements, and then it turned out that he loved the job.

I am not saying that Sir Isaac got to the office one morning and said, "What this country needs for the next two hundred years is to be the world's banker, and so this morning I am going to invent a key currency." But I am treating it as more than one of those odd, quirky footnotes in history because Sir Isaac was a genius obsessed with the

occult and with alchemy; volumes he wrote on these subjects have been held at Cambridge University, still unpublished by his order. To alchemists, gold is the key to
transformation. And certainly Sir Isaac pursued counter-
feiters with religious zeal and delighted in seeing them
hanged.

Newton's guinea was, by its design, unclippable. A
clipped coin is one that has had a bit of the metal clipped,
shaved off, usually around the circumference. If you
saved up all the shavings and melted them down, you had
a kind of royalty on the money that passed through your
hands. Currencies have throughout history been backed
by some form of precious metal, but the kings who wanted
some extra revenue could find a way to clip the coins. Of
course, then the currency would be debased, and the citizens would spend the clipped coins as fast as they could
and save the unclipped ones. Sir Thomas Gresham, Sir
Isaac Newton.

Sir Isaac's unclippable guinea rang if you dropped it; it
was solid; the world began to collect it. The guinea rivaled
the Spanish silver dollar. But you need more than precious
metals to have a key currency; you have to want to be the
Bank, and history has to give you a place so that you can
be the Bank. In the eighteenth century, traders around
the world sent money to London, to be held in "sterling,"
which is what the British currency came to be called. That
name has come to mean "pure, noble, of quality," and is a
definition of the purity of silver. All sorts of things have
been called sterling, including a men's after-shave. Sterling derives from Easterling, an Estonian trading family
that stamped its name into bars of silver. For part of British financial history, sterling was fixed in terms of silver:
11 ounces, 2 dramweight of silver was 20 shillings thrup-
pence.

Only twice, in the period from 1717 to 1931, did the
British suspend the convertibility of their currency. Each

time they needed more money to fight a war than the tight hand of convertibility would permit. They suspended the convertibility to fight Napoleon and to fight the Kaiser. Each war produced paper money and inflation, as wars tend to do.

After Waterloo, sterling met every test of a key currency. The government was stable, the institutions honored and intact. The Royal Navy sailed the world; trade followed the flag. Britain was first into the industrial revolution, so its manufactured goods spread over the world. The battles were always at the fringes of the empire.

Every time there was a small crisis about the pound, the monetary authorities would raise the interest rates sharply. That might depress the domestic economy, but the high interest rates would draw in foreign exchange, and the pound would retain its value. Britain bought the raw materials, the commodities, and sent back the manufactured goods; and since the price of raw materials gradually declined, the pound increased in value.

The British government issued "consols," perpetual bonds. Fathers gave them to their sons, and those sons gave them to their sons, and the bonds actually *increased* in value as time went on. "Never sell consols," said Soames Forsyte, Galsworthy's man of property.

The world brought its money to London and changed it into sterling. London banked it and insured it. Cartographers colored Britain pink on world maps, and the world was half pink, from the Cape to Cairo, from Suez to Australia. In 1897, at Victoria's Diamond Jubilee, the fleet formed five lines, each five miles long, and it took four hours for it to pass in review at Spithead.

British capital went everywhere. It financed American railroads and great ranches in the western United States. British investors held not only American ranches, but Argentine ones, too. Their companies mined gold in South Africa and tin in Malaya, grew hemp in Tanganyika and apples in Tasmania, drilled for oil in Mexico, and ran the trolley lines in Shanghai and the Moscow Power and Light Company.

The British spent a very long time in Stage One, when everybody wants the currency and nobody wants to cash it in.

World War I was enormously costly. The tin mines of Malaya, the western ranches, the Mexican oil, had to be sold for artillery shells and other items unproductive in an economic sense. The Moscow Power and Light Company passed to other ownership. The pound was no longer worth a pound.

It is hard to become a key currency; it is also hard to stop being a key currency. Through the 1920s the British tried to maintain the value of the pound at $4.86; they even tried the old nineteenth-century formula; put the interest rate up, attract more foreign capital, slow the domestic economy down. It didn't work; the effects on the domestic economy were too painful. The stock market crash and credit collapse in 1929 and 1930 ended the long reign of sterling.

In 1931 the British let the pound "float"; they abolished its convertibility. It was not pegged to gold via a fixed exchange rate, and on any given day it would sell for whatever buyers and sellers agreed on. The international monetary system collapsed. There was no key currency. Trade died. In the United States a quarter of the work force was unemployed.

Yet the reign of the pound was so supreme that the memory lingers on, and so do some of the relationships. The British navy is gone from the Persian Gulf, but Kuwait and Abu Dhabi still do their banking chiefly in London.

The British pound was not the only key currency in its heyday; the French franc was also used in its own area of influence. But for two hundred years it was the pound that was supreme. The Bank of England stood for riches and power. In the Depression the world broke up into blocs, and each bloc tried to gain an advantage by depreciating its currency so that it could increase its exports and put its people back to work. That game is called beggar-thy-neighbor, and it was a disaster.

With World War II the dollar became the key currency. Gold came to the United States, which fed the world and was untouched by war on its own territory.

W. Michael Blumenthal, the former Secretary of the Treasury, has a personal memory of this transition. He was born in Berlin; before World War II his family left for China. After a Middle East trip he recalled this: "I remember every stop we made on the *Haruna Maru*," he said. "Port Said, Suez, Aden, Bombay, Colombo, Singapore, Hong Kong, and Shanghai. And at every stop the Union Jack was flying and a British officer in knee socks, with a topee and a swagger stick, would come aboard and say, 'Howjado.'

"And now the British are gone, and everywhere you go, at the top levels of government, they have their eyes absolutely fixed on the United States. What is U.S. policy going to be? What is the American President going to do? We are absolutely bigger than life; their expectations of what we can do are bigger than life."

In 1944 the finance and treasury ministers of forty-four countries met at the mountain summer resort of Bretton Woods, New Hampshire. And all the currencies were set in a fixed relationship. If you were a central banker and you brought $35 to the United States, you could have an ounce of gold. (Americans could still not own gold.) All the other currencies were pegged to the dollar.

The dollar met all the criteria of a key currency. The United States honored its obligations. It had military and political power. Its institutions were stable. It had every opportunity for economic growth and price stability. And there was an even more overwhelming criterion: there wasn't anything else.

Pegging a currency to a precious metal doesn't make it a key currency, but it helps to restrict the printing of paper money, because the amount of metal is finite, and thus it might be one sign that some faith with the currency will be kept. But the South African rand is partially backed by gold, and no one deals in it who does not have to; it is too subject to controls and restrictions. The Swiss franc and several other European currencies have some gold backing, and there is some devotion to keeping those currencies stable, but Switzerland is a small country, without military power or political influence. The world is so hungry for something to denominate in, for something to be the key currency, that the Swiss, with a stable franc, have taken in money from all over the world and profited by handling it. But there simply aren't enough Swiss francs to finance the world's trade.

Lord Keynes, who had called himself a Cassandra when he saw the dire Depression coming, brought to Bretton Woods a plan for international prosperity that he hoped would satisfy national ambitions and yet prevent a return to the 1930s. He proposed an international currency, "bancor," and an international bank, an International Clearing Union. "Bancor" was a bit too radical for its time; it called for the United States to put in some money and have the devastated Europeans borrow it. The plans that were adopted did not go that far.

But the nations that met at Bretton Woods wanted to avoid the currency wars of the 1930s and to have cooperation. Out of the agreements at Bretton Woods came the international institutions of the System: the International Monetary Fund, to govern international monetary relations; the International Bank for Reconstruction and Development, to rebuild the world; and the General Agreement on Tariffs and Trade.

With magnificent generosity the United States gave the money for the world to rebuild, through Marshall Plan grants and loans. (The Marshall Plan also preserved the dominance of the United States more than participation in a Clearing Union might have.) The System grew and prospered: growing banks, growing networks of communications, growing trade. Economists worried about a "dollar gap"; how would the world get enough dollars to trade? It seems a very long time ago, but in the 1950s the United States was producing half of the world's oil, half of its automobiles, and 40 percent of its industrial output. When American tourists went abroad, shady characters would beckon them into alleyways, saying, "Psst! Wanna change dollars?" and they would offer a premium over the official rate.

By 1958 the System was so successful that trade was booming, all the major currencies were convertible into each other, and the dollar was better than gold. Better, because why bother with gold? If you really wanted it, you could turn dollars in for it; but gold is sterile, it earns no interest, you have to pay storage charges on it. It was dollars everyone wanted. Now it was the American navy that prowled the world, American banks with their flags in all the foreign capitals, and American companies that owned, worldwide, the nickel mines and auto-parts plants.

Americans were quite happy to spend those dollars abroad. American businesses bought industrial plants and equipment and raw materials overseas. The Pentagon sent dollars out to pay for its bases and its troops. Through the 1960s more dollars went out than came in. Thus began the "overhang" of dollars abroad, the deficit in the balance of payments.

The foreigners, gradually, no longer needed dollars to buy half the world's automobiles from the United States;

there were now Volkswagens and Datsuns and Renaults. They no longer needed dollars to buy from Texas half the world's oil; there was oil everywhere. In fact, the Americans themselves were sending dollars out to buy Volkswagens and Datsuns. The foreigners might reassure themselves by the American guarantee that their central banks could have an ounce of gold for $35 if they wanted it, but gradually, as the dollars piled up abroad, more of them cashed in the dollars and took the gold.

Leave it to economic historians to debate the motives and sequences of President Nixon's departure from the gold-dollar link. Were the actions at the official "gold window" forcing exchange rate realignments? Were they to head off a sudden gold hemorrhage? Were they, like many of Treasury Secretary John Connolly's actions, not completely thought out? The exact reasons, for our purposes, do not matter. In August 1971 the United States Treasury stopped selling gold for dollars altogether. The potential claims on the gold were too great. The claims, from overseas, were in the form of a curious currency called a Eurodollar, which was simply a dollar abroad. Brought to the United States, it was like any other dollar, except that in foreign official hands it could be presented for gold. When the United States cut the tie between the dollar and gold, the key currency no longer had any kind of backing in a precious metal.

The Wonderful Country of Euroland

It was a stateless currency, one that respected no borders, as hard to control as drops of mercury, as organically given to growth as lilies on a pond or ragweed in August. The identity of its inventor is as anomalous as finding the greatest scientist of his age as Master of the Mint. The Eurodollar was invented by the Russians.

Like everyone else in the mid-1950s, the Russians used the dollar in their international transactions. It was the key currency; no one wanted rubles. If you earned dollars, you could take those dollars to the United States and get oil, aircraft, wheat, soybeans, automobiles; you could also get, if you wanted it, gold. You could leave the dollars in a New York bank and get interest. Like everyone else, the Russians had some dollars in New York.

After the Hungarian revolt in 1956, a Russian bureaucrat moved his country's dollar balances to the Moscow Narodny Bank in London, a bank with a British charter owned by the Soviet Union. He probably thought that if the cold war got worse, the Americans might freeze those dollars in New York, so he had better keep them in Europe, beyond the reach of politics. I once pursued this faceless bureaucrat who deserves a footnote in history. The pursuit looked promising when a Russian banker said, "Dregasovitch didn't invent the Eurodollar, the people under him did; he just took all the credit," but the trail grew cold after that. The Eurodollar's inventor has disappeared into the complex world of Russian banking; perhaps he has a dacha and a supply of Cuban cigars; perhaps he feels he is not honored in his own country and tells his grandchildren that he might have been president of the Bank of America if he had grown up in California.

Pressed for details, the Moscow Narodny Bank replies with very dry tracts on "the development of socialist banks." It no longer matters. On February 28, 1957, the Moscow Narodny Bank in London put out to loan, through a London merchant bank, the sum of $800,000. This minuscule amount was borrowed and repaid outside the American banking system. The Soviets also owned a bank in Paris, called the Banque Commercial pour l'Europe du Nord, whose Telex address was "Eurbank." The Paris Russian bank took some Narodny dollars and lent them; the dollars were known as Eurbank dollars, and finally Eurodollars.

At that point we can retire the Russians from the history of the Eurodollar; the capitalist bankers all loved the idea. The charm of Eurodollars, to bankers, was that they didn't belong anywhere and owed no allegiance to anyone; therefore, nobody regulated them. They were beyond the reach of the Federal Reserve, the Bank of England, the Bundesbank, and all the other government authorities. The Federal Reserve can require banks to put up a portion of their deposits as reserves; other agencies govern the character and size of loans. But not in Eurodollars; these dollars could be deposited, lent, and repaid, all while the Federal Reserve looked on from afar.

If the Federal Reserve was trying to stop too many dollars from flowing out, it could say to its member banks, "No dollars go abroad to buy those plants in Europe for a while, okay?" The member banks would have no choice but to agree.

But the would-be borrower could borrow for his needs, not in domestic dollars, but in Eurodollars, from Canadian banks, Dutch banks, the London Moscow Narodny Bank (not very likely), and even from Eurobanks sponsored by American parents—anybody who had Eurodollars and wanted to lend them.

If the Federal Reserve was trying to get a grip on the money supply, it might say that all banks have to ante up another 2 percent in reserves. Or that no bank can pay interest on a time deposit until it's been there thirty days. Or it would set an interest rate ceiling.

Those regulations sent American banks into London, and into the Eurodollar business, where there were no interest rate ceilings and reserve requirements. If the Federal Reserve tried to create penalties against the hometown banks for the London activities, the American banks could say, "Do you want the British and the Germans and the Dutch to get all the business?"

The American banking authorities could regulate the American banks wherever they were, in some respects.

The Comptroller of the Currency, for example, could issue rules designed to protect, in his opinion, the safety of the banks. The banking statute might say, "No bank can lend more than 10 percent of its capital to any one borrower," but the Comptroller could make the rule more restrictive; a bank could get a reprimand if the Comptroller thought its loan portfolio was beginning to get shaky. If the Chase Manhattan had a foreign branch, the Comptroller would include its loans with the parent office.

In Germany the Bundesbank could not even do that. In the Nazi era the German banks even outside Germany reported back Jewish bank accounts, so in the postwar reforms, in a desire to protect individuals, the new German authorities forbade their banks to collect information over the border.

So the regulation of the banks varied from country to country. But the *currency*, once escaped, was gone: there was no way to whistle it home. If threatened with regulation, the Eurodollars would flutter up like a frightened flock of warblers and alight in some other country.

Beyond the wonderful country of Euroland was a still more wonderful country called Offshore. In Euroland the dollars were lent and deposited beyond the reach of the monetary authorities. Offshore was beyond the reach of the taxing authorities. For the dollars that belonged nowhere, there were now countries with hundreds of banks whose banking systems did not exist, like the Bahamas, the Netherlands Antilles, and the Cayman Islands. The borders of the two countries, Euroland and Offshore, were very fuzzy and overlapping, and in any case the two countries existed by their nonexistence in the filing cabinets of big law firms in New York and London. The Netherlands Antilles would get to sell a charter, and some annual stamps, so it was happy; and the bank was happy because it was in the Big Rock Candy Mountain of banking, where bankers are free as the breeze. The banks might be small, or they might have recognizable names: Chase, Citicorp, Barclays, Bank of America, Deutsche Bank, Algemeine Nederland—all chartered Offshore and doing business in Euroland.

The currency for Euroland came from the balance-of-payments deficit, that is, from more dollars going out than coming in. If the extra dollars for the Volkswagens had all come back to New York to be lent or invested, there would have been no Eurodollar. But some of those dollars, sent out, never came back; they arrived in Euroland with Caribbean tans.

This phenomenon began with the $800,000 loaned by the Moscow Narodny Bank in London, and now there are somewhere around three-quarters of a *trillion* dollars of this very fecund currency, and there are also Euromarks and Euroyen and Eurofrancs, all looking rested and tanned and showing no desire to go home.

The problem with those Eurodollars is that they *could* come home; they did not have to stay contained in their own wonderful world.

What if there were too many of them?

The Perimeter Defenses

The Euro form of dollars may have made the currency more fecund by freedom from family planning. Its defenders, the commercial bankers, say the Euros financed the world's greatest boom. Central bankers, the governments' bankers, itching to regulate the commercial bankers, saw the Euros as the devil's offspring. Guido Carli, governor of the Bank of Italy, said they were the root of all evil.

Euro or not, dollars were taken everywhere because they were the key currency. If you were a Peruvian and you wanted to buy a Volkswagen, or a plant in Germany, the Germans might not want your local sols. Mine some copper, or catch some anchovies, earn some marks or dollars, and you could have your VW. But the Americans did not have to sell something first; all they had to do was issue the dollars. Those dollars were just as good as the dollars earned by the Peruvians mining copper.

General de Gaulle objected to this. He said the American key-currency status was "an exorbitant privilege." What was to stop the Americans from printing money and buying up France?

Even in the dollar's sunny heyday, there were some economists who saw some trouble for the Bank—the American key currency—and for the System that depended on it. Gold was at its 1935 price, $35 an ounce, and dollars were convertible into gold. Was that price high enough? What if a run started on the Bank, if countries began to cash in their dollars? One of the economists was Sir Roy Harrod at Oxford, Keynes's biographer. One was a Harvard-educated Belgian with a pleasant, skeptical look, Robert Triffin. Triffin's writing manners were abrasive when addressing other economists; he believed that using American payments deficits and dollar outflows to meet the world's need for reserves was a prescription for disaster.

An American, Milton Gilbert, worked as chief economist for the Bank for International Settlements in Basel, the bank for central banks, from 1960 to 1975. He proposed doubling the price of gold to hold the fixed-rate system together, because he could see the French openly draining gold from the United States, while the other industrial nations worried that there were more claims against the United States than there was gold. They were reluctant to bring up the subject with the Americans, because the Americans were the bulwark of NATO, and they did not want the American troops withdrawn from Europe. "I failed to convince my own countrymen," Gilbert said in 1975, after he retired. "They couldn't clear their minds of domestic politics, and they came to treat me, not only as wrong, but as kind of a half-traitor."

In the 1960s the French wine dealers, the Italian shoemakers, the German Beetle makers, and the Japanese TV makers found good business selling to Americans. If the Americans didn't earn enough dollars, they printed the difference. The Toyota exporter in Japan with a batch of dollars wanted to play golf in Japan, and the golf course would take yen, so he took his dollars to the Bank of Japan, got yen for them, and went off to play golf. If the Bank of Japan already had enough dollars, it would complain that it was having to print extra yen for these dollars that were being brought in; the Americans were exporting a bit of inflation. Then the Bank of Japan used the dollars to buy U.S. Treasury bonds. The U.S. Treasury would take the dollars back, giving an IOU—a bond—and a promised date for repayment. That financed the deficit.

Robert Roosa was John Kennedy's Undersecretary for Monetary Affairs, a mild, bespectacled former Rhodes scholar who speaks in long sentences. Roosa began to devise what he called "perimeter defenses" to stop a possible run on the dollar. He generated a gentlemen's agreement atmosphere with the foreign banks: the dollars could pile up there, but they wouldn't be taken to New York and presented for gold.

Roosa devised special issues of Treasury bonds, denominated in Swiss francs, which sopped up some dollars. The Treasury would issue a "Roosa bond"; that is, it would take in the foreign dollars and promise to repay at some future date in Swiss francs. (The device worked, but it was costly: the Swissies appreciated so much it took a billion extra dollars.) Roosa also arranged some "swap lines" with other central banks. If there were too many dollars for the French franc or the Dutch guilder, the Treasury would take them home, owe the lender who held them, and guarantee any losses if the dollar went down.

By using the examples of Volkswagens and French

wines, I intend something concrete and therefore, I hope, easy to understand. The dollars that went out and got to be too many were not all spent on consumer high living, nor were the spenders good-time-Charleys living it up at the Tour d'Argent in Paris. The spenders were American multinational companies, with familiar names like IBM and Exxon, that were developing subsidiaries abroad, as well as the Pentagon. The defenders of the policies that weakened the dollar could say that Germany and Japan had no military umbrella of their own; we were paying for it.

The British, in their long reign as the Bank with the currency, chose to defend the currency. The Americans had other priorities.

Vietnam, for example. The foreign bankers could see that the war was not financed by taxation; therefore, there were going to be still more dollars around. American administrations might try to stop the dollar outflow; there was a Voluntary Foreign Credit Restraint Program— "Please don't take any more dollars out"—and then a Mandatory Foreign Credit Restraint Program—"DON'T TAKE ANY MORE DOLLARS OUT"; but the Euros multiplied, and ungentlemanly characters, with Gresham's Law ahead of the Pledge of Allegiance in their minds, kept borrowing dollars to buy the stronger currencies, the Swiss franc and the deutsch mark.

By May 1971 the German central bank, the Bundesbank, could—or would—no longer take in dollars and give out marks. The international monetary system didn't break down, but it stopped for a while. The German, Dutch, Belgian, Austrian, and Swiss exchange markets all closed on May 6. When they reopened, the Swiss and Austrians had revalued their currencies upward, the French had forbidden their citizens to deal in foreign currency

except through the Bank of France, and the Germans cut
the relationship between the mark and everything else.

The neat, classical world devised in 1944 at Bretton
Woods had had the dollar as its centerpiece, gold at $35
an ounce backing the dollar, and all the other currencies
fixed in their relationship to the dollar. Now that system
was coming apart. There were too many dollars for the
gold; everyone could see that if the Euro holders all
cashed in their dollars, Fort Knox would be bare in a day.
In August 1971 the Nixon administration cut the tie between gold and the dollar.

"When we left the pound, we could go to the dollar,"
said Jelle Zijlstra, then of the Bank of the Netherlands.
"But where could we go from the dollar? To the moon?"

The ten leading industrial countries met at the Smith-
sonian Institution in Washington. They tried a replay of
Bretton Woods: a higher price for gold, a devaluation of
the dollar, and new fixed rates for all the currencies. But
the fix did not even last for eighteen months. During the
period of the fix, the world's money supply took another
flip upward. Remember the Toyota exporter in Japan who
wanted to play golf. When he brought in his dollars, and
the dollar-yen rate was fixed, the Bank of Japan would
have to print more yen to match the dollars.

More yen, more marks, more everything, in fact. Critics
said the United States should have tightened its credit;
money was cheap and the inflation rate relatively low. Borrow dollars and buy; the yen and the marks and the francs
and the dollars all went out into the marketplace. The
Reuters Commodity Index—foodstuffs, fibers, minerals
—went up 65 percent from the end of 1971 to the spring
of 1973. Only oil did not go up.

One by one, the world's central banks peeled out of the
fixed-rate relationships. The exchange rates floated everywhere. A dollar was worth, on any given day, what the
buyers and sellers said it was worth.

The Floating World

Floating rates were greeted with great approval by one whole tribe within the academy. *This* will fix it, they said. A German banker known to me said he preferred the natural cynicism of the marketplace to the political optimism of governments.

The trouble with floating rates is that they bounce all over the place. Let some bad trade figures come out, and the dollar will start to sink. Let the Russians scare their neighbors by rolling 100,000 troops over the border, and the dollar will get bid up by folks who are suddenly ready to sacrifice factor number two (liquidity, constant value) for factor number one (safety, the bank is still there). The deutsch mark may look solid, but when the Russian tanks get to Frankfurt, it's Kleenex.

If OPEC raises oil prices sharply, the dollar will go up at first, because although the United States imports a lot of oil, it still *has* a lot of oil. Germany and Japan have no oil, so their deficits will increase until they export enough to pay for the oil. Then in a later stage the dollar will sink, because the Germans and Japanese will have sold enough exports to pay for their oil, and we will still be printing to pay for it. That's the way it's worked so far.

If you are a manufacturer, you might think a 10-percent profit was okay. But if you're manufacturing in one country and selling in another, with floating rates the currencies could move that much *in one day.* Here it took you eight months to make this widget and another four to sell it, and a currency bounce wipes out your profit.

The theory is that a forward market develops and protects you. If you sign your widget contract in 1981, you buy a forward currency contract for 1982, when the widgets will be ready, that hedges your widget sale, and what you pay for the hedge is just like an insurance contract, part of the cost of doing business. These forward contracts can be bought through various brokers, banks, and exchanges.

Do they work? Usually, but not always. They work when things are calm. If everybody tries to hedge his way out of pounds or dollars or whatever at the same time, the futures market stops functioning just because it's a market.

With floating rates, all the opinions on a currency were instantly visible on a computer screen. For example, during the Arab oil embargo, the dollar at first went up (safety, world rumblings) and then down, as our oil imports increased and we sent more and more and more dollars abroad for the oil.

The markets were following old Sir Thomas Gresham. Sell the weak currency and buy the strong one. Better, borrow the weak currency—pay it back when it's still weaker—and buy the strong one.

The defenders of American policy, held to account for a 30-percent drop in the world's key currency, said: "The Germans and the Japanese aren't such heroes, their money supplies are growing even faster than ours. The Swiss have paid a price for protecting their currency; they haven't grown since 1973. The Germans and the Swiss have less inflation than we do, in spite of their growing money supplies, because they can cut back their economies with no social damage. Their factories are filled with Turks and Portuguese and Italians, so when they cut back, they just send the Turks and the Portuguese home. That way there's still no unemployment in Germany and Switzerland; the unemployed are back in Istanbul. We can't do that because our unemployed are American citizens. Socially, we don't have the fear of inflation that the Germans and the Swiss do. That fear helps them with their unions and their consensus policies. As for the Japanese, they have that damn beehive society that can blast out products and sell them all over.

"You say we've dropped 30 percent against the strong currencies, which is a disaster for a key currency; why don't you look at the world as a whole? We're doing fine against the bolivar, the zloty, and the Canadian dollar."

But the world was not denominated in zlotys and Canadian dollars; it was largely denominated in U.S. dollars. And in the United States there were two irresistible free rides going on. The first was that the rate of inflation was higher than the interest rate. If you could borrow money at 10 percent and inflation was at 12 percent, money was free. The second free ride was in the price of gasoline, which was controlled, so that it was half free. Leave aside energy policy debates; gasoline is no small thing in the United States. The United States consumes a third of the world's oil; one out of every eight barrels in the free world burns up on our highways. We sent the dollars for the oil: higher imports, higher deficits, weaker dollar.

The energy policy debate thus took on financial and psychological significance. The foreign dollar holders who could see no end to the gas consumption, and the deficits, would say, "The Americans don't have an energy policy, the deficits are going to get bigger, more dollars, think I'll sell me some dollars and buy me some Swissies. I don't think the Russian tanks are rolling to Zurich this year, and I can always change my mind."

The financial world was headed for panic in October 1978 from the run on the dollar. The Americans put their interest rates up, used $30 billion in swaps and credits—remember the Roosa devices—and that fix lasted until the 1979 crisis.

Defending the currency isn't easy because it hurts someone at home, usually someone who votes.

You, let us say, are the chairman of the Board of Governors of the Federal Reserve System of the United States.

The markets are watching the Thursday money-supply figures, hawklike. You have to spend time on the Hill, before various congressional committees. You have to preside over your regional banks. You hear rumblings that the trade figures are not being greeted well abroad. Out on the perimeter the roads are not safe after dark.

And then the phone rings at your bedside at three o'clock in the morning. The markets in Tokyo and Singapore are open and there is a run on your currency—all sellers, no buyers. And then the London market is open, and your currency doesn't have a friend left. The sellers go right through the perimeter defenses without a swig from their canteens; you throw your swaps and your lines and they eat them all up and keep right on coming, the swaps only slow down a platoon here and a platoon there, the rest of the sellers look like the Chinese army, they just keep coming, no respect for human life. You call up the Bundesbank and the Bank of England and the Bank of Japan and you say, "Mayday! You guys could at least make a little clatter in the background, some smoke, some action, divert them, somebody just ran by my bedroom." You call up your board and tell them to get their shoes and socks on and meet you at the office.

Then you call the President and tell him you have just seen fingers come over the windowsill, this is it, you are about to put the interest rates up to 20 percent and drain all the money out of the banks.

The President is no economist, but he can understand what an interest rate at 20 percent means. "Are you crazy?" he screams. "You'll throw the country into a depression! Car dealers can't pay twenty percent on their showroom cars! And the tires—the glass—Michigan! There goes Michigan! Steel! Pennsylvania! There goes Pennsylvania! Home builders . . ."

You say, "Then you'd better be prepared to close the exchanges, maybe the banks; this bunch went right through the perimeter defenses; and otherwise I don't want to be responsible and I resign."

The President says he'll deal with you later.

So you put the interest rates up, which breaks the panic. The money that couldn't wait to leave at 10 percent now thinks if it can get 20 percent interest, why not hang around and collect it and see what happens? The dollar's not going down another 20 percent. The markets calm down, the raiders retreat.

And you think, Pshew! That was close! There must be a better way to save the currency than slamming a mallet on the economy's forehead as if it were a stupid mule. Wonder what it is. Wonder what's for breakfast; that was a rough night.

Have a good breakfast, because a lot of people are mad at you. They don't care about the currency. They're home builders, and the savings banks have all just taken the phone off the hook. The car dealers are hoping to stretch car payments out to eighty-six years, so that nobody will notice the new interest rate. The economy starts to stagger.

One day I happened to be in the office of the secretary of the chairman of the Board of Governors of the Federal Reserve System, to use the full symphonic title, and I noticed a neat stack of lumber in the corner, pieces maybe four inches by a foot. "Oh, that?" said the chairman's secretary. "The builders keep mailing those in, to remind us about the interest rates; they say we put them out of work."

Saturday Morning Serenade

The dollar has faded as the key currency, and so have its privileges. It is now the key currency by default; 80 percent of the currency used as reserves in the world is still dollars, but nobody is happy about it.

We really didn't want tc be the Bank. Unlike the British, we never depended on foreign trade; it was only 8 percent of our gross national product. So we didn't have the conviction and the priorities that made sterling sound like sterling. (Parenthetically, if Soames Forsyte's descendants had repeated to themselves, "Never sell consols," in the years *after* the pound was so sterling, they would have lost 96 percent of their purchasing power in the later British inflations.) We were relatively self-sufficient. Ironically, we are less self-sufficient now, because of our need for oil and bauxite and manganese and trace minerals, just as the world is really fed up with the dollar as the key currency.

The world believes our Bank will be there (safety), but it doesn't believe the currency will hold its value. So it tries to figure out how much value it will lose. Ten percent a year? Put the interest rates at 16 percent, then, and the money will come back, but at a stiff price for all the businesses that have to borrow. Let the rates go down, and the businesses at home may be happier, but the international money will exit from the dollar and the raiders will regroup.

When you stop being the key currency, you may have to give back some of the goodies you had as the Banker. The British gave back the Argentine ranches and the Shanghai Trolley Company. So we are vulnerable now.

Thirty years ago one of our friends on the Persian Gulf with a small inherited spread—sand, flies, and a concession to the oil men—might have been sitting in front of his mud palace, fanning himself, conducting his *majlis*, listening to two of his tribesmen dispute over three goats, deciding the complaints of the father and the husband of a runaway wife. Meanwhile the Stars and Stripes was snapping in the breeze on the fantails of the world's greatest fleet, the one that replaced the Royal Navy, and a dollar was something over which you could erect, if not a cathedral, at least a handsome temple with Greek columns, like our nineteenth-century banks.

And today, if the same Persian Gulf friend (he would

want it called the Arabian Gulf), now very rich from oil, begins to move a computer blip representing part of his billion-dollar savings account from New York to Frankfurt, hence is selling dollars and buying marks, the builders in our country have to stop building, the car buyers stop buying, the banks rein in the credit, and small businesses can't borrow—a very cumbersome process.

It is too late for the dollar to be the only key currency. Even if we ran surpluses and had balanced budgets, faith has eroded, and the sole-key-currency role doesn't match our role in the world anyway. So the burden has to be shared. And in fact, people are collecting deutsch marks and yen and sometimes francs and pounds. The central bankers of the countries whose currencies are being collected are not happy with the idea of being a reserve currency; they like their jobs and they do not want those disagreeable domestic pressures, either.

Nobody wants to be the Bank. Nobody wants to have the key currency, because it's hard to run an industrial democracy and a Bank at the same time. The British did it, but even they don't want to do it again. So we have an ad hoc system of multiple key currencies.

The master financial mechanics at the International Monetary Fund thought up a way for dollar holders to leave quietly, a "substitution account" in which governments would trade in their dollars and get Special Drawing Rights, a hybrid reserve asset. The "substitution account" is still on the runway.

The Master Mechanics have some other ideas. (Nothing deprecating about that phrase. Henry Ford and Thomas Edison were Master Mechanics. They do fixes within the system. The Isaac Newtons think up the whole system.) Here are some of the fixes: Central banks could issue securities outside the exchange markets. There could be other versions of the old "Roosa bonds," foreign (or externally) denominated securities guaranteed against exchange losses. Or you could use the IMF's own gold holdings, now somewhere between $60 and $80 billion, as a backing for the substitution account, creating a kind of Super Bank dependent on its own assets instead of those of its individual members.

Not much enthusiasm for that one. Super Bank? Who would run it? What if we don't like what they do? The IMF has always been considered the preserve of Western Europeans, even though it has 140 members. More recently, with some of the Arab nations so rich and some of the developing countries so vociferous, the Westerners do not have such firm control. The Arabs press for status for the PLO; the developing countries press for longer, easier loans. The hard-money crowd worries: What if the IMF were indeed a Super Bank, and what if it fell more into the hands of the Third World; wouldn't it be tempted to spin out more and more money?

Central bankers have a cozy club, and they talk to each other at dinners, but no central banker is elected to his job; he is appointed. Somebody else is elected, and that somebody can usually fire the central banker or make life unpleasant for him. Central bankers do not pass the tax laws or the spending programs or face the electorate.

Meanwhile, the markets sniff from currency to currency like a dog after a hidden bone, but basically the markets distrust *all* the currencies and *all* the governments, just some less than others. The central banks used to be bigger than the markets, but the paper money in the markets has grown so boldly that the markets are now much bigger than the central banks.

If a currency appreciates, it appreciates in relation to something. The denominator, the dollar, is worth less, which means our relative standard of living goes down.

There is a little moral to this Saturday morning serenade. We have to get our own house in order. The grand seigneurial days of the key currency are over, which means we are one country among a lot of countries, and we have to produce and sell. To produce, we have to have productivity, good workmanship, savings and investment, a positive attitude—all those nice Puritan things. We have to make an effort to sell abroad, which historically we never bothered much with because home was enough.

This shouldn't be so hard. This is still a very rich and powerful country, which you can forget if you just watch our key currency fluctuate. We have an enormous "overhang," which is "hangover" transposed. We can't continue to let that get bigger. Rich does not just mean 265 million ounces of gold, which is what we have left. Rich means talent and brains and energy, universities and courts and a business system.

The mechanical devices could buy some time; it is all the unfashionable Puritan virtues—work, saving, investment—that create the currency.

You've learned enough international finance now. The rest is filling in the details. You know that if, like my Boston lawyer, you think the dollar is no place to have money, you have a way out. The major currencies are still convertible. So there's nothing to stop you from having a savings account in another currency, or buying some Eurobonds. The Euro markets are not as smooth as American markets, and the prices bounce around. I am promoting Puritan virtues, not currency speculation; but it is not totally an American world anymore. Other countries share the risks, the prosperity, and the rewards.

When my Boston lawyer brought in Edgar, his Swiss banker, the meeting did not turn out as I thought it might.

Edgar's Choice

Edgar carries three little notebooks. He is so well tailored that none of them makes a bulge. One has the telephone numbers of bankers and clients all around the world. The second has the names of new restaurants he has heard about and wants to try. The third has the telephone numbers of agreeable companions who might want to try the places listed in the second. We met in a restaurant that had been an antiques store.

"Your analysis is very good," Edgar said. "Our desert friends are piling up the money unbelievably. After the first big oil boost, they spent the money or put it in dollars. Now they are becoming more restive. We saw the next wave go through gold and silver. Gold went from two hundred fifty dollars to eight hundred fifty dollars in only eight months, and silver from six dollars to forty-eight dollars in a year. If you had a few contracts before the wave came, you made a fortune."

I made a note of the marine metaphor. There are good waves and bad waves, just as Gresham's Law has good money and bad money. A good wave is one you ride right. A bad wave is one that spills you.

"Now we see the money spreading out," said Edgar, "into copper, rubber, sugar, and zinc. Sugar is up from ten cents to twenty-four cents in only six months. It didn't take much money to send gold and silver up, compared to how many dollars there are."

I trotted out my D-mark bond portfolio.

"Very nice," said Edgar. "But you may have a wait. The Germans do not want the mark to go up, yet the demand for the mark is there. So the Bundesbank is issuing bonds directly to Middle Eastern buyers who don't have to bid in the marketplace. Now, the Bundesbank doesn't want people bringing it dollars, and the Bundesbank and the Federal Reserve in New York have it figured so the whole exchange is a wash, and the investor doesn't benefit. You get, say, fifteen percent on a dollar bond today, and you get five percent on a German bond. So the D mark would have to go up ten percent for you to break even. By the time the pressure builds up on the D mark, maybe the

International Monetary Fund will be stronger; maybe there will be a scheme under the IMF into which you can go from dollars. That way the system would keep going."

I asked Edgar what currency he liked.

"The dollar," he said.

"The *dollar?*"

"The dollar," Edgar said.

"But our energy imports, our deficits . . ."

"True, and that may bring down the whole system in the long run," he said. "And six months ago you would have been right—anything but the dollar. But now I see the Russians in Afghanistan—if they would go into Afghanistan, maybe they would make trouble somewhere else. Maybe the Russians wouldn't send tanks into West Germany, but maybe they can create enough of a fuss that you have some sort of emergency, a disruption of everyday business. If there's a disruption, I'd rather be in the States.

"That's the negative side in Europe. Then there's the positive side for yourselves. Maybe you'll come to your senses. Maybe you'll put in a gas tax and get gas to two dollars and fifty cents a gallon, as it is in Europe, and that will cut the usage. Someday you'll have an energy program. And meanwhile I can get fifteen percent on my dollars, maybe more if the rates go higher. My desert clients are more sophisticated now than in 1973. With oil at thirty dollars a barrel, they can buy all the economists and think tanks they want. And they are telling me, 'Edgar, buy us a farm in Iowa, buy us a company somewhere in America.' "

"What if we don't come through with the gas tax and the energy program?"

"Then you may pump too many dollars out, and no one will want them; but I am a Swiss, and you know how we Swiss are. We have been holding gold a long time. If it got to eight hundred fifty dollars so easily, where *could* it go?"

I do know how the Swiss are, and I should confess that I am not enamored of Swiss bankers. Edgar could discard the dollar tomorrow. The hard-money, dire-days-coming crowd always tells you to get a Swiss bank account. I may have been too early. I was once part owner of the fastest-growing bank in Switzerland, the United California Bank in Basel, whose president was Paul E. Erdman and whose majority shareholder was the second-largest bank holding company in the United States. That bank went bust through the actions of its nimble 100-percent Swiss traders. There is no Federal Deposit Insurance Corporation in Switzerland, and the lawyers and auditors I met subsequently in trilingual wrangles were very Swiss, and I would not want to meet any of them even in a well-lit alley. The Swiss popularized the anonymous bank account; they have hosted deposed Latin American dictators and Arab princes and Asian generals and smaller people as well; the secret bank account was a product for which a weary and corrupt world apparently lusted. So the Swiss bankers do know which way the money is flowing, sometimes. I never met a Swiss who didn't love gold.

Many years ago I published an interview with the Gnome of Zurich, who believed only in gold. The interview made him very famous. He predicted, in 1966, that the Treasury would cut the dollar from gold, and that the stock market would go down, and gold would go up, and all the reasons why. "Whether we have a crisis or not," he said, "depends on who wins the race between belief and disbelief. The dollar is the real international currency because the alternative is shambles. We [gnomes] stand for disbelief. We are basically cynical about the ability of men to manage their affairs rationally for very long."

Gold, said the Gnome, was reality, a brake on printed money. Alas, in the 1970s the Gnome was right. Disbelief won; the crises came; the markets went down and gold went up twenty times and can go anywhere that fear and paper money will take it. Keynes called gold "a barbaric relic"; he believed that rational men could conduct their affairs rationally. Western industrial governments have not been enamored of gold as a standard because it is too confining; it gets in the way of their programs and benefits the two major gold producers, South Africa and the Soviet Union. The industrial democracies do not want to depend on those two countries for the additional gold they would need to increase the reserves behind a currency.

The Soviet Union, in fact, has the largest unmined gold reserves in the world: about 5 billion ounces in the ground. The total unmined gold reserves in the world are estimated at 7 billion ounces. Thus the Soviets have gold, at current prices, worth roughly $3 trillion. On a full gold standard, the Soviets could give up skirmishing with the West and buy it.

If gold was a brake on the spending of governments, what else could be a brake? There is no automatic brake. The answer is a social consensus in a society that understands the effects of inflation and is willing to take the measures that end it.

We've seen how the deficits under the fixed-rate, key-currency system gave the first push to inflation, and how the system evolved into the floating world of paper money. My suspicion is that this era of infinitely inflatable currencies will not go on forever, and in fact, that it is rather late in the era. My other suspicion is that this floating world, this looseness, reflects the society around it. Its virtues are flexibility and mobility. But we are told that people now are used to instant gratification; capitalism by its very definition is based on some postponed gratification, whether by governments or people, so that the capital can be originated, invested, and compounded. We are told that our respect for institutions is declining, and that those institutions—marriage, schools, courts—are not what they used to be. Yet the smooth functioning of capitalism needs permanent institutions, so that the time can be granted for seeds to be planted, to sprout, and to grow up, for investments to mature.

We shape our houses, and then they shape us.

When the atomic physicists began to describe the subparticle universe of quantum mechanics, they needed a description of the existing world as a base reference. They called it "Newtonian": classical, balanced, fixed. The Newtonian universe; think of old Sir Isaac, bullying the Royal Society, going off with glee to see some counterfeiter hanged, and you will see what a brief period we spent as the Bank with the key currency. We paid far too little attention to our privilege, and we did not use it well for very long. But the problems of the ailing dollar were soon to be compounded by a more serious threat.

7

HOW OPEC STARTED, AND GREW, AND ENGINEERED THE GREATEST TRANSFER OF WEALTH IN WORLD HISTORY

Wanda Jablonski and I are bent over the coffee table in her apartment. Wanda is a lady of considerable knowledge and influence in the oil trade, as the proprietor and publisher of the *Petroleum Intelligence Weekly*. She is also a lady of some gumption, as she started and built up that publication alone, before the top business schools let in women and the current batch of women entrepreneurs was trained. Wanda and I are about to run, jointly, a colloquium called "The Impact of OPEC Pricing on Western Economies," under the sponsorship of a foundation. Serious numbers crunchers from all over will be arriving: the chief economists of Exxon and Mobil, some experts on the

144

Middle East, people from the international banks and the Fed and smaller oil companies, and even a dash of Europeans.

It seems to me sometimes that all I do is to worry about the Impact of OPEC Pricing on Western Economies. I can remember when the dollar was King Currency and Saudi Arabia was where they had camel races. A few short years later, fifty men in Riyadh, maybe not even fifty, can decide whether we will be in a depression or not; the banking system is in jeopardy, money has gone from solid to liquid to gas, sovereign countries are flirting with bankruptcy, a cheap house costs $100,000, and Milton Friedman is hoping that everybody will forget that he said, in 1974, that OPEC would collapse and oil would never get up to $10 a barrel. We have seen the greatest transfer of wealth in the history of the world, practically without a shot being fired.

If we know where the price of oil is going, we have some clues as to whether the banking system will survive, and whether the $100,000 house is going to cost $500,000 or $5,000, and what happens to the stock market and central heating and Western civilization.

So I am going to ask our conference my usual questions: Can OPEC hold together? Can they manage the price? Where do you think the price will go? Ten years ago it was $1.80 a barrel, and then they quadrupled it, and then it was at $12.70 for a while, and at conference time it's $28. Where next? Fifty dollars a barrel? A hundred? What about Mexico and Canada and the oil outside OPEC? Won't that help? And so on. Then our plan is to bounce all the oil numbers into the financial group, to see if the world's banking system can survive OPEC.

Wanda brushes a blond lock from her forehead.

"Do you know where OPEC started?" she says. I say Baghdad, 1960, because in my files are all the OPEC utterances and that is when they start.

"No, in my suite out at the Nile Hilton in 1959, because

that was where I introduced Perez Alfonso to Abdullah Tariki."

"Did you have to?" I asked, because it seems to me that this is a bit like saying that you were the one who gave Admiral Yamamoto the guided tour of Pearl Harbor back before he had *that* idea.

"Oh, it would have happened anyway," Wanda said.

The Man Who Invented OPEC

Indeed it would. For OPEC did not really begin in the Middle East, and it was not really invented by the Arabs. The OPEC story is almost unknown in this country, and it is full of ironies, not the least of which is the way it was modeled on one of our own institutions.

The man who invented OPEC was a precise, scholarly Venezuelan lawyer called Juan Pablo Perez Alfonso. The four names do not sound as four in Spanish; Juan Pablo is John-Paul, and in the Spanish form Perez is the patronymic and Alfonso the matronymic. Juan Pablo Perez Alfonso was born in Caracas in 1903, the grandson of a prosperous coffee grower and importer. By the time he was in his teens, however, his father was having trouble with the importing firm, and Juan Pablo had to leave the university for several terms to help in the family business. As the oldest son, he also had to take the responsibility for his eleven brothers and sisters. Responsibility at an early age, and limited resources, produced a careful attitude in Juan Pablo toward those resources.

Perez Alfonso went back to the Central University in Caracas and graduated with a law degree, older, because of the interruptions, than any other member of his class. He taught civil law, became a city councilman and, in 1938, a congressman. He appears, in early pictures, as a slim, handsome man, his hairline already receding. Later he was to grow the prototypical Latin pencil mustache and to wear the horn-rimmed glasses favored by Latin American intellectuals.

It was natural for Venezuelans to be concerned with oil. Venezuela was the world's leading oil exporter, and oil provided the bulk of the government's revenues. The first major oil strike had been in 1922, so oil had been a presence for nearly two decades by the time Perez Alfonso got to Congress. Perez Alfonso was a leading member of the *Accion Democratica,* a new opposition party, and he made himself his party's oil expert, as well as someone who could turn out a closely reasoned juridical thesis.

Perez Alfonso had a hand in framing the 1943 Venezuelan oil law, which Venezuelans consider a landmark. When the *Accion Democratica* won the election in 1945, the reformer Romulo Betancourt became president, and Perez Alfonso became Minister of Mines and Hydrocarbons, the oil minister. Perez Alfonso's first action was to cut his own salary 20 percent and to suggest that the other ministers cut theirs, so that the people would know the reform party was serious.

Perez Alfonso's next action was to send for the chief engineer of the Texas Railroad Commission. Even in 1945 Perez Alfonso saw oil as a finite resource, and he wanted to apply the conservation techniques of the Texas Railroad Commission with regard to gas flaring, how much oil to take out of a reservoir, and the safest procedure for abandoning a well.

It sounds strange to have an agency called the Texas *Railroad* Commission come into this story, until you realize that it is also the oil commission. In the 1930s there was so much oil being produced in Texas that the market was chaotic, the price sometimes as low as 10 cents a barrel. In the competitive fervor, oil men drilled into each other's leases, the legs of the derricks sometimes overlapped, and the engineers complained about depletion and wastage.

The Texas oil industry turned to the state government for help and supported a move to give the Texas Railroad Commission—whose business had been, obviously, railroad regulation—the power to regulate drilling and production. The rationale for the activities of the commission was conservation, and the commission did enforce rules to prolong the life of the wells. The existence of the commission was a tribute to the political power of the independent oil men.

There were, in Texas, major oil companies that not only drilled for oil but refined it and marketed it through their own gasoline stations and sales agents. There were also independent oil men who only drilled, and then sold oil in the marketplace. Sometimes the independents and the majors would have wells tapped into the same pool of oil, like two straws in a drink, since the underground oil naturally did not follow the contours of the surface ownership. If the demand slumped, the major oil company could keep lifting oil, because it had its own outlets to sell through. The independents, if they had to stop drilling because there was no market, would then complain that the major was sucking up their oil.

The independents were much smaller than the majors, but, as individuals, some of them were multimillionaires, much richer than any oil company executive, and hence able to spend well in political contributions. H. L. Hunt and John Mecom were among the independents, and they were to be among the richest people in the country. So the independents could get their cause to be heard.

The Texas Railroad Commission did not set a price for oil, but it determined what could be produced. The early appointments to its board developed a reputation for fairness, from the point of view of the producers. When the demand dropped, the Texas Railroad Commission gathered the industry and polled it as to what the real demand might be. It then set an allowable rate of production, so many days per month, that oil could be produced. Thus conservation produced a mechanism for stabilizing the market.

If the price of oil started to sag, the Texas Railroad Commission would reduce the number of days per month that oil could be produced. "It became the policy of the Commission," *Fortune* wrote in 1959, "to keep oil prices high enough for the 'little man'—the marginal Texas producer—to make money. This of course was a wonderful arrangement for the nonmarginal (i.e., the major) U.S. producers. It enabled them to clear as much as 50 per cent per annum. And it was even more wonderful for the major companies overseas."

It was wonderful for the companies overseas because the Texas price was the American price, called the "Gulf" price, back when the Gulf meant the Gulf of Mexico, not the Persian Gulf or the Arabian Gulf. And the Texas price became the world price, so oil was leaving the other Gulf, the Persian Gulf, in the tankers of Exxon (the oil companies, to prevent confusion, are here called by their current names) and Gulf, at $1.80 a barrel—the Texas price— when it cost only 10 cents a barrel.

The trouble was that so much oil was being found in the world that the "Gulf" price, out of Texas, wasn't always sticking. Somebody was always trying to cut the price. The Texas Railroad Commission could keep the American price up by ordering a cutback in production, but oil could still land in the United States from abroad, and move cheaply. The American oil companies then limited imports, by voluntary agreement, which later became mandatory by order of the U.S. government. They constructed, said the British economist Paul Frankel, "an invisible dike against the outside world."

In 1948 the military dictatorship of Perez Jiminez took over in Venezuela, and Juan Pablo Perez Alfonso went into exile, first in Washington, D.C., and then in Mexico City. He lived modestly, writing tracts and articles, sometimes receiving checks from his real estate in Caracas. His children remember him prowling the house, snapping off the television set, and telling them to do something useful. Perez Alfonso was in exile for ten years, reading, writing, and studying the activities of the Texas Railroad Commission. This is a paraphrase of what he wrote:

Venezuela is not in control of its own destiny. It ought to be. We may be the richest country in Latin America, but we still have poor people, and the oil will not last forever. Lake Maracaibo drops a foot a year, with all that oil pulled from under it. Then the money comes back to us at levels we don't control, depending on the world oil market. Sometimes there isn't enough, and sometimes there's too much all at once and it spills into high living in Caracas. Everything should match neatly: the supply, the demand, and the money for social needs.

If Venezuela was not in control of its own destiny, who was? The International Oil Cartel; if the Venezuelans gave it any trouble, the cartel simply cut back in Venezuela and took the oil from somewhere else in its vast empire. For most of Venezuelan history, though, the relationships between the oil companies and the Venezuelan government had been so cozy that no such action was necessary. The cartel members operating in Venezuela were Exxon, Gulf, Texaco, Royal Dutch, and Mobil.

The cartel had been formed in September 1928, when Sir Henri Deterding, the chairman of Royal Dutch/Shell, invited the heads of Exxon (then Standard Oil of New Jersey) and British Petroleum to his estate in Achnacarry, Scotland, ostensibly for some grouse shooting. What the grouse shooters did, however, was to agree on an unsigned document that specified principles for eliminating "destructive competition." The three original members later admitted Texaco, Gulf, Mobil, and Socal—Standard of

California—to make up what Enrico Mattei, the Italian oil man who could not break their grip, called the "Seven Sisters."

In 1952 the United States Federal Trade Commission reported that the cartel "controlled all the principal oil producing areas outside the United States, all foreign refineries, patents, and refinery technology, and divided world markets between [sic] them." The committees of the cartel, in London and New York, set production quotas and coordinated distribution of the world's oil. A Department of Justice lawyer called the cartel agreement "a grand policy blueprint for a corporate world government of the petroleum industry." The Department of Justice criminal antitrust case against the five American members, in 1952, was later downgraded to a civil complaint and settled by consent. When the Shah, with CIA assistance, deposed Iran's Prime Minister Mossadegh in 1953, the United States National Security Council, Action Memorandum 875b, ordered "a solution which would protect the interests of the free world in the Near East" and, in effect, got the Department of Justice to drop its antitrust actions so that the oil companies could act in concert in Iran.

None of this was lost on Juan Pablo Perez Alfonso; he studied it intently from his exile houses in Washington and Mexico. Some of the history was not made public until the mid-1970s, when the Senate Subcommittee on Multinational Corporations, chaired by Senator Frank Church, held its hearings. By 1959 the Venezuelan military junta had fled the country, its suitcases stuffed with cash, and Romulo Betancourt was back as El Presidente, and Juan Pablo Perez Alfonso was back as his oil minister. (Betancourt, his admirers later said, was the only Venezuelan ever to leave the presidency with a net worth of $383.)

Juan Pablo Perez Alfonso got on the phone to Austin, Texas, and invited one of the members of the Texas Railroad Commission to come for a visit, to dispense advice and counsel. Then he began to issue directives in his cramped, careful hand.

First, he paid his respects to conservation, in the style of the Texas Railroad Commission.

Next, he said that he wanted, on behalf of Venezuela, "to avoid monetary losses due to unjustified price reductions." That means just what it sounds like: we don't want the price to go down, because then we get less money.

Then he said that in the United States the price of oil was shored up by state and government controls that allowed all the producers a share of the market, and that is what Venezuela should do, too.

So Venezuela got some new oil laws. But it still faced the old International Cartel. And it was still utterly dependent on oil revenues, and the population was growing, and it couldn't always get its oil *into* the United States, the biggest market, the biggest consumer, because of that damned invisible dike. And if the Venezuelan producers, especially the independents, couldn't get the oil over the damned invisible dike, they had to dump the oil somewhere else in the world market, which meant less money for Venezuela.

Perez Alfonso did not smoke or drink, and he suffered from insomnia. He kept a pad and pencil by his bedside, so that he could work on problems when he could not sleep, and he sometimes read through the night and got up at dawn. Jotting on his notepad, Perez Alfonso hatched a grand scheme of absolutely breathtaking audacity. It would be an international Texas Railroad Commission, without the Texans! A Texas Railroad Commission for the whole world! If the price of oil started to go down, all the members would hold back their production until the price went up again. And together, united, the *producers* of the oil—by which Perez Alfonso meant the countries in which the oil was located—together could stand up to the great industrial nations with their great oil companies.

Venezuela had, at that time, 7 percent of the world's oil

reserves, and the Middle East had 70 percent. Venezuela could cut back until it was blue in the face and it wouldn't matter; it would be like Pennsylvania starting the Texas Railroad Commission.

Juan Pablo Perez Alfonso had his plans and his tracts and Venezuela's new oil laws all translated into Arabic.

And while Juan Pablo Perez Alfonso was getting all the materials translated into Arabic, Abdullah Tariki was fuming.

The Odd Couple

Abdullah Tariki was in the first wave of Saudi oil technocrats who went to the West to study. He had been to the University of Texas, had been briefly married to an American girl, and had, for one bitter period, even been a Texaco trainee. Tariki had absorbed all the arguments about the oil companies in the 1952 report of the Federal Trade Commission. Now, in 1959, he was director of the Office of Petroleum Affairs for Saudi Arabia, and he was, for that time and that country, a radical. He wanted Saudi Arabia to have an integrated oil company of its own, and not just to let Aramco bring up the oil and take it away. Aramco was the partnership of Exxon, Mobil, Socal, and Texaco.

Tariki was fuming because the oil companies had just *reduced* their prices. Saudi Arabia did not have very sophisticated management, to say the least. King Saud married at least 125 times, and each wife got a house and an allowance. When the king needed money, a courtier would call up Aramco and ask for an advance. Saudi Arabia was perilously close to being out of cash, and Tariki was getting the phone calls, and the oil companies were *cutting* their prices, which was going to cost Saudi Arabia $34 million.

Perez Alfonso gathered thirteen aides and the multilingual translations of the Venezuelan oil laws and got everybody onto a plane for Cairo—tourist class, of course—to attend the very first Arab Oil Congress.

Abdullah Tariki, still smoldering, got onto a plane for Cairo with some Saudi oil technocrats.

And so, on April 16, 1959, Wanda said, "By the way, Abdullah Tariki, do you know Juan Pablo Perez Alfonso?"

But it was clearly going to happen anyway, since once the two oil ministers had traded a few pleasantries about Texas, Perez Alfonso's aides began handing out documents in Arabic to Abdullah Tariki's aides. Two of Perez Alfonso's aides had been to the University of Texas with Abdullah Tariki.

Juan Pablo Perez Alfonso began to detail his plan for a worldwide Texas Railroad Commission. Conserve and cut back, unite and control. If you want more money, do not sell more oil; sell *less.*

Abdullah Tariki listened intently. How would it work? Who would decide how much each country would cut back? How could the cutbacks be enforced?

It was decided that Tariki would go out and preach this plan to the Iraqis and the Kuwaitis and the Bahrainis and all the other tribes with oil. These tribes were more used to quarreling than cooperating, and they were used to calling up the awesome oil companies as one would a parent. Kuwait was a small city-state, and the Emirates were right out of the Middle Ages—mud palaces and goats. The Union Jack hung from the flagpole at Aden, and British destroyers slid through the waters of the Gulf. So it was a radical idea to go out and preach unity and cooperation and shutting the oil in.

But Tariki was a radical. "I think it could work," he said, and he went out to preach.

Tariki went through the Arab states, and Perez Alfonso went to Iran, where he held a press conference even before he got to see the Shah. Later he went even to Moscow.

The Russians were as hostile as the major oil companies. Perez Alfonso had to explain that OPEC was not a front for the oil cartel.

In August 1959 *Fortune* magazine noticed the itinerant preachings of the Odd Couple. Its tone was one of amusement and skepticism, its point of view, as usual, that of big business. To read it is to enter an astonishing time warp.

The problem, *Fortune* said, is the Glut. Too much oil. Furthermore, said *Fortune*, "the glut is certain to last a long time." The reason: "too much oil underground too easy to get at, ready to flow at very little additional expense." The ratio of reserves to consumption had formerly been twenty to one; that is, for every barrel shipped there were twenty barrels underground. Now it was forty to one; in the Middle East it was one hundred to one. Even if nobody ever drilled another well, there was so much oil that the ratio of reserves to consumption wouldn't go back to twenty to one for another decade.

"The international oil companies do not propose to take a beating lying down," said *Fortune*. "They are redoubling their efforts to increase the use of petroleum products." General Motors and Socal had already bought the Los Angeles mass transit rail system and shut it down. Exxon promised a tiger in a tank. Everywhere there were campaigns to increase driving and heating. "Glut without end?" read the *Fortune* subhead. "Today, for the first time in years, the companies are cracking down on salaries, expense accounts and office overhead." The Highway Trust Fund helped by building the interstate highway system. Farther out, suburbs were springing up, requiring more driving.

"A Strange New Plan for World Oil," *Fortune* headlined its article:

> The proposition, baldly stated, is that the great oil-producing countries outside the U.S. should get together

to limit production and maintain prices. The rationale of this proposal is clear enough. Crude oil prices outside the U.S. have been falling like overripe fruit. Inside the U.S., however, prices have been holding relatively high and steady because the mighty Texas Railroad Commission, supported by other state and federal bodies, in effect adjusts the supply of U.S. oil to the market. . . . An international Texas Railroad Commission could keep crude oil production in line with demand, allocate production equitably among producing countries and companies, and so maintain prices at or close to the elegant level maintained in the U.S. The high irony of the proposition is enough to raise a guffaw from even the sourest oilman . . . such a global scheme, granting it is at all feasible, obviously runs against just about every principle of free enterprise economics in the book . . . the basic interest of the consumer in cheaper oil, made possible by the discovery of ever larger reserves, would be thrown to the winds.

"Taking everything together," *Fortune* said, "the proposal of Messrs. Perez Alfonso and Tariki is not only impractical but bad economics." What *Fortune* proposed was that the United States *import more* oil. That would take the pressure off world prices, and they could find a more realistic level.

Fortune may have been in a time warp, but its suggestion, in 1959, to import oil made some sense. The dollar was strong, oil could have been imported at less than $1.80 a barrel, the world market might have been helped, and a finite resource might have been preserved. Today we pay out $30 a barrel to import oil, and we even pump some of that oil into the salt domes of Louisiana as a reserve. Twenty years ago we took it out of the ground here and burned it up; now we bring it in a tanker, at twenty times the 1959 cost, and put it back into the ground.

But the domestic American oil independents did not

want to import more oil in 1959. They wanted the protec-
tion of the "invisible dike." Independents operating
abroad, in Libya and Venezuela, were finding oil, and so
were the Seven Sisters.

Fortune's "glut" numbers obviously came from the oil
companies, and the vision of its writer was appropriately
limited. But it was certainly right in one respect. The
"strange new plan" of Perez Alfonso and Tariki did not
worry about the oil consumer, and it ran against every
principle of free enterprise in the book. But if it ran
against every principle of free enterprise, what about the
model on which it was based? That was the irony, because
the oil companies were the source of so much rhetoric
about free enterprise.

One other note from the time warp. The price cut that
so angered Abdullah Tariki cost $34 million a *year*. Saudi
Arabia now takes in $166 million a *day*. Keeping that scale
in mind will help to explain the age of paper money.

They were an odd couple, Perez Alfonso and Tariki,
but they got along. Here was this precise, brilliant, balding
Latin with his horn-rimmed glasses and his pencil mustache, intense, nervous, his bedside pad always ready to
receive his thoughts when he could not sleep; and here
was his Arab sidekick, somewhat swarthy—he had sometimes been taken for a Mexican in Texas restaurants—
with thick hair and a generous nose. Tariki was as careless
as Perez Alfonso was precise. He loved speaking to crowds,
though he was personally shy; and when he was speaking,
he would drum out, "Aramco—is—stealing, Aramco—is
—stealing," and then would rattle off statistics. The statistics bore no particular relationship to reality. "They sound
good, no?" he said. "So what? The oil is ours." Tariki lived
alone in Jidda, in a house with a walled garden that contained gazelles, chickens, turkeys, and various lame animals which he nursed. His Saluki dogs had the run of the

house, and the Salukis remained in their chairs even when visitors entered. Tariki was also a violent Arab nationalist. "I am an Arab, not a Saudi," he said.

The Odd Couple flew together from country to country, preaching, "Unite and control, conserve and cut back," and they spelled out their plan in, of all places, Tyler, Texas, in the spring of 1960. The Texas Independent Producers convention listened with attention and skepticism.

Sitting in his elegant boardroom in Rockefeller Center in New York, Monroe Rathbone must have heard the sounds of the Odd Couple as that of two annoying mosquitoes. "Jack" Rathbone was the head of Exxon—Esso, as it was then called—and all he could see, that summer of 1960, was the Glut. The Russians were selling oil; the Italians were selling oil; odd tankers everywhere were dumping the stuff for whatever it would bring.

Petroleum Week, where Wanda then worked as a senior editor, smelled a price cut coming and said there would be an uproar.

A couple of Exxon directors, Howard Page and William Stott, warned that the budgets of a lot of countries were based on the oil price.

Jack Rathbone was a chemical engineer, like most of the Exxon board, not a diplomat. The top ranks of Exxon came from the "Exxon Academy," the great refinery at Baton Rouge.

Exxon cut the price, without calling up any of the producing countries, as was the tradition in those days. The other oil companies followed.

The budgets of the Middle Eastern countries went out the windows, with a clamor from those countries. The entire atmosphere in the Middle East was transformed. The Odd Couple's preachings were recalled. Tariki called a meeting in Baghdad for September 9, 1960.

The price cut was serious for Iran, with its growing population, and for Saudi Arabia, which was planning a major program of social services.

Fifteen years later, the Shah of Iran recalled the moment to the British journalist Anthony Sampson. "Even if the price cut was basically sound," he said, "it could not be acceptable to us as long as it was taken without our consent." He had been angry, and not at all confident of the power of the oil producers. "We were just walking in the mist. Not in the dark, but it was a little misty. There was still that complex of the big powers, and the mystical power and all the magic behind the name of all these big countries."

With the Odd Couple as militant hosts, five nations—Saudi Arabia, Iran, Iraq, Kuwait, and Venezuela—met in Baghdad and declared the birth of OPEC, the Organization of Petroleum Exporting Countries, "a cartel to confront the cartel," said one delegate.

"We have formed a very exclusive club," said Juan Pablo Perez Alfonso. "Between us we control ninety percent of crude exports to world markets, and we are now united. We are making history."

That was considered so important by the press of the world that it was barely reported at all. For the great event of September 9, Reuters mustered up a dispatch on September 24. *The New York Times* published a back-page squib on September 25.

The OPEC declaration of independence rings with the indignation of the colonists dumping the tea into the harbor, but here the excesses of Mad King George are those of the oil companies. OPEC, says its first words, can no longer "remain indifferent to the attitude heretofore adopted by the oil companies." It demanded that the companies "maintain their prices steady," in fact, "restore prices to the levels prevailing before the reductions." Those reductions were 9 cents a barrel, an amount that would later seem ludicrously small. But so was the tax on the tea at Boston harbor.

Oil, said the newly born cartel, was needed to finance development and balance budgets; it was a depleting asset and had to be replaced by other assets.

Later the rhetoric was to get more strident, with more talk of colonialism and grievances and the Third World and independence. In the beginning OPEC wanted the price to go back to where it had been before the Exxon board cut it.

If the American public slumbered through this momentous beginning, it can hardly be blamed for its lack of awareness. Its presidential candidates, Richard Nixon and John F. Kennedy, were vigorously debating the status of two tiny islands off the coast of China, called Quemoy and Matsu.

The oil companies were trying to think up more ways to sell petroleum products, to burn off what *Fortune* had called the Glut Without End.

"We Have Formed a Very Exclusive Club"

"We have formed a very exclusive club," said Juan Pablo Perez Alfonso. That is exactly what OPEC was, and is: a Club.

What were the qualifications for membership? Obviously, to be in the Organization of Petroleum Exporting Countries, you had to be a Petroleum Exporting Country. The original language said a country with "a substantial net export" of oil. The second criterion was that the applicant have "fundamentally similar interests" to those of the members. So it was not just *any* Petroleum Exporting Country that could become a member. Canada and the Soviet Union would not do, for different reasons. Both lacked "similar interests" to the members.

OPEC's rules were that an applicant had to be accepted by three-quarters of the Full Members, but a blackball by any Founding Member would keep him out.

Like any really exclusive club, "fundamentally similar interests" later began to mean more than the charter title, "petroleum exporting." The sheikhdom of Qatar, not a "substantial net exporter," was to be admitted, as was the small West African country of Gabon, also not a substantial exporter. But the Western Hemisphere islands of Trinidad and Tobago were blackballed; they did not have "fundamentally similar interests."

OPEC began with an office in Geneva. The Swiss treated it as a Club and not as an international organization: "the Swiss government," OPEC's secretary, Abdul Amir Kubbah protested, "considered that OPEC's objective was to defend the private and sole interests of its Member Countries and that it had no international interest." OPEC wanted the status of an embassy: extraterritoriality, immunity from legal process, freedom from customs and taxes, the right to have codes and couriers and commissaries. The Austrians granted this, and in 1965 the Club moved to Vienna, to a building called Texaco Haus, after its principal tenant.

Three of the five Founding Members—those with the charter privilege of blackball—were Arab states, as were, eventually, seven of the twelve Full Members. And while the Arab states later formed OAPEC, the Organization of Arab Petroleum Exporting Countries, as an adjunct to OPEC, there has never been much question of some aspects of what "fundamentally similar interests" means.

To show that it was a good member, with "fundamentally similar interests," Venezuela announced right away that it would not sell oil to Israel.

OPEC had an office, a structure, a procedure for meetings. It commissioned a study on pricing by the consulting firm of Arthur D. Little. In 1962 Abdullah Tariki was fired and told to leave Saudi Arabia. The Saudi royal family did not appreciate his admiration for Egypt's Gamal Nasser, or his radicalism. He was replaced by Sheikh Ahmed Zaki Yamani, who was only thirty-two at the time. Tariki went to Cairo and became a consultant.

Yamani was less radical, less abrasive, much more to the liking of the Western interests. The son of a judge in Mecca, he had been educated in Cairo, and at New York University and Harvard. His neat, pointed beard was like that of an opera star. He was to become the first great international contemporary oil celebrity.

Juan Pablo Perez Alfonso stepped down as oil minister when Betancourt left office in Venezuela, but his staff remained in place, and Perez Alfonso became the *eminence grise* of Venezuelan oil policy. He continued to hold press conferences, to scold the government for being too lax with the oil companies, and to lead the next wave of tax reform.

But as for OPEC, it was no Texas Railroad Commission. Production programming in oil is an enormously complex process, requiring sophisticated market analysis and a willingness to compromise. The OPEC Secretariat tried two plans of prorationing—cutback and control—and got nowhere. The Saudis, in particular, said any such scheme violated their sovereignty. The clerks in Vienna, they said, could do what they wanted; clerks did not dictate to the royal family. The Iraqis quarreled with the Iranians, the Iranians with the Saudis. The Kuwaitis were suspicious of the Iraqis, who claimed, in fact, ownership of Kuwait. The Iranians and the Saudis passed Venezuela as the world's leading oil exporters.

Juan Pablo Perez Alfonso complained that Venezuelan leadership and influence in OPEC was declining, and that the Arabs were contemptuous of Venezuela. Oil, he insisted, had an intrinsic value, and the industrial nations would soon realize it.

But the price of oil did not go up; in fact, it declined, all through the 1960s. The "posted price" of $1.80 a barrel in the Persian Gulf was for tax purposes; sometimes the oil was discounted to as low as $1 a barrel. Behind the "invisible dike," in Texas, oil sold, at the end of the decade, for $3.45 a barrel.

A contributing factor to the declining price of Middle Eastern oil was the improved ways of carrying it. The tankers in the middle 1950s had been perhaps 20,000 tons. Japanese shipyards then developed the jumbo tanker, and then the VLCC supertanker, 250,000 tons, which sharply reduced the cost of oil as it landed at the refineries.

It took two wars, a gradual change in energy habits, and a French bulldozer to bring about the control first envisaged by Perez Alfonso.

The change in energy habits was from coal to oil, and no wonder. Coal was bulky, hard to transport, and left irritants in the atmosphere when burned. Mining it was an unpleasant and hazardous task, whether in Pennsylvania or Wales or Lorraine, and there was always trouble with the miners.

The automobile population of the world was increasing geometrically, as if the idea of bigger families had also spread to vehicles.

In 1940 coal accounted for two-thirds of the world's energy. In 1970 it provided less than a third. In the United States coal as a percentage of total energy consumption dropped from 47.2 percent to 18.6 percent in the same period.

All during the 1960s, OPEC and the seven great oil companies squabbled over a few cents a barrel. The Shah developed a major spending program and needed more revenue to support it. The Saudis eyed his program nervously. During the Six Day War, in 1967, the Arabs set up a boycott, and the Suez Canal was closed. The boycott was relatively ineffective. The end of the Six Day War left OPEC standing, but in tatters; the Iranians and the Venezuelans had increased their exports at the expense of the Arabs.

In the United States, in the early 1960s, the rate of inflation was about 1 percent a year.

The Balance Tips

If the world's oil producers were squabbling, the United States had a cushion: the extra days per month that the Texas Railroad Commission said not to pump. Then oil was discovered in the North Sea, and the independent oil producers who had found oil in Libya made further handsome discoveries there. Slowly, like the first tremors of an earthquake, the balance began to change. There were stray factors not easily integrated: more wells that came up dry. American oil production was peaking. There were more dry holes—or less prolific ones—in Libya and Algeria. Those countries began to consider the wasting asset more seriously.

The Suez Canal was closed, but there was a pipeline from the great Saudi fields to the Lebanese town of Sidon as well as the supertankers lifting oil in the Persian Gulf. And there was Libya, right across the Mediterranean from Europe—no canal necessary, no supertankers necessary. Libya was supplying a quarter of Europe's oil.

The United States was preoccupied with Vietnam.

Within a twelve-month period the balance had tipped, and yet very few noticed.

On September 1, 1969, a radical colonel in Libya, Muammar el-Qaddafi, seized power from King Idris, who had granted the concessions to the oil companies. Libya had a large foreign-exchange surplus from selling its oil. It was under no financial pressure. The new prime minister, Suleiman Maghrebi, had a Ph.D. from George Washington University, had worked at one time as a lawyer for

Exxon, and had even been in jail for organizing an oil workers' strike. Colonel Qaddafi decided to take on the Western oil companies, both as an ideological move and as a financial one. He made noises about a deal with the Russians.

In May 1970 a French bulldozer on a job in Syria accidentally broke the "Tapline," the Trans-Arabian Pipeline running to the Mediterranean. The Syrians refused to repair it until they got higher transmission fees. The Nigerians were in a civil war, with their own oil province of Biafra the chief battleground, and Nigerian production was off. Suddenly—or what seemed suddenly—the cushion was gone. There was still no shortage of oil in the world, but political events had interrupted the delivery of oil.

The new regime of Colonel Qaddafi confronted the oil companies: it wanted an extra 40 cents a barrel, to make up for the convenience of delivery to Europe the companies enjoyed from Libya. The oil companies offered 5 cents. The Libyans looked over the companies to which they had given oil concessions; the most successful of the independents was Occidental, whose strikes had made it the biggest producer in Libya. Most of Occidental's oil went to Europe, in competition with the Seven Sisters. The Libyans decided to pick off the companies one by one. In the familiar name of conservation, Colonel Qaddafi ordered Occidental's production cut back. Occidental went to Exxon and asked whether Exxon would supply it, roughly at cost, from elsewhere in the world if Occidental resisted the Libyan demands. Exxon offered a higher, third-party price, but turned Occidental down on the deal it proposed. Occidental had no other major source of crude, and it then capitulated to the Libyans.

We know this history better than we normally would because of the extraordinary hearings conducted in 1974 by the subcommittee of the Senate Foreign Relations Committee chaired by Senator Frank Church. Shell resisted the Libyans; its production was cut off. Shell's chairman was a precisely articulate, monocle-wearing British aristocrat, Sir David Barran. "Our conclusion," he wrote later to Senator Church, "was that sooner or later we, both oil company and consumer, would have to face an avalanche of escalating demands from producer governments, and that we should at least try to stem the avalanche."

The oil companies met at the State Department in Washington to see what support they could muster. The companies were astonished to find the State Department opening the discussion by bringing up the plight of the Palestinians, which seemed irrelevant, but which was part of the radical Libyan rhetoric. The State Department was not eager to support the oil companies. It was trying to reestablish relations with the Algerians, next door to Libya, and to obtain a supply of Algerian natural gas. The Libyans, said James Akins, the State Department's oil expert, were "competent men in a strong position, who played their hand straight, and found it a winning one." Their demands, said Akins, were reasonable. One by one the oil companies capitulated. The first rolling rocks of the avalanche were in motion. The game of Leapfrog in oil prices, which is still going on, began.

"The Libyan success was an embarrassment to other OPEC countries," wrote Abdul Amir Kubbah. OPEC, said Kubbah, had been too moderate. "We wasted ten years, not following what our Venezuelan friends had told us," said Kubbah. "Now Colonel Qaddafi had shocked us into action."

The Shah of Iran was miffed at the Libyan initiative. Among his own self-given titles were Shahanshah, King of Kings, Shadow of God on Earth; and here was an upstart colonel leading the Club. His power in the area, he said, was ten times, no, twenty times as great as that of the British had ever been. He warned the consuming countries not to get together behind their oil companies; he warned the oil companies not to get together to defeat the legitimate demands of the producers. The companies, he said, would now negotiate with the Persian Gulf states. That way he, the Shahanshah, could restrain the "wild men" of OPEC. The "wild men," Iraq and Algeria among them, were already leapfrogging their prices to match those of the Libyans. When OPEC met in Caracas in December, though, there was little difference between the "wild men" and the "moderates." A month later the oil companies met the Persian Gulf states in Tehran.

The Shah could see that the British and American governments had left the oil companies without diplomatic support, and he was a grimly determined host. The Libyans had found the way to transfer the wealth of the world; they had used a *temporary* market condition to kick up the prices. Theoretically, the Tapline break was temporary, the Nigerian civil war was temporary, the Suez Canal closing was temporary, and even the European demand in the summer of 1970 seemed temporarily above normal. The Americans could be complacent, even shortsighted, because almost all of their oil at that time came from the Western Hemisphere: from their own oil states, and from Canada and Venezuela. Only 3 percent came from the Middle East. The Libyans had also shown that a "negotiation" between strong producers and divided consumers scarcely had to be a negotiation at all; it was the exact reverse of the oil situation Perez Alfonso had found when he first got elected to Congress in Venezuela, when the oil cartel dictated the prices. The Shah said that the proper price for oil was perhaps *ten times* the current price, which would bring it to the level of the price of alternative fuels.

The oil companies quietly got together in New York to rehearse some strategy, together with their rivals, the independents, and the German, Spanish, Japanese, French, and Belgian oil companies. The text sent to OPEC by the oil companies had, considering the old history of the oil cartel, an ironic twist: it said that the oil consumers and producers both needed stability, and this business of Leap-frog was very unstable; OPEC should act together and bind its members! The companies did not want to have two sets of negotiations as the Shah suggested; they feared another round of Leapfrog. A State Department spokes-man, John Irwin, was sent to Tehran to explain why the oil companies were getting together and why they should have only a single negotiation. The Shah talked Irwin out of it; the companies had no choice then but to follow the Shah's plan.

The oil companies were not used to acting in concert, even though they had once been a powerful cartel. They had to obtain a Justice Department antitrust waiver just to be able to talk to one another. Tentatively they discussed cooperation and a "safety net." So they ranged along one side of the table in Tehran, the Seven Sisters, led by Lord Strathalmond, more familiarly known in the oil industry as Billy Fraser, the popular, gregarious director of British Petroleum, whose father had made an oil fortune in Iran. On the other side of the table was a formidable negotiating team representing countries, not companies: Sheikh Zaki Yamani, New York University and Harvard, smooth and poised; Jamshid Amouzegar, a lean, craggy, ironic Iranian with B.A. and Ph.D. degrees from Cornell; and Saadoun Hammadi, an unsmiling, austere Iraqi with a Ph.D. from the University of Wisconsin. The American-educated members of the OPEC team were their respective coun-tries' oil ministers.

The negotiations went on for thirty-three days. The oil companies made their headquarters in London, in British Petroleum's skyscraper, with messages going to and from their field team in Tehran. And while the discussions went back and forth, OPEC had a threat that its delegates were not afraid to put forth: if it did not get what it wanted, it would shut off the oil. It promised "concerted and simultaneous action by all member countries."

"*That* was a surprise," said a British observer. "We were used to these chaps always quarreling among themselves, the Iraqi hotheads and the conservative Saudis. The Western countries were not prepared at all for economic blackmail. We knew the Iranians were spending twenty percent more than their income, so they had to get a raise, but we were surprised at how very tough all of them had become."

Though the parley went on for thirty-three days, the OPEC members actually came out with a higher price per barrel than they had asked for the first day. OPEC would get another 50 cents a barrel. The companies hoped they had won five years of peace. But even that was fragile; a dozen years before, an American lawyer, Frank Hendryx, had been legal adviser to Abdullah Tariki's department and had brought up the concept in Western law that sovereign governments have the right to abrogate commercial contracts that run counter to the legitimate interests of their citizens. Even at that time the Arab governments were well aware of the principle.

The agreement was signed on February 14, 1971. It might have been called the St. Valentine's Day Massacre.

The importance was not in the 50 cents a barrel; it was that OPEC now dictated the terms.

The oil company teams, who had felt, in Tehran, that they were "bargaining in front of a loaded gun," now had to go to Libya for another round of negotiations; Tehran had covered only the Persian Gulf nations. The Libyans thought that OPEC had been far too gentle at the St. Valentine's Day Massacre. Every day the Libyan oil minister, Ezzedin El-Mabruk, began with an hour's harangue on the sins of the West, its support for Israel, its years of exploitation. With the Tapline wrecked, Europe was more than ever dependent on Libya. Mabruk said he was about to turn off the oil. "We lived five thousand years without it, and we can continue to live without it," he said.

Only the other OPEC members stopped him from asking for an increase *three times* that of the one agreed upon in Tehran. He got a bigger one than the Gulf states, even so. The oil companies went home. They still had the tankers, the refineries, the petrochemical plants, and the filling stations.

But they had lost control of the oil.

Unite and control, conserve and threaten to cut back. It worked! In Caracas, Perez Alfonso read the OPEC accounts with some satisfaction.

I have a reason for reciting the advanced degrees of OPEC's negotiators. The image of the Arab in the West was that of the "raghead," watering his camel and lusting after small boys. The Six Day War had produced the television image of Egyptian soldiers running back to Egypt barefoot through the sand. "Exxon seemed certain the Arabs could never get together," a former Exxon executive recalled. "Their image of the Arabs seemed as though it was taken from the movie *Lawrence of Arabia.*"

But on the other side of the table, at Tehran, were these three ragheads who had gotten Ph.D.'s and other advanced degrees from American universities in a foreign language, which is to say, English. Not that advanced degrees in a second language are necessary signs of great negotiating skills, but in this case the gentlemen were formidable and knew the cards they held. "It was not until we realized our strength that we *had* our strength," a Saudi aide said later.

Sheikh Yamani had told an Exxon director, George Piercy, "You know you cannot take a shutdown." But the West could have taken a shutdown far better in that winter of 1971 than it could ever take again.

The Atlantic Richfield Company had not been a party

to the negotiations. The Arco directors met in their Manhattan boardroom to hear an account of what had happened on Valentine's Day. One director traced on his notepad an abstract pattern, like the abstraction in the James Beyer tapestry on the wall. When the recitation was finished, he said, sarcastically, "Well, we really held the Arabs to their own terms."

The price rise of the St. Valentine's Day Massacre did not dampen demand; indeed, that demand went up and up, all over the world. Behind the "invisible dike" the price of Texas oil was $3.45 a barrel, frozen by the price and wage controls imposed by the Nixon administration. The United States was now importing 23 percent of its oil, but most of that still came from Canada and Venezuela. The Middle Eastern oil was $2.20 a barrel at Ras Tanura in Saudi Arabia, still cheaper than the Texas oil.

All through the 1960s the oil companies had worried about the Endless Glut. Michael Haider, chairman of Exxon, said at its annual meeting in Houston, in May 1967, "I wish I could say I will be around when there is a shortage of crude oil outside the United States." A memo from Standard of California in December of 1968 warned that Arctic oil would keep the Glut going.

By 1972 the Glut was gone. The Texas Railroad Commission did not have to worry about how many days a month the wells could pump; they were going flat out, every day. The demand was right across the board: gasoline for automobiles, kerosene for jets, chemicals, weed sprays, fertilizers, plastics.

Richard Nixon was reelected by forty-nine of fifty states. His energy task force, headed by George Shultz, had reported there was little danger of an Arab boycott and that import restrictions should be liberalized.

It is a curious experience to review the technical literature of the early 1970s. The specialized oil journals are preoccupied with the day-to-day business of concessions, and tax rates, and participations. Not much about the days of dire ahead. A whole generation of oil men had grown up with the Glut.

The warnings appear in that dry Establishment quarterly, *Foreign Affairs*. The oil consultant Walter Levy warned, in 1971, that the *governments* of consuming countries—not just the *companies*—must pay attention to those changing ratios. James Akins, the career State Department official who had counseled the companies to make their peace with Libya, defended the State Department position, also in *Foreign Affairs*. World oil consumption, he said, in April 1973, would be as great in the next twelve years as world oil consumption through all of previous *history*. The loss of production from any two Middle Eastern countries would cause a panic, and the price of oil could go to $5 a barrel.

Akins's critics said he was an Arabophile. He had told an OPEC meeting, "I don't think you have any reason to be ashamed of your success so far" and then counseled the oil producers "to continue to bend, not to break, this steel rod [the oil companies]." Akins's critics said he was giving the Arabs a blueprint for blackmail.

The article was certainly read all over the world. Juan Pablo Perez Alfonso passed it out all over Caracas. But the oil countries scarcely needed an American article to tell them what was going on. The volume of oil in international trade had gone up like this:

1950	3.7 million barrels a day
1960	9.0 million barrels a day
1970	25.6 million barrels a day
1973	34.2 million barrels a day

The "invisible dike" around the American oil began to shudder and shake. It had been built to keep the cheap

foreign oil from coming *in*. Now it blew away, not from
the supply pressure *outside,* but from the *demand inside.*
The import restrictions were lifted, and what went roaring
out, of course, was dollars. Those dollars went out and
competed for oil supplies that were already tight. The administration in Washington did nothing to control the
scramble. It had other problems on its mind. It was about
to go on trial.

The chairman of British Shell told a Harvard seminar
that the energy problem was now a political problem, and
that the consuming governments should get together. The
State Department in Washington had been trying to arrange talks with the Europeans, and indeed, in June 1973,
the OECD, the Western organization with the title Organization for Economic Cooperation and Development, set
up a group to discuss energency oil policy, to report back
in November.

It was too late.

The demand for oil was running ahead of the most
extreme predictions. Independent oil companies tried to
beat the seven great oil companies to the wellheads. Japanese trading companies tried to beat the independent oil
companies. Only Aramco, in Saudi Arabia, had spare capacity, and it had little. By September 1973 the market
price had for the first time overtaken the official "posted"
price. OPEC could easily read what this meant politically.
Its former secretary-general, Nadim al-Pachaci, told a conference, "The Arabs now hold the keys to the energy and
monetary crisis. They will know how to use both as a political weapon."

Anwar al-Sadat of Egypt flew to Saudi Arabia to discuss
his military plans with King Faisal. The ruler of Kuwait,
Sheikh Sabah ibn Salim al-Sabah, also visited Faisal, then
went on to Cairo to promise Kuwait's oil weapon in the
forthcoming battle with Israel.

In October the Egyptians turned their high-pressure

West German fire hoses on the sand embankments of the Israelis' Bar-Lev line, literally dissolved the sand foundations, and crossed the Suez Canal. The United States' resupply of Israel was done in the face of warnings of embargo. OPEC met in Kuwait and announced a cutback of 5 percent and a price rise. Saudi Arabia announced a still bigger cutback.

For the first time in history, the OPEC bureaucrats met with nobody on the other side of the table. No Exxon, no Mobil, no Texaco, no BP, no Shell. They were not invited. There were no negotiations. The price of oil would be, said OPEC, $5.12 a barrel. By ukase, by fiat, by order of the high command. The press release was prepared only in Arabic.

There was, in Kuwait, at that moment, a British observer who was a friend of mine. He is so understated that his graces seem to have descended upon him, but this is a pose. "I thought it might be useful to learn a spot of Arabic," he says, but what he means is that he went to the British Arabic training school in Lebanon for eighteen months, sixteen hours a day, seven days a week. My British friend sat afterward with an Arab friend from OPEC, who described this moment: "We declared the new price of oil. It was a little strange, because the companies were not there. We knew this was the biggest rise that the price of oil had ever taken. Now remember we have grown up with the British fleet on our doorstep, we have been to schools in Britain or America, we are from small countries, without armies and hospitals. And now we have nearly doubled the price of oil.

"And we sit there for a moment, and *unconsciously we are listening for the whine of jets overhead,* as if we will be punished.

"Of course nothing happened. But I remember that moment. Those giant countries! Now we will never be afraid again."

"Vietnam," said my British friend later, "took the edge off, the great giant brought down by an army in sneakers."

Within a few weeks OPEC had doubled the price again. It was easy. The Arabs had embargoed oil destined for the United States and the Netherlands, to punish their support of Israel, in addition to the cutbacks. Though the cutbacks amounted to less than 10 percent of world supplies, frantic buyers were bidding wild prices. The Iranian oil company had auctioned oil as high as $17 a barrel. The Japanese trading companies had slept on the doorstep the night before the auction.

The OPEC meeting in Tehran, in December 1973, a few weeks later, was like the triumphal march in an opera. The great black limousines purred to the front door, to discharge the elegant Sheikh Zaki Yamani in his blue tailored raincoat and the craggy Jamshid Amouzegar. The Western diplomats and observers scrambled through the side doors, trying to find out who was saying what to whom and what was happening. As for the press, it was not just *Platt's Oilgram* and the *Middle East Economic Survey* and Wanda anymore, it was everybody—CBS, the BBC, *Mainichi, O Globo*.

The Shah, said Jamshid Amouzegar, had ordered a study of alternative fuels. "We were struck," said the eminent Cornell alumnus, "by the fact that in 1951 coal was fifty-one percent of the fuel in the United States, and now it is nineteen percent. Because of cheap oil, alternative sources are being neglected. No one in the West is worrying about what happens when the oil runs out." The embargo had showed the weakness of the West. OPEC's economic commission had determined that the price should be $17 a barrel.

Sheikh Yamani was apprehensive at so large a boost. "I was afraid the effects would be even more harmful than they were, that they would create a major depression in the West. I knew that if you went down, we would go down," he said. Yamani tried to get in touch with King Faisal, but was unable to. If he kept the price down, it might break OPEC but leave the Saudis isolated. Yamani remained within OPEC, insisting on a smaller price increase, and was later reprimanded by Faisal. But Yamani was stunned when, while the OPEC ministers were still meeting, the Shah called a press conference.

The price of oil, the Shah said, would be $11.65 a barrel. That was even more than Yamani had agreed to. The Shah's arrogance astounded the assembled diplomats and reporters. The new price of oil, he said, was very low and "was reached on the basis of generosity and kindness." As for the Western consumers, it would do them good to economize: "All those children of well-to-do families who have plenty to eat at every meal, who have their own cars, who act almost as terrorists and throw bombs here and there, will have to rethink all these privileges . . . they will have to work harder."

"We were amazed to find ourselves the objects of so much attention," said Abdul Latif al-Hamad, a former student of a friend of mine at Claremont Colleges, California, and the director of the Kuwait Fund. "We got as great a shock as you did. We thought we were pygmies, facing giants, and now we found that the giants are ordinary people and the Rock of Gibraltar is papier-mâché. And we had been protected by the oil companies from the world; now they were gone, and we had to decide everything ourselves. It was like being a rich orphan."

There were stunned reactions all over the world. One was recalled to me some years later by Janos Fekete, deputy director of the National Bank of Hungary, an extremely shrewd banker, a good Communist, a man with a puckish sense of humor.

"I went to my office," he said, "and I said to my staff, 'Now we will see the mighty West rise up! They cannot lend themselves to this *fraud*, where the price is so far from the cost! It is a hoax!' I was excited.

"My staff was much more sober. They said, 'Janos, now we have to do the budgets all over, we are in deficit.' And I said, '*A fene egye meg!*' Of course we are! Damn! Because we import oil from the Russians, and they use the OPEC price! Now we must pay the Russians four times as much for our oil! *A fene egye meg!*"

In the Third World, Fekete's experience was duplicated, with variations. First, a feeling of jubilation in all those countries of Asia and Africa. What an upset! Ragheads, 66; Giants, 0! Wahoo! So much for the blue-eyed devils in the cold-weather countries! So much for the arrogant long-nosed bastards! So much for the imperialist exploiters who wanted us to be a nation of busboys!

And then somebody—maybe the financial people, like Fekete—would say, "But now we have to pay four times as much for the oil, and *we* have no oil. Where do we get the money?"

An exercise just like that was the genesis of this book. The price at Howard's Mobil station had not quadrupled, but Howard wasn't getting much gas that frosty winter. There was a line three blocks long leading up to Howard's Mobil. Howard himself was bleary-eyed from dealing with angry customers. First I drove by, to see how long Howard would be open, because I didn't want to spend two hours in a gas line and then find a sign that said "No Gas." Howard said, "Go to the end of the line; we can make it today."

The gas line sat and crept, sat and crept, and the snow came down around us. I finished reading all the bank letters. I finished *The Wall Street Journal, The New York Times,* and *The Economist.* There was still a block and a half to go.

First I thought, This gas line is burning up a lot of gas just trying to get more. Then: How do we pay for the oil quadruple? That is, we, the United States? Well, we could sell something to the Arabs. What are we good at growing or making and selling? Aircraft, wheat, soybeans, maybe some high-technology equipment. Now, what are they buying? Who's in OPEC? We can forget Gabon and Ecuador and Qatar—not significant. Who are we talking about? Iraq: cross off, no relations with them. Libya, Kuwait, Saudi Arabia, Iran. Libya: fewer than 2 million people. Kuwait: fewer than 300,000. Saudi Arabia: 6 million. Small countries. Don't have big airlines. Sell a couple of 727s, a 747 or two; that's about enough oil for ten minutes of gas lines. Wheat, soybeans—small countries don't eat much; we have 120 million cars, each car is sitting in a gas line with its motor running; you could sell all the wheat and soybeans Libya, Kuwait, and Saudi Arabia could eat and only move the whole national gas line one block. Less. Maybe thirty feet. Of course, Iran . . . 33 million people . . . Shah—aircraft? A couple more airplanes, a little more wheat—aircraft, *arms.* We could sell arms to the Shah.

But not enough to the other folks. No, what we will buy the oil with is dollars, because the world takes dollars, trades in dollars. And the oil folk will have the dollars, and then they can come and buy what they want. But nobody realizes the *scale.* Let's just say we pay the import price for half of the oil needs, at let's say, $10 a barrel, carry the 3, times 365 days in the year; my goodness, in one year OPEC could have $100 billion extra, maybe $200 billion soon, then they could come and buy half of the stocks on the New York Stock Exchange, almost half. And that's only one year. The next year the 120 million cars are back at the gas pump, and OPEC has *another* $100 billion, and they keep piling up those claim checks until they *can* buy the whole New York Stock Exchange. They keep the claim check, and we move the cars around. *We are going to sell America for a product that burns up in the atmosphere.* We will be a colony.

No, that can't be right. Something else has to happen.

I was up to the gas pump.

"Just don't swear at me," Howard said. "I only run a filling station."

I didn't swear at Howard. I was trying to figure out what was wrong with that idea: *We are issuing claim checks on our country for something that burns up in the atmosphere.*

As it turns out, unhappily, very unhappily, years later, columns later, economists later, congressmen later, Department of Energy officials later, sheikhs and oil men and bankers later, the idea was not wrong. Nor was it unique to me, needless to say.

The triumph of the Club is something quite unparalleled in history. When else was there such a transfer of wealth? When the Spaniards brought back the gold and silver of Peru? When the British raj ruled India?

Those were transfers of wealth, but none happened so quickly. From the day the Odd Couple met at the Nile Hilton to the day the French bulldozer broke the Tapline was less than eleven years. From that to the St. Valentine's Day Massacre was less than two, and in less than another three the triumph was complete. It was the greatest transfer of wealth in the history of the world. And it is hard to communicate. If you say oil went from $1.80 a barrel to $11.65 a barrel, that's a big percentage, but it's still just ten bucks. And if you say this year we will send out $90 billion for oil, that's an abstraction; you can't divide $90 billion into orange juice and come out sounding anything but silly.

Unite and control, conserve and cutback—the preachings of the Odd Couple—were scratched out first by the tidy Venezuelan lawyer who admired the Texas Railroad Commission. But you will notice, by their absence, missing elements in this staccato little capsule history. Those elements are the governments of the West. The conventional wisdom is that they were out to lunch, that they had delegated their role to the oil companies. In Churchill's phrase, they presided over the liquidation of an empire.

Or they did not preside at all. They were weak and divided.

"The French were too anti-American," said one of Mobil's veteran negotiators, "the British too bemused by their debt to Pompidou, the Italians too governed by Mattei's legacy of dislike for the Seven Sisters, the Japanese too scared of OPEC . . . the Americans, British, Germans, and Dutch preferred to hope that the hurricane would pass . . . none saw that what was really needed was solidarity among all of them." Unite and control, conserve and cut back, may have begun in the West, but it was forgotten.

There is also an unconventional view, which is that at least some elements in the West were quite happy to see the price of oil go up. The thesis of this view is that Richard Nixon and Henry Kissinger made a deal with the Shah of Iran. It was developed first by the columnist Jack Anderson, and then by the CBS television show "60 Minutes." At least one of the sources, if not the principal source, was James Akins, the foreign-service officer, Arabist, and oil specialist, who had written "This Time the Wolf Is Here" in *Foreign Affairs*. Akins had become ambassador to Saudi Arabia and then, in 1975, was fired by Kissinger.

Nixon and Kissinger stopped off in Iran on the way home from the Moscow summit in 1972. What they saw was a dangerous situation. The British had withdrawn from the Persian Gulf at the end of 1971; the United States was still involved in Vietnam. There was a power vacuum in the strategic Middle East. The Shah could take it over and would get the arms to do so.

How would the Shah pay for the arms? By raising the price of oil. No American Congress would have voted billions to arm Iran, it was thought, while troops were still in Vietnam. James Akins reported that the Saudis were worried both by the Iranian buildup and by the prospect of a high price for oil, which they thought would damage the stability of the West, on which their bank accounts and survival depended.

William Simon, Secretary of the Treasury at that time, said later, of the oil-price-for-weapons idea: "There could be some truth in that. We were heavily involved in Vietnam. We were trying to extricate ourselves. We had a President who was being besieged in the closing days of Watergate. We didn't need any trouble in other parts of the world and we had to make sure our allies were in strong positions, so that the Russians could not take advantage of our domestic problems, our Vietnam problems, and become mischievous as they're prone to do in other parts of the world."

Of Simon, a staff member at the Council of Economic Advisers said: "Bill is no intellectual and he is also a fervent free enterpriser. He thought a higher oil price might bring up more oil, and that would help to break the cartel. We would get the money we paid for oil back through selling arms, and the oil surpluses would go to our banks and drive interest rates down to four percent. Bill says, 'We all make mistakes; Henry really blew that one.' But so did he."

Kissinger and Simon did push forward the International Energy Agency, a group of twenty Western countries, hoping to cut joint consumption and thus confront the Club. But its efforts were feeble.

If a quadrupled oil price was the cost of arming the Shah, it was one of the most expensive blunders in history. The scale of the transfer of wealth is hard to comprehend, and in this instance the arithmetic makes no sense. If $90 billion a year sounds silly divided into orange juice, it does not make much more sense divided into F-14s.

If you raise the price of oil $10 a barrel, times the OPEC production of roughly 30 million barrels a day, you have raised OPEC's revenues by $109.5 billion in one year. Granted, OPEC is a whole group of countries, both high and low absorbers.

Now go to the Grumman plant on Long Island. Walk around an F-14, kick the tires; there it is, completely equipped, tinted glass, white sidewalls, AM-FM, avionics, radar. In 1974 the flyaway cost of an F-14 was just under $9 million, air-to-air missiles not included. Grumman could turn out eighty F-14s a year. Bring pilots and fly a year's worth away. That's $720 million.

Now go to McDonnell Douglas in St. Louis. Bring more pilots, McDonnell Douglas can turn out more aircraft than Grumman; bring more money, an F-15 is a very hot airplane, costs $12 million in 1974, ready to fly away. Price tag for a fleet of one hundred F-15s: $1.2 billion. You've spent a shade less than $2 billion on airplanes, but round it out; you need spare parts and extra tires.

What else? How about the biggest ticket in defense, a nuclear-powered aircraft carrier? That retails, in 1974, for $771 million to $1.354 billion, depending on the model and the options. Take two. Take some destroyer escorts for the nuclear carriers, take a couple of missile cruisers. Have some submarines.

Guess what: you have a very hot air force, a sleek fleet, and you still have around $100 billion left. This year. Some of those airplanes are going to last more than a year, and next year you have another $100 billion *extra*.

So the West could transfer to OPEC one air force, one navy, and still owe $100 billion *every year*.

I believe the Kissinger-Shah story has an element of truth but is too simple. I have gone back some distance to show how the growth in oil demand created the opportunity for Perez Alfonso's Club. Given that demand, and given the belligerence of many members of the Club, the price of oil was bound to go up, but nothing like as much as it did. There is no question that the Nixon administration set the Shah up as the military power of the Middle East, and once the Shah was set up, he could not be neatly controlled, so he was able, with the other OPEC price hawks, to dictate the price of oil. There were people who were not sorry to see the price of oil go up, because it might, they thought, in the long run, create alternatives to OPEC oil. Or maybe they had other motives.

But the oil price quadruple was a shock, and few expected it to stick. Surely OPEC would break up, as Milton Friedman so confidently predicted. The hurricane would pass. The answer to the question about the arithmetic is that no one worked out the arithmetic.

"Consuming governments preferred to wring their hands," said the Mobil observer, ". . . to bicker among themselves . . . to contemplate *sauve qui peut* initiatives against one another . . . [they] had no conception of the scale of the disaster to which their lack of initiative and solidarity was exposing them."

The Western industrial economies now had the worst of both inflation and recession.

The higher oil prices acted as a fiscal drag, a tax. Higher prices for oil meant higher prices for fertilizer and plastics as well as gasoline and heat. If your gasoline bill and your heating bill and your food bill went up, you might defer buying a car; then the automobile manufacturer laid off some workers, who in turn cut back on their own purchases. The recession of 1974–75 was the worst since the Depression of the 1930s.

And at that same time, inflation went up sharply. In the United States direct and indirect energy costs amount to 10 percent of pretax household income. A 100-percent rise in energy costs meant 10-percent inflation, all by itself. Not all the energy was oil, and not all oil came from the Middle East; but the price of OPEC oil had just gone up 400 percent, and the OPEC price became the world price.

Except in the United States. The "invisible dike" had been blown away, but the Texas prices were now *lower* than the world price. Regulation from Washington permitted the Texas price to rise only gradually. Some sections of the United States used domestic oil and gas, some

used imported oil, and Washington tried to find a price
and structure that would spread the cost across the whole
country, and it did not want the oil producers to have a
sudden bonanza.

"Just Go in There and Take it"

Suddenly, it seemed, that cold winter of 1975, the West
discovered that half the oil it used didn't belong to it, and
that discovery led to an outburst of jingoism. (*Jingo* came
from a nineteenth-century British music-hall song: we
don't want to fight, but by jingo if we do . . .) By jingo, if
they wouldn't give us the oil, maybe we would just *take* it.
"I am not saying there are no circumstances in which the
United States might resort to force," said Henry Kissinger,
in careful double negatives.

Hawks got to play war room. The focus of the war game
was the Persian Gulf.

"The main operation," wrote *The Economist* of London,
"would probably be carried out by a naval task force with
three or four aircraft carriers . . . helicopter-borne marines from assault ships . . . occupy selected positions in
the Ghawar oilfield, take possession of the Ras Tanura
refinery and terminal." Writing in *Harper's* under the
pseudonym Miles Ignotus ("Unknown Soldier"), defense
analyst and Johns Hopkins professor Edward Luttwak also
picked the Ras Tanura refinery and the Ghawar field.
"British Leyland Motors, the largest industrial combine in
Britain," he wrote, in "Seizing Arab Oil," "was built up
through the work of tens of thousands of English workers
over a period of more than seventy years. [It could be]
acquired by a single family in Kuwait with only six days'
worth of oil production. Why should we countenance the
transfer of hundreds of billions of dollars' worth of real

estate and industry to the ownership of reverse colonialists?"

And so the Unknown Soldier wrote of marines, the Eighty-second Airborne, fire-fighting teams to put out the fires in the oil wells, and an International Oil and Aid Organization to lift the oil, allocate funds for investment, distribute money to poor countries, and "give some money to the Saudis et al. to pay for essential imports." And if we could not do this, what were the armed forces good for? Why pay $85 billion a year for impotence? Ironically, the fantasy military-operation schemes were directed against the price "dove," Saudi Arabia, which increased its production to meet the demand, which put its surpluses promptly into Western banks, and which seemed to worry more about the stability of the West than the West did itself.

The success of the Club not only inspired the military-fantasy spasms, it inspired imitation. The uranium producers already had a plan for a cartel. The copper producers began talking to one another. In the most ungentlemanly move of all, the Bordeaux wine growers, the Conseil Interprofessionel du Vin de Bordeaux, got together to do something about a good vintage in Bordeaux. M. Jean Michel Courteau, its director, announced that the association, which counted among its members Château Lafite-Rothschild and Château Mouton-Rothschild and Château Latour, was taking "certain steps to regulate the market and stabilize prices." Wine glut! The growers were to conserve and cut back.

OPEC cannot be blamed for this one. Ten of its thirteen members were Muslim countries where wine drinking was officially proscribed.

Was OPEC really such a monolithic, all-powerful cartel? It existed for ten years and was not effective at all, until, with the Suez Canal closed, the French bulldozer wrecked the Tapline. Once supplies were tight, the organization and the idea were ready for the circumstances. The cutbacks necessary for control did not come from cool, prehensile fingers reaching for a marketplace; they came first from the passions of politics, what the Arabs called the Ramadan War—the Yom Kippur War. The oil price quadruple was such a shock to the Western economies that demand fell, and by April 1975 OPEC was producing at 35 percent less than its total capacity.

One can see—maybe—why Milton Friedman thought it was about to break up. There were two small producers, Ecuador and Gabon, that needed all the money they could get. Then there were the medium-size producers, at about 2 million barrels a day—Algeria, Indonesia, Venezuela, Nigeria—all with growing populations, all wanting to conserve oil, but needing money. If the demand dropped, wouldn't they cut into one another's markets?

It wasn't necessary. Kuwait and Saudi Arabia cut back. Saudi Arabia, alone, was a third of OPEC. The international Texas Railroad Commission had found its Texas, but it did not work nearly as neatly, determining the prorationing and the markets. The oil companies sought out the markets, delivered and refined the oil. "Why should we abolish the oil companies," said Iran's Jamshid Amouzegar, "when they can find the markets for us and regulate them? We can just sit back and let them do it for us."

Even with an excess capacity of 35 percent, OPEC held the price up. And OPEC's Secretariat in Vienna now had several economic studies in progress. The Caracas firm of Parra, Ramos & Parra, was looking into OPEC's oil and other energy sources, as was Chem Systems International of New York. The Hochschule für Welthandel and the Battelle Research Institute of Geneva had a contract, for 28 million Austrian schillings, to construct OPEC's World Energy Model.

The Receiving End

The owners of the oil, everywhere in the world, were four times as rich after Tehran; soon they would be ten times as rich. Sometimes this made a dramatic difference in life-style.

Take Sheikh Rashid of Dubai. Dubai is one of what the British called the Trucial States when, in the nineteenth century, they established a military presence in this lightly populated area of desert and salt marshes on the Persian Gulf. Sheikh Rashid, before the oil, had derived his income from the *dhows,* the wooden sailing ships that called at his customs house, on the way to "reexport"—some said smuggle—gold and silver to India. Before the oil—the first strike was not until 1957—Sheikh Rashid feuded with Deira, the rival village across the creek. The weapons used in this feud were the cannons from old ships, some of them hundreds of years old. The cannons were stuffed with rags and pistons from hijacked cars, and since cannonballs were in short supply, a nightly truce after sunset prayers permitted the combatants to comb the battlefields and retrieve the cannonballs.

One day, in the pre-oil era, Sheikh Rashid accepted a dinner invitation across the creek, and then had his men kill off his hosts. In the best Middle Eastern tradition—and not unlike Richard III—he consolidated his victory by marrying the thirteen-year-old daughter of the vanquished ruler of Deira to his brother. The Sheikha Sana, as she is called, is a high-spirited woman who once shot her husband's fourth wife. She says, of her early years, that her experiences made her strong, and she has now built up a thriving taxi fleet. Sheikh Rashid married his daughter, Miriam, to the neighboring Sheikh of Qatar, who lent him the money for a bridge across the creek.

Even before the oil, Sheikh Rashid was considered a wise ruler.

A man of some charm, Sheikh Rashid is accessible to his people. He lists himself in the Dubai telephone directory, with numbers for living room, bedroom, yacht, and garden. On his desk is a little plaque that says, "It's NICE to be IMPORTANT, but it's IMPORTANT to be NICE." For his people Sheikh Rashid has built two harbors, two international airports, a cement factory, and an aluminum smelter.

Sheikh Rashid's income is now about $1 billion a year, and no one hunts for cannonballs anymore in Dubai. His in-law, the Sheikh of Qatar, produces more oil and is even richer. In the nineteenth century the British navy sailed the Persian Gulf to protect the routes to India; now their former Persian Gulf wards come to London. Sheikh Rashid's ambassador, Mohammed Mahdi al-Tajir, drove the British press to xenophobic frenzy by purchasing $60 million in English real estate in two years: town houses, country houses, and the centuries-old castles of dukes. "Arabs like beautiful things," he said simply. The British press shuddered deliciously at the new, Mephistophelian image of its visitors. The *Daily Mirror* warned of "schoolgirls missing after dating Arabs," whisked off to "exclusive restaurants in Rolls Royces."

This mythology—the Arab as Mephistopheles—was not limited to Britain. In the popular film *Network* the Saudis bought an American TV network. And the investigators who offered bribes to congressmen and videotaped the bribes in "Abscam" were decked out as "Arab sheikhs."

While the popular British press detailed "Ordeal of Sheikh's Love Slave," the British in the aggregate benefited from the new oil price, because it had cost so much to establish those offshore platforms in the icy waters of the North Sea. For the moment they were paying more for imported oil, but at $11.65 a barrel, the North Sea oil was now a solid investment; it meant self-sufficiency and a strong pound. The Norwegians, too, were happy, because they owned the other half of the North Sea field.

You would count, as happy, all the other oil-field owners. Mexico might be able to handle its exploding population, Louisiana could reduce its income tax, Alaska would abolish its income tax, and under Texas there were 12 billion barrels of oil rising toward the OPEC price as fast as Washington would let them.

You would have to count, as happy, the oil companies. In the mid-1970s they aired their unhappiness in full-page ads; they constructed charts to show they were making only pennies on the dollar. But they were still carrying and refining the OPEC oil, and they owned, themselves, a lot of oil outside OPEC. They were the biggest corporations in the world, and their gross volume was going up, because the raw material was going up.

With their enormous cash flow, the oil companies were also buying other resources—coal, uranium, oil shale, and timberland—assets "whose potential profit increases inexorably with the rising value of the reserves," said the National Bureau of Economic Research.

Count, as happy, the investment bankers who sold the bonds for the pipelines, and the makers of drilling rigs and drilling mud and logging instruments and offshore platforms.

Count, as happy, the armorers and sutlers to the Middle East. Iran signed up for $19 billion in arms over several years, Saudi Arabia for $15 billion; and although that did not wipe out even half of one year's surplus for OPEC, the phones rang at the armorers.

Count, as happy, the thirty biggest banks in the world. The Saudis and Kuwaitis, being conservative, wanted time to think, and they put money into the banks. Since bigger, they thought, is better, the bigger banks could use the petrodollar deposits to strengthen their position in banking. The banks had the money on short-term deposit and were lending it long-term, which posed a potential problem.

Count, as happy, the builders who got the multibillion-dollar construction contracts: Bechtel of San Francisco; Fluor of Irvine, California; and Ralph Parsons, Inc., of Pasadena.

Count, as happy, the agents and contact men who made the deals. A Bombay Parsi with the unusual name of Shapoor Reporter was so useful to the British in getting contracts from the Shah's Iran that he was knighted and became Sir Shapoor Reporter. The fees were very high. The Senate Subcommittee on Multinational Corporations found that Lockheed had paid one Saudi, Adnan Kashoggi, $106 million for assistance. Kashoggi's former wife said in her divorce suit that her former husband had built up a net worth of $2.4 billion, which would have made him easily the most prosperous member of his Stanford class. His $44-million yacht had a helicopter landing pad, and his $3-million apartment in Manhattan's Olympic Tower boasted a swimming pool. He had a Korean bodyguard and a valet who shaved him every morning in a special chair, replicas of which were in each of his twelve houses.

When Texas oil man Nelson Bunker Hunt embarked on his scheme to invest heavily in the world's silver market, some said to corner it, former Texas governor John Connally arranged a meeting with another Saudi, Sheikh Khaled Bin Mahfouz, who took over a floor of Washington's Mayflower Hotel for his forty bodyguards.

On a more modest scale—perhaps seven figures instead of nine—were the New York and Washington and London law firms that sometimes matched buyers and sellers and sometimes drew up the contracts. The big ones stayed invisible; among the visible were Fred Dutton, Kennedy aide turned Washington lawyer, and Gerald Parsky, Assistant Secretary of the Treasury turned Washington lawyer;

and who is this, pacing the floor of the Intercontinental in Riyadh, waiting for his contact? Is it, can it be—Spiro Agnew?

You would have to count as content, if not happy, the energy and oil experts, and the foundations, for they soon turned out more than 120 full-length studies of the oil situation, of which only the first 36 were collected for this book.

Every game has winners and losers. The losers were all of us without a stake in energy. We paid higher gasoline prices and higher heating and air-conditioning bills, higher airline fares, higher prices for the derivatives of oil. Our standard of living went down. The winners were not just those who had the oil, but those who could service the owners of the oil.

They were not just Americans; in fact, Americans did not do very well. Fewer than 2 percent of the construction contracts in fourteen Middle Eastern countries were won by American firms—fewer than firms from Brazil and Yugoslavia, and far behind South Korea.

The president of France, Valéry Giscard d'Estaing, made a triumphant tour through the Arab states, plugging the Palestinian cause and winning factory orders; in the 1960s France had had a special relationship with Israel. A Scandinavian floating exhibition steamed into eight Arab ports, displaying products to 100,000 visitors.

Muhammad Ali, the boxer Muhammad Ali, barnstormed through Saudi Arabia, promoting Toyota cars.

With every passing day, someone else had an investment in the status quo.

"I Feel Like Renouncing My Offspring"

There is one character in the story who was not particularly happy. That was Juan Pablo Perez Alfonso. When he left the government, he retired behind the walls of his estate in Los Choros, in Caracas, the estate itself a small farm he had bought in 1941. The oil boom had brought the expanding city out to and beyond his farm. He still kept his austere habits, reading through the night and rising at dawn. He was a recognizable figure on the streets of Caracas, because he had shaved off his thinning hair and looked like a Venezuelan Yul Brynner, or Kojak. When his party offered to run him for president, he refused. How, he asked, could Venezuela have a president who did not own a dinner jacket, who lived so simply, who would not cut a ribbon or go to a cocktail party?

He had admired the Texas Railroad Commission, he said, for its conservation practices, and he wanted OPEC to be a club that would give oil its proper value and extend its life. It was intended to wrest the power from the great oil companies, and to show the industrial nations how they wasted resources.

"The nations of OPEC," he said, "should be an example to the rest of the world in the way they live."

But OPEC was not a proper example. It was setting itself up in the mode of the wasteful industrial world. It burned oil itself at a ferocious rate, an affront to the careful, conservative Perez Alfonso. He scolded the Venezuelans.

The *Norteamericanos* were sitting in gas lines, their cities had brownouts, they were finally learning about oil as a resource, and what was Caracas doing? It was keeping the lights on all night! Big American cars were speeding on the highways! And what of Venezuela's leadership of OPEC? It was disappearing! Leadership should not come from the number of barrels of oil pumped every day; it should come from *moral fiber*. Was OPEC to be just Arabs?

Toward Perez Alfonso the Venezuelans felt real affection, but it was the affection Americans feel when they read of Boston Brahmin grand dames rising to learn

Greek and Hebrew at six o'clock in the morning, or walking from Boston to Providence in midwinter, because it is good for them. Plain living and high thinking were admirable, but un-Latin, no? And Perez Alfonso was a little eccentric, with his bald head and all this scolding about resources and saving everything, and walking around Caracas in Boy Scout shorts. And getting up at dawn—well, with oil bringing in four times as much, that was when you were going to bed, Caracas was a party, the *tropicales* were dancing on the tabletops, H. Stern and Gucci were doing a thriving business, luxury apartments with dazzling views of the sea were springing up, money was everywhere. A Venezuelan newsmagazine put that serious bald head on its cover; no subtitle, just "Perez Alfonso"—you knew what you would get inside, sober thinking, worrying about the future—wasn't that good, for Venezuela to have its own Ralph Waldo Emerson? What an irony for the man who began the great transfer of wealth to be so spartan.

Perez Alfonso did not like the Shah, or Sheikh Yamani. "I have no taste for emperors," he said. They were not preserving the resource, and they were squandering its proceeds. He worried about the influx of wealth into Venezuela. "Wealth distorts the values of people who do not work for it," he said.

And as for OPEC, it seemed devoted to maximizing its prices, it was neglecting what was done with the revenues received, it was not conservationist enough.

"I may be the father of OPEC," he said, "but now sometimes I feel like renouncing my offspring."

Juan Pablo Perez Alfonso died of cancer in 1979, leaving a wife and five grown children. That upright, un-Latin, austere Puritan conscience was evident even in his last instructions.

He was to be cremated in the United States, to avoid any public expression of sorrow in Venezuela. His house was to go to a small foundation, the Center for Permanent

Learning. People were to come and enjoy the garden and notice the beauties of nature; from there they could look out at the smog over Caracas.

Abdullah Tariki, the other half of the Odd Couple, continued his consulting business. The Saudi government, with Bedouin generosity, continued to pay his old salary, even while he was in exile. Saadoun Hammadi, the unsmiling Iraqi oil minister, University of Wisconsin Ph.D., became his country's foreign minister and later warned the United States against helping Iran. Sheikh Yamani's balancing instincts served him well, and he survived even his worldwide celebrity. Jamshid Amouzegar, the Cornell-trained Iranian who hosted the St. Valentine's Day Massacre, fled Iran when the Shah fell. The present Iranian UN embassy did not know where he was—somewhere in the United States. "The swine is hiding," said the Khomeini representatives.

The executives of the Seven Sisters are still in place, or are in prosperous retirement. Howard's Mobil did not survive. Howard was very bitter about his treatment by this particular Sister; they had canceled his contract, he said, because he had not sold enough gas.

The Second Oil Crisis

It was a military fanatic, Colonel Muammar el-Qaddafi of Libya, who set up the First Oil Crisis of the 1970s. A devout Muslim who sometimes went to the desert for a month to meditate, he horrified the Western democracies by his support of the incredible Ugandan dictator Idi Amin and by his support of terrorist groups everywhere. His militancy had goaded the OPEC nations into their triumph at the St. Valentine's Day Massacre, which taught them their strength and gave them the cohesion for their actions in the 1973 Arab-Israeli war.

It was a religious fanatic, the Ayatollah Ruhollah Khomeini, who precipitated the Second Oil Crisis of the late 1970s and whose regime, in a way it did not particularly intend, reiterated the preachings of the Odd Couple.

OPEC meetings during the 1970s featured debates between the hawks, who wanted the price to go up right away, and the doves, who wanted to keep it down. The Libyans and Iraqis, revolutionary military regimes, contested the leadership of the Saudis, a traditional monarchy with an enormous income and a stake in the stability of the West.

Until the Shah fell, there was a modest surplus of oil in the channels of the world. Higher prices had forced some cutback in demand, and there was additional oil from Alaska and the North Sea. OPEC watchers noted that the cartel was getting less real money, because the Western currencies were depreciating faster than the oil price was going up.

But Iran was among the large producers, at 6 million barrels a day, and when the Shah was deposed, production from Iran's oil fields dropped to a fraction of the previous totals. That missing 6 million barrels a day was enough to create a shortage again, and the scramble resumed.

Most world oil, in the 1970s, was sold through the Seven Sisters, the great oil companies, and on long-term contracts. The British economist Paul Frankel, who had given us the phrase "the invisible dike," came up with a metaphor for the situation of the oil companies. "They had lost the heights," he said, "but they still controlled the plains."

But the Ayatollah Khomeini's revolution affected the control of the plains. Politically, it sought to disturb the traditional regimes in Saudi Arabia and Kuwait. And it made oil deals, not with the Seven Sisters, but with the nations that scrambled to Tehran and to the "spot" market.

In the oil trade the "spot" market is called "Rotterdam," because oil can be bought, on a daily basis, from the huge

tankers anchored in the Rotterdam harbor. The "Rotterdam" market, though, is all over the world. It is really the
Telex, through which the trades are made. Among the
major traders are Mitsubishi, the enormous Japanese combine, and Philipp Brothers, the commodity arm of the
international firm of Engelhard; but there are many others.

The Iranian shutdown had made supplies tight. The
Israelis and the South Africans could no longer buy Iranian oil, and they were looking for oil wherever they could
find it. The Italians had only two weeks' worth of supply
in the tanks, and the Spaniards and the Swedes were also
low.

The new Iranian regime, with no loyalty to the old contracts with the Seven Sisters, began to sell to the "spot"
market. On Monday, May 14, 1979, the Iranians sold oil
at $23 a barrel, above the posted OPEC price of $13.34.
On Tuesday it was $28. On Thursday it was $34. Ironically, the Seven Sisters were among the bidders; a subsid-
iary of Texaco secretly made a deal for 2 million barrels at
$32. At Kharg Island in the Persian Gulf, there was the
usual long line of tankers waiting to take on Iranian oil.
The tankers with long-term contracts were told to stay
anchored. (They were paying, incidentally, $35,000 a day
in parking fees.) The tankers with "spot" contracts went
right to the head of the line.

Not surprisingly, the "spot" market began to attract the
oil. American oil companies with refined oil in the Caribbean began sending it to the "spot" market, seeking to
maximize profits. The price in the "spot" market went as
high as $42 a barrel.

The Carter administration, knowing that Americans get
irritated when there are gas lines, abruptly offered a subsidy of $5 a barrel to get the Caribbean oil back again; the
oil it sought was heating oil, for the next winter, but it did
not want the summer gasoline supplies hurt by refiners

who had to switch their mix because of the heating-oil diversion.

The International Energy Agency might as well have passed out boxing gloves, or hockey sticks. Janos Fekete, the Hungarian banker, had once gone to the office expecting to hear reports of the Mighty West rising up. The Mighty West rose up now, into an internal donnybrook. The Germans, totally dependent on foreign oil, said that the American subsidy was just helping to drive up the price and hinted that maybe the Americans wanted the price up because it helped the American oil producers and hurt German industry. They offered the British industrial investment for a cut of the North Sea oil. The British refused. Accusing fingers were pointed in all directions.

Other OPEC nations pulled some oil from long-term contracts and sold it in the "spot" market. Some of the OPEC nations saw the dangers. OPEC was losing control! Libya and Algeria broke the $23.50-a-barrel *ceiling* set by the cartel. "Prices are out of control," warned Ali Khalifa al-Sabah, the oil minister of Kuwait. OPEC was breaking apart, but on the *up* side. No one had thought of that.

At the Department of Energy in Washington, officials totted up supply and demand. There should have been an excess of a million barrels a day, so why were prices going up? "The spot price reflects uncertainty, not shortage," said one analyst there.

The world was on a binge of tank topping. The Japanese bought twenty oceangoing tankers and pumped them full. Every retired tanker of dubious ancestry found someone willing to take it home. Independent oil companies found themselves cut back by the Seven Sisters, who were in turn getting cut back, and they had to hustle up their own sources.

Eventually the binge lost its momentum, because there were no more tanks to top. The OPEC ministers met and raised the price again. The "spot" market was supposed to be only for day-to-day purchases, but it was determining the price of oil.

The binge of the Second Oil Crisis, you will now see, is very relevant to this discussion of paper money. Remember Sir Thomas Gresham, whose law said bad money drives out good, meaning bad money drives good money out of circulation and into savings. The bad money is spent. In the Second Oil Crisis what was saved was *oil,* and what was spent was *money. The store of value had become oil.* The yen, the marks, the dollars, the francs, were spent; the oil was saved.

The lesson was not lost. Oil was the good currency, money the bad. When the Iranians restored production, they made more money producing at 3 million barrels a day than they would have made at their former rate of 6 million barrels a day. The Kuwaitis said they might cut back by 500,000 barrels a day, the Nigerians said they would cut back 200,000 barrels a day, the Venezuelans 150,000 barrels a day.

Oil does not make very good money. It does not sit neatly in bank vaults. You cannot trade a quart of it for a tuna sandwich, or a barrel for a pair of shoes. On a very large scale you might be able to trade it for a million pairs of shoes, but the trade would be cumbersome. Gold became money because it was so destructible and finite; the destiny of oil is to burn. Ironically, monetizing the oil helped to produce the age of paper money, and the destiny of paper money is also to burn, except that paper money is really a misnomer, because the money is really blips in a computer, and blips do not burn. Not literally.

But let us see what you think is a store of value. You can have $1,000 in dollars, and we will pay you 10 percent in interest. If you take the $1,000 in sterling, we will pay you 14 percent. For yen, and marks, and Swiss francs, we will pay you the appropriate interest rate. Or we will let you have $1,000 worth of oil, stored anywhere you want.

If you choose the oil, you get no interest, and interest compounds. Knowing what you do, would you rather have the money or the oil?

The First Oil Crisis, in 1973–74, took oil from $2.69 to $11.65 a barrel, about a quadruple. The Second Oil Crisis, following the arrival of the Ayatollah Khomeini, produced roughly a double, to about $28 a barrel in 1979.

The Club was keeping up the game that worked so well: Leapfrog. Cut back the production, and supplies will be tight. Cut back the deliveries, and the oil consumers who can't get oil will go to the "spot" market, which is relatively small compared to the volume of world oil. The price in the "spot" market pops up. Then you say, well, that's the true value of oil, and you call a meeting of the oil ministers and move the OPEC price of oil up toward the "spot" market price. But if the "spot" market moves down again, you don't move the official price back down, because now you have a new long-term OPEC price. And you have room to do this because, taking OPEC as a whole, you need only 22 million of your 30 million barrels a day to pay your bills. The other 8 million barrels are "discretionary," and you can mess around with them, shut in some of them if necessary. Yet Leapfrog was not designed by OPEC ministers; they merely followed political events and took advantage.

The great oil companies are in a curious and ambiguous position. On the one hand, they are getting bigger and bigger, in dollar terms, because the cost of their basic material is going up. Every OPEC boost makes their non-OPEC oil, which they still own, more valuable. But OPEC is now going "downstream," into tankers and refineries and petroleum products. OPEC controls the heights, and has, since the St. Valentine's Day Massacre. Now, skirmish by skirmish, it is moving into the plains. It can say, "We

want you to charter tankers for us, we want you to build a
refinery for us, we want you to buy our refinery products
and liquefied petroleum gases, and we will tell you the
price."

The great oil companies controlled, in 1974, 78 percent
of the oil in international trade. By 1979 they controlled
only 44 percent, and their control was fast fading. "We're
not even sure we can guarantee a supply to our own affil-
iates," said a vice-president of Shell, "our own refineries,
our own filling stations."

Who bought the oil the majors did not buy? The Western governments themselves, and their trading companies. The French signed a ten-year contract with Iraq, and
then hustled off to Saudi Arabia and Venezuela. The
Swedes, the Germans, and the Japanese were on the same
circuit. When the Iranian militants seized American hos-
tages, the United States cut off trade with Iran. Japan
bought the Iranian oil, with what the Carter administration charged was "unseemly haste." Japan, the Japanese
Ministry of Trade and Industry pointed out, defensively,
uses 80 percent of its oil for industry, its very life; in the
United States only 20 percent is used for industry. Japan's
use of energy, said the MTI, was quite sparing.

When the other industrial countries looked at the
United States, they felt very insecure.

One out of every eight barrels of oil produced in the
free world burned up on American highways.

The Americans paid for their imported oil by printing
dollars and sending them out. That was weakening the
international monetary system.

The Americans had no real energy policy, couldn't get
it through their Congress; and with American demand so
high, OPEC could keep popping the price.

The Americans were less vulnerable than the rest of the
world, because their own oil met half their needs. Japan

had no energy at all; Germany imported two-thirds of its energy, all its oil. Each pop of the OPEC price made some Americans richer; in fact, the Americans who owned those domestic oil wells were now $400 billion richer than when the price of oil began to move.

The Americans owned five of the Seven Sisters: Exxon, Texaco, Gulf, Mobil, and Standard of California. With Aramco they had some access to OPEC oil. The British owned all of one Sister, BP, and half of Royal Dutch/Shell. The Dutch owned the other half of Royal Dutch/Shell, and the British had the North Sea oil and the Dutch some North Sea gas. The damn Anglos had it made.

Will American oil greed doom the world? asked *The Economist* of London. Quite properly, it answered the question by warning its readers that the American economy grew and bought the world's goods and needed oil to do so, and that domestic American oil production was declining, so the Americans needed more from abroad.

But the *image* of America was that of a careless giant in a ten-gallon hat driving a sixteen-cylinder Cadillac at ninety miles an hour, and getting richer in the process.

The international institutions of the Mighty West, the OECD and its International Energy Agency, thus became even weaker. Its members felt they did not have the delegated powers to deal with the situation. The International Energy Agency was working on plans for the West to cut its imports and to allocate supplies, and the Western governments allowed their delegates to go to Paris or Geneva or Brussels, check into hotel rooms, go to meetings, talk to each other, and put the summarized discussions in plastic binders. But meanwhile the governments went out and signed up oil on a country-to-country basis.

When the International Energy Agency met, it presumed some flexibility in the distribution of world oil. It could say, "Let's all agree now, we cut back here and here,

Japan gets a little more, the United States gets a little less," and each point could be debated. But as 5 and 6 million barrels a day were signed up on a country-to-country basis, that flexibility diminished. Long-term deals were in place. When the Seven Sisters ran the world, they were able to allocate the oil. But the Seven Sisters no longer ran the world.

With the West so divided, the members of the Club could do the following:

They could determine how much oil to give their former masters, the Seven Sisters.

They could decide how much to compete with the Seven Sisters in refining and marketing, and take it or leave it.

They could ask for technical assistance, financing, and anything else on a shopping list.

They could tear up any contract they did not like, even if the contract was only a month old and was supposed to run for ten years, on the grounds that it no longer matched the needs of a sovereign people. They could change the terms of contracts *retroactively;* they could say, "We have decided you owe us a billion dollars more for 1977," and there would be no appeal.

They could determine how much new oil to explore for, and in some places nobody is in any hurry to explore for new oil, because the game is going just fine the way it is.

They could say, "The price of oil is going to go up by the rate of inflation, *plus* some more, because we want a real return for our asset."

And they could also grant favors for the correct opinions outside the oil trade: What do you think of nuclear power? What do you think of the current situation in the Middle East? How do you feel about Yasir Arafat and the Palestine Liberation Organization?

We ask, Can OPEC hold together? The economists have said no, it can't, it's a cartel, cartels don't survive, it says so right here in this book. But the economists knew only numbers, not *asibaya*, not an Arab sense of community, not the Third World flexing its muscles. We ask, Where will the price go? Ten years ago not a single economist could foresee a tenfold increase in price. OPEC is a Club, not quite a cartel, not as well organized as the Texas Railroad Commission, sometimes more like a bunch of eighteenth-century privateers waiting for the fat Spanish galleons to pass. It has survived a 35-percent drop in demand for its oil, in 1975; it has survived late-night screaming among its members at meetings; it has survived even a real shooting war between two of its major producers. For all its quarrels, it has held together better than the Mighty West. It will survive until the oil consumers develop energy independence and the diplomatic cohesion and skills that are appropriate to major powers.

In the next chapter we will see whether we are close to such independence, and what we could do if we were. Meanwhile, the price will go not only where economic demand takes it, for the reality of the world is more ragged than the world of economists. The price will go where OPEC takes it, and that price is determined not only by economic demand but by political opportunity. The present secretary-general of OPEC says he has looked over the numbers, and he thinks maybe $60 a barrel would be fair, and, like the economists', his guess is as good as anybody else's.

OPEC brings to mind a rather monolithic image now. But OPEC is people, just as the Seven Sisters were.

Abdul Aziz, the oil minister, drives his car to his office. Maybe he gets driven to his office, because the streets are crowded, and he can do some reading. He is part of the educated elite of his country. He may think something like this, which happens to be exactly what one such minister said: "My mother died of typhoid because there was no doctor in town. She was only twenty-eight. I almost lost my sight because there was no eye doctor. There were scorpions in our house: I was stung more than once. The infant mortality rate was sixty to seventy percent. A family had six or seven children in order to end up keeping one of them. We had no electricity. Unless you bear in mind this yearning of our people for a better life, you will not understand what is going on."

Then he gets to his office and his male secretary says, "Mr. Ichiban of Japan, Mr. Lundquist of Sweden, Mr. Costanzo of Brazil, and Mr. Munchausen of Germany are all waiting to see you."

Abdul Aziz looks into his outer office, where each of the gents is sitting with a black briefcase. They are all eyeing each other nervously. They are well scrubbed and well dressed. Abdul Aziz knows that each one is going to say, "I just read about the new Israeli settlements in the West Bank. Terrible, terrible." Then he will open his briefcase, this well-scrubbed, neatly suited Westerner, and make a pitch. The others will still be in the waiting room. Abdul Aziz is already an hour late, because time has a different importance in the Middle East. No matter; Abdul Aziz rather likes keeping all the Westerners in the waiting room. He knows that each of the buyers has been told, "Secure the oil now, we don't want any gas lines, we must keep our industry going, politically we can't risk a cold winter." Abdul Aziz looks out the window and enjoys the moment. Twenty years ago the Seven Sisters would have told his country how much oil it could produce.

Only twenty years! he thinks. How much has happened in twenty years!

8

WHY THE "ENERGY CRISIS" IS MISNAMED, AND WHY IT IS A FINANCIAL THREAT NO MATTER WHAT THE NAME

The Club was triumphant. It had engineered the biggest transfer of wealth in the history of the world, because it was sitting on the biggest pool of liquid fuels when the demand rose. Then it used political crises, Middle Eastern political crises at that, to raise the price. The producers' cartel replaced the Seven Sisters' cartel. If Perez Alfonso had not met Abdullah Tariki, would the natural quarrels of the producing countries have led to a different result? That is conjecture.

Most people were introduced to the "energy crisis" by the gas lines of 1973–74, when the Club, certain members of the Club, cut back production and embargoed certain destinations. That demonstrated our dependence. The threat of the Club's control is not the inconvenience of waiting in gas lines; it is that we are issuing claim checks on the country for a product that burns up in the atmosphere. We assume we can go right on issuing them. We have already issued the claim checks for Illinois, North Carolina, Arkansas, Wisconsin, and Georgia. The dollars we issue are too great in number to be divided into orange juice or F-14s. The threat of the "energy crisis" in the next decade is a financial crisis: a breakdown of the trade and banking systems, a galloping depression.

Let's sharpen the focus on the "energy crisis." First, let's put to one side the argument that the *planet* is running out of resources. That is a supermacro ecological thesis, which became the subject of intense debate with the publication of the projections of the Club of Rome's computer model. The time horizons of this discussion are farther away— into the next century. Let's agree that long-term, we should certainly be considering the resources of the planet.

The phrase "energy crisis" provokes a glazed expression in many people; doubt that there is one is widespread. I think the problem is that we have given the situation the wrong name. A "crisis" is a turning point, a condition of instability leading to decisive change. But as "crisis" wears on and on, we lose patience. Further, we have enough *potential* energy. If the United States has four hundred years' worth of coal, it has enough potential energy. Then what is the crisis? Is there really a crisis?

There is. What we have is a liquid-fuels crisis, an oil crisis, leading to a possible financial crisis. We are set up to use oil. We use more oil than we produce, so we use the Club's oil, which the Club sends us for dollars. We send the Club more than a billion dollars a week. We hope the Club keeps taking the dollars. The Club can cut off that oil and raise its price. To relieve our dependence on the

Club, we need time, money, and political will. We're not prepared to burn coal enough to lessen that dependence, and we have no other alternatives ready.

Let's look at two simple tables. The one on the left is oil consumed in international trade. The one on the right is the production of metric tons of coal. The two tables illustrate a point: the world has switched from coal to oil for much of its fuel. Oil is up ten times in usage, coal only twice, while the world population and world industry have grown dramatically.

TABLE A Oil (in millions of barrels per day)		TABLE B Coal (in millions of metric tons)	
1950	3.7	1950	1,580
1960	9.0	1960	2,191
1970	25.6	1970	2,397
1973	34.2	1973	2,483
1979	35.4	1979	2,932

Coal could lessen our dependence on imported oil, and because we have so much of it, we could export it and earn the money to reclaim Wisconsin and Georgia. The United States has enough coal for three to five hundred years, depending on whose estimate you use. The world has enough coal for two hundred years. *The World Coal Study,* edited by Carroll Wilson at MIT, calls for a tripled use of coal by the year 2000.

We know why the world switched from coal to oil. Coal is bulky and inefficient, is hard to produce, has dangerous emissions when burned, and may even affect the atmosphere in its production of carbon dioxide. Its emissions may contribute to "acid rain," which kills plant life and freshwater fish. To produce coal, we must begin to solve the pollution problems of coal right away.

The American coal industry operates below even its cur-

rent capacity and counts 20,000 miners out of work. The
first and easiest use of coal is by electric utilities, but that
conversion, or reconversion, is going very slowly, for reasons we have come to label as "political."

We do not now have the infrastructure for a coal-based
economy that would curb our dependence on oil. We need
miners and mines, new miners, new mines. We don't want
to mar the landscape or injure the miners. We have to
train thousands of new miners.

We have to move the coal across the country, so we need
unit trains, the mile-long hundred-car trains that carry
coal in bulk. That means rebuilding the railroads. It also
brings political problems, because a lot of towns don't want
frequent hundred-car trains rumbling through their middle.

We have eager buyers for our coal, if we want to export
it. To export it, though, we need coal ports. We have no
West Coast coal port at all. We have relatively minor facilities on our other coasts, and our great Virginia coal port,
Hampton Roads, is backed up.

We need a fleet of coal-carrying ships, a new generation
of ships, perhaps fifty a year for twenty years. Think of
the vast tanker fleets at sea right now, hundreds of tankers
all over the world. To move coal, we need a similar coal
fleet.

We need the money to invest in the mines, the miners,
the pipelines, the railbeds, the railroads, the coal ports,
and the ships. We need the building skills to accomplish
this, and time to do it in.

Now we get to the most important item. We need a sense
of national purpose, of intention, because otherwise the
natural conflicts cancel each other and nothing gets done
at all.

The coal towns in Montana and Wyoming can say, "We
like our landscape now; what do we care what Common-
wealth Edison and Detroit Edison and Consolidated Edi-

son and New Jersey Public Service use for fuel?" The
towns that straddle the rail lines can say, "Not through our
town, you don't." The environmentalists can go to court
and ask for an injunction and a five-year study; one such
group calls its tactics, frankly, "analysis paralysis."

If we have the money to send to the Club for the oil,
and currently we are sending out $80 billion a year, then
we have the money for the mines, the miners, the pipelines, the railbeds, the railroads, the coal ports, and the
ships, though it would mean spending more while we got
them built. Right now we are using our building skills to
build whole industrial petrochemical cities for the Club, in
its own lands. So it's all do-able, from both the financial
and engineering standpoints. Let's do it.

Who wants to start by giving up something?

Coal will be here, but not tomorrow.

Then there is nuclear power. One of my neighbors is a
physicist in charge of a great laboratory with a nine-figure
budget. He's working on fusion, which would solve many
of our energy problems. He's already up to 70 million
degrees Fahrenheit, and all he needs is 100 million degrees and maybe the process will work. I ask, "When do
you get the last thirty million degrees?" And he says, "The
last thirty million degrees are the hardest; give me another
fifteen years."

We have nuclear power plants, seventy-four of them,
and they are a subject of intense debate. New England, the
upper Midwest, and the southern Atlantic states already
get almost a third of their electricity from nuclear power,
and utilities will continue to use more. But the problem of
nuclear waste had held up the expansion of nuclear
power, even before Three Mile Island. That phrase itself,
or that locale, has become world-famous. "In the United
States," says the Harvard Business School energy study,
"there is simply no reasonable possibility for massive con-

tributions from nuclear power for at least the rest of the twentieth century." The politics of coal are nothing, in intensity, to the emotions aroused by nuclear power.

Incidentally, the French have gone flat out in building nuclear power. A "scenario" written by an independent consultant for one of the Seven Sisters predicted as "probable" a nuclear accident within the next ten years. The location of the surmised accident was France, because the French are pushing their program so fast. When the French got wind of this, they were understandably furious. "We are building a lot of nuclear plants," they said, "but we staff them with the highest-level people, and you staff yours with garage mechanics." That got people here mad at the French, those who knew about it.

If the existing problems of nuclear waste aren't solved, we begin to lose even the nuclear power we now have, within five years.

Let's just say, without taking sides, no *extra* help from nuclear power in the next ten years, no significant additional contribution.

Solar. Ah, solar. Everybody loves solar power. Sounds so natural and healthy. Fuels from biomass: plants, woods, and waste. Windmills. Photovoltaic cells, solar cells, solar thermal electric. Forty percent of our energy by the year 2000, say the folks who organized International Sun Day, could be solar. "Won't have the impact of a mosquito bite on an elephant's fanny," says *World Oil*.

Solar power is *renewable* power. Let's not underestimate natural America. (*The Greening of America* predicted the surge of denim, the blue-jeaning of the country.) Some solar uses are feasible right now. Let's say all the suggestions of Professor Modesto A. Maidique, Harvard Business School, are taken. Let's say we get from solar 5 to 15 percent of our energy by the year 2000, an optimistic projection. Solar power could have an impact, and we should start now; but the real impact would be in the 1990s. We need some more technology here, and nobody sees a solar car. Solar: not much help for a decade, and even then we won't have solar America.

Conservation. To a lot of people, "conservation" suggests a bunch of granola-eating Sierra Clubbers telling everybody to get a bicycle or hiking boots. Conservation is a favorite of the energy numbers crunchers, because the numbers always work out. You can cut energy usage by a third, maybe more, and still keep more or less the same life-style. Turn down the thermostat eight degrees in the winter, and you save enough energy to equal the output of Indonesia. Inflate the tires properly, tune the engine, stick to the speed limit, and you get a small sheikhdom, bigger than Bahrain and not as big as Abu Dhabi. Pull the curtains, and you get another small sheikhdom. The first section of conservation is just cutting back.

Double the mileage of the cars, and you're talking big numbers. Now, instead of burning up one out of every eight barrels of oil in the world, you're only burning up one out of every sixteen. Now you're up to the oil capacity of an Iran or an Iraq. The second section of conservation is to get new equipment that uses less energy, like small cars.

But it takes a while to turn over the automobile fleet, even if you offer a federal bounty for junking gas guzzlers. (That one works out too, in the numbers.) We could sell business the idea of no ties and short-sleeved shirts in the summer, but it only works from an energy point of view when you open the windows and save on air conditioning. It takes a while to design and build new buildings, because you can't really pay people to drive an old building to the junkyard.

Good news and bad news. The good news is that conservation is already happening. Industry will buy new equipment if it saves money, so Robertshaw and Honeywell and IBM are making money producing instruments and computers that control temperatures and processes in a way that saves energy—enough energy to make up the cost of the controls. General Motors, wounded by Japanese imports, is going to have a fleet of thirty-one-mile-per-gallon cars by 1985. The imports already deliver this. Full-sized cars have already dropped from 40 percent to 4 percent of total sales.

The really good news comes in a ratio that has been falling apart. "Conservation" also sounded to some people like "no growth," because it used to be thought, to be simple for a moment, that you needed a unit of energy for a unit of growth. (The unsimple way of saying this was that the GNP energy coefficient was inelastic.) But energy use has been dropping off more than national growth has been slowing, and that helps remove it from the growth–no growth argument.

That's the good news. The bad news is that the easy part gets done first. The gains in industry will be slower from here on. Driving habits, the automobile fleet turnover, new buildings, all take time. The really bad news is that, as one government official said, "there is no organized conservation industry." The oil industry can paper the country with full-page ads and prowl the corridors of Congress. Much of the coal industry is owned by the oil industry. There is lobbying for conservation, but it doesn't have the wonderful clarity of the oil industry.

Now we come to something that continuously amazes me. In 1980, three years after President Carter declared the "moral equivalent of war," seven years after the Arab oil embargo, eight years after the St. Valentine's Day Massacre, half the American people did not believe there was any crisis about energy. Seven in ten Americans thought that gasoline shortages were deliberately contrived by the oil companies.

Nearly four in ten Americans didn't know we needed to import oil, according to a Gallup poll.

The polls of Messrs. Gallup and Yankelovich, which we reviewed over a ten-year history, reveal an almost continuous resistance to a perception of the situation. Is there a crisis? No. Who causes the problems? The oil companies; next, the government. OPEC? Thirteen percent, in 1979, responded to the acronym OPEC. That was at least up from 6 percent in 1974.

You're not going to have real conservation if most of the American people believe the whole affair is a plot of the oil companies.

Why don't the American people believe the truth? I don't know. Daniel Yergin, the coauthor of the Harvard Business School energy report, says it is a failure of the media to teach the people. He quotes the example of an editor rejecting a lucid article because the readers couldn't handle it, it's boring. That's certainly true. But "readers" is already a limited example. Most Americans get their news from television. Energy is a complex and abstract subject. It can't compete with instant replay, let's go to the videotape, swish! Goal! Touchdown! It can't compete with sexual revelations, or revolutions.

Sixty percent of college-educated Americans now believe there is an energy problem, says the Gallup organization. And half of them have modified their behavior because of the cost of energy.

So, if you have read this far, you need not feel quite so lonely. But you have already *read* more about energy than most of your fellow Americans ever will.

When various experts look at world energy, they always come back to American usage. We say, "The United States is the Saudi Arabia of coal"; abroad, they say, "The United States is the Saudi Arabia of *consumption*." Sheikh Yamani and Johannes Witteveen both say, "What about no Sunday driving? Or rationing?" Those are Hamiltonian solutions;

that is, they presume an elite leadership devoted to rational solutions and preserving the currency.

The American people themselves need not feel guilty about their past use of energy; they were sold the use of it in the days of the Endless Glut. Guilt sometimes gets in the way of seeing the problem clearly. They need not feel guilty *if* they become conscious of the problem. I have the subjective feeling, undocumented by Gallup polls, that in the past the people were more ready to move than the leadership could lead. American energy consumption can be modified without a severe strain on the life-style, but every year that goes by as if nothing has happened is a year for the locust; the strain will be felt in the dollar, in the life-styles of future years.

We've just touched on various alternatives to oil: coal, nuclear, solar, and conservation. We might also have mentioned natural gas, the so-called prince of hydrocarbons. Natural gas is a very efficient fuel, but most energy studies consider the reserves, in the United States, to be limited, just as the oil is. Only recently have prospectors looked for gas by itself; until now it has been a by-product of oil exploration. Some experts think the natural gas supplies have been underestimated, because there is also gas that is much more expensive to produce: deep-drilled gas, below 15,000 feet; gas in "tight sands"; and gas from shale. But that takes investment and time, and it isn't sure.

Remember that most of the crowd making decisions about spending money in energy grew up with the Endless Glut. They look at the OPEC price of $30 and wonder if somebody isn't about to bring on a huge field somewhere that will crack the price. They think, If we *knew* that oil was going to be up to $50 a barrel, and stay there, we could commit money to coal, heavy oil, shale, deep-drilled gas. But what if the oil price fell, and we spent the money? Then everybody goes back to oil, we're busted and out of a job. The small coal operators who opened mines in the mid-1970s are already in trouble.

It takes time and money—and technology and skills—to create alternatives to oil, and *people* have to make those decisions. The results take ten years to be realized, and the *people* get elected, or reelected, in two years, or four years; and if they're businessmen, they may be retired or their successors in place before all the results are seen.

There is one question that brings forth passions like those stirred by the theological debates in sixteenth-century Germany, Martin Luther at Marburg or Leipzig. The oil industry is passionate, and so are its opponents.

If you raise the price, does that coax more oil out of the ground?

Only if the oil is there.

The price of oil could go to $500 a barrel, and if you drilled for it on Park Avenue or Peachtree Street or Lake Shore Drive it wouldn't make any difference.

Obviously, some oil gets produced at $30 a barrel that wouldn't be produced at $3 a barrel. It becomes economical to go back to abandoned wells, inject them with steam or water, and bring up what oil remains. It becomes economical to prospect in new and difficult places. The Overthrust Belt, with its zigzag formations, is very promising.

But within the United States, the oil men say, "the easy oil has been found." The entire country has been mapped, prospected, and punched. More than 2 million holes have been drilled in its surface. We have old oil fields, and the wells don't flow after a while, they drip; and the national usage of oil keeps right on going. The average well in the United States now yields 17 barrels a day. The average well in Venezuela yields 186 barrels a day. The average well in Saudi Arabia yields 12,405 barrels a day.

Since the First Oil Crisis, the Texas price of "new oil" has quadrupled, and the "old oil" has been allowed to double and will eventually rise to the market price. With oil at $30 a barrel, the independent drillers are back with the greatest enthusiasm they have shown since the 1950s, and the companies that supply oil-field services are booming. But production in the United States is still declining.

Excluding northern Alaska, our oil reserves have dropped every single year since 1966, as these estimates of past production and future production from the Petroleum Industry Research Foundation show:

1973	9.0 million barrels a day
1979	7.2 million barrels a day
1985	6.3 million barrels a day
1990	5.9 million barrels a day

These figures are based on the assumption that the oil industry gets the price it wants. They assume higher world prices, decontrol of oil prices in the United States, and the location of 2.3 to 2.4 *billion* barrels of oil a year in the United States outside Alaska, which would be more oil than we've been finding recently.

Alaskan production will also peak and decline. There are other areas in the Arctic, such as the Beaufort Sea, that remain to be explored, and where oil may be found, if the wrangles between the oil companies and the legislators are resolved. We should resolve these wrangles quickly. The Alaska pipeline was held up for years, yet even a naturalist like John McPhee, who bears a great love for the state, described the Alaska pipeline in size and impact as resembling a thread across Staten Island. Oil on federal lands is a controversial subject. But even with the use of federal lands and additional areas of Alaska, American production will decline. There is not a single expert who expects it to rise. The range in estimates brackets the rate at which it will fall. The most pessimistic estimate is 4 million barrels a day in 1990.

Our usage of oil has dropped as the price of oil has climbed. But the expected drop in production is going to

keep the gap there over the next decade. Here is part of a
1978 conversation with John O'Leary, who was then second in command at the Department of Energy. I was asking whether a free-market price wouldn't bring up a lot of
oil, and whether there weren't non-OPEC areas of the
world that would supply us.

"William Simon says," I said, "that if you just freed the
price, the market would take care of it. The oil companies
say that, too."

"Well, they would."

"Simon says we don't need a Department of Energy. It
just gets in the way."

"That's an agricultural observation, that is, an observation from the economics of agriculture. Agriculture goes
season by season. Here we have a finite resource. You have
to plan."

There was, at that moment, one of the periodic mini-
gluts.

"North Slope oil is piling up in California," I said. "In
the ports the tanker crews are playing backgammon."

"The surplus is a hiccup," O'Leary said, "a good summer day's driving, fifty thousand barrels. It will disappear.
The scale is different from what it used to be. A bonanza
isn't what it used to be. When our economy used a million
barrels a day, a strike in Texas of a hundred-thousand-
barrels-a-day field would rock the industry. Oil could go
down to ten cents a barrel. But now we have an economy
that uses seventeen million barrels a day. There are no
bonanzas big enough to rock it; we've only found one on
this continent in a hundred and twenty years, the North
Slope."

"Mexico," I said. "Mexico has just hit ten for ten on the
drilling. The president of Mexico says he's going to have
more oil than Saudi Arabia."

"It's natural to embrace Mexico. We have Mexico down
for two and a half million barrels a day in 1985. Will it be
more? Don't forget the lead times and the investment. If

they spend the money on the society, they may not plow all the money back."

"Mexico," I said, to that conference Wanda and I led. The financial types around the table were doodling. The Exxon economist was making notes. The Mobil man was adding some figures.

"I just got back from Mexico," said the most youthful of my oilmen. "It's going to be terrific. Elephant-size structures. An offshore Saudi."

The Mobil man put his glasses back on and riffled through some of his figures.

"Unofficially," he said. "Okay, unofficially? I'll give you another three and a half million barrels a day from *all* the non-OPEC countries by 1985. Most of that will go to developing countries. Korea and Brazil buy oil, too. Even if the U.S. demand is constant, *world* demand is going to go from 51 million barrels a day to 66 million. World demand will pick up three and a half million barrels a day easily. You can *find* more oil, but that doesn't mean whoever has the oil will bring it up and *sell* it."

In Caracas, at the end of 1977, Sheikh Yamani led the doves in holding the price at an OPEC meeting. But he warned that demand would grow, and that prices would double in a decade. He was wrong. They doubled in two years.

"There are only two main questions in the entire oil situation," John O'Leary, of the Department of Energy, said. "One is, What will the demand be?"

Whenever we have a recession, demand falls off. Automobile plants that have been shut down do not use any power. Laid-off workers do not drive and fly as much as workers who are being paid full-time and overtime. So we have periodic mini-gluts, well publicized by the newspapers, which leads people to believe the problem has gone away, or was all an oil company plot. But we don't want to live in a state of permanent recession.

"The other question," said John O'Leary, "is, What will the Saudis do? Because what the Saudis do determines the supply. The North Sea, the North Slope, Mexico—we can see the limits to these. We can see the capacities of most major fields. But the Saudis have the capacity to take us through a decade. They are the only country with the reserves."

We are back to the Club. All the rules we were taught about cartels said that they break up. The members quarrel and begin discounting to get a bigger share. And this Club's members certainly quarrel. Iran and Iraq went to war, bombing each other's oil facilities, but neither Club member resigned, and the other Club members noted calmly that this Persian Gulf war, with its damage to oil facilities, would surely raise the price of oil.

It is an extraordinary point in history when the world's leading industrial powers are so dependent on a handful of families.

On one side of the Persian Gulf are Iran and Iraq, both hostile to the West and warring with each other. When the Iranians and the Iraqis attack each other, the state radio of each calls for *jihad,* holy war, and accuses the enemy of being in league with the racist Zionist imperialist Americans. Anyone who has lingering doubts about the necessity for energy independence should read the transcripts recorded by the BBC of the broadcasts from Baghdad and Tehran.

On the other side of the Persian Gulf are the so-called conservative states, the family proprietors: the al-Salim al-Sabahs of Kuwait, the Rashids of Dubai, the Zayed-bin-Sultan-al-Nahyans of Abu Dhabi, and dwarfing them all, the Saudis, who named Arabia after themselves. Who are these people upon whom we have now become so perilously dependent?

9

THE SAUDI CONNECTION: THE KINGDOM AND THE POWER

I know of only one place referred to reverently as the Kingdom, and it is not the kingdom of heaven. Nor is it Sweden or Nepal or whatever kingdoms are left. The Arabists call Saudi Arabia simply the Kingdom.

There are only two questions, the Department of Energy had said. One is, What will demand be? The other is, What will the Saudis do? Only the Saudis have the reserves.

If, when the demand rises, the Saudis open those reserves, they help to hold down the price. If they do not open the reserves, the price rises more sharply. A sharply rising price of oil accelerates inflation. It also helps to produce a recession, because part of the income that went for other products and services must be diverted to oil when the price rises, and the factories and enterprises produc-

ing those products and services then close down. What the
Kingdom decides can thus determine the level of industrial activity in the West, whether the Communists make
gains in France and Italy, how intense inflation may be,
what happens to interest rates, the securities markets,
housing—extraordinary leverage for so small a country.

The Kingdom, in terms of oil, is roughly one-third of
OPEC. Together with its neighbors and in-laws up and
down the coast of the Gulf, it is one-half of OPEC. Unlike
the other half of OPEC, this half does not need all the
money it can earn from the oil. Venezuela, Algeria, and
Indonesia need all the money they can get. The Kingdom
does not. So its decisions are not economic, they are political. What the Kingdom decides will influence the economy of the 1980s.

The Kingdom is the size of the United States east of the
Mississippi River. One corner of it, the southwestern province of Asir, has some green valleys. The very southwest
of the Arabian Peninsula, Yemen, was the "Arabia Felix"
of Roman times. The Jebel al-Hijaz range blocks the mois-
ture from traveling east, leaving one of the world's largest
deserts. The desert is so extensive that the southeastern
section of the Kingdom is called Ar Rub al Khali, "The
Empty Quarter." The Kingdom does not have a single
river. Summer temperatures of 120 degrees Fahrenheit,
with no rainfall, are common. Because the climate was so
harsh, the population remained small. Today it is about 7
million; no one knows for sure.

In 1928 the Standard Oil Company of California, Socal,
had failed to find oil in Mexico, Ecuador, the Philippines,
and Alaska. As a last resort, it bought a concession from
Gulf on the island of Bahrain, twenty miles off the coast
of Saudi Arabia, and found some oil. Socal sought out
Harry St. John Philby, a local Ford dealer and sometime
British agent, who was a friend of the Saudi finance minister, Sheikh Abdullah Sulaiman. Philby needed money

for the education of his children, one of whom, Kim, was to become a famous double agent, a "mole," in World War II. For 35,000 gold sovereigns, Socal got the concession for Saudi Arabia. Sheikh Abdullah Sulaiman counted out the coins himself.

Socal's Damman Number 7 struck oil at 4,727 feet in 1937. The first tanker was loaded in 1939. Damman Number 7 is still flowing. Since Socal did not have a ready market for its oil, it traded a half share to Texaco for an increased share of the cartel's market. Socal and Texaco admitted Exxon and Mobil for a still bigger share of the market. The four oil companies, Socal, Texaco, Exxon, and Mobil, all good Sisters, formed Aramco, the Arabian-American Oil Company. Within thirty years Aramco had found, in Saudi Arabia, crude reserves of more than 180 billion barrels, one-quarter of all the oil reserves on the planet.

But no one knows how much oil is really to be found in the Kingdom.

Few places on earth have changed as rapidly as Saudi Arabia. In the 1930s, when it was possible to take a train from Tel Aviv to Cairo, when Cairo itself was a relatively civilized center, the Saudis still lived largely as they did in biblical times. Perhaps a quarter of the population was nomadic; half were small cultivators or shepherds, semi-nomadic tribesmen, and village craftsmen. And a quarter lived in the small cities. The traveler might take the train from Tel Aviv to Cairo, but in Saudi Arabia he would be riding a camel, and warily. The mud-walled brick towns closed their doors at sunset; the gates were barred at nightfall. If you were traveling and saw a stranger, you looked for some prearranged signal—waving a headcloth, throwing up handfuls of sand; if you did not see it, you galloped away. Raiders and feuding tribes made journeys hazardous.

Abdul Aziz ibn-Saud, the king who united Saudi Arabia, grew up in exile in Kuwait. He grew up also in the austere, puritanical form of Islam derived from the doctrines of an eighteenth-century reformer, Mohammed ibn Abd al-Wahab. Ibn-Saud was six-five and loved desert sports and desert warfare. In 1901, at the age of twenty-one, with only forty men, he recaptured the Saudi home city of Riyadh from the rival Rashid tribe. In the name of Wahabism and in battle he gradually conquered the country, and in 1932 he renamed it Saudi Arabia. He had to restrain the tribes who pledged him allegiance from engaging in holy war and war as sport; he had also to decide whether to permit the first incursions of the twentieth century: radio, telegraph, and automobiles. Ibn-Saud's conquests of the holy cities of Mecca and Medina alarmed the Islamic world outside Arabia, lest Wahabism change those traditional seats of learning, but ibn-Saud did his best to reassure the alarmed delegations that came to visit, and he made the *hajj* safe for pilgrims.

Before Damman Number 7, before the oil, Saudi Arabia lived off goats, dates, and pilgrims, a million pilgrims a year. Since Mecca is the birthplace of the Prophet, Saudi Arabia takes extremely seriously its role as the keeper of the holy places; with its austere Wahabism, it thinks of itself also as Keeper of the Faith.

Life is changing in Saudi Arabia. Twenty years ago King Abdul Aziz's Swiss steward wrote that he had eunuchs helping him in the palace kitchens. Twenty years ago slave dealers still occasionally brought their commerce from Africa. Slavery was officially abolished in 1962. There were no public women's schools in 1962, and when the first women were admitted to segregated schools, the National Guard had to be called out to protect the school from irate fathers. Even with the oil flowing, twenty years ago the Saudi treasury was virtually bankrupt; hence Abdullah Tariki's annoyance with the price cuts of the oil companies.

For a major industrial enterprise, Aramco was relatively enlightened. It produced its oil and it stayed to itself. It arranged for Saudis to have schooling in the United States, largely in those western and southern American universities where the Aramco executives had studied. When not on the job, the Aramco employees stayed largely in their Dhahran compound. The compound seems not only incongruous in Saudi Arabia; it is not even contemporary America. More like *Saturday Evening Post* America, or like a military base, with sprinklers flicking water onto the green lawns, and the houses that seem very much like officers' quarters. The Aramco compound reminded me of a July day in Fort Shafter, Hawaii. In Saudi Arabia women do not drive cars, except in the Aramco compound. Nor within the compound do they have to dress as severely as outside; elsewhere, to keep within Wahabi modesty, long skirts and long sleeves are recommended.

We are accustomed to the drama of oil from old movies, *Boom Town* and *Giant,* the gusher suddenly spouting a black geyser, the symbol of the oil derrick. But when you take off from Dhahran in a propjet to tour the world's greatest oil field, there is little to see. The sun glares from the water at Ras Tanura, where the tankers line up. And then you can see the Strait of Hormuz, through which the tankers pass, Iran on the far side. And then, below, miles and miles of light-brown sand, a sea of sand on a sea of oil, the occasional barracks of construction workers, disciplined armies of Koreans. A black line snakes across the desert, a pipeline, and this is it: the Ghawar field, with oil enough to bring the Russians to the Gulf, to make the banks tremble, to change the history of the world.

No derricks, no symbols, very quiet. A lonely black pumping station. A bright burning spot where gas is flared. The oil is so easy, the oil men say, you can dig it with a teaspoon, so pressured from its geologic formation you do not need to pump it. In Kuwait it runs downhill to the tankers. It costs the Saudis 15 cents a barrel, from the ground to the tanker. Sixty percent of this oil runs through only eight pumping stations. It is not comforting to think that the financial stability of the West rests on eight pumping stations.

Some lucky factors, for the West, were operating in Saudi Arabia. Because the Wahabis who rule the Kingdom are so fanatically opposed to communism, they sought out the West. Because Aramco was relatively enlightened, it did not generate ill will as times changed. Because the United States was never a physical presence in Saudi society—as, say, the French were in Algeria—a "special relationship" could flower.

But we can't take these factors for granted. Libya's Qaddafi is an ascetic Muslim, and after he deposed a religious king, he called the Russians. The Soviet presence in Muslim Iraq has been pronounced. The Ayatollah Khomeini's fundamentalism in Iran has caused us great discomfort. What will the Saudis do?

Every Muslim, once in his lifetime, more often if he is able, should make the journey to Mecca, the birthplace of the Prophet. Once he makes the pilgrimage, the *hajj*, he can call himself a *hajji*.

In recent years the senior officials of the United States Treasury have undertaken their own version of the *hajj*. Their concerns are material, not spiritual; but the destination is also Saudi Arabia—Riyadh, the capital, not Mecca. The American *hajj* is usually in the autumn. Respects are paid to the Saudi reserves, the Saudi bank accounts, the financial surpluses. Entreaties go out to hold down the price of oil. I went, in late 1977, on one such *hajj*, with the Secretary of the Treasury, then W. Michael Blumenthal, and then Undersecretary Anthony Solomon, and Assistant Secretary C. Fred Bergsten. I made out a check to the Treasurer of the United States for the air fare plus one dollar—the Treasury does not compete with the airlines. It uses an air force plane equipped with Xerox machines and IBM Selectrics; and no voice ever says "This is your captain speaking."

The *hajjis* called on Sadat, on the Israelis, on the Shah, and on the Kuwaitis. The finance minister of Kuwait is Abdul Rahman Salim al-Ateeqy. He has a big black mustache. In the negotiations before the St. Valentine's Day Massacre, Billy Fraser, Lord Strathalmond, would say, "Here comes Groucho Marx." Al-Ateeqy has a reputation as a tough old bird. "The oil companies took our oil at a dollar a barrel," said the tough old bird. "BP and Gulf would come and say, 'You can pump a million barrels a day; that's all we will sell.' That power is gone now. We try to help the world by producing more oil; we think about the declining dollar. There is no alternative to the U.S. as an investment."

The finance minister fingered his *misbaha,* his worry beads. "We are not producing at capacity. Oil in the ground is better than paper money. We are not the saviors of the Western economies; what can we do about trade unions in Britain, or the problems of Italy? We will be good trading partners. One more thing. For stability in the Middle East there must be a settlement, the Palestinians must have a state. If I have a bad Palestinian, where can I expel him to?"

The per-capita income in Kuwait is $13,500. In the United States it is $6,339. There are as many Palestinians working in Kuwait as there are Kuwaitis.

Abdul Aziz al-Qūrashi is governor of the Saudi Arabian Monetary Agency. He has great personal magnetism, a rich, deep, British-accented voice. We spoke with him and Muhammad Ali Aba al-Khayl, the minister of finance, in Riyadh. Both were in *thaubs,* the customary starched white gown, and in *kaffiyeh* headdresses, their ankle socks and loafers visible. Al-Qūrashi could replace Walter Cronkite for resonance. Or Alistair Cooke.

What do the Saudis want?

"Peace. Stability. Technology, for development. We will never be self-sufficient in agriculture, so we will always import rice, sugar, wheat."

Governor al-Qūrashi smiles. "And camels."

"You import camels?"

Governor al-Qūrashi is having a good time. Why camels?

"We eat them."

Governor al-Qūrashi is a graduate of the University of Southern California. His smile is as wide as it will go. He must have played this scene before.

Minister Aba al-Khayl insists the Saudis will spend the oil money. They have an ambitious development plan. They will contribute more to the IMF and the African and Asian development banks. Then comes the theme we heard all over the Middle East, even in Israel.

"All we need to pump is three million barrels a day. That will take care of us. Everything over three million barrels a day is a gift."

In 1980 the Saudis were pumping 9 million barrels a day. Perhaps their needs were up to 4 million barrels a day, or even 5. Five million barrels a day is $55 billion a year.

"We would rather keep the oil than have the paper money," says Minister Aba al-Khayl.

In the boom-camp atmosphere of Riyadh, the capital, something is missing: the sight of women. There are a few Bedu women on the streets, moving like nuns, everything but their eyes veiled. Their eyes are made up with kohl. In the offices the secretaries are men. The women are at home, practicing the arts of the extended family.

Riyadh is a forest of construction cranes, with as much rubble as Berlin in 1946. "That's funny, there was a street here yesterday," says an embassy friend, turning a corner only to meet a pile of rubble and some construction cranes. He goes another half block. "And this street wasn't here yesterday." Riyadh—outside the original town—has been designed by Constantinos Doxiadis, the city planner. Riyadh has six-lane highways with arc lights. Texas architects have provided government buildings with a style that is a mixture of contemporary and classic Arabic. (There is, occasionally, the feeling that Houston is being stamped out of metal, attached to concrete, helicoptered in, and bolted down in the desert kingdom.) Banged and disabled automobiles are part of the roadside scene; they grow faster than the ranks of the trucks to take them away. There is the usual brag—"We have the worst drivers in the world"—explained: "You take a boy who has been tending goats, teach him to drive, put him behind the wheel, and the accelerator falls naturally to the floor."

The Treasury left; I stayed. I was talking to young Saudi technocrats. They took for granted the private ten-passenger business jets, the Hawker-Siddeleys and Gulfstreams that were available to them. On the highways we would see new Datsun pickup trucks, with camels trussed up in the back. How does the camel cross the desert? By Datsun. The camel-in-the-Datsun theme reappeared with variations. A deputy minister bought a house in Riyadh; his father came to visit and pitched his tent on the front lawn, refusing the remonstrances of his son to share the brick house.

My host was an American corporate representative. He had a pleasant, newly furnished, five-bedroom house on three-quarters of an acre. A nice house, nothing special. The rent was $100,000 a year. Not the purchase price—the rent. "They overpaid," I was told. "The rent on that house should only be seventy thousand a year."

The rent was in scale, in Saudi Arabia. The technocrats were young, but they had the responsibility for billions of dollars. They were the bridge between the desert kingdom and the Houston of the Middle East. It was as if some recent Stanford and Harvard classes had taken over the Pentagon and HEW. One technocrat had, for some reason, ended up in Cape Girardeau, Missouri, at Southeast Missouri State University. He loved it. He got to see the real America, he said.

Most of the Saudis go to Texas and California; that is where Aramco sent their cousins and older brothers. Now they know the way, and they like the climate. Colloquial Americanisms pour from be*thaub*ed Arabs. I could not believe the passion for football; video cassettes of the previous Saturday's game are traded from hand to hand. The true enthusiasts prefer not to know the outcome ahead of time.

Is the interest in football that real, or is it part of the Saudi gift of trying to please the visitor? "It's real," said an Arabist at the embassy. "They really get hooked on the motion, the pomp, and the drama of big-time football. The previous sports here were hawking and camel racing."

When the petrodollar flood began, the ranks to administer it were thin. Consequently, this phenomenon of young, American-educated Arabs administering billions.

"We have a lot to learn, but it's not so bad, because we all know each other. For example, I went to USC. I think USC is probably the most popular school for Saudis. And if I want to get something done at Planning, I know a guy who was down the hall from me at USC; the guy at Finance was my roommate at USC; and we know the ringer from Ohio State because he is married to my roommate's sister. You know, the Saudi cabinet has more American-trained Ph.D.'s than the U.S. cabinet."

The speaker is a deputy minister. His office has Knoll furniture, stainless steel and leather, and looks as if it were very recently uncrated. In fact, the building, with its Belgian elevators and its wet-smelling cement, looks as if it were very recently uncrated. Perhaps it was; a leading Saudi entrepreneur is planning to build prefabricated hotel rooms in Texas, complete with furniture, fly the rooms to Saudi, and stack them into hotels.

Another deputy minister comes in. They are both in crisp white *thaubs* with cuff links in the sleeves, and loafers. They speak in Arabic. Then they switch to English.

"Who do you play Saturday?"

"Texas."

"Texas will kill you. We will be number one."

"No chance. You still have to play Notre Dame. We will be number one."

They ask my opinion. No use. They follow the bowl contenders far more closely than I do. They follow senators, too—especially senators who concern themselves with Israel and the Middle East. There they sound moderate: "Well, we must have a settlement, we must recognize Israel, they must have a plan for the Palestinians. If the Israelis reach a settlement, they will not only have peace in the Middle East, they will make a lot of money. They have great skills in agriculture and medicine and banking."

Could anyone love his college as much as the Saudi technocrats seem to? I suppose, if you came from a big Saudi extended family, with your father and your uncles running things, and your mother and your aunts and your cousins watching out for marriageable girls, then you would have a real culture shock upon landing in America. (If you landed at JFK in February in a blizzard and got continually beaten in the race for taxis, as happened to one of my friends, you might want to turn around and go home.) Then the American university scene would have intoxicating freedom and wild diversity, not to mention women with bare legs and bare faces. And if you work hard and go back to Saudi with your degree and get married and start working long hours in a ministry, the "bright college years with pleasure rife" might really be that; you might want to hang on to some residue of that experience. And this becomes a factor in the calculus of imports, exports, deficits, surpluses, and the price of oil.

John Hubbard, the former president of the University of Southern California, made a trip to the Middle East. In the government alone he could count four cabinet ministers and fourteen deputy ministers as USC alumni, plus some of USC's most prosperous businessmen. He was the guest at a banquet: lamb and pilaf. He brought with him the filmed highlights of recent USC seasons. One was a USC–Notre Dame game, when USC trailed 24–6 at the half. The bearded and be*thaub*ed audience groaned. The USC Trojans came back with forty-nine points in the second half to win. The audience cheered, play by play, touchdown by touchdown. When the lights went on, the host of the alumni meeting, filled with the spirit of victory, made a pronouncement. "Gentlemen," he said, "Allah is a Trojan."

The Saudi connection was later to cause Hubbard some severe embarrassment. J. Robert Fluor, builder of a $5-billion gas-gathering system in Saudi, chairman of the USC Board of Trustees, attempted to set up a $22-million Middle East Study Center at USC, with a former Aramco vice-president as its head, and with funding from those who had business with Saudi Arabia. The autonomous character of the proposed center, and the crude way in which Fluor tried to raise the money, led the USC faculty to rebellion and created a scandal in southern California. But it was the sellers to the Saudis, not the Saudis themselves, who created the scandal.

Princeton had only a handful of Saudi alumni, but among them was Prince Saud al-Faisal, the handsome foreign minister. Princeton was conscious of the sensitivities and handled its Saudi connection with skill. The grant of

$5 million from the Saudis, to help the University of Riyadh, created no fuss at all.

Money alone is not the governing factor. "Everyone can get a government loan for a house. Every taxi driver can be an investor," said Prince Muhammad bin Faisal, a young entrepreneur. "But what about the inner life?" The technocrats may speak colloquial American, but the religious police still patrol in Riyadh, enforcing the five-times-a-day call to prayer, rapping with their canes on the shutters of shopkeepers who are tardy in closing for prayer. The same canes may rap the legs of women immodestly dressed. The manpower for growth is in short supply; already there are 2 million foreigners, Yemenis, Pakistanis, Baluchis, in Saudi. Across the Gulf there is the sobering example of Iran, which was industrializing and growing, up to the point the Ayatollah Khomeini took power and reminded the populace of the inner life.

The technocrats administer Saudi; they do not run it. The Kingdom is run by the king, the royal family, the Koran, and a whole language of cultural assumptions. We see the side the Saudis present to us, and it is difficult to predicate the economic future on present assumptions.

Presiding over a vast area with a small population and a great treasure, the Saudis value nothing so much as stability. They write checks to radicals and conservatives alike within the Arab world. When they look around, they see, across the Red Sea, a Marxist-oriented group of lieutenant colonels in Ethiopia. On their own southern border is the People's Republic of Yemen; the ubiquitous Cubans are there, advising. The Russians are in Afghanistan, and across the Persian Gulf the radical Iraqis and the disarrayed Iranians war with each other. It helps to have powerful friends.

What will the Saudis do? In a famous simile, Sheikh Yamani said the Saudi relationship with the West was like a Catholic marriage: with disagreements, but basically indissoluble. Sheikh Yamani's other comparison was that of a rapidly changing society and a speeding car. A well-designed car might start to shake at a hundred miles an hour, and at some speed above that it would shake apart. The Kingdom watchers in American universities began to schedule seminars on the stresses in Saudi society.

The Midas Curse

When Sheikh Yamani spoke of a car shaking as it moves above a hundred miles an hour, he meant the impact of wealth on Saudi society. The Saudis have one of the most curious problems ever faced by a people. They have too much money. King Midas wished that everything he touched might turn into gold, and when the wish was granted, he nearly starved to death because he could not eat gold. If the Saudis pump their oil at the rate of 10 million barrels a day, the $110 billion (at $30 a barrel) which that produces *in a year* is really more than they can use. If they spend the money, that too-rapid spending begins to tear the society apart. Yet they cannot escape their Midas touch, for if they cut their production back to 5 million barrels a day, that would create a shortage; then the spot price would move up, the OPEC ministers would declare a new level for oil, and shortly the Saudis would get as much money for their reduced production as they did for their original production. No matter which way they turn, the Saudis cannot escape their money, and the money makes them a target, both internally and externally. The more money they have, the less safe they may be. So they move cautiously.

The Saudis have been accommodating. When the Iranian revolution cut back Iran's oil production in 1979, the Saudis increased their oil output. Young technocrats opposed the high rates of production; they said the Saudi society could not absorb the money, that so much money was perilous, that the Saudi output should be more closely matched to the country's needs. But the oil policy was decided by political factors, not economics; the Saudis wanted to maintain their dominant role in OPEC and to remind the West of their own importance. When the Iranians and Iraqis bombed each other's oil facilities in 1980, the Saudis once again stepped up the production rate to 10 million barrels a day.

In the mid-seventies American policy makers hoped the Saudis would increase their capacity to 16 or 18 million barrels a day, to float us through the 1980s, until new energy technologies could help. Then it was noticed that the Saudis were not ordering the capital equipment for expansion very quickly. If they did not have the capacity, they could not be diplomatically pressured to deliver it. The U.S. General Accounting Office then came forth with a more modest projection: 14 million barrels a day in 1982. We do not hear much of 14 million barrels a day in 1982 anymore. The Saudis are accommodating, but they keep their own counsel.

There are limits to the "special relationship" between the Saudis and the United States. In the 1973 Yom Kippur War the Saudis embargoed Aramco's shipments to the U.S. Navy, as well as to the United States, and the Pentagon had to call unembargoed British Petroleum to reassure itself of fuel for the Sixth Fleet. Later, the Saudis sought to put some distance between the Americans and themselves. High-level Saudi delegations went on state visits to France and Germany. The Saudis let it be known that they were unhappy. They had spent, they said, $19 billion on arms, all on American advice, and did not have much to show for it; the Americans, said some of the American-trained Saudis, were training their small army as if it would have to fight on the plains of Western Europe. The Saudis watched the debate on the U.S. Rapid

Deployment Force that was meant to reassure them; they could quote the generals who said the Rapid Deployment Force could not get anywhere very fast and could not last thirty days when it got there. They could also quote the generals who said the United States Army was understaffed, underequipped, semiliterate, and not ready to fight. The Saudis complained that the lack of a settlement between Israelis and Palestinians left them vulnerable to the radical regimes that espoused the Palestinians and said they could not afford to be identified with the United States in the Arab world. They did not, they said, want an American military presence in Saudi Arabia because it would make them too vulnerable; they were distressed that the Americans had not been able to retrieve their own citizens who were trapped in the embassy in Tehran. And finally, they were annoyed at the leaks from American intelligence services that worried so much so publicly about the survival of the Kingdom.

But when the Iraqis and the Iranians went to war, the Saudis were glad to have some AWACS (Airborne Warning and Control System) radar planes. Thomas McHale, a former senior adviser to the Kingdom, had dinner with Prince Saud al-Faisal, the Princetonian foreign minister. The Germans and the French and the Japanese had all been wooing the Saudis; were the Saudis going to be weaned from the Americans? Saud al-Faisal narrowed his eyes for a moment, looking like his hawklike desert grandfather.

"How many ships in the Japanese navy?" he said.

In spite of the California connection, in spite of the visits by bankers and construction company vice-presidents, it is not easy to know what is going on in the Kingdom. In a society without a parliament and a press, information comes out as the king wishes. Only one television crew has filmed there; few writers have been allowed access. Kremlin watchers see who stands next to whom at the May Day review and can read nuances in *Pravda* and *Izvestia*. Kingdom watchers learn similar nuances.

When the pivotal importance of Saudi Arabia became evident, after the First Oil Crisis, an irregular group of Kingdom watchers began to meet: some oil types, two stray Brits, some career and former career foreign-service officers, and some professors who are Arabists. (I was one of the two who did not speak Arabic. I noticed that the Kingdom watchers switched to Arabic when the bill came and it was time to decide who would pick up the tab. You begin to learn some Arabic under such circumstances, but it is of very limited use.) The Kingdom watchers gather intelligence much the way intelligence was gathered in the days when most of the world consisted of kingdoms: from their own occasional trips, from travelers, from court gossip, from whatever information the traveling princes of the realm dispense. It would be hard to find another time in history when we were so dependent on a single country, let alone one so far from the Western, Protestant-ethic tradition. Gradually, the question became not only, What will the Saudis do? It became, Will the Saudis survive?

The Kingdom watchers have a nightmare scenario. All the bankers say the world cannot survive a Third Oil Crisis. By "the world" they mean the present financial system. In the Second Oil Crisis the militants took over Iran. Oil production fell to practically nothing, and when it resumed, it had been cut by 3 million barrels a day. We saw the militants at the embassy on television, shaking their fists at the cameras. When the Iranians cut back, the Saudis opened the reserves by a million barrels a day, but the scramble was so intense the price of oil doubled. Now the only reserve left is in Saudi Arabia, and to a minor extent in its immediate Gulf neighbors.

The nightmare scenario is not that the Russian tanks rumble out of Afghanistan and down to the Gulf. The nightmare is called Bad Crowd in Riyadh. The Bad Crowd does just what it did across the Gulf. It burns the Stars and

Stripes, and maybe the Union Jack for good measure. It shakes its fists at the television cameras. It chants slogans about imperialism. It has a leader, maybe a priest, maybe a colonel, maybe a religious colonel, like Muammar Qaddafi, and the leader says: "We're buried in Western *junk,* Western corruption; look at them, they have no family honor and all their women are easy, Satan has touched them! Let us not be seduced, to be ruled by their promises! Out with the rotting corruption! Back to the cool, the noble, the pure; back to the Word of God! Back to God!"

Even as the Americans get airlifted out, even as the crowds roam the streets, trashing the visible signs of the Westerners, even so, would they not still have to sell the oil?

No. Certainly not 9 million barrels a day. They may have $100 billion in their bank account. Before the oil they lived off dates and pilgrims, and the pilgrims still come. It's not likely that they would have to support themselves by a pilgrim tax. The Iranians made more money delivering 3 million barrels a day than they did at 6 billion, because the very action of cutting back doubled the price.

When the Iranians cut the supplies, the Saudis were still there. But the Saudis are nearly a third of OPEC, and there is no one to replace them. That's why we could survive the Second Oil Crisis but not the Third. Bad Crowd in Riyadh gives you oil at $100 a barrel, gasoline rationing with gasoline at $6 a gallon, a third of all airline flights grounded, lines around the block at the banks, the Chase Manhattan sinking from sight, the stock market dropping sixty points a day: general unpleasantness, followed by real depression.

So the Kingdom watchers phone each other and meet for lunch. Paul comes back from the Kingdom and says he has good news and bad news. We do not discard even trivial information.

Good news: the telephones work. Pretty soon, video

screens, Saudi operators, even directory assistance. That's what money can buy: a $7-billion telephone system. Directory assistance is not so easy in a country that has no street names, no house numbers, no town planning. It's a tribal society, and everybody loves talking on the phone. When the telephone contract was first awarded, the American consortium was angry that the prize went to the Dutch and the Swedes. It was said the Americans had the low bid but had the wrong prince as agent. It was said the commissions alone, just for delivering the contract, would total several hundred million dollars. Ancient history.

More good news: the new Jidda airport works, bigger than Heathrow, bigger than O'Hare. When I visited Paul in Saudi Arabia, he saw me off at the old Jidda airport. Only one door was functional in the old airport building. There was a crowd trying to get through this single door, the exiting passengers. Another crowd, of which we found ourselves a part, was trying to enter, to get through the same door. Paul is built like an NFL fullback. Our crowd lined up behind him and pushed him, and Paul had no choice but to open the hole off tackle. Our crowd poured through, leaving the exiting crowd sprawled on the floor, fetally clutching its suitcases, its baby goats, its bags of oranges. You do hate to trample people as part of an airport departure. No more of that. Let all the *hajjis* come, let O'Hare and Heathrow sulk; this is what money can buy.

More good news: Mansour al-Turki, formerly deputy finance minister, is the new head of the University of Riyadh. Mansour is a burly man, whose *thaub* swings like a cassock when he walks, so that he moves like an Italian bishop. Nice, ironic sense of humor, very smart, very hardworking. Give Mansour $5 billion and you'll have a hell of a school. Five billion dollars, the budgeted capital. Take a little while, but you'll get it.

Not so good news: "The Saudis think the President is sandbagging them because we promised progress in getting the Palestinians autonomy on the West Bank, and instead the Israelis are building settlements."

News: preemptive Islamic austerity. No more dog food at the market. Dogs unclean. No water in the hotel swimming pools. Too much risk of mixed bathing, men and women. No women working, too likely they might meet men.

Bad news: "There really is an impact from across the Gulf. Khomeini's broadcasts get recorded, and the cassettes passed around. The Shiites in the eastern province are giving the royal family a lot of trouble; they think they're being treated as second-class citizens by the Sunnis." The oil is in the eastern province. The Saudis are Sunnis; the Shiites are Muslims like those in power in Iran.

"The Khomeini cassettes are also getting to the foreign workers in the Kingdom—mostly Yemenis, but Baluchis and Pakistanis, too. Because they're mostly Arab, and all of them Muslim, they feel they have a claim on the wealth, that they're not just invited guests, that they ought to be able to participate. But the really bad news is the mosque."

Say "the mosque" to a Kingdom watcher, and you mean not only the grand mosque in Mecca, the holiest place in Islam, but the seizure of the mosque, in the fall of 1979, by a group described as religious fanatics.

"I hear," Paul said, "that they weren't just religious nuts; they were really trying for a coup. It's said they had some support in the army. It took the Saudis three weeks to clean them out, and they had to call French security forces to help; that's what I heard. [A French Kingdom watcher says the French supplied fewer than a dozen specialists from a counterterrorist unit, as advisers.] And I hear the corruption at the top is beginning to irritate people. The royal family spreads the largess around, but they're taking so much that, in this environment, it makes them vulnerable."

A Saudi prince—there are at least 1,400 princes—came

to talk to a group; not only our Kingdom watchers, but others. "How do we know you, the royal family, will still be around in five years, or ten years?" he was asked. "We thought the Shah was in Iran for good."

Prince Bindar bin Sultan said: "We are not Iran. The Shah was an upstart, the son of an army colonel, who installed himself as ruler after a coup. Our family has ruled the Kingdom for years. We are at one with the people."

The Kingdom watchers used to take this for granted. There were 5,000 members of the royal family, and they covered all the bases in the society. There was no parliament or congress, but there was the institution of the *majlis* —anybody with a grievance or a problem could go to the king and get a hearing, if not with the king, with a prince, or a sheikh; thus everybody felt a part of society and had a connection with those in power. The laws of Islam ruled, and the king was on the throne.

"It still works," Paul said, "but when there are deals in the hundreds of millions of dollars, it doesn't work quite so well."

In the Equestrian Club, in Riyadh, smoked glass filters the glare of the desert sun, turning it into ice-blue light that falls on luxurious leather sofas and splendid carpets. In the $10-million clubhouse are swimming pools, squash courts, music rooms, and meeting rooms worthy of $300-million deals. There are only 183 members, all royal or big business, and no small deals.

But the office of Amir Abbas Hoveyda was equally plush; book-lined, with impeccable eighteenth-century French antique furniture, carpets for a museum. That was in Tehran. I had a private conversation with Hoveyda, the former prime minister, the minister of the court, an elegant, cultivated man in elegant British tailoring. He lectured me on conservation. "The price of oil will rise because conservation in the West will fail," he said. "The problem is leadership, *discipline.*" We talked not only about oil but about books and film; Hoveyda's brother had been a respected film critic in Paris before he had become his country's ambassador to the UN. Hoveyda was a part of the Shah's government, but since he had never been accused of the Shah's excesses, he did not leave Iran when he could have.

Sometime later I was to see this elegant gentleman's picture on the front page of *The New York Times.* He looked tired and haggard. Right after the picture was taken, he was stood up against the wall of the prison courtyard and shot.

We can count on the Saudis to be accommodating, but not to float us through the 1980s without serious efforts on our part. They know, themselves, that thirteen of the present rulers of Arab states removed their predecessors by force. The scale of oil revenues changed the world's money and made the House of Saud the richest family in the world, and one of the most vulnerable. Its customs are not ours, but with the extreme scenarios in mind, we can say fervently, *Allah yittowil umrak,* "May God lengthen your life."

I asked one of our stray Brit Kingdom watchers what he thought the odds were of a Third Oil Crisis, and of the Saudis surviving the decade intact. He puffed on his pipe and dismissed the exercise. Did I think he was a London bookmaker? Then, without further prompting, he puffed some pipe smoke and said, like a bookmaker, "Six-five, choice, too close to call."

10

RECYCLING THE PETRODOLLARS: TREACHEROUS SEAS, GALE-FORCE WINDS, FIRE!

It seems very unfair. First we have to worry about the richest family in the world, the Sauds, for fear of getting something worse. And now I am about to tell you that we have to worry about the Rockefellers. You are going to tell me the Sauds and the Rockefellers will always be able to afford a nice house, going out to dinner, tuition, travel, and the other amenities, and you are absolutely right. But we do have to spare a worry for David Rockefeller and his bank, the Chase Manhattan.

I am using the Chase Manhattan only symbolically, for what we are talking about is all the banks; Chase Manhattan happens to be a good example because it is a very big international lender. In 1979 almost half of its profits came from overseas. We are talking about the survival of the System again, this time from a different point of view. Awhile ago the System was looking for a key currency to believe in. *Credere.*

This problem is called Recycling the Petrodollars. The connection between the Sauds and the Rockefellers is that the Saud family puts its money in the Rockefeller family bank. Then the Rockefeller family bank lends the money around the world, sometimes to the people who need more money to pay the Saud family the new price of oil. Gertrude Stein said once that the money is always the money, only the pockets are different.

If the oil consumers could sell enough to the oil producers, the trade would come out even. If the Kenyans could raise the price of their coffee enough to pay for the increased price of gasoline and fertilizer, and the Saudis would drink enough coffee at the higher price to match that, no problem. But there aren't enough Saudis to drink that much coffee at any price. As we've seen, the oil producers who are "low absorbers" can't buy enough to make up for all the petrodollars they've suddenly earned.

The Saud family is richer and puts the money in the Rockefeller family bank. The Kenyans can't pay for the gasoline at the new price, so they go to the bank for a loan. Now they owe the Rockefellers, who are holding the money for the Saudis. It would be simpler if the Kenyans just owed the Saudis, but that isn't the way it has happened. The bank trusts that the Kenyans will cut back on their gasoline use and increase their earnings enough to pay off the loan. Then the petrodollars will have been recycled.

The problem is that the banks are in the middle, and the *scale* has gotten so large. Remember that game called What OPEC Could Buy. OPEC could buy, in 1975, the whole New York Times Company for one and a half hours' surplus. It could buy the Washington Post Company, with *Newsweek* and all its TV stations, with another one and a half hours' surplus. It could buy all the American media, ABC, CBS, the *Los Angeles Times*—the works —in a week, and it could buy all the stocks on the London exchange in eight months, arithmetically speaking. It takes a big scale to rock a big System.

When the price of oil goes up, it creates more money in several ways. We'll come back to those ways in a moment. The oil money that isn't spent goes into the banks, the banks lend the money, and borrowed money is just as good as earned money in bidding for more oil. With more money around, the Club says, "Hey, that's inflation, we have to raise the price of oil again to get even," and the cycle goes around again in bigger and bigger swings.

Oil becomes a quasi-currency, and then both the Sauds and the Rockefellers worry about the System. David Rockefeller even went for the marine metaphor in a speech. "Treacherous economic seas," he said, in his marine forecast, "and gale-force financial winds, strong enough to capsize even successful countries."

Pinstriped bankers meet in worried conclaves. Can the System handle the petrodollars? If it doesn't, will there be a Great Depression, like that of the 1930s? Is there a way to slow the process? Would the world accept slower growth —or permanent recession—to save the System? What's the alternative? More and more inflation? First the million-dollar house, and then, someday, the million-dollar hamburger?

Oil Creates Money

Ordinarily, oil should be a commodity like any other. But the current scale of the oil transfers, sent through the banks, creates more money.

A higher price for oil sucks money out of an oil-consuming country. That country then has less money to spend for cars and apples and gasoline. Less money, less activity, recession, unemployment. *Deflation*—the oil price increase acts like a tax. In the oil-consuming country there is less money; in the oil producer there is more. So far it balances.

Things being what they are, the tendency is for the oil-consuming country to print a little more money to ease the pain of recession. That's politics, not economics or banking. Sending out real assets for the oil means very hard work. The central banker himself may want to tough it out, but the prime minister is already under attack by the labor unions and the parliament is restive.

The oil producer still has the money paid for the oil, though, and doesn't need it. Into the bank it goes. Now the bank has a deposit, let's say, just to reverse all that OPEC gigantism, of $100. The Federal Reserve says that bank has to keep 10 percent of the deposit as a reserve. You walk in and borrow $90. You put that money in your checking account; now it's a deposit there, and your cousin Charley can walk in and borrow $81, because that fractional reserve is set aside each time. Your cousin Charley deposits his loan in *his* checking account, and the bank lends $72.90 to the next borrower. That's the way the multiplier works, and it keeps on going. If the Federal Reserve wants more money in the banks, it lowers that fractional reserve, so that you can borrow $95 instead of $90, and your cousin Charley can borrow $85.50 instead of $81. If the Federal Reserve wants there to be less money, it raises that fractional reserve.

Question: What's the multiplier in Euroland? Theoretically, it's infinite. The Rockefeller bank of Euroland gets an OPEC deposit of $100, and it can lend the whole $100 to you; and when you deposit the $100 in the Deutsche Bank Luxembourg, that bank can lend the whole $100 to your cousin Charley, who puts it into the Banco d'Espagna of Euroland, and so on, so the original OPEC $100 gets quite a bit of mileage.

In practice, it is said, the prudence of the banks cuts down that flow. Or some of the deposits leak back into the reserve-system banks of the world, and then they get wound down in the regular way. But nobody really knows, because there is no uniform reporting system out of Euroland.

If you think this is dizzying, so do the bankers. David Rockefeller is dizzy, too. Treacherous seas, he says.

Bankers do not like to be gloomy. Somebody might get frightened and take his deposit out of the bank. The bankers are particularly uneasy because they thought they had this all worked out.

The point in What OPEC Could Buy is not that it was going to buy CBS. The point is that with a stroke of the pen, at least one OPEC country had leaped ahead of the major industrial countries in terms of their external assets, their ability to hold foreign exchange.

The West Germans, the thrifty, hard-working West Germans, had gone to the office and the factory, and hammered and blowtorched and bolted, and they had infested the world with their Beetle Volkswagens, their machinery, and their chemicals, and they had earned, by 1975, a surplus of $40 billion.

And the Japanese, with their beehive cooperation, had gone to the factory early in the morning and sung "Hail to Thee, O Matsushita," the company song, and done their group calisthenics, and hammered and buzzed around and swamped the world in television sets and stereos and cameras and little cars, and after years of work they were on their way to multibillion-dollar surpluses.

The United States and Britain and Italy didn't have any such surpluses at all (though the United States did have the long-term investments from its key-currency heyday).

And now, suddenly, one country—one family—had an exchange surplus of $60 billion! Without even working!

That was unconsciously confusing, because the Protestant ethic and the spirit of capitalism have been mixed, blended, and intercausal since the sixteenth century, as Max Weber pointed out. Success enables you to see if you are in a state of grace, and work is honorable because it leads to success. Even the Japanese were Protestants in this way of thinking, Robert Bellah wrote in *Tokugawa Religion*. If you have been working until midnight and now have triumphed with a $2,000-a-year raise, and the fellow down the block suddenly inherits $1 billion, you may have metaphysical doubts about the rewards of work.

In the days following the First Oil Crisis, the financial people were very fearful. The economists had a rapt audience. Everybody wanted to know: How much money is OPEC going to have, and what is going to happen to the world? So the economists flexed their equations, plugged in the computers, and came up with these numbers.

The staff economists at the Organization for Economic Cooperation and Development said that OPEC would have $740 billion by 1980.

The staff at the World Bank said OPEC would have $654 billion by 1980 and $1.2 trillion by 1985.

The Morgan Bank was conservative and said OPEC would have $250 billion in 1978.

Those who could understand the process then went into a quiet panic, because numbers like those would break the System—doors closed, lines around the block, bank holiday, apples on the street corners. The banks would float away on this tide of money. They would lend the money to the countries without oil, and those countries wouldn't be able to repay the loans, and the banks whose loans weren't repaid would be insolvent, and the System would come apart, one joint at a time. Dire. This time the wolf is here.

The problem with the economic forecasts was that the

mathematics were elegant, but the reality wasn't. Not one forecast was even close. The economists had left something out.

Christmas Morning in Arabia

Right after the First Oil Crisis, I had a visit from a young Saudi, whom we called Abdul Latif III, to differentiate him from Abdul Latif al-Hamad, the director of the Kuwait Fund, and Ahmad Abdul Latif, at the Saudi Arabian Monetary Agency. He was not dressed in a white *thaub,* and he did not have a beard and sunglasses like the Arabs in the cartoons. He was dressed, in fact, in a $700 made-to-order pinstripe suit from Dunhill Tailors on 57th Street in New York, the model with the sleeve buttons that button, favored by the world's bankers, which made him look rather elegantly Italian. He had been in an investment-management class at the Harvard Business School, where I had lectured some years before, and he was looking me up, he said, because his family was looking for a bank.

Abdul Latif III was not a prince and not a sheikh. He was from a trading family well-off enough to send him to school in the United States. "My grandfather walked beside his camels, with the goods on them, like the peddlers in the United States in the last century who went from farm to farm in a horse and buggy. My father set up a store, just as the sons of the peddlers set up stores. And now we're in banking and construction, and we have the franchises of General Electric and Siemens and Phillips.

"You have to remember that the government has the oil, not the citizen. So we don't see all this oil revenue until the government spends it. But it does spend it. I have a friend at the American embassy who says it's like Christmas morning at eleven o'clock, wrapping paper everywhere. The ports are backed up for ninety days. It costs five riyals to bring a bag of cement by helicopter from a ship, and the cement itself only costs seven riyals. The cost of living is going up. We even had to import sand; we didn't have the right kind of sand for building.

"The first thing we noticed after the embargo was lifted was that these carpetbaggers had arrived, staying anywhere, sleeping anywhere, assuming the Arabs were so ignorant and so rich they would buy anything. That's faded. The second thing was, there was money around. Some of the old trading firms, fifty and seventy years old, would have been lucky in the 1960s to have a hundred thousand riyals [about $28,000] in the bank. Now they had a lot more.

"The money showed up first in real estate. If somebody bought a corner for five hundred riyals, the next day he would be offered two thousand, the next week ten thousand. Three months later he could get a hundred thousand riyals. My father and my uncles and my cousins would meet, and what they would talk about was real estate. My uncle would say, 'A hundred thousand riyals for that corner? Crazy!' "

"You want a bank," I said. "You could buy the Bank of America with one week's surplus; that is, you could buy half of sixty-nine million shares currently selling in the market for one point two billion dollars." I was joking, though the arithmetic was right.

"We had in mind a small, friendly bank," said Abdul Latif III.

It occurred to me that the Arabs could solve the surplus simply by the right company selection. They should buy the Penn Central, Lockheed, Chrysler, and the U.S. Post Office, and then all the recycling problems would be solved.

Abdul Latif III went home without a bank. His family did establish a bank in Bahrain, off the coast of Saudi Arabia, and that bank went into syndications in Europe.

The next time I saw him he had put on weight, and he had lost much of the rather sweet quality he had had as a student. His half brother Mahmoud was in Germany, negotiating an industrial deal; his half brother Gamal was in London; and the business was expanding so fast it was running out of capable family members, even though it had gone to the ends of cousindom. The family was still looking for an American bank. Even though Mahmoud and Hassan and Abdul Latif III all used the phrase *Im'shallah,* "as God wills," they were working as hard as if work produced a glimmer of the state of grace.

The bank set up in Bahrain by the family of Abdul Latif III had a lot of company. On the once sleepy island there were now 120 banks, the Bank of America and the Bank of Tokyo, Citicorp and Barclays, and David Rockefeller's Chase Manhattan. And beside them were the new Arab banks, some of them big-league banks indeed, such as the Arab Banking Corporation, whose capital was $1 billion. Some of the Arab banks also went to Europe; suddenly there were 32 Arab banks in Paris.

All of these banks had the same objective: they wanted the petrodollar deposits.

What the economists left out was this: they didn't know anybody would import *sand* into Saudi Arabia. Abdul Latif III's family had these buildings halfway up in Jidda and no cement; the cement was so far out in the backed-up harbor that it cost 5 riyals to bring in a 7-riyal bag of cement, and that process was repeated throughout the Middle East until Christmas morning was over and life was better organized. OPEC spent enough to throw off the projections. And because the higher price of oil meant less money in the West for everything else, there was a deep recession, which meant that some industries cut back, laid off workers, and used less oil. So the OPEC surplus didn't get to a trillion dollars, and the System functioned, and the wolf did not come.

But even with cement at 12 riyals a bag, OPEC still had a lot of money in the banks, and the bankers had two fears. One was irrational but didn't seem so, and the other was quite real.

The irrational fear was: Look at these Arab deposits piling up, we take the Arab deposits and we lend them out for ten years to Turkey and Brazil, but the money is only in there for thirty days at a time. What if the Arabs yanked the money the first of the month?

A banker cannot make a loan unless he has a deposit. It seems a little silly to state that so baldly, but if three college-educated Americans in ten don't know we have to import oil, I don't feel so bad about saying something bald. Banks do not lend their own money. They lend the money somebody else has left there.

If you have just bidden good-bye to a happy bunch of Brazilians, for whom you have bought a nice dinner and to whom you have given a big loan, and from whom, on the front end, you have gotten a big fee, you must have somebody else's money on deposit to cover that loan. If all the somebodies take their money out of your bank, and you can't get any more, that's a run on the bank; hang up the "Closed" sign.

If the Arabs yank their money out of your bank, and you have that Brazilian loan on your books, you'd better get another deposit right away. But if you are a member of the System in good standing, you can get that Arab money right back again. The Arabs have taken it somewhere—to Britain or Switzerland—and you can call up and borrow it back again, from another bank. You have to pay more, of course, and naturally it may not be the exact very same money, but all you want to do is cover your Brazilian loan.

In the early oil days, the Gulf sheikhs would demand to be paid in gold and silver coins, and they would put the chest of coins under their beds. No more. Now they put the money in the bank, or start a bank themselves.

So the money has to stay in the System, and if it is in the System, a bank that is in good standing can borrow back the deposits that have been yanked away. If the bank is not in good standing, it doesn't get its phone calls returned. If that happens, the banking authorities, the Federal Reserve, the Bundesbank, or the Bank of England put that sick bank into Intensive Care and the other banks close ranks around it. But the System still functions, as long as it's only one bank. If it happened to a lot of banks at the same time, obviously there wouldn't be enough Intensive Care units, and the effect would be like an epidemic or plague.

So much for the irrational fear; an individual bank could be burned, but Arabs yanking deposits don't bring down the System because there's nowhere else to put the money.

The rational fear was: Maybe the System can't handle all this money. What if it gets so much money that it can't find prudent places to lend it?

The borrower has to be able to pay the money back. If the Kenyans borrow for their oil bill, we presume they are going to tighten their belts and sell some more coffee and sisal, because you can't just borrow the money and then burn it up in Sunday driving.

The largest pile of OPEC money was at the Saudi Arabian Monetary Agency, whose chief was Abdul Aziz al-Qūrashi, he of the handsome features, the Saudi Alistair Cooke. Al-Qūrashi sat with his American adviser, David Mulford, formerly of Merrill Lynch White Weld, and worked out, under royal instructions, a cautious policy. They set aside money for the development plans, they bought United States government bonds and Bundesbank notes, and then they made a list of the biggest banks in the world and started at the top. They put money into the five biggest American banks, the three biggest Swiss banks, the three biggest German banks, and the two biggest British banks, and then they went on to the next tier of banks.

The banks formed syndicates—you take part of my deal and I'll take part of yours—and they lent the money out.

A panel of economists headed by Paul McCracken, the former chairman of the Council of Economic Advisers, studied the phenomenon. "The private banks of the OECD," they said, the Western countries, "acted as a turntable for the OPEC surplus funds." The Brazilians and the Koreans and the Kenyans didn't have any oil and their oil bills went up, but they stayed in business because the private banks lent them the money they got from the oil producers.

The chief turntable mechanism was the banks of Euroland. The banks were big enough for conservative depositors. The Deutsche Bank, for example, is the biggest bank in West Germany. Its headquarters are in Frankfurt, but it has 13,042 other offices and 146 billion deutsch marks in assets. But the Deutsche Bank in Luxembourg grew even bigger than its parent! The depositors liked Euroland because there are no politics in Euroland, no nasty overtones about where the money came from, and the rates are better.

The borrowers liked Euroland because the terms are easier. If Peru went to David Rockefeller's Chase Manhattan in New York, the Comptroller of the Currency might be looking over the Chase's shoulder, and the Chase would have to be stringent. If the Peruvians went to an international agency like the IMF, they might find a stony-faced banker telling them what to do politically: raise taxes, cut imports.

In Euroland, if you've got the loan, you've got it; it's up to the bank to measure its own risks.

Some said the banks were so eager to get the business that they made loans that were risky, and hence endangered the System. One banker, Wilfried Guth, of the

Deutsche Bank, fretted publicly: "The discrepancy between the wealth of wisdom on the macroeconomics of international lending and the scarcity of information on individual banks' experiences is paralleled by an interesting phenomenon which might have delighted Sigmund Freud. Prominent bankers have long expressed grave reservations with respect to the unsound state of affairs in the rollover markets, while at the same time their banks continue to be very active participants in these very markets."

In other words, the bankers were sounding grave about unsound loans and telling each other to slow down the lending, and then they would go right ahead and lend. "Let's cut back; you first," they would say to each other. If the Germans and the Americans got suddenly prudent, there would be an eager Spanish or Italian or Japanese bank willing to step in.

The bankers had a problem. Imprudent banks are supposed to be punished by the marketplace, by going out of business. But the banks were so interdependent that an imprudent bank could cause the collapse of the System.

I am going to give you only the very primitive elements of the mechanics. It is easy to understand the musical-chairs element: if Bank A owes Bank B $100, and Bank B owes Bank C $110, and Bank C owes Bank D $120, the music has to keep going. Not only the music, but the tempo. Velocity is also part of money, so if a slowdown occurs, it has to happen in a controlled way, or some bank doesn't get paid in time. Then Bank D says, "The money didn't come in" to Bank C, which says it to Bank B, and so on.

The central banks of the Western countries went to Switzerland and agreed on something called the Basel Concordat—wonderful name, right out of the early days of the Protestant ethic. The Basel Concordat is a volunteer fire department. The central bankers warned that they were not there to bail out some profligate bank, but to preserve the System. "The main thing," said Wilfried Guth of the Deutsche Bank, "is to extinguish the fire very quickly before heat or explosion endangers all surroundings."

When you start up a bank, you have to put in some capital. Then you get some deposits, and then you lend the deposits. In a proper bank these three items bear a prudent relationship to one another. If you are a little country bank with a capital of $100,000, it would be very imprudent of you to loan Brazil $50 million. So you want a prudent relationship between the capital and the assets, which is to say the loans on the books, and between the loans and the deposits. In the Western countries the financial agents of the government are there with a definition of prudence.

Euroland is not only free of such annoyances; it is very, very competitive, and the banks began to lend more and more money in relation to their own capital, the money the shareholders had put in. You can see how competitive it is by looking at the crunch that followed the Second Oil Crisis. The international bank borrowing rate is called LIBOR, London Interbank Offered Rate. It's like the prime rate. In the United States, General Motors borrows at the prime rate, and a small company might pay two points over prime, or three. The extra points are the bank's margin for the risk. After the First Oil Crisis, industrial countries were paying 1¼ percent over LIBOR, and the newer, developing countries, 2½ percent over LIBOR. That gave the banks a little cushion. But the banks were so eager to get the business that they elbowed each other, offering better and better terms, and after the Second Oil Crisis the industrial countries were paying only .5 percent over LIBOR, and the developing countries only .68 percent.

The Euromarket got the world through the First Oil

Crisis by taking the OPEC funds and lending them, and it is working through the Second Oil Crisis.

If Zaire or Turkey got into trouble and couldn't repay, the banks sat down with them and said, "That's okay, take longer to pay back." That's called rescheduling. The bank has gotten its placement fee on the first day, and it gets its interest, and the borrower gets longer to pay back.

Let's tot up what happened. First, the banks got the OPEC surpluses and lent them. Economic activity went down because of recession; and all other things being equal, you would have expected *deflation,* not *inflation.* Deflation is unpleasant, so the central banks loosened up a bit. Then there was all that money in the banks, and the money was lent. Banks create money by lending it, so the money was there even with recession.

Then the price of oil went up again, and oil is a quasi-currency: more oil, more bank deposits, more money.

Then the banks gave a boost to the supply of money by increasing the loans they made in relationship to their own capital. Let's say that relationship was five to one, nice and conservative these days. You have the deposits and you've made the loans, up to the level Grandfather thought was all right. Now some more borrowers come in. Do you say no? You could make more money with those loans, and if you don't make them, those scrappy Japanese banks will make them, and then they'll build a relationship with the borrower and it might be hard to get the borrower back at some future date. So you make the loans, and your ratio goes to ten to one. The scrappy Japanese banks hustle more, and their ratio goes to twenty to one. So, by increasing the ratio of loans to capital, the banks put more money out into the world on the same base.

Now we have more money out from all these factors: first, the tendency of consuming countries to inflate a bit to offset the depressing effects of higher oil prices; second, from the lending in Euroland, where more of the deposit is available to lend, because there are no official reserves required; and third, from the lending, by the banks, of more money in relationship to their own capital.

Since the OPEC countries picked the biggest banks first, those banks increased their share of the market, and the other banks had to hustle to compete, and that competition drove the lenders to make riskier loans.

The banks were spinning out money like cotton candy. In one year, 1978, the Euromarket grew by $200 billion. The Brazilians alone had borrowed $52 billion and were growing ferociously. One Brazilian banker said, "If you owe enough money, they can't afford to let you go broke."

The banks drew up a list of countries that might have trouble paying back, and there were seventeen countries on the list: Brazil, the Philippines, Korea, Turkey, Thailand, Poland, Pakistan, Nicaragua, Panama, Egypt, Jamaica, Ethiopia, Kenya, Morocco, Yugoslavia, Sudan, Zaire. Those countries are good customers of the United States and of Western Europe. If trade slows down, somebody's unemployed. That's the list at the moment; it may get longer. Those developing countries need money to grow. But *half* of all the new loans are now going only to pay off the old loans. Obviously, the developing countries can't keep borrowing just for oil and the old loans, or the loans never get paid.

The borrowing countries are not unhappy with inflation. It lets them pay back with cheaper dollars.

There's the cycle: oil, banks, loans, inflation, new price for oil, banks, loans, inflation.

Is there a way to stop the wheel without stripping the gears?

As unpleasant as inflation has been, we have not yet felt the impact of the Second Oil Crisis, in 1979, because it takes a while for credit expansions to work through the System. It takes one year, says the IMF, before the expanded monetary reserves actually increase the money supply, and it takes about thirty months before those increases in world reserves turn into world inflation.

So the impact of the Second Oil Crisis will be felt in 1982–83, at which time the shocked oil producers will say, "Look at this inflation," and they will raise the price of oil again. Thirty months after that we will have another burst of inflation, and . . .

"Lifelong practices," wrote Keynes, of bankers, "make them the most romantic and least realistic of men. It is so much their stock in trade that their position should not be questioned, that they do not even question it themselves until it is too late. Like the honest citizens they are, they feel a proper indignation at the perils of the wicked world in which they live—when the perils mature; but they do not foresee them. So, if they are saved, it will be, I expect, in their own despite."

The individual banker, looking at his loans, says, "This one is secured by coffee in transit; this one is secured by a shipment of shoes; this is a debt of a sovereign government, and sovereign governments never default."

"Sovereign governments never default" is not true. Leaving aside the Cubas of the world, which default and go to the other side, sovereign governments do default when they cannot make their payments. But if they want to stay in the System, they are apologetic about it. Then they sit down with the banks and work out a plan; they get a new loan to pay the old one back, and the banks hope that coffee or sisal or copper goes up, and the banks will be paid back.

In one respect the world is now going through a period of economic history that has some parallels with the United States in the last century. The United States was then a capital-short country. Individual banks could issue their own currency; a Chicago dollar might sell in New

York for 80 cents. The debtor farmers wanted greenbacks, cheap money, so that they could get money and pay it back easily. "Free silver!" was the rallying cry of the West; the eastern bankers wanted sound money, limited in quantity.

When William Jennings Bryan electrified his presidential convention by declaring, "You shall not crucify mankind upon a cross of gold," he was speaking for the greenback borrowers, against the hard-money gold lenders.

The United States went from boom to crash, from banking panic to banking panic. After the Panic of 1907, Congress established a National Monetary Commission and finally, in 1913, the Federal Reserve. The Federal Reserve Act says its purpose is "to furnish an elastic currency." The creation of the Federal Reserve with its "elastic currency" coincided with World War I, when the European governments abandoned the gold standard and went to paper money so that they could pay for the war. The Federal Reserve's "elastic currency," its own notes, were money in addition to Treasury notes and silver dollars, and thus the Federal Reserve could give the banks an infusion if the depositors suddenly lined up to take their deposits out. In the banking crisis of the 1930s, the Federal Reserve failed to prevent those bank failures. Its critics said it was mismanaged. The New Deal buttressed the system with banking reforms and deposit insurance, and now the banking system has the faith of the country. *Credere,* belief. And the Federal Reserve is the Lender of Last Resort.

Aggressive bankers think things will sort themselves out. Conservative bankers pull out their pocket watches and say it's getting late. This is what they see: The nonoil countries of the Third World have borrowed $183 billion from the World Bank, and from governments, under fairly stringent conditions. They have also borrowed another $190 billion from multinational banks. The bulk of that is

due within the next three years. The multinational banks
are up to their lending limits. Prudently, they can't lend
more. How can the developing countries get the money to
continue to grow, and still pay off their loans?

The confident bankers say, "Look at all that talk of
gloom and doom back in 1975; we did it before and we
can do it again. We handled the First Oil Crisis and we can
handle the Second Oil Crisis. The mechanism works; why
do you want to tinker with it? Sure, the bureaucrats at the
central banks would like to get their fingers into our business. But no banks have failed because of bad loans; banks
fail because they speculate in the foreign-exchange markets, or they make the wrong investment decisions."

Oil—bank deposits—bank loans—inflation. When I
tried this thesis on some Latin American bankers, their
reaction was so different it was surprising. It was: "So
what? We live with inflation. Lend us the money. You can't
stop developing countries from growing, just because of a
few little worries about some banks. And what if you have
a shake-out of some marginal banks, so what? Inflation, so
what? A crash, so what?"

Here the vision is not of the Mighty West, but of the
Mighty North.

"The North is a fat man, used to eating two steaks a day,
while some people starve," said one of my Latin bankers.
"It will do the North good to cut back. Maybe the fat
North needs a shock to its system, like a crash starvation
diet."

"A crash would remove your buyers, and so would a
banking collapse, or a banking slowdown," I protested.

"Then nationalize all the banks and start over."

That's a very different point of view, so different it's
disorienting.

It was unsettling for me to have these dialogs. I start
from the position that the System must survive, and then
I find a lot of folk from the South and the East—the world
South and the world East—so determined to play Catch

Up and Get Even that they don't share that premise. What System? David Rockefeller's System? Maybe the Arabs will devise their own System.

All the bankers say the International Monetary Fund will have to help. Borrowers do not like the IMF because it is hard-nosed: it dictates political conditions. Some years ago the IMF set stringent conditions for Egypt, the Egyptian government stopped subsidizing bread and salt, and the crowds went out into the streets and burned buildings. Same thing in Peru. If you are a government, and you look out the window at the crowds burning the buildings, you worry first about the crowds and second about the bankers at the IMF.

The International Monetary Fund is not a central bank. It gets its funds from its members, 140 of them, and congress and parliament and assembly have to vote the contributions. It is hard to get those contributions. The IMF has $33 billion, which makes it a very modest fire department, given the size of the area it has to cover.

Jelle Zijlstra, the Dutch banker who became the head of the Bank for International Settlements, assessed the situation in 1980 at the fiftieth birthday of that bank. The banks, he said, would work through the Second Oil Crisis. The growth in the West would be only half of what we were used to. If the OPEC surplus gradually worked down, it would be a sluggish world but it would survive.

But the System could not survive a Third Oil Crisis, said Zijlstra. Given that, inflation would go up, the recycling to the oil-short nations would be almost impossible, world trade would crumble, and so would the System. Three strikes, out.

Would not OPEC see the danger and back off from a Third Oil Crisis?

That presumes rational men acting rationally. It is not rational for the United States to burn up its patrimony on the highways and watch its currency shrink, but speed limits are still protested; that's politics.

OPEC is even more political and less rational. The politics of some of its members are volatile, even savage. The Ayatollah Khomeini lived quietly in a Paris suburb, but the Ayatollah's followers do not permit such luxury of their own opponents; they gun them down on the streets of Paris. In Bethesda, Maryland, an Iranian exile answers his door to get a special-delivery letter from someone dressed as a postman and is shot at point-blank range. The former prime minister of Syria is shot as he enters his Paris office. In London and Paris, embassies are seized by alternate groups of Iraqis and Iranians, and gun battles ensue.

It would be rational for the private banks of the System to step away from serious risk and let OPEC lend the surplus itself. It would be rational for the Arab surplus countries to make heavy contributions to international institutions, so that those institutions could lend the surplus to the oil-short countries. But the Arab contributions have been tied to political ends.

The USC alumni with their video cassettes of the football games make for sympathetic reading, but the Iraqis and Libyans and Iranians are more numerous, and far more hostile. A prominent Arabist, Professor J. B. Kelly, reminds us that Muslim jurisprudence divides the world into *dar-Islam,* Muslim territory, and *dar al-harb,* hostile territory, whose chief constituent is Western Christendom; and he says that a basis of Middle Eastern politics is "the enduring and deep-seated resentment felt by the Muslim states for the Christian West."

Suppose the System did not survive; suppose the West fell into trade wars. OPEC might be able to break the West apart. It has no love for it anyway; one need only listen to the calls for *jihad,* holy war, that ring out over various official radio stations. With its own banks OPEC could control not only energy but capital, and with capital it could make its own alliances with whichever Western nations needed oil the most.

This time the wolf is here, goes the refrain. Not *this* time, say the bankers.

But the wolf is out there.

I went to see my banker mentor. In this instance I am not to identify him, but the furniture in his office is all antiques, antiques with brass handles; on the walls there are lithographs of the great clippers, and the only drink served at lunch is sherry.

"Walt Wriston says nothing works as well as an aggressive bank taking care of itself," he said of the president of Citicorp. "Wilfried Guth proposes a safety net for the banks, and David Rockefeller says to Wilfried, 'You're making loans I wouldn't make.'"

I had with me the complete file of metaphors: fire and water, Rockefeller's gale and Guth's firestorm. And the British banker Lord Armstrong, saying money was gaseous rather than liquid, literally uncontrollable: "Yet it is like fire; you must prevent it from getting out of hand."

"The oil price increases have made the System fragile," said my banker. He handed me a sheet of paper. "Here are the sixty biggest banks in the world. Within the next three years at least one of them will be in serious trouble. So we hope the fire trucks are ready."

What happens then? I wanted to know.

"All the central bankers have agreed that each will be the lender of last resort in his country. And each one is going to try to know the total position of all of his banks —not easy, because so many of the banks are over the border." In Euroland, that is.

What are the chances of serious trouble?

"I'd say at least two out of three. I don't think it will be an American bank, or a German bank, though the Bundesbank has no control over German banks outside Germany. There are a lot of very big banks in the world now.

"After the First Oil Crisis, the bankers got quite confident, as those OPEC surpluses went down. Nobody really expected the Ayatollah and the Second Oil Crisis, which shows that events have a way of breaking loose."

Are the various central banks equal to the task?

"Some of them aren't."

Then who will they turn to? There is no Lender of Last Resort for the world.

"We hope that OPEC is reasonable and that the IMF has more resources."

That's a lot to ask for. What if OPEC isn't reasonable and the IMF gets lent out?

"There will be no choice. The Federal Reserve will call the other central banks for help, but it will be the Lender of Last Resort."

To the world?

"To the world."

Where will the Federal Reserve get the money?

"It will print it."

But that's superinflation!

"The System must survive. A burst of liquidity at the right time can save the System and buy time to solve the problems. Otherwise we will have a massive depression, and the Western nations will battle one another for the scraps, as they did in the Depression."

"An Act," I said, "to provide for the establishment of Federal Reserve banks, *to furnish an elastic currency,* to establish more effective supervision of banking, and for other purposes."

"You have been reading the Act," said my banker.

"We certainly have an elastic currency," I said.

"We do. The men who framed the Act were shaped by money panics, and they thought that a central bank, a Reserve Bank, with, as you say, an elastic currency, could keep the faith of depositors and prevent runs on the banks, and a banking collapse. I suspect the instrument they created may have a wider use than that which they intended."

But with more dollars being printed, wouldn't people flee those dollars?

"We hope that a burst of liquidity, properly handled, would restore confidence, not destroy it. Everything will depend on what people believe. A run on the dollar is the end of the System; but remember, there is nowhere else to go. So rationally, everyone will *have* to believe, because there is no other choice."

But the world is not always rational.

"No, it isn't. It may just be that unthinkable things will happen."

Do you think people understand this situation—the monetized oil, the multiplier on the money, the money spinning out over the world, then the oil going up again because of inflation?

"Not at all. Not even in the government. A very few congressmen and senators; I could count them on one hand. A handful of people in the Treasury. Abroad, same thing. And those who understand cannot explain."

It's dizzying, this recycling business, especially with gale warnings and fire departments and wolves that show up when they're not expected. You can see that the System is fragile, and vulnerable at some key points. If it begins to come apart, you will not see that on television news. You can't get the System into three minutes of prime time. What you might see is that the President has taken some bold action to offset unemployment, or there are riots in Egypt and Peru, or there is bold action to do something or other about banks, or the President says boldly that patriotic people will not travel this year.

If there is a Third Oil Crisis, the announcement of good news in the next chapter is canceled until there is more visibility.

All the world's a stage, and the play the pinstriped bankers have been cast in is, absurdly, that children's classic, *Peter Pan*. For you will remember that when Peter's invisible friend Tinker Bell is dying, he steps out of the play, goes to the footlights, and addresses the audience directly. "Do you believe?" he asks. "Say you *believe!* Clap your hands if you believe!"

"What happens," I once asked a Broadway actress who played Peter Pan, "if the audience doesn't clap?"

She said, "The show would not go on. They have to clap. But they know that, so they do."

11

THE STOCK MARKET: WHAT DO WE DO ON MONDAY MORNING?

Many years ago I ran a small mutual fund whose real boss was one of the canny, original talents on Wall Street. His persona was that of good-ole-boy country shrewdness, all catfish, huntin' dawgs, and hard tradin'. He had been born in Sedalia, Missouri, and did not often reveal that he had spent two years at the Harvard Business School. I am sure he got to be more good-ole-boy in Manhattan than he ever was in Sedalia. He considered the years I spent at Harvard and Oxford as a handicap that could be overcome with serious effort, so when I arrived at his house on Saturdays, having digested Walter Lippmann and Raymond Aron and the other heavies, his eyes would narrow when I gave him the cosmic overview. Khrushchev really say that? De

Gaulle really say that? Holy cow! What do we do on Monday morning?

If he were alive now, I can hear this man say, "Oh, my, there is no governing economic theory; the savings have gone into the houses and the houses have gone to the moon; they made the dollar the key currency and now they don't want it; it is in gloomy old Stage Three and there are no new candidates for Stage One; the Club has control of the energy prices and won't let go; the Mighty West looks like warm mozzarella; the banking system is skittery; the Eurobanks can spin money like cotton candy; only eight people understand all this and they can't explain it; and I'll add one: the Giants don't have a quarterback who can throw worth a damn. Umm."

I still flinch. I can hear that voice say, "What do we do on Monday morning?"

To which I might say, "Let's look at the stock market. Could be a real party."

That sounds, I know, a bit like the ball the Duchess of Richmond gave on the eve of the Battle of Waterloo.

The duchess had rented a splendid house in Brussels that summer of 1815. Napoleon and his fearsome army were just nine miles away; there were 200,000 soldiers in the Belgian countryside, preparing for this battle that would decide the fate of Europe; over the horizon, guns thudded and boomed. But when the duchess asked whether she could give her ball, the British commander-in-chief, the Duke of Wellington, said, "With the greatest safety, and without fear of interruption." He brought all of his officers, and as the champagne flowed and the music played, some of them had to leave for their regiments in their dancing slippers. With his supreme nonchalance and confidence, Wellington asked, when he finally left the dance floor, "Have you a good map in this house?"

Be prepared and confident and light on your feet, and you can come to the party.

Before everybody gets totally into the party mood, we had better issue the usual warnings. We assume that everyone is snug in his quadruply subsidized, social-consensus house, which he intends to live in, not speculate with. We assume everyone has Blue Cross, insurance enough for disasters, and cash enough for hamburgers and the credit-card bill. We have another warning as well: this is a message in a bottle. We can put the message into the bottle and float it out, but we do not know when it is going to wash ashore. If books were instantaneously transmitted and received, such a caveat would not be necessary. A book is a sixteenth-century invention delivered by nineteenth-century transportation. Months go by while the typesetter sets type, galley proofs are corrected and sent back, the pages are printed and bound, and finally the whole product is given to a nice gentleman with a carriage and two matched gray geldings, who says giddyap and takes the books to bookstores, during which time please read the papers, because now you know enough to know what's going on, and you know that something likely will, which you can then fit in.

The stock market party may go on even with threats over the horizon. But in the worst-case scenario, a Third Oil Crisis, a banking crisis, a deflation and depression, the party would be postponed. If the Mighty West breaks up, every country goes out for itself, protectionist walls go up, and world trade slows down; then you have a recession or depression so serious that you would have to wait for some visibility. Such a recession might give an extraordinary opportunity to bond buyers; classically, in recession, bonds go up. When economic activity falls, the demand for money goes down, interest rates drop, the new bonds come out with lower rates, and the old bonds, with the higher rates, go up. Disaster is thus an opportunity, but only for the very, very nimble: this is not a classical period, and governments are unlikely to let economic activity stay low without themselves borrowing and spending, which limits the bond market rally.

Without the worst-case scenario, you can make a very cheerful case for the stock market.

Over the next decade the stock market could triple. That is, the broad-based popular averages could triple, which would mean that the Dow Jones Average, just over 900 at the Message-in-the-Bottle moment, would reach 2,700. That particular average includes many old and mature companies, so more volatile companies could make more radical moves. Some already have.

The Dow Jones Average—as well as the other popular averages—tripled a generation ago, from 1954 to 1961. That made shareholders feel wonderful and quite smart. Inflation rates were low, and so were interest rates, by current standards. When the United States government priced a bond issue to yield 5 percent, the bonds were called "magic fives" and everybody grabbed them.

Alas, a triple is not what it used to be. Nobody calls any government bonds at all magic anymore, so there are no magic tens or magic twelves. If you have a bond yielding 10 percent, and you invest each coupon in more bonds yielding 10 percent, you will double your money in seven years, which makes a triple look a little less breathtaking, because you also have to give some to the tax man.

Even a triple that isn't what it used to be, though, should create enough motion for the brokers to be happy. In the triple of a generation ago, trading volume ran fewer than 5 million shares a day on the New York Stock Exchange. During the Cuban Missile Crisis it got up to 7 million shares a day. During the most panicky days of the 1929 crash, it reached 16.5 million shares a day. Now it is possible to see trading of 100 million shares a day, with peak trading of 150 million shares a day, which should cheer up Wall Street enough for it to forget that a triple doesn't buy what it used to. And that cheer could have a contagious element.

The Invisible Crash

The stock market is not on most lists of inflation hedges. Here is one such list; note where the stock market is on it.

INFLATION HEDGES
COMPOUND ANNUAL RATE OF RETURN (PERCENT)

	10 Years	Rank	5 Years	Rank	1 Year	Rank
Gold	31.6%	1	28.4%	3	104.0%	1
Oil	31.6	2	17.7	7	92.4	2
Silver	23.7	3	27.3	4	76.8	3
U.S. Stamps	21.8	4	31.0	2	43.2	4
Chinese Ceramics	18.8	5	38.7	1	13.1	11
Rare Books	16.1	6	12.7	10	14.0	10
U.S. Coins	16.0	7	21.9	5	25.3	5
Diamonds	15.1	8	18.3	6	25.0	6
Old Masters	13.4	9	15.2	8	17.4	7
U.S. Farmland	12.6	10	13.4	9	14.3	9
Housing	10.2	11	11.6	11	10.4	13
Consumer Price Index	7.7	12	8.9	12	14.5	8

Source: Salomon Bros.

The reason the stock market isn't on that list is that all those investments have gone up, the stock market hasn't, and the chart is retrospective. Both individuals and professionals got burned in the stock market in the 1970s, and they feel like Mark Twain's cat, which sat on a hot stove and then wouldn't sit on a cold one, either.

Let's take a look at what happened.

The stock market crashed in the 1970s, and no one noticed. The people in it noticed, of course, and they felt a certain amount of pain, but "crash" suggests a national calamity, specifically the 1929 Great Crash, which wiped out a generation of investors and helped to bring on the Depression. The crash of the 1970s did not have a sharp, disastrous slide and did not create a national calamity; but curiously enough, the stock market statistics say it was worse. If the first crash was a dramatic leap from a sixty-story building, the second was like drowning in a bubble bath. The bubble-bath drowning sounds less scary, but you end up just as dead.

In the Great Crash the stock market fell sharply in the autumn of 1929, rallied back 50 percent in 1930, and then slipped slowly down to the point in 1932 where the Dow Jones Average had lost 83 percent of its peak value. Since many investors were on margin, using credit, very few had anything left. Those who did found, through the rest of the decade, their dollars appreciating and services to buy with the dollars very cheap; maids were $5 a week. In the 1970s the dollar depreciated and services went up faster than anything else.

In the decade of the 1930s, the value of stocks on the New York Stock Exchange, from the end of 1929 to 1939, fell 31 percent, because after the early 1930s the stocks edged back up. In the decade of the 1970s, the value of stocks on the New York Stock Exchange fell 42 percent.

Of course, the securities holders of the 1970s didn't feel like those of the 1930s because their world was more than securities. Their houses went up, and their jobs didn't disappear. The stock market crash of the 1970s was masked by the age of paper money.

In the 1970s the taxes were much higher than in the 1930s. Federal and state taxes were levied on both dividends and capital gains, when there were any capital gains, and given the rate of inflation, that was a tax on capital. After inflation the return on both stocks and bonds was negative. You might have gotten the checks, but prices went up faster.

So it's no wonder that 7 million investors left the stock market. *Business Week,* in a dramatic 1979 cover story, "The Death of Equities," pronounced the market killed by inflation and dead forever. Profits fall because of inflation, said *Business Week;* businesses can't raise prices fast enough; investors are putting their money into "collectibles": diamonds, gold, works of art.

Business Week's thesis was disputed. Professor James Lorie, at the University of Chicago, figured that business profits went up from $41.8 billion in 1969 to $85.8 billion in 1979—better than double, but not as much as inflation. It wasn't business profits that went down, it was what investors were willing to pay for those profits. It was the prices of the stocks that collapsed, not the earnings of the companies whose shares were traded.

Depressed Stagehands

We'll come back to the case for the market in a moment. The invisible crash of the 1970s left Wall Street itself a depressed place. The crash itself missed a climactic resolution: the stock market stood relatively still while everything else "went up." The securities industry itself was depressed, even apart from the pieces of paper in which it dealt.

First, one of its privileges was taken away. Formerly it had been cushioned by the fixed-rate commission. The commissions were the same on a one-million-share trade as on a one-hundred-share trade, even though the costs of executing both trades—the telephones, the clerks, the services of the floor traders—were about the same. That made the million-share trade very, very profitable, and brokers were more than happy to buy hockey tickets and Caribbean jaunts for institutional investors who might have some million-share orders to give. Then the fixed-rate commissions were eliminated, by government order. True competition developed, and the profits from commissions got very thin, at the same time that 7 million individual investors were leaving the market. Many Wall Street firms could not adapt to the new climate of fierce competition, and they merged or went out of business. Fewer firms, fewer individual investors, fewer analysts calling on companies, fewer phone calls from brokers to clients. Lord Keynes once said that the natural "animal spirits" of men were part of what made business go, and the animal spirits of Wall Street were low.

A second reason for the low state of the securities industry—the stagehands for the stock market performances—was a loss of intellectual respectability. Previous generations had thought that the shrewd old foxes of the Street learned how to pick stocks and manage portfolios. Banks and mutual funds sold the services of the investment managers on that basis. Then the financial academic community began to study the investment performance of professional managers with its new tool, the computer. Ironically, some of the money that sponsored the work came from the old Wall Streeters who had made it and wanted to give something to the alma mater. When the statistics came in, the computer runs said the portfolios assembled by professionals were doing no better than randomly chosen portfolios of stocks. All that buying and selling and phoning around was for naught. Tack up the stock page on the wall; a monkey with a handful of darts can do just as good a job as that lad in the three-piece suit from the Stanford Business School.

The market, said the finance professors, is "efficient." All the opinions of all the investors are already in the prices, so you can't beat the market. You can go up with the market or down with it, but you can't beat it. The market is a "random walk." If you had a good market, you might be happy to ride with it, but the 1970s did not produce good markets on the whole. The professional managers very frequently did worse than the market averages.

The students of the finance professors graduated and got jobs in the banks and insurance companies and told the Wall Streeters they were spinning their wheels; the market is efficient, what value did they have? So some of the purveyors of managed funds gave up trying to buy and sell stocks; they created computer indexes of the whole exchange and sold "index funds" that simply duplicated the market. The live money managers who still said they were picking stocks, and whose results were close to the market, were said by their enemies to be "closet indexers": they weren't really picking the stocks, they had a computer in the closet shadowing the market.

The bedraggled Wall Streeters began to adopt the statistical vocabulary of their attackers. There was, for example, "beta." Beta is a Greek letter, and the attackers were much given to the use of Greek letters in their equations. "Beta" measured the sensitivity of stocks to market swings and equated risk with volatility, so you tuned in the degree of risk you were willing to accept, and that gave you the "beta" of a portfolio and enabled the purveyors of securities to speak in the same Greek letters as their attackers. "Beta" came from Modern Portfolio Theory, which was even more advanced statistically. If you left in the 1960s, and you are thinking about coming back in the 1980s, you may not even have to worry about Modern Portfolio Theory. Recently another academic crowd came along with its own computer runs and said that "beta" didn't work and Modern Portfolio Theory didn't work, which created a huge controversy in very limited circles, because some banks had already sold their services to institutional clients on the basis of their sophistication with Modern Portfolio Theory. In unfriendly markets the advanced mathematics and computer runs gave some clients the comfortable sound of engineering and persuaded them that scientific care was being taken of their investments.

The computer is a tool that has changed contemporary life. We cannot do without it. My old market mentor used to say, in his affected backwoodsy way, "A good dawg is wonnerful for huntin', can't do without him, but you doan give the *gun* to the *dawg.*"

Individual investors, of course, did not follow closely the uses of and disputes about Capital Asset Pricing Models. Told that the market was down 35 percent but that his stocks were down only 30 percent, which was superb for his particular beta, the investor would say, "A pox on your beta; I don't want to lose 30 percent," would take the rest out and head for the casino, or the supermarket.

The gloomy mood on Wall Street, the declining self-image of portfolio managers, and the confusing buzz of techniques were only secondary to the invisible crash, problems among the stagehands.

The primary reason for the market decline was this: the market had to adjust to the age of paper money. It worked this way.

The Yale economist Irving Fisher, who worked in the 1920s, articulated the idea of the rate of return. He said that a bond had to yield a true rate over the rate of inflation. If there was no inflation, the true rate of a top bond would be about 3 percent. A lot of statistical work subsequently supported this.

If you had a 10-percent inflation rate, then, you would expect a bond return of 13 percent, or even 15 percent, if you allowed for taxes. Riskier bonds would have to yield more. Since common stocks are supposed to be riskier than bonds, they would have to have a higher yield than the bonds. The stock doesn't have to "yield" the money in a coupon like the bond; it doesn't have to pay dividends equal to bond interest. But the profitability of the company, the return on capital, ought to be higher than a bond.

For many years this was wonderfully true in the stock market. In the two decades after World War II, the rate of inflation was low, so bonds yielded 3 or 4 percent, and the return on equity capital in stocks was 10 to 11 percent. The early investors got a double benefit: not only were they getting a high return on investment, but they got a bonus when other investors realized the nice deal and came into the market, and moved prices higher.

With increased inflation, though, the situation had to change. Investors demanded a higher return, so when new bonds came out, they yielded 8 and 10 percent, and the old bonds were marked down in the marketplace until they, too, had higher yields.

Bond prices adjust very quickly, because the leading bonds—government bonds—are traded in such large volume and are so fungible, so able to substitute for one another. If a new, three-year U.S. government bond comes out with a yield of 10 percent, the old government bonds with the same maturity date will be marked by the marketplace to approximately the very same yield.

In the 1970s bond prices fell when inflation went up. You would expect that. If inflation is 5 percent, and bonds are at 8 percent, then if inflation is 10 percent, bonds will go to 13 percent, and the old bonds, the ones that yielded 8 percent when they came out, will go down until they, too, yield 13 percent.

While the bond prices were falling, the managers of stocks could debate whether the old maxim that stocks were an inflation hedge was true. Professor Franco Modigliani of MIT and Professor Richard Cohn of the University of Illinois at Chicago were arguing that stocks were undervalued because the market wasn't taking into account the inflationary bonus of corporate *debt*, all those bonds the corporations had issued in earlier days, which could now be paid back with cheaper dollars. But it was also argued that inflation had disguised the costs, so you couldn't trust the earnings reports. If you drive a $5,000 car and you have it on the books at that sum, your balance sheet gets a sudden shock when you've depreciated the car and you have to spend, not $5,000, but $10,000 for a new one.

Meanwhile, some stocks went up and some went down, but group by group, day by day, the whole stock market was getting marked down. A manager in Boston would sell some stocks that had behaved badly and park the money in government bonds, where he was "locking in" a high yield of 9 or 10 percent, which seemed like a good return when stocks were going down. A manager in Chicago would buy bonds at 10 percent with new pension contributions because they satisfied his actuarial requirements, and because 10 percent seemed like a high number to him; he could remember the "magic fives."

At the beginning of the 1970s, the institutional investors had invested nearly 80 percent of their funds in common stocks, and at the end of the 1970s they held only 60 percent in common stocks.

Stock prices fell until they were in line with bond yields, which in turn were in line with the new age of paper money at that particular level. This is an overall statistical snapshot. Nobody had the theory lined up until the data was in.

Some businesses have a high return on equity, and some do not. Some adjusted easily to inflation: they rode on it like a cork. Advertising agencies, for example, get 15 percent of each advertising dollar spent. If inflation goes up, so does the cost of a television commercial or a full-page ad, but the advertising agency doesn't need a new factory; its commission rides on the sum of dollars, the same way that real estate agents make more money as house prices escalate. Monopoly newspapers—same thing. If there's only one paper in town—deplorable from the point of view of the citizens—Sears and A & P have to advertise their sales and pay the going rate; in effect, the newspaper can float on the higher prices at Sears and the A & P. Other industries trimmed their costs and pushed up their prices. The profits went up; the return on equity went up.

The return-on-equity statistics of popular averages show that the companies represented have adjusted to inflation. Remember that in the 1950s stocks had a return on equity of 10 to 11 percent, but interest rates were only 3 to 4 percent. In the past five years the return on equity of the Fortune 500 stocks rose to nearly 16 percent. The return on equity of Standard & Poor's industrial stocks rose in the past five years from roughly 13 percent to 19 percent. (In that average the oil stocks are more heavily weighted, and the oil companies, as we've seen, have prospered in the recent environment.)

How does this translate? The return on stocks is once more in line with the return on bonds, which is more or less in line with inflationary expectations. In fact, the stocks are better priced.

(You can see why we need the Message in the Bottle: prices change. That is why you look, not for tips, but for a way of thinking.)

Institutional investors now hold around $2 trillion in assets. Some of it is in real estate, some in mortgages, some in bonds, some in stocks; recently, $415 billion was in stocks, though that figure varies with the market. If these investors shift a percentage of their funds into common stocks, that naturally brings more money to the market. Furthermore, we now have the largest work force in our national history, most of it covered by pension plans. Corporations and state and local governments make new contributions to those plans every year. The U.S. Department of Labor estimates private pension-fund assets at $889.5 billion by 1985, and state and local government funds at $327 billion by that date; and it estimates that by 1995 the total of pension funds will be nearly $4 trillion. Pension funds are only one form of institutional assets; thus the $4 trillion does not include voluntary savings in life insurance and mutual funds.

If the institutional investors returned the percentage of common stocks held from 60 percent to 80 percent, that would be an enormous flow of funds.

Of course, if inflation accelerates, the government would have to sell its bonds at higher and higher prices, as would other borrowers, and those higher bond rates would again compete with common stocks, as they did in the last cycle. In a real financial crisis, common stocks do not perform well, because they so directly reflect the anxieties of the marketplace. Financial crises destroy bond markets; sick bond markets can kill stock markets.

Those are the institutional investors; what about the individual investor, and houses, and inflation hedges? That tide of paper money has *already* ripped through postage stamps, Chinese ceramics, old bronzes, Chippendale chests, diamonds, gold, modern art, Old Masters, cigar bands, comic books, antique cars, silver, Meissen figurines, Kewpie dolls, Art Nouveau postcards, guns, canes, and anything else anybody wants to collect. The Dow Jones Average sells for its 1967 price, and no cigar band, no Chippendale chest, no Meissen figurine—and probably no house anywhere—sells for its 1967 price. The stock market has this dubious and residual virtue: it is the last game in town.

Bankers, trust officers, used to sit down with their clients to go over lists of securities. Today the bigger banks will help you buy, if you have a substantial trust account, works of art, Oriental carpets, antique furniture, and other niceties sold at Sotheby's. Fifteen banks will help you put diamonds in your retirement plan. Your portfolio could now include a carpet, a chest of crawers, and a nice stone. That's real flight from money.

If you put the time and energy into collecting carpets, or thoroughbred horses, or modern art, you may do very well. But in financial terms the "spreads" are very large. The bid side and the asked side on a $1,000 bond, or on shares of stock, are only a few dollars apart. An art dealer may sell a painting at $1,000 and bid $600 for the same painting. And you can't always find a buyer for your racehorse or your Cézanne the day you want to sell. If Winford Blueford III at the bank is ready to advise you on carpets and drawings, I bet the opportunities are somewhere else.

Incidentally, paper money is worldwide. The Meissen figurines and the Chippendale chests are up everywhere. A nice house in Geneva can run you a million dollars, and a handsome condo on the water in Rio, half a million. Compared to many places, the United States is now cheap. It is cheap to foreign dollar holders because it pushed out all those key-currency dollars and left them overseas, and then pushed out another batch of dollars to the oil countries, and the dollar holders sold the bad currency and put away the good, which made the dollar cheaper, just as Sir Thomas Gresham said in 1566. So the Germans with cheap dollars came and bought the A & P and the Bantam paperback book company and drug companies and more farmland in the United States than there is in East Germany. American real estate prices may seem crazy to Americans, but they are reasonable if you don't pay in dollars.

The Kuwaitis are not going to buy the house next door, unless it is in Beverly Hills or in the Olympic Tower in New York. The Kuwaitis are going to put money in a Swiss bank, or start a bank of their own and go partners with a Swiss bank, and the Swiss banker is going to look around the world for opportunity. Almost all the other stock markets in the world have had a good rise—that is, the major markets. (In the minor markets Spain is down and Hong Kong is through the roof.) The United States still has the broadest, most efficient, most honest securities markets in

the world. The foreigners hold back sometimes because
they aren't sure that they understand the rules, or that
they know what the dollar will be worth.

We need only modest assumptions for a stock market
triple. We assume that profits after taxes are about 10
percent, or roughly the same area we're already in. We
assume the profits are reinvested, and that investors will
pay slightly more for the same earnings; if they pay seven
times earnings now, they may pay eight and a half times
earnings or nine times earnings in ten years. Three potential kinds of investors have buying power: institutional,
individual, and foreign.

It used to be said that the individual investors were always wrong. Services were sold that told what the Little
People were doing, so the Smart People could do the opposite. You no longer hear about the dumb Little People,
because so many of them departed for the condo market,
the racetrack, and the options market, and because the big
Smart People did so badly. It is natural, and quite healthy,
for the individual investors to be wary. They can take
heart from two factors. The first is that the smart professionals have somebody looking over their shoulder, quarter by quarter, whether a boss or a client. That makes their
time horizon very short. As a corporate director, I have
heard several different treasurers come in and report that
the pension fund was divided among five managers; three
beat the market, two didn't; we're firing the bottom two
and looking for two more. That costs institutional managers serenity.

The second factor is that institutional investors are very
large animals, and most of them do not like to tread where
the ice is thin. They also need a lot of room; in securities
terms, they have to be able to sell in volume, and therefore
many of them do not like smaller companies, which do not
have many shares outstanding relatively, and where buying and selling can produce large percentage moves. If the

amount they can commit to a situation is limited, it may not be worth the time and money of their staff.

The Underground Bull Market

This small section is a footnote to the main argument and should be discounted for my own biases. The fund I once ran had what today would be a very high beta. When a portfolio almost twenty years old fell out of a file cabinet I was weeding, I could barely recognize a third of the names. Those companies had disappeared. Dixie Dinettes? Mother's Cookies? Did I really buy 30,000 shares of Mother's Cookies? Whatever happened to Mother's Cookies? I hope it is happy, wherever it went. Then I began to relax a bit, because I could remember where some of the companies had disappeared to. Hermes Electronics was bought by Itek, which survived and did very well. TRG was bought by Control Data, which became a very big company. Eberline Instrument became part of Thermo Electron, which prospered brilliantly, though you would have sat a very long time with the Eberline. And then there were the two little oil-service companies, Texas Instruments and Schlumberger. (In a previous incarnation Texas Instruments was classified that way.) Texas Instruments went on to become a billion-dollar giant in semiconductors, and Schlumberger ranged the world's oil fields. I hope my successors kept the Schlumberger, because it is up fifty times, 5,000 percent, but I bet they didn't. Now with oil at $30 a barrel, the drillers all want those seismic logging techniques, and everybody loves Schlumberger; but they didn't when "growth stock" meant Alcoa.

What made the smaller stocks fun, in spite of the very grave risks they incurred, was that many of them were part of real innovative excitement, with the growth and problems of adolescence. Sometimes they ran out of money; sometimes the entrepreneurs who started them had the ability to get them off the ground, but then could not run a middle-size company, or they got bored, or divorced, or sometimes IBM growled at the whole field. The investors had to suffer through some sickening declines and to keep their heads in periods of giddy trendiness when new companies sprang up everywhere, the weeds looking much like the flowers.

Joseph Schumpeter, one of the great economists of the century, wrote, at the time when the prospects for capitalism were also very gloomy, that what would save it was its ability to innovate. He called it "creative destruction"; the markets are not saturated because innovation makes the old products obsolete. If you go to the Science Museum in Kensington, in London, you will see the stream of mechanical and electrical inventions that Britain produced in the nineteenth century—valves, gears, pumps—each innovation giving the industrial revolution another push. Frequently the new pump or the new valve also produced prosperity for an inventor or a company. The postindustrial revolution is in information processing; it may equal the industrial revolution in its impact. Many of the small companies have been real pioneers; they have brought a new product or service to the world market. For the risks they took, investors in computers and semiconductors and biomedical devices have been well rewarded.

"It has been established," wrote *Fortune* in 1980, "that the stocks of small companies outperform the market, no one knows why." The magazine suggested that the difference between the small stocks and the big ones was a "liquidity premium"—harder to buy and sell. Also harder to find out about, though the sum of unassimilated news should theoretically be neutral, the unknown bad news and the unknown good news canceling out. The markets in the very large stocks were very "efficient," they had more news available, and that made large investors comfortable.

The University of Chicago, citadel of the "efficient market" theory, studied this "underground bull market." Professor Roger Ibbotson found these results over twenty-two years: the Standard & Poor's 500, up 504 percent; the "second tier," up 967 percent. Over fifty-four years, said Professor Rolf W. Banz, the smaller stocks provided twice the return of the Big Board companies. When his efficient-market colleagues said, "That's fine, investors accept greater risks in these stocks, so they are rewarded for those risks," Banz ran another study with the smallest companies adjusted for risk. They still came out ahead, even statistically adjusted for risk.

Yet for all their stellar performances, these actors, the smaller companies, lacked audiences. Many played to empty theaters. The securities industry keeps track of who follows what; Merrill Lynch, the industry giant, follows 1,117 stocks. To do that it uses eighty analysts. The next-largest group of analysts is at Salomon Brothers, with twenty-six analysts covering 679 stocks, most of the stocks the same as Merrill's.

There are 21,000 public companies, and you can see that most of them are ignored. Of the top 2,800 companies, 30 percent are covered by only one analyst. More than 12,000 companies faithfully keep their records up to date at the Securities and Exchange Commission, but nobody comes calling on most of them. Probably nobody will; they may be country banks, or regional supermarkets, and by now they have gotten used to performing for a few close relatives and some cousins.

Commercial services take the data from the Securities and Exchange Commission and publish them, even put them into the data bases of computers. If you have a home computer terminal, you can subscribe, over the phone lines, to services that produce all this information. Home computer terminals are coming into the same price range as good television sets, and the subscription costs to the investment services are charged at an hourly rate. As in residential phone service, the night rates are cheaper. So far, nobody cares. It's just spiffier microphones and better lighting for the actors without audiences.

How do we know, by a market clock, where we are with the more junior stocks? There is certainly a time when enthusiasm for them runs to excess, and they become risky. When we began the draft of the message for the bottle, the secondary stocks sold at a price-earnings ratio that was *less* than that of their big brothers in the Dow Jones Average. By subsequent drafts of the message, they were more expensive, selling at perhaps 1.2 or 1.3 times the ratio of their big brothers. Convertible debentures were issued with big premiums built in, so the discovery cycle is on its way. Historically, when the junior stocks are up to 2.0 times the big seniors in relative price, that is a danger signal.

When and if the institutional investors boost their percentage of common stocks, and when the Kuwaitis and the Germans are enthusiastic about the stock market, and when your neighbor is sitting up late tapping on his den computer, when the stock market seems logical, then this message in a bottle is rescinded. The bourgeois French adage was *Achetez aux canons, vendez aux clairons*—"Buy on the cannons, sell on the trumpets." The cannons are the enemy artillery pounding your city; the trumpets are those that sound the defenders' charge that routs them. It takes psychological fortitude to do the reverse of what seems to be called for. Contrarian philosophy—don't go with the crowd—has provided adage wisdom for a long time.

The Lost Universe

What you have read here are some reasonable arguments for the stock market catching up. Reasonable arguments do not cause markets to go up. An important element has changed.

Formerly this was the spectrum of financial instruments:

If you wanted to invest without risk, you bought U.S. government bonds and accepted that return. Slightly riskier—not much—were triple-A corporate bonds. Then there were "blue chip" stocks: American Telephone & Telegraph, United States Steel, General Motors, Alcoa, du Pont, Standard Oil.

You could pay a bit more, in terms of earnings, for a company that was growing faster: IBM, Minnesota Mining and Manufacturing.

Getting riskier, you could go to the red chips and the white chips, the American Stock Exchange, the over-the-counter market.

The investment universe was neat and certain and Newtonian.

All gone. The Newtonian universe is gone.

Bonds will still pay you back dollar for dollar when they mature, but you don't know what the dollar will be worth. Meanwhile, if the chairman of the Federal Reserve gets a phone call before dawn that the raiders have come through the perimeter defenses, you might find the rates at 20 percent, which sends the bond market into a tailspin. So bonds can fluctuate like volatile stocks used to, as some professional managers found to their sorrow. Same with those tax-exempts.

As for what used to be "blue chips," what is blue? Companies like American Telephone, with secure dividends, used to be considered "growth bonds"; the dividend was secure, so the stock sold like a bond, and the dividend was even occasionally increased. American Telephone is going to do well, but bonds fluctuate. Of the twenty-two most modern large steel facilities in the world, fourteen are in Japan and none is in the United States. Who could put away U.S. Steel? IBM became a religious artifact, but its price fell because investors were willing to pay less for the earnings, and other companies make computers. General Motors found that Datsuns and Toyotas and VWs could carve a share of the market; the game has become world-wide.

This doesn't mean stocks can't go up. Many will. It means the frame of reference has changed. The market is much more volatile, and volatility can produce opportunities, if not sound sleep.

All investments are speculations in the age of paper money.

Soames Forsyte could say, "Never sell consols," and transmit the advice across generations. Today, it is doubtful that he could say anything that would still be true in a year. The King is not on the Throne, the pound is not worth a pound, all is not right with the world. Index funds and beta and Modern Portfolio Theory—and three more computer-derived techniques now a-borning—are all quests for certainty, for orientation, for classical science, for the lost Newtonian universe.

Bring your dancing slippers to the party, *but leave your boots in the hall.*

As for the great duke, he left the party, had a brief nap, got on his chestnut charger, and won a great battle—"a damn close thing," he said. A carrier pigeon took the news across the Channel to the man who had helped the duke finance his campaign. Nathan Rothschild gave the bird a pigeon bonbon, went to the exchange, sold a little just to create a mild panic, then threw his fortune on the buy side, after which there was a bull market that lasted for ninety-nine years. That is the real way to buy on the cannons.

12

WHAT PAPER MONEY MEANS

Myopia: Borrow and Buy

Good luck with the stock market, the house, the real estate, the Swissie and the yen, the gold, the silver, the coins, the modern art, the racehorse, and the Meissen figurine. As individuals, we did not make the world the way it is, we did not each create the paper money, and we have to use our wits. Houses can be lived in, fixing up houses can be productive work, the stock market can be seen as a productive investment. I hope your modern art gives you pleasure and that your racehorse wins.

But what may momentarily serve us as individuals doesn't help us collectively. You have been persistent enough to read abstractions and large numbers, and you will have skills enough to do well in the years ahead. To live comfortably, though, we need more than a big bank account. We need the milkman, the policeman, the baker, and the teacher as well, and they will not all be able to hedge themselves against the currency. If they are not content, they will be on strike, or will not do their jobs in some other way, and our standard of living will go down just as if our bank accounts were melting. So we can't leave out these fellow citizens even from a materialistic viewpoint.

In the early days of paper money, they keep up, lagging slightly. They are "indexed." Their unions win COLA, cost of living adjustments; they get raises according to COWPS, the Council on Wage and Price Stability. Commercial contracts and real estate deals are tied to CPI, the Consumer Price Index. The Latin bankers had said, "Why don't you just print the money, index everything, and stop worrying?"

If I raised my prices yesterday, and you're my competitor, and the government says, "Simon says, freeze!," I have a big advantage over you. Next time you will jump the gun, and I will follow. It's very hard to find the index numbers by which everything should move, because some products and processes don't naturally move at the same speed as others. It's tough to police. For example, in Latin America the savings rates tend to lag behind the inflation rates; when inflation in Brazil was 100 percent, the savings rate was only 50 percent. Such instability frequently helps to bring military government. Every South American country has had a military junta running it at some point. Military juntas get to suspend the normal processes, and to govern by edict and bayonet, which is outside this discussion. There is no perfectly indexed, optimally functioning economy.

In the longer run, in collective terms, there's something obviously wrong with the whole approach of hedging, of asking, How do I beat inflation, how do I stay ahead? Hedging depends on a continuous supply of gulls, of suckers, of greater fools, of people who haven't gotten the word. Think a minute: somebody has to sell you that "inflation hedge," somebody who already owns it. Why should he? Why should I sell my house for your depreciating dollars? The advice that tells you to go out and borrow, buy *things*, that's the way to beat it, presumes that the lender hasn't heard what's happened to the money. Maybe the lenders are the foolish children with the 5-percent bank passbooks and the 6-percent $50 Treasury E bonds. When the foolish children find that the skates they were saving for have doubled in price while they were saving, when all the foolish children together find they lent you the money through their savings bank for a condo that's gone way up and they still don't have their skates, they will say the hell with it. When they get old enough to vote, they're going to remember what fools they were and come looking for you with a candidate who has blood in his eye.

Hedging only works when there is *unanticipated* inflation. Sir Thomas Gresham presumed somebody would take your bad money so that you could save the good. Maybe somebody will. Maybe the lenders will always lend, the way retrievers will always chase a ball. Let's say the lenders still lend.

Everybody gets the word: borrow, beat inflation. If everybody heads for one rail of the boat, the boat's going to tip. Your Uncle Sam is right there with the rest of the crowd on the rail; he's a quarter of all the borrowing.

I have been saving the biggest number until now, but I have no way to dramatize it, no orange juice, no F-14s, no nuclear carriers. The number is $4.3 trillion: $4,300,000,000,000. That's the outstanding debt in the credit markets. That's you, me, the car payments, the Master Charge and Visa payments, all the corporations, and your Uncle Sam with all of his family, among whom you only met Fannie and Ginnie and Freddie, who are well behaved compared to some of their cousins, like their military cousins, their HEW cousins, and their farm cousins. That $4.3 trillion is especially large in relation to capital, equity capital, which hasn't grown much in the past ten years, and which is about $1 trillion. Here's the way the debt has grown:

> In 1960 the debt was $750 billion.
> In 1970 the debt was $1.5 trillion.
> In 1980 the debt was $4.3 trillion.

Some of that jump from $1.5 trillion to $4.3 trillion went to finance growth, but most of it financed consumption, and what was consumed is gone. We have borrowed to live the way we wanted to. We still live on the nicest spread in the county, but the old farm is mortgaged to the hilt, the banks are nervous, and the boll weevil is out there in the cotton. Our inheritance looks vast, but it's all mortgaged.

If we look at a chart of the American household, we can see that the line representing household borrowing crosses the line of household savings for the first time in the 1970s. Household borrowing finances consumption and assets that don't produce additional wealth, such as houses not rented to others, cars, silver, and Kewpie dolls.

Uncle Sam, with the noblest of intentions, borrows for that whole panoply of good works. He relieves the poor, soothes the sick, guards the consumer from fraud, supports the farmers, regulates the threats to health, gives money to states and cities. He does this with our money, with our explicit taxes, income, estate, gift, gas, and so on, and with our implicit tax of inflation. He has not really measured the cost of his good intentions.

Borrowing has gotten more popular. Lending has gotten less popular. Since there must be a lender for every borrower, the price of the money, the interest, has gone up, and the lender wants it back faster. This time horizon of the lender has been mentioned before, because it is a very significant symbol.

ANNUAL NET INCREASE IN HOUSEHOLD SAVINGS AND BORROWINGS, 1952–1979 ($ Billions)

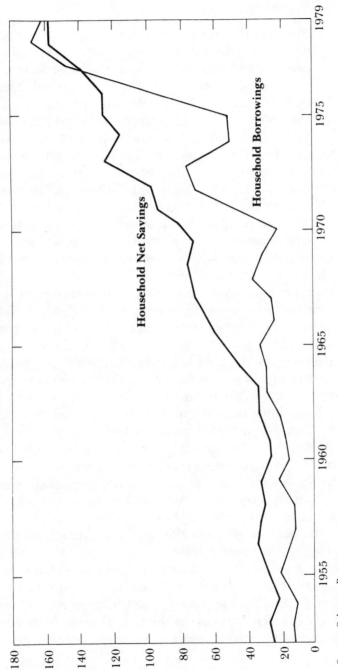

Household Net Savings

Household Borrowings

Source: Salomon Bros.

People save; they also borrow. In a healthy economy, they save more than they borrow. What is startling about this chart is that the lines cross. There's a limit, naturally, to how much households can increase their borrowing.

In the nineteenth century the British government could borrow money and say it would *never* pay it back, and its credit was so good that the bonds went up. Those were the perpetual "consols." After World War II the United States could borrow money for forty years and pay the lender 2½ percent. Now it pays 13 percent to borrow for ten years. The time horizon of the lender parallels the foreshortening of goals. Lenders do not want to lend long-term; corporate managers do not think long-term, they think more in near-term three-year slices. Building up capital and cutting back on debt is a tough and painful process. When it happens in the business cycle, the sufferers, whether business or farm or labor, complain and the government accommodates with more money. So the cycle of adding to the debt continues.

Serious people wonder: How do we break this cycle? We are not an isolated, self-sufficient island. As the debt building goes on, we become more vulnerable to some external shock, an oil crisis, a banking crisis, the fatigue point of the takers of the debased key currency. Without a shock we will continue to have more borrowers than lenders and to move to greater vulnerability. With a shock—and it could be a domestic malfunction, as well as an external shock—the System could break down.

We shape our houses, and then they shape us. The building of the debt creates more dollars, which creates a distrust of dollars, which erodes the credibility of the currency as a store of value. We become more concerned about getting through the next crisis, next year, than about the next decade and the next generation, and that works against our better instincts.

Those instincts—to work and save, to accumulate—are strong in productive societies. They have to do with children and trees. People want to plant trees they may not see mature, to leave things for the next generation, to take advantage of increasing herds and compounding interest.

Though they do not think of it in exactly this way, they want the money itself—not gold, not silver, not Kewpie dolls, not canned goods or even houses—to be the store of value, because they do not want to spend their time figuring out how to escape or manipulate the currency. Somebody else will always manipulate faster and leave them the loser, and anyway, they would rather be doing what they do, building or selling or plowing or singing. The trouble with paper money is that it rewards the minority that can manipulate money and makes fools of the generation that has worked and saved.

Keynes worried about the other side of the problem, how to reliquefy the economy, how to loosen up the savings, and he thought the Protestant ethic extreme. "We have been trained too long to strive," he said, "and not to enjoy," and he looked forward to the day when the "social customs and economic practices . . . useful in promoting the accumulation of capital, we shall be free, at last, to discard." He really thought those practices were a bit gross. We have arrived at the day Keynes was waiting for, but by the wrong way, the shortcut. The day Keynes spoke of was in the twenty-first century, after a hundred years of getting rich through the benefits of science and the compounding of past earned wealth. Now we have "social customs and economic practices" designed for distributing the production—in the name of fairness—and discouraging the accumulation that was supposed to set us free. We enjoy, by flying now and paying later.

What We Want the Money For

We are, as a country, well clothed. We are, as we've seen, well housed, although the use of housing as a speculative medium may threaten that sense of being well housed. We are certainly well fed. Forty million of us go on a diet every year, agriculture is our biggest export, and the Department of Agriculture makes the old Texas Railroad Commission look like a sandlot team. (The Texas Railroad Commission polled its industry and cut back production; the Department of Agriculture *pushes* the milk prices at a flick of the CPI.)

If we have food, clothing, shelter, 140 million vehicles on the road, saturation in television sets, stereos, appliances, what is it we want money for? I think we are trying to buy something that can't be bought. That something is *community*, *asibaya* in Arabic, *danketsu* in Japanese. (Economists misjudged OPEC in 1974 because they thought of it only in economic terms, not as *asibaya* among its members.) Community is social cohesion, solidarity, personal intimacy, emotional depth, moral commitment, continuity in time, a vision of man in his wholeness rather than in one or another of his roles.

How do we try to buy community? One example: We pay for crime, or flee it; we don't seem to be able to solve it. More than a million cars a year are stolen, and the insurance companies find it cheaper to pass the costs through than to get us to solve the problem. Our crime statistics go up every year, and we've gotten used to them. We want to live where it is safe, where our houses and children are safe, so we keep moving. "Retirement villages" sometimes resemble guarded stockades. In our bigger cities we have come to take a calloused attitude toward street assaults, mayhem in dark parking lots, murders in the subway—a disregard for life we used to associate with the Orient.

In the Orient, in Japan, the crime rates are going *down*. You can walk anywhere in Tokyo, it is reported, without looking over your shoulder, and taxi drivers don't hesitate to carry a lot of cash. A Harvard sociologist looked into the phenomenon. *"Danketsu gai tsuyoi,"* he said, the capacity to work together. The Japanese neighborhoods are very strong, family relationships are very strong, the police are part of every neighborhood, and criminals are expected to turn themselves in so as not to shame their parents.

Those who so confidently predict apocalyptic depression for us are confident we have no sense of community; it is the missing element in all their dire tales. A Great Depression is coming. Stock your basement with vitamins, beef jerky, canned tuna, silver coins, and penicillin. When the stores are bare and the power is off, you will be snug with your portable generator and your food and your shotgun, and if your neighbor is starving and asks for a can of tuna, he should have joined the ark before it started raining; give him a blast over his head. A sober insurance company executive, in a sober little book warning of financial crisis, suggests you look for a country retreat in the hills, "preferably above a bridge that can be defended and, if necessary, destroyed." It doesn't seem to be part of the vision that you get along with your neighbors, that people meet at the church or the school, that if you have the tuna your neighbor might have the peach cobbler.

We are certainly a more violent society than the Germans were in 1923. They were so law-abiding that when a band of revolutionaries took over the subway to overthrow the government, they lined up nicely to buy their tickets and obeyed the signs that said "Keep Off the Grass." (That group did not succeed, perhaps because of the mentality that caused them to buy tickets and ride the subway to overthrow the government.) The Germans did not have a hundred million handguns, as we have, or urban unemployment generations old. Hyperinflation dissolved their "social glue," in Arthur Burns's phrase, and we would certainly not have to get as far as the hundred-million-dollar bill to have very serious trouble. If the Teamsters are on strike, the stores will be bare; if the power company stays on strike long enough, your portable generator may come in handy. But I keep thinking of an interview with the German actress Lotte Lenya, who was in Berlin in 1923. Did she remember it? "Oh, yes, Brecht was working on his play and I was rehearsing in another play." What about the inflation? "Oh, that was all politics." No country since has had a violent hyperinflation unless it first had war or revolution.

The Longer View

Paper money has an enormous constituency. The people who owe the $4.3 trillion don't mind at all if the dollar cheapens, because they profit by it. There does not seem to be a unified constituency for preserving the integrity of the currency. So it will take concentrated energy to get the battered System through the next decade, *and this is something we must do.* That's right, the System must survive.

Far more is at stake than just bank accounts. Remember the Dutch banker who said, "Where can we go from the dollar. To the moon?" When you travel outside the country, you become more aware of our responsibility. This is still the country that is looked to. No searchlights and barbed wire keep its people in. There is no other leader of the West. What attracts the rest of the world is still this country's energy and capacity for opportunity and generosity and even compassion, even though those qualities are not always well mobilized. They have been in the making a long time.

We think of the Arabs as taking our money, as holding us up for oil; a thousand years ago they gave us something even more valuable and more necessary than oil: numbers. They brought from India the ingenious tool called the zero, as well as the numbers we now call "arabic," 1, 2, 3, 4, 5, 6, 7, 8, 9.

In the thirteenth century a traveler from Pisa, one Leonardo Fibonacchi, brought the numerical system to Tuscany in northern Italy, which enabled the Tuscans to have books that did not multiply CXXV by MCMXXXIII; they could have complex accounts, double-entry bookkeeping, a system. The Tuscans developed banks, with bills of exchange, credit notes, like medieval traveler's checks, so that the traveling merchants did not have to carry cash.

Soon the Tuscans and the Florentines and the Venetians are banking all over southern and middle Europe, and then this particular *geist* or spirit goes fluttering over the Alps to Holland, because the Spaniards have conquered the southern part of the Netherlands and burned all the farms and the Dutch refugees have moved into Amsterdam, with cousins in cities around Europe, and when the boom starts in Europe there is an energy crisis, which consists of everybody chopping down all the trees of southern Europe for fuel, so many trees that the glassmakers are forbidden to build fires to make glass, and the Dutch take to the water and sail to the Baltic for more wood to solve the energy crisis with the trees from Finland and Sweden. And, as James Burke has written, the Dutch soon monopolize the wood trade, turning adversity to advantage, and their little ships are taking the wood south and the wine north, and pretty soon Amsterdam is the richest city in Europe, all this trade financed by the pieces of paper adapted from the northern Italians with the numbers on them brought by the Arabs from India.

The British take to the sea, too, raising the money on their lands, using the system brought by the French, remember the *mort-gage,* and the *geist* is getting a boost from John Calvin, who is preaching that work, successful work, gives you a glimpse of whether you are in a state of grace. The Dutch ships sail off to America, where the Dutchmen buy an island owned by the Manhattan Indians, and build a wall across the northern boundary of their little settlement, and the muddy path along the wall is, naturally,

Wall Street. When the British have had enough of the Catholic Stuart kings, they send to Holland for the handiest Protestant, the Prince of Orange and Nassau, and then they have not only William and Mary as rulers, but they also have the Dutch coffeehouse crowd that comes along with William and is soon mixing it up with the English coffeehouse crowd. You can find all the shipping news in these coffeehouses, you can borrow money, lend money, invest money, hear music, drink coffee, meet girls, meet men, everything. The Dutch ships and the English ships are away a long time sometimes (their hulls classified, by risk and soundness, with a system in the coffeehouse known as Lloyd's), their cargoes financed by the pieces of paper called bills of credit, the money raised by *mort-gage* on the newly registered lands of England, the bills themselves deriving from the ones used by the Hollanders taken from the northern Italians with the numbers on them brought by the Arabs from India.

The Russians have been in the story before, too. The Russians want a warm-water port, so they march across Finland, which ruins the wood trade built by the Dutch to solve the energy crisis. Europe needs not only the wood for fuel and ships, it is having trouble with *Teredo navalis,* a little water mollusk that eats the hulls of the wooden ships, but if the hulls are coated with tar and pitch from pine trees, *Teredo navalis* can't eat them. Now the Russians have the Baltic pine forests, and so the handiest place to get the tar and pitch is from the pine forests of the Carolinas, which is how the North Carolinians got to be known as Tarheels, though that nickname comes later, and more and more ships sail the Atlantic. New Amsterdam becomes New York, the Puritans become Yankee traders, and to trade in the pieces of paper, they meet under a buttonwood tree in 1692 which shades the muddy path known as Wall Street, and they call the area right under the tree the Stock Exchange.

With all this shipping going on, there are a lot of bills of credit floating around, upon which you can raise cash until your ship comes in, and to organize this procedure an informal association has been meeting in London, in the Nag's Head saloon, on Cateaten Street, down the road from the coffeehouses. In 1694 they need a better name for the association, and so they call it the Bank of England. One day on Cateaten Street, the boys are sitting around in the Nag's Head, and somebody says, "Who do you think should be the next Master of the Mint?" Another fellow says, "What about Isaac Newton? He's paid his dues." Another fellow says, "Isaac *Newton?* The Isaac Newton from Cambridge, with the math formulas and the papers about optics and light? Isn't he a little strange about gold?"

Meanwhile, in a tavern in New York . . . but wait a minute. This is where you came in. You know enough of the rest of the story. It helps to remember, on our dour days, what a long story it is, what a marvelous adventure. It's not over yet.

NOTES

CHAPTER 1: IF TIMES HAVE BEEN SO GOOD, WHY DO WE FEEL SO BAD?

p. 17 Arthur Burns, inflation, "social glue": Arthur Burns's inflation causes are union power, business concentration, the stagnation of productivity, the intervention of government in the economy, the size and persistence of federal budget deficits, the excessive growth of the money supply, the devaluation of the dollar, bad harvests, and the cartel power of OPEC. These he describes as cited by others. Burns's own three favorite causes of inflation are all attributable to the government: "its philosophical and permanent bias toward stimulating the economy, its interference with market competition, and its legislation of expensive environmental and safety laws." Statement by Arthur F. Burns, Scholar at the American Enterprise Institute for Public Policy Research, before the Committee on Banking, Housing and Urban Affairs, United States Senate, March 14, 1980.

p. 19 Gallup polls: *Gallup Opinion Index,* no. 167 (June 1979), pp. 23–24.

p. 20 Inflation: *Statistical Abstract of the United States* (Washington, D.C.: U.S. Department of Commerce), various issues.

p. 20 President Johnson: David Halberstam, *The Best and the Brightest* (New York: Random House, 1972).

p. 24 Real income . . . money illusion: "We're Better Off than We Think," editorial, *The New York Times,* November 29, 1979. Also in Lester Thurow, "The Distributional Consequences of Inflation," in *The Zero-Sum Society* (New York: Basic Books, 1980), pp. 47–54.

p. 24 Work harder: Robert M. Solow, "Why Do We Feel So Bad?," unpublished paper. See also Robert M. Solow, "All Simple Stories about Inflation Are Wrong: Lessons for Our Economy," unpublished paper. An abbreviated version of "All Simple Stories" is in *The Executive,* the journal of the Cornell University Graduate Business School (Summer 1980).

p. 26   Two measures of money supply: No one is quite sure these days exactly what money is. There used to be a distinction between deposits in banks, upon which you could write a check, and time deposits, which would be left for a specific period. Now, with checking available against money market funds and NOW accounts, the definitions are blurred. The two definitions here are M1B, time deposits against which checks can be written, and M2, time deposits against which checks cannot be written. Here are their rates of annual growth since 1973:

	1973	*1974*	*1975*	*1976*	*1977*	*1978*	*1979*
M1B	5.5	4.3	4.8	6.5	8.1	8.2	7.7
M2	7.0	5.6	12.8	14.1	10.9	8.2	8.8

We can see that M1B leveled off and M2 actually turned down, even though the rates of inflation accelerated during those periods. Perhaps there is a lagging effect from money growth. Monetarists insist that if you restricted the supply of money long enough, you would begin to control inflation. But no one knows exactly how long that period is, nor whether the society would tolerate the economic slowdown thus produced. Nor do we know whether the Federal Reserve can really control the supply of money as the textbooks say.

CHAPTER 2:   WHY NOT CALL UP THE ECONOMISTS?

p. 30   Experimental science: James Bryant Conant, *On Understanding Science* (New Haven: Yale University Press, 1947).

p. 31   "Macro" magnitudes: Sir John Hicks, *Causality in Economics* (Oxford: Blackwell, 1979).

p. 31   An economist: Will Rogers, "Recession and Inflation," in *The Will Rogers Scrapbook,* ed. Bryan B. Sterling (New York: Grosset and Dunlap, 1976), p. 59.

p. 36   Elasticities: also see Hendrik Houthakker with Michael Kennedy, in *Directions in Energy Policy,* ed. Kursunoglu and Perlmutter (Cambridge, Mass.: Ballinger, 1980); and Hendrik Houthakker, "The Relationships between Energy Growth and Economic Growth" (unpublished paper, 1980), and "Introduction to World Energy Model" (unpublished paper, 1977.) See also Sergio Koreisha and Robert Stobaugh, "Limits to Models," in *Energy Future: Report of the Energy Project at the Harvard Business School,* ed. Robert Stobaugh and Daniel Yergin (New York: Random House, 1979).

p. 37   Hopi language: Benjamin Lee Whorf, "An American Indian Model of the Universe," *International Journal of American Linguistics,* vol. 16, 1950, pp. 67–72. See also Benjamin Lee Whorf, *Language, Thought, and Reality* (Cambridge, Mass.: Technology Press, 1956).

p. 38   Keynes: See Robert Lekachman, *The Age of Keynes* (New York: McGraw-Hill, 1975); Sir Roy Harrod, *The Life of John Maynard Keynes* (London: Macmillan,

1951); and E. A. G. Robinson, *John Maynard Keynes: Economist, Author, Statesman* (New York: Oxford University Press, 1971). For letters between Keynes and Kahn, see John Maynard Keynes, *The Collected Writings*, 16 vols. (New York: St. Martin's Press, 1971).

p. 41 Godkin lectures: Walter Heller, *New Dimensions of Political Economy* (Cambridge, Mass.: Harvard University Press, 1966), p. 1.

p. 41 *Time* magazine: "We're All Keynesians Now," *Time*, December 31, 1965, pp. 64–67.

p. 41 Samuelson's textbook: Paul Samuelson, *Economics* (New York: McGraw-Hill, 1973); and *Readings in Economics* (New York: McGraw-Hill, 1973). See also *Business Week*, December 28, 1974, p. 51.

p. 43 Stanley Fischer: Stanley Fischer and Rudiger Dornbusch, *Macroeconomics* (New York: McGraw-Hill, 1978).

p. 44 Sustained innocence: George W. Ball, "An Overdose of Economists," *Washington Post*, April 7, 1980.

p. 44 Leontief: Personal conversation. See also Thomas Mayer, "Economics as a Hard Science: Realistic Goal or Wishful Thinking?" *Economic Inquiry*, vol. xviii, April 1980, pp. 165–178; and Wassily Leontief, *American Economic Review*, March 1971, pp. 1–7.

CHAPTER 4: THE CHILLING SYMBOL: A WHEELBARROW FULL OF MONEY

p. 55 The material for this chapter was culled from the following sources: Fritz Ringer, ed., *The German Inflation of 1923* (New York: Oxford University Press, 1969); Adam Fergusson, *When Money Dies; The Nightmare of the Weimar Collapse* (London: Kimber, 1975); William Guttmann, *The Great Inflation, Germany 1919–1923* (Farnborough, England: Saxon House, 1975); and Karsten Laursen and Jorgen Pederson, *The German Inflation, 1918–1923* (Amsterdam, 1964).

CHAPTER 5: WHY HOUSES BECAME MORE THAN HOUSES

p. 69 Sixty percent of all homes: U.S. Bureau of the Census.

p. 70 Hoover . . . Roosevelt: Martin Mayer, *The Builders* (New York: W. W. Norton, 1978), pp. 366–368.

p. 71 FHA: Ibid.

p. 72 Levittown: Eric Larrabee, "The Six Thousand Homes That Levitt Built," *Harper's* September 1948, p. 85.

p. 72 Decent housing: U.S. Department of Housing and Urban Development (HUD).

p. 72 Johnson: Mayer, *The Builders*, p. 382.

p. 73 Government-guaranteed bonds: Wertheim and Co., New York.

p. 83   A colleague of mine: Richard Reeves, who then became an ex-colleague and wrote "Boom," *The New Yorker,* December 24, 1979, pp. 74–78, from which the Goodkin and Popejoy quotes are taken.

p. 84   No boom: "Real Estate: A Time to Beware," *Forbes,* June 11, 1979, pp. 53–61.

p. 84   Bubbly: Victor F. Zonana, "Basic Price of $100,000 for 3-Bedroom House Prevails in Some Areas," *The Wall Street Journal,* August 17, 1979.

p. 85   Real estate crash: See, for example, Chris Welles, "The Housing Bubble: Will It Really Burst?," *Esquire,* July 3–19, 1979, pp. 47–56.

p. 86   Housing prices:

AVERAGE SELLING PRICE FOR EXISTING HOMES,
1975–1980

1975	$39,000
1976	$42,200
1977	$47,900
1978	$55,500
1979	$64,200
June 1980	$75,700

Source: National Association of Realtors

AVERAGE SELLING PRICE FOR NEW HOMES,
1975–1979

1975	$39,300
1976	$44,200
1977	$48,800
1978	$58,100
June 1979	$68,200

Source: U.S. Bureau of the Census

See page 00 for chart of prices 1979–1989

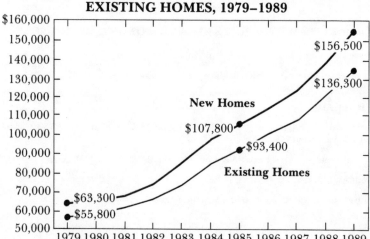

PROJECTED MEDIAN PRICES OF NEW AND EXISTING HOMES, 1979–1989

Source: NAHB Econometric Forecasting Service, table 16.

p. 88 Table: "Business Outlook," Townsend-Greenspan and Co., Inc., New York, February 1, 1980.

p. 89 Stocks listed: Source: New York Stock Exchange.

p. 93 Chart: U.S. Bureau of the Census.

p. 94 86 million houses: U.S. Bureau of the Census.

p. 95 Table: "Business Outlook," Townsend-Greenspan.

p. 96 Passbook savings: Salomon Brothers, New York.

p. 98 4 million houses: Townsend-Greenspan and Co., Inc., New York.

p. 99 Table: Federal Reserve Chart Book.

p. 100 Jay Janis: Zonana, "Basic Price of $100,000."

p. 101 56 million households: U.S. Bureau of the Census.

p. 102 National Association of Home Builders: Michael Sumichrist, "Housing in the 80's," National Association of Home Builders.

CHAPTER 6: THE PROLIFERATING DOLLAR: HOW THE KEY CURRENCY GOT DEBASED

p. 109 Witteveen: "Group of Thirty," Consultative Group on International Economic and Monetary Affairs, Inc., February 1980; and Johannes Witteveen Speech, "Energy and Money Relationships," New York, May 16, 1980.

p. 112 Three stages: C. Fred Bergsten, *The Dilemmas of the Dollar* (New York: Council on Foreign Relations, New York University Press, 1975).

p. 114 Newton: For a complete history see Sir Albert Feaveryear's *The Pound Sterling* (Oxford: Clarendon Press, 1963).

p. 116 Consols: John Galsworthy, *The Forsyte Saga* (New York: Scribners, 1933), vol. 1, *The Man of Property.*

p. 116 The fleet: Sir William Laird Clowes, *The Royal Navy* (London: Marsten and Co., 1903), p. 85.

p. 116 British capital: Martin Mayer, *The Fate of the Dollar* (New York: Times Books, 1980), p. 31.

p. 119 Bretton Woods: J. Keith Horsefield, *The International Monetary Fund: 1945–1965*, vol. 1 (Washington, D.C., 1969), pp. 89ff.; and *The First Ten Years of the International Monetary Fund* (Washington, D.C.: IMF Publications, 1956).

p. 119 Bancor: Richard N. Gardner, "Bretton Woods," in *Essays on John Maynard Keynes*, ed. Milo Keynes (Cambridge: 1975), p. 209.

p. 122 Moscow Narodny Bank: Personal correspondence.

p. 125 Three-quarters of a trillion dollars: *World Financial Markets* (Morgan Guaranty newsletter), July 1980.

p. 126 Robert Triffin: Robert Triffin, *Gold and the Dollar Crisis* (New Haven: Yale University Press, 1961).

p. 126 Milton Gilbert: Richard Janssen, "What If Gold Prices had been Raised in the 1960s as a BIS Aide Suggested," *The Wall Street Journal*, September 30, 1980.

p. 129 Jelle Zijlstra: Quoted in Mayer, *The Fate of the Dollar.*

p. 132 Money was free:

INFLATION VS. INTEREST RATES

Fed Discount Rates

1970	Nov.	5¾	1977	Aug.	5¾
	Dec.	5½		Oct.	6
1971	Jan.	5	1978	Jan.	6½
	Feb.	4¾		May	7
	July	5		July	7¼
	Nov.	4¾		Aug.	7¾
	Dec.	4½		Sept.	8
1973	Jan.	5		Oct.	8½
	Feb.	5½		Nov.	9½
	May	6	1979	May	9½
	June	6½		Aug.	10
	July	7		Sept.	10½
	Aug.	7½		Oct.	11¾
1974	Apr.	8		Nov.	12
	Dec.	7¾	1980	Feb.	12½
1975	Jan.	7¼		Mar.	13
	Feb.	6¾		June	12
	Mar.	6¼		July	11
	May	6		Aug.	10
1976	Jan.	5½			
	Nov.	5¼			

Inflation, annual percentage change, seasonally adjusted

1970	5.9
1971	3.4
1972	3.4
1973	8.8
1974	12.2
1975	7.0
1976	4.8
1977	6.8
1978	9.0
1979	13.3
1980	21.2 (June, percentage change from previous six months)

Source: Council of Economic Advisers, Economic Indicators, July 1980.

p. 132 One out of every eight barrels: American Petroleum Institute; Federal Highway Administration, *Highway Statistics, 1979* (Washington, D.C., 1980).

p. 138 265 million ounces: International Monetary Fund, *International Financial Statistics,* August 1980.

p. 141 Gnome of Zurich: See Adam Smith, *The Money Game* (New York: Random House, 1968).

p. 142 5 billion ounces: Charles G. Stahl, "Pray You Never Have to Use It," *Forbes,* September 29, 1980, pp. 103–104.

CHAPTER 7: HOW OPEC STARTED, AND GREW, AND ENGINEERED THE GREATEST TRANSFER OF WEALTH IN WORLD HISTORY

p. 147 Perez Alfonso: See Romulo Betancourt, *Venezuela: Oil and Politics* (Boston: Houghton Mifflin, 1979); and Franklin Tugwell, *The Politics of Oil in Venezuela* (Stanford, Calif.: Stanford University Press, 1975).

p. 147 Texas Railroad Commission: James E. Anderson et al., *Texas Politics* (New York: Harper & Row, 1971); Stuart McCorkle, *Texas Government* (New York: McGraw-Hill, 1974), pp. 301–305; Wilbourn E. Benton, *Texas: Its Government and Politics* (Englewood Cliffs, N.J.: Prentice-Hall, 1972), pp. 328–332; and C. McCleskey, *The Government and Politics of Texas* (Boston: Little, Brown, 1975), pp. 326–333.

p. 149 *Fortune:* Gilbert Burck, "A Strange New Plan for World Oil," *Fortune,* August 1959, pp. 94–97, 146, 148.

p. 149 $1.80 a barrel: Organization of Petroleum Exporting Countries (OPEC), *Annual Statistical Bulletin,* contains historical data on Persian Gulf oil prices.

p. 149 10 cents a barrel: The 10-cent figure is from the sixties and was probably an accurate figure until OPEC governments became heavily involved in oil production. See also *Petroleum Intelligence Weekly,* May 12, 1980, p. 7.

p. 150 The cartel: Burck, "A Strange New Plan," p. 97.

p. 151 Federal Trade Commission: *The International Petroleum Cartel,* a staff report to the Federal Trade Commission, submitted to the Subcommittee on Monopoly of the Select Committee on Small Business, United States Senate, August 22, 1952. This report was reprinted by the U.S. Government Printing Office in 1975.

p. 151 Action Memorandum: Much of the early history of the oil cartel can be found in the reports of the Senate Sub-Committee on Multinational Corporations; for example, *The International Petroleum Cartel, the Iranian Consortium, and U.S. National Security,* February 1974.

p. 152 Unjustified price reductions: Tugwell, *Politics of Oil,* p. 55.

p. 153 Abdullah Tariki: See "New Triumph for Tariki—He's Oil Minister," *Oil and Gas Journal* 59, no. 2 (January 1, 1961); and Harold H. Martin, "The Oil of the Arab World," *Saturday Evening Post,* February 17, 1962.

p. 155 *Fortune:* Burck, "A Strange New Plan."

p. 159 Shah of Iran: Zuhayr Mikdashi, *The Community of Oil Exporting Countries* (London, 1972), p. 33; and David Hirst, *Oil and Public Opinion in the Middle East*

(London, 1966), p. 112, quoted in Anthony Sampson, *The Seven Sisters* (New York: Viking Press, 1975), p. 160.

p. 159 A cartel to confront: Quoted in Sampson, *Seven Sisters*, p. 156.

p. 159 OPEC: OPEC, Resolution 1.2, Conference Resolutions, Baghdad, September 1960.

p. 160 Membership: OPEC Resolution 1.2; see also Article 7 of OPEC's Statute, Vienna, 1971.

p. 161 The Swiss government: Abdul Amir Q. Kubbah, *OPEC: Past and Present* (Vienna, 1974), p. 18.

p. 162 Yamani: See Oriana Fallaci, "A Sheik Who Hates to Gamble," *The New York Times*, September 14, 1975; Sally Quinn, "The Astrology of Oil and the Art of Survival," *Washington Post*, October 23, 1979; and William D. Smith, "Mastermind for Arab Oil," *The New York Times*, October 8, 1972.

p. 163 Coal: United Nations, *World Energy Supplies, 1929–1950;* and National Coal Association, *Coal Facts 1978–79.*

p. 166 Barran: Senate Sub-Committee, *The International Petroleum Cartel.*

p. 166 Akins: See also J. B. Kelly, *Arabia, the Gulf and the West* (New York: Basic Books, 1980).

p. 166 The Libyan success: Kubbah, *OPEC*, p. 54.

p. 169 Concerted and simultaneous action: OPEC Resolution XXI.120, Vienna, 1971.

p. 169 How very tough: Gurney Breckenfeld, "How the Arabs Changed the Oil Business," *Fortune*, August 1971, pp. 113–116, 190, 197–201.

p. 170 Five thousand years: Quoted in Sampson, *Seven Sisters*, p. 177.

p. 170 *Lawrence of Arabia:* Idem.

p. 171 Their own terms: Breckenfeld, "Arabs Changed the Oil Business," p. 113.

p. 171 Haider: Quoted in Sampson, *Seven Sisters*, p. 240.

p. 172 Changing ratios: Walter J. Levy, "Oil Power," *Foreign Affairs*, July 1971, pp. 652–668.

p. 172 Akins: James E. Akins, "The Oil Crisis: This Time the Wolf Is Here," *Foreign Affairs*, April 1973, pp. 462–490.

p. 172 Table: *BP Statistical Review of the World Oil Industry 1979* (London: British Petroleum Company, 1980), p. 27.

p. 173 Nadim al-Pachaci: See Kelly, *Arabia.*

p. 175 Amouzegar: Quoted in Sampson, *Seven Sisters*, p. 257.

p. 175 Yamani: Quoted in Kelly, *Arabia.*

p. 176 Shah: Quoted in *Middle East Economic Survey*, December 28, 1973.

p. 176 al-Hamad: Personal interview.

p. 180 The French: Quoted in Sampson, *Seven Sisters,* p. 229.

p. 180 "60 Minutes": "The Kissinger-Shah Connection," *60 Minutes,* vol. 21, no. 34 (May 4, 1980). See also Jack Anderson, "Kissinger's Cleared Iran's Oil Gouge," *Washington Post,* December 5, 1979.

p. 181 Simon: "Kissinger-Shah Connection."

p. 183 *Sauve qui peut:* Quoted in Sampson, *Seven Sisters,* p. 229, and rechecked.

p. 183 10-percent inflation: Thurow, *Zero-Sum Society,* p. 41.

p. 184 Kissinger: "Kissinger on Oil, Food, and Trade," *Business Week,* January 13, 1975, pp. 66–76.

p. 184 *The Economist:* "If Compromise Doesn't Work," *The Economist,* May 1975, pp. 35–36.

p. 184 Miles Ignotus: Miles Ignotus, "Seizing Arab Oil," *Harper's,* March 1975, pp. 45–62.

p. 185 Bordeaux wine: Terry Robards, "Wine Talk: A Blow to the Law of Supply and Demand," *The New York Times,* May 7, 1980.

p. 186 Amouzegar: Quoted in Sampson, *Seven Sisters,* p. 301.

p. 187 Rashid: Andrew Duncan, *Money Rush* (New York: Doubleday, 1979), pp. 20–21.

p. 189 National Bureau of Economic Research: Avram Kisselgoff, "The Propagation of Prices in the Oil Industry, 1958–1976," National Bureau of Economic Research, 1980. See also Leonard Silk, "OPEC's Prices and Oil Profits," *The New York Times,* June 11, 1980.

p. 190 Kashoggi: Ibid., p. 236.

p. 193 Renouncing my offspring: *The New York Times,* September 4, 1979. I am grateful to Juan Pablo Perez Castillo, the son of Juan Pablo Perez Alfonso, for some of the material in this section.

p. 195 Frankel: Quoted in "Oil's New Power Structure," *Business Week,* December 24, 1979, pp. 82-88.

p. 196 Texaco: Anthony Sampson, *The Seven Sisters* (New York: Bantam, 1980).

p. 197 al-Sabah: Joseph Kraft, "Letter from OPEC," *The New Yorker,* January 28, 1980.

p. 197 Spot price reflects uncertainty: James Tanner and Rich Jaroslavsky, "Why the Price of Oil Continues to Increase Despite Ample Supply," *The Wall Street Journal,* November 2, 1979.

p. 200 Vice-president of Shell: "Oil's New Power Structure," p. 88.

p. 200 Japan: Ibid.

p. 201 American oil greed: *The Economist,* July 8, 1978, p. 67.

p. 203 One such minister: Colin Legum, ed. *Middle East Contemporary Survey,* vol. 2 (New York: Holmes and Meier, 1979), p. 343.

CHAPTER 8:   WHY THE "ENERGY CRISIS" IS MISNAMED, AND WHY IT IS A FINANCIAL THREAT NO MATTER WHAT THE NAME

p. 206 Resources: See Adam Smith, "The Last Days of Cowboy Capitalism," *Atlantic,* October 1972; and *Supermoney* (New York: Random House, 1972).

p. 206 Doubt that there is one: The pollster Louis Harris told the author, "Cynicism about the oil crisis is very deep. Ironically, only when some Establishment sources began to say there was no real energy crisis did the public *then* begin to believe that there really was one; the public had built in such skepticism that it reversed what it was told."

p. 207 Oil table: *BP Statistical Review of the World Oil Industry 1979,* p. 27. Coal table: United Nations, *World Energy Supplies,* annual.

p. 207 Tripled use of coal: Carroll L. Wilson, ed., *Coal—Bridge to the Future: Report of the World Coal Study* (Cambridge, Mass.: Ballinger, 1980).

p. 208 Infrastructure: "The Coal Goal: How?," *The New York Times,* June 29, 1980.

p. 209 Analysis paralysis: Thurow, *Zero-Sum Society.*

p. 209 Nuclear power plants: U.S. Department of Energy, Energy Information Administration, *Monthly Energy Review,* May 1980, pp. 69–73.

p. 209 Harvard Business School: Robert Stobaugh and Daniel Yergin, eds., *Energy Future: Report of the Energy Project at the Harvard Business School* (New York: Random House, 1979), p. 135.

p. 210 Elephant's fanny: R. W. Scott, *World Oil,* June 1978.

p. 210 Harvard Business School: Modesto A. Maidique, "Solar America," in *Energy Future,* ed. Stobaugh and Yergin, pp. 183–215.

p. 212 40 percent to 4 percent: Daniel Yergin, *The Dependence Dilemma* (Cambridge, Mass.: Center for International Affairs, 1980).

p. 212 Growth–no growth: John G. Myers, "Energy Conservation and Economic Growth—Are They Incompatible?" *The Conference Board Record,* February 1975, pp. 27–32.

p. 212 Conservation industry: Roger Sant, former assistant administrator for Conservation at the Federal Energy Administration, remarks to the Conference Board, September 30, 1975.

p. 213 Polls: Various polls demonstrate this point. See *Gallup Opinion Index,* no. 104 (February 1974); no. 167 (June 1979); and no. 170 (September 1979). See also *The Harris Survey,* February 7, 1974; September 2, 1974; and *ABC News–Harris Survey,* vol. 1, no. 52 (April 30, 1979); vol. 1, no. 70 (June 11, 1979); and vol. 1, no. 62 (May 24, 1979).

p. 213 Failure of the media: Daniel Yergin, "The Real Meaning of the Energy Crunch," *The New York Times Magazine,* June 4, 1978.

p. 214 Gas from shale: U.S. Department of Commerce, *Natural Gas from Unconventional Geologic Sources,* sect. 4 (Washington, D.C.: National Academy of Sciences, 1976).

p. 215 Average well: "World Oil Review," *Oil and Gas Journal,* December 1979. Figures for the United States are from *The Petroleum Industry in Your State,* 1979, and from Energy Information Administration, *Monthly Energy Review.*

p. 216 Table: "Oil in the U.S. Energy Perspective—a Forecast to 1990," prepared by the Petroleum Industry Research Foundation, New York, May 1980.

CHAPTER 9: THE SAUDI CONNECTION: THE KINGDOM AND THE POWER

p. 222 How much oil: The U.S. Department of Energy estimates that Saudi Arabia has proved crude oil reserves of 166.5 billion barrels. By contrast, the United States has only 26.5 billion barrels. Energy Information Administration, *Annual Report to Congress,* 1979, vol. 2, p. 36.

p. 223 Swiss steward: Jose Arnold, *Golden Swords, and Pots and Pans* (New York: Harcourt, Brace and World, 1963).

p. 226 Per-capita income: See also Adam Smith, "The Arabs, Their Money and Ours," *Atlantic,* February 1978.

p. 231 John Hubbard: Anthony Cook, "The California-Saudi Connection," *New West,* July 3, 1978, pp. 43–49.

p. 231 Robert Fluor: L. J. Davis, "Consorting with Arabs," *Harper's,* July 1980, pp. 39–48.

p. 231 Princeton: *The New York Times,* March 4, 1980.

The following books provide background material on the Kingdom: H. St. John Philby, *Saudi Arabia* (London: Benn, 1955); Bayly Winder, *Saudi Arabia in the Nineteenth Century* (London: Macmillan, 1965); David Howarth, *The Desert King: A Life of Ibn Saud* (London: Collins, 1964); and Peter Habday, *Saudi Arabia Today: An Introduction to the Richest Oil Power* (London: Macmillan, 1978).

CHAPTER 10: RECYCLING THE PETRODOLLARS: TREACHEROUS SEAS, GALE-FORCE WINDS, FIRE!

p. 244 David Rockefeller: Quoted in Richard F. Janssen and Philip Revzin, "World's Bankers Face Big Task of Recycling OPEC Surplus Fund," *The Wall Street Journal,* February 20, 1980.

p. 247 Exchange surplus: International Monetary Fund, *International Financial Statistics*, August 1980.

p. 247 Japanese were Protestants: Robert Bellah, *Tokugawa Religion* (Boston: Beacon Press, 1957).

p. 253 Paul McCracken: Quoted in Norman Gall, "How Much More Can the System Take?" *Forbes*, June 23, 1980, pp. 91–98.

p. 253 Euroland: The mechanics of the Euromarket are explained more fully in Geoffrey Bell, *The Euro-Dollar Market and the International Financial System* (New York: John Wiley and Sons, 1973); and in "The Euromarket," *Columbia Journal of World Business*, vol. 14, no. 3 (Fall 1979). I wish to thank Geoffrey Bell for his assistance.

p. 253 Wilfried Guth: Wilfried Guth, "The Problems Raised by the Growth of International Bank Lending," speech given on the occasion of the International Monetary Conference, June 2, 1980. See also Robert A. Bennett, "A 'Safety Net' for Banks Is Proposed," *The New York Times*, June 3, 1980.

p. 255 LIBOR: Guth, "Problems Raised."

p. 257 $200 billion: *World Financial Markets*, July 1980.

p. 259 Panic of 1907: Milton Friedman and Anna Jacobson Schwartz, *A Monetary History of the United States 1867–1960* (Princeton: Princeton University Press, 1963), pp. 170–173.

p. 260 Lending limits: See Janssen and Revsin, "World's Bankers Face Big Task"; and *World Financial Markets*, December 1979.

p. 261 $33 billion: *International Financial Statistics*, August 1980.

p. 262 Jelle Zijlstra: Quoted in Paul Lewis, "Banker Warns on Oil Price Rise," *The New York Times*, June 10, 1980.

p. 262 *dar-Islam:* Kelly, *Arabia.*

p. 263 Sixty biggest banks in the world:

THE WORLD'S LARGEST BANKS, BY DEPOSITS, 1979

Rank		Country	Deposits (U.S. $ millions)
1	Banque Nationale de Paris	France	$87,185
2	Credit Agricole	France	85,730
3	Deutsche Bank	W. Germany	85,148
4	BankAmerica Corp.	U.S.	84,984
5	Credit Lyonnais	France	80,965
6	Societe Generale	France	76,961
7	Citibank	U.S.	70,556
8	Dresdner Bank	W. Germany	66,464
9	National Westminster Bank	U.K.	58,982
10	Barclays Bank	U.K.	58,444

Rank		Country	Deposits (U.S. $ millions)
11	Westdeutsche Landesbank	W. Germany	57,569
12	Commerzbank	W. Germany	55,306
13	Dai-Ichi Kangyo Bank	Japan	51,540
14	Chase Manhattan Bank	U.S.	49,354
15	Fuji Bank	Japan	47,300
16	Sumitomo Bank	Japan	46,900
17	Bayerische Vereinsbank	W. Germany	45,409
18	Mitsubishi Bank	Japan	44,500
19	Centrale Rabobank	Netherlands	43,715
20	Sanwa Bank	Japan	43,330
21	Amsterdam-Rotterdam Bank	Netherlands	42,445
22	Bayerische Landesbank	W. Germany	42,231
23	Industrial Bank of Japan	Japan	42,060
24	Royal Bank of Canada	Canada	40,678
25	Hypo-Bank	W. Germany	40,580
26	Algemene Bank Nederland	Netherlands	40,422
27	Midland Bank	U.K.	40,093
28	Banca Nazionale de Lavoro	Italy	39,800
29	Swiss Bank Corp.	Switzerland	37,922
30	Manufacturers Hanover Trust	U.S.	37,800
31	Canadian Imperial Bk. of Com.	Canada	37,421
32	Union Bank of Switzerland	Switzerland	35,878
33	Lloyds Bank	U.K.	35,575
34	Long-Term Credit Bank	Japan	34,290
35	Banca Commerciale Italiana	Italy	33,300
36	Bank of Tokyo	Japan	32,490
37	Tokai Bank	Japan	32,010
38	Societe Generale de Banque	Belgium	31,893
39	Credit Suisse	Switzerland	30,467
40	Morgan Guaranty Trust	U.S.	30,298
41	Bank fur Gemeinwirtschaft	W. Germany	29,971
42	Mitsui Bank	Japan	29,880
43	Taiyo Kobe Bank	Japan	29,750
44	Mitsubishi Trust & Banking	Japan	29,370
45	Chemical Bank	U.S.	28,987
46	Bank of Montreal	Canada	28,721
47	Credito Italiano	Italy	28,300
48	Sumitomo Trust & Banking	Japan	27,880
49	Bank of Nova Scotia	Canada	27,365
50	Daiwa Bank	Japan	27,030
51	Mitsui Trust & Banking	Japan	26,020
52	Standard Chartered Bank	U.K.	25,246
53	Banco di Roma	Italy	25,200
54	Hessische Landesbank	W. Germany	24,128
55	Continental Illinois	U.S.	23,751
56	Bq. de Paris et des Pays-Bas	France	23,665
57	Monte dei Paschi di Siena	Italy	23,510
58	Bankers Trust Corp.	U.S.	22,437
59	Nippon Credit Bank	Japan	22,270
60	Norddeutsche Landesbank	W. Germany	21,971

Source: *Institutional Investor*, July 1980.

p. 266 Broadway actress: Sallie Brophy.

CHAPTER 11:   THE STOCK MARKET: WHAT DO WE DO ON MONDAY MORNING?

p. 268 Waterloo: Elizabeth Longford, *Wellington* (New York: Harper & Row, 1969).

p. 270 Trading volume: Friedman and Schwartz, *Monetary History;* and Standard & Poor, Inc., New York.

p. 271 Table: Salomon Brothers, New York.

p. 271 Crashed in the 1970s: James H. Lorie, "The Second Great Crash," *The Wall Street Journal,* June 2, 1980.

p. 273 *Business Week:* "The Death of Equities," *Business Week,* August 13, 1979, pp. 54–59.

p. 273 Lorie: Lorie, "Second Great Crash."

p. 274 Random walk: Burton G. Malkiel, *A Random Walk Down Wall Street* (New York: W. W. Norton, 1973); and "What the Hell Is a Random Walk?" in Smith, *Money Game.*

p. 275 Beta: Anise Wallace, "Is Beta Dead?," *Institutional Investor,* July 1980, pp. 22–30; and "Beta, or Speak to Me Softly in Algebra," in Smith, *Supermoney.*

p. 277 Irving Fisher: Irving Fisher, *Theory of Interest* (Clifton, N.J.: Augustus M. Kelley, 1956).

p. 277 Bonds yielded 3 or 4 percent: Warren E. Buffett, "How Inflation Swindles the Equity Investor," *Fortune,* May 1977, p. 251.

p. 277 Stocks were undervalued: Franco Modigliani and Richard A. Cohn, "Inflation, Rational Valuation, and the Market," *Financial Analysts Journal,* March–April 1979, pp. 24–44.

p. 278 80 percent of their funds: Securities and Exchange Commission.

p. 279 Institutional investors: Salomon Brothers, New York.

p. 279 Pension-fund assets: U.S. Department of Labor; *Pensions and Investments* magazine; Towers, Perrin, Forster and Crosby, Philadelphia.

p. 281 Farmland . . . East Germany: Doesn't match the official figures, but supposedly true under other names. See "Drang Nach USA," *Forbes,* July 7, 1980.

p. 284 Joseph Schumpeter: Joseph Schumpeter, *Capitalism, Socialism, and Democracy* (New York: Harper and Bros., 1942), pp. 81–86.

p. 284 *Fortune:* A. F. Ehrbar, "Giant Payoff from Midget Stocks," *Fortune,* June 30, 1980, pp. 111–114.

p. 285 Ibbotson . . . Banz: Ibid.

p. 285 Merrill Lynch: Robert Metz, "Finding the Value of a Stock," *The New York Times,* January 24, 1980.

p. 285 21,000 public companies: Securities and Exchange Commission.

p. 286 *Achetez aux canons:* Thanks to John Train.

CHAPTER 12: WHAT PAPER MONEY MEANS

p. 293 Chart: Salomon Brothers, New York.

p. 296 A Harvard sociologist: Professor Ezra Vogel. See *Japan As No. 1* (Cambridge, Mass.: Harvard University Press, 1979).

p. 297 A sober insurance company executive: Ashby Bladen, Guardian Life, in *How to Cope with the Developing Financial Crisis* (New York: McGraw-Hill, 1980).

p. 297 A bridge that can be defended: Ibid., p. 139.

p. 299 James Burke: James Burke, *Connections* (Boston: Little, Brown, 1978).

p. 300 *Teredo navalis:* Ibid.

BIBLIOGRAPHY

References to daily newspapers and to weekly and monthly magazines are in the Notes and are not repeated in this bibliography.

Akins, James E. "The Oil Crisis: This Time the Wolf Is Here." *Foreign Affairs,* April 1973.

Anderson, James E., et al. *Texas Politics.* New York: Harper & Row, 1971.

Arnold, Jose. *Golden Swords, and Pots and Pans.* New York: Harcourt, Brace and World, 1963.

Bank for International Settlements. 49th annual report. Basle. June 1979.

Bell, Geoffrey. *The Euro-Dollar Market and the International Financial System.* New York: John Wiley and Sons, 1973.

Bellah, Robert. *Tokugawa Religion.* Boston: Beacon Press, 1957.

Benton, Wilbourn E. *Texas: Its Government and Politics.* Englewood Cliffs, N.J.: Prentice-Hall, 1972.

Bergsten, C. Fred. *The Dilemmas of the Dollar.* New York: Council on Foreign Relations, New York University Press, 1975.

Betancourt, Romulo. *Venezuela: Oil and Politics.* Boston: Houghton Mifflin, 1979.

Blair, John. *The Control of Oil.* New York: Pantheon, 1977.

British Petroleum Co. *BP Statistical Review of the World Oil Industry.* Annual.

Brownlee, W. Elliot. *Dynamics of Ascent.* New York: Knopf, 1978.

Chase Manhattan Bank. *Eurocurrency Financing.* The corporation, 1975.

Clowes, Sir William Laird. *The Royal Navy.* London: Sampson Low, Marsten and Co., 1903.

Collin, Fernand. *The Eurodollar Market: Source of Inflationary Demand.* Committee for Monetary Research and Education, Inc. June 1978.

Conant, James Bryant. *On Understanding Science.* New Haven: Yale University Press, 1947.

Craig, Sir John. *The Mint.* Cambridge, 1953.

Dillard, Dudley. *Economic Development of the North Atlantic Community.* Englewood Cliffs, N.J.: Prentice-Hall, 1967.

Duncan, Andrew. *Money Rush.* New York: Doubleday, 1979.

Einzig, Paul, and Quinn, Brian Scott. *The Eurodollar System.* London, 1977.

Feaveryear, Sir Albert. *The Pound Sterling.* Oxford: Clarendon Press, 1963.

Federal Energy Administration, Committee on Finance. *Energy Statistics.*

Federal Highway Administration. *Highway Statistics.* Annual.

Fergusson, Adam. *When Money Dies: The Nightmare of the Weimar Collapse.* London: Kimber, 1975.

Fischer, Stanley, and Dornbusch, Rudiger. *Macroeconomics.* New York: McGraw-Hill, 1978.

"Focus: the Euromarket." *Columbia Journal of World Business,* Fall 1979.

Friedman, Milton, and Schwartz, Anna Jacobson. *A Monetary History of the United States 1867–1960.* Princeton: Princeton University Press, 1963.

Galbraith, John K. *The Great Crash, 1929.* Boston: Houghton Mifflin, 1972.

Gough, Robert, and Siegel, Robin. "Why Inflation Becomes Worse." *Data Resources Review,* January 1979.

Guttmann, William. *The Great Inflation, Germany 1919–1923.* Farnborough, England: Saxon House, 1975.

Habday, Peter. *Saudi Arabia Today: An Introduction to the Richest Oil Power.* London: Macmillan, 1978.

Halberstam, David. *The Best and the Brightest.* New York: Random House, 1972.

Harrod, Sir Roy. *The Life of John Maynard Keynes.* London: Macmillan, 1951.

Heller, Walter. *New Dimensions of Political Economy.* Cambridge, Mass.: Harvard University Press, 1966.

Hicks, Sir John. *Causality in Economics.* Oxford: Blackwell, 1979.

Hirst, David. *Oil and Public Opinion in the Middle East.* London, 1966.

Horsefield, J. Keith. *The International Monetary Fund 1945–1965.* Washington, D.C., 1969.

Howarth, David. *The Desert King: A Life Of Ibn Saud.* London: Collins, 1964.

International Monetary Fund (IMF). *The First Ten Years of the International Monetary Fund 1945–1955.* Washington, D.C., 1956.

International Monetary Fund. *International Financial Statistics.* Monthly.

The International Petroleum Cartel, the Iranian Consortium, and U.S. National Security, report of the Senate Subcommittee on Multinational Corporations, February 1974. Washington, D.C.: U.S. Government Printing Office, 1974.

The International Petroleum Cartel, a staff report to the Federal Trade Commission, submitted to the Subcommittee on Monopoly of the Select Committee on Small Business, United States Senate, August 22, 1952. Washington, D.C.: U.S. Government Printing Office, 1975.

Kaufman, Henry; McKeon, James; and Foster, David. *1980 Prospectus for Financial Markets.* New York: Salomon Brothers, 1980.

Kelly, J.B. *Arabia, the Gulf and the West.* New York: Basic Books, 1980.

Kenen, Peter. *Reserve Asset Preferences of Central Banks and Stability of the Gold Exchange Standard.* Princeton: Princeton University Department of Economics, 1963.

Keynes, John Maynard. *The Collected Writings,* 16 vols. New York: St. Martin's Press, 1971.

———. *The Economic Consequences of the Peace,* London: Macmillan, 1919.

———. *The General Theory of Employment, Interest and Money.* London: Macmillan, 1936.

Keynes, Milo, ed. *Essays on John Maynard Keynes.* London: Cambridge University Press, 1975.

Kisselgoff, Avram. "The Propagation of Prices in the Oil Industry, 1958–1976." National Bureau of Economic Research, 1980.

Kubbah, Abdul Amir Q. *OPEC: Past and Present.* Vienna, 1974.

Laursen, Karsten, and Pederson, Jorgen. *The German Inflation, 1918–1923.* Amsterdam, 1964.

Legum, Colin. *Middle East Contemporary Survey.* New York: Holmes and Meier, 1979.

Lekachman, Robert. *The Age of Keynes.* New York: McGraw-Hill, 1975.

———. *Economists at Bay.* New York: McGraw-Hill, 1976.

Leontief, Wassily. "Theoretical Assumptions and Nonobservable Facts." *American Economic Review,* March 1971.

Levy, Walter J. "Oil Power." *Foreign Affairs,* July 1971.

———. "Oil and the Decline of the West." *Foreign Affairs,* summer 1980.

Longford, Elizabeth, *Wellington.* New York: Harper & Row, 1969.

McCleskey, C. *The Government and Politics of Texas.* Boston: Little, Brown, 1975.

MacCorkle, Stuart. *Texas Government.* New York: McGraw-Hill, 1974.

McKinnon, Ronald I. "The Eurocurrency Market." *Essays in International Finance,* no. 125, December 1977.

Malkiel, Burton G. *The Inflation Beater's Investment Guide.* New York: W.W. Norton, 1980.

———. *A Random Walk Down Wall Street.* New York: W.W. Norton, 1973.

Mayer, Martin. *The Builders.* New York: W.W. Norton, 1978.

———. *The Fate of the Dollar.* New York: Times Books, 1980.

Mayer, Thomas. "Economics as Hard Science: Realistic Goal or Wishful Thinking?" *Economic Inquiry,* vol. xviii, April 1980.

Mendelsohn, M. S. *Money on the Move.* New York: McGraw-Hill, 1980.

Middle East Contemporary Survey, vol. II.

Middle East Economic Digest. Weekly.

Middle East Economic Survey. Weekly.

Mikdashi, Zuhayr. *The Community of Oil Exporting Countries.* London, 1972.

Modigliani, Franco, and Cohn, Richard A. "Inflation, Rational Valuation, and the Market," *Financial Analysts Journal,* March–April 1979.

Morgan Guaranty Trust Co. *World Financial Markets.* Monthly.

Myers, John G. "Energy Conservation and Economic Growth—Are They Compatible?" *The Conference Board Record,* February 1975.

National Coal Association. *Coal Facts,* 1978–79.

Odell, Peter. *Oil and World Power.* New York: Taplinger, 1975.

"The Oil Crisis: In Perspective." *Daedalus,* Journal of the American Academy of Arts and Sciences, Fall 1975.

OPEC Bulletin, Vienna. Monthly.

OPEC. *Review and Record.* Vienna. Monthly.

Organization of Petroleum Exporting Countries (OPEC). *Annual Statistical Bulletin.* Vienna.

Philby, H. St. John. *Saudi Arabia.* London: Benn, 1955.

Ratner, Sidney; Soltow, James; and Sylla, Richard. *The Evolution of the American Economy.* New York: Basic Books, 1980.

Ringer, Fritz, ed. *The German Inflation of 1923.* New York: Oxford University Press, 1969.

Robinson, E. A. G. *John Maynard Keynes: Economist, Author, Statesman.* New York: Oxford University Press, 1971.

Roosa, Robert V. *The Dollar and World Liquidity.* New York: Random House, 1967.

Rustow, Dankwart A., and Mugno, John R. *OPEC: Success and Prospects.* New York: New York University Press, 1976.

Sampson, Anthony. *The Seven Sisters.* New York: Viking Press, 1975.

Samuelson, Paul. *Economics.* New York: McGraw-Hill, 1973.

———. *Readings in Economics.* New York: McGraw-Hill, 1973.

Schumpeter, Joseph. *Capitalism, Socialism, and Democracy.* New York: Harper and Bros., 1942.

Sherbiny, N. A. *Arab Oil.* New York: Praeger, 1976.

Smith, Adam. *The Money Game.* New York: Random House, 1968.

———. *Supermoney.* New York: Random House, 1972.

Spero, Joan Edelman. *The Failure of the Franklin National Bank.* New York: Columbia University Press, 1980.

Starr, Roger. *Housing and the Money Market.* New York: Basic Books, 1975.

Sterling, Bryan B., ed. *The Will Rogers Scrapbook.* New York: Grosset and Dunlap, 1976.

Stern, Carl H.; Makin, John H.; and Logue, Dennis E. *Eurocurrencies and the International Monetary System.* Washington, D.C.: American Enterprise Institute for Public Policy Research, 1976.

Stobaugh, Robert, and Yergin, Daniel, eds. *Energy Future: Report of the Energy Project at the Harvard Business School.* New York: Random House, 1979.

Thurow, Lester C. *The Zero-Sum Society.* New York: Basic Books, 1980.

Triffin, Robert. *Gold and the Dollar Crisis.* New Haven: Yale University Press, 1961.

Tugwell, Franklin. *The Politics of Oil in Venezuela.* Stanford, Calif.: Stanford University Press, 1975.

Turner, Louis. *Oil Companies in the International System.* London: Royal Institute of International Affairs, 1978.

United Nations Statistical Office. *World Energy Supplies.* Annual.

United States Central Intelligence Agency. *The International Energy Situation: Outlook to 1985.* Washington, D.C., 1977.

U.S. Department of Commerce. *National Gas from Unconventional Geologic Sources.* Washington, D.C.: National Academy of Sciences, 1976.

U.S. Department of Commerce. *Statistical Abstract of the United States.* Washington, D.C.: U.S. Government Printing Office. Annual.

U.S. Department of Energy, Energy Information Administration. *Report to Congress.* Annual.

———. *Monthly Energy Review.*

Whorf, Benjamin Lee. *Language, Thought, and Reality.* Cambridge, Mass.: Technology Press, 1956.

Wilson, Carroll L., ed. *Coal—Bridge to the Future: Report of the World Coal Study.* Cambridge, Mass.: Ballinger, 1980.

Wilson, Neill C., and Taylor, Frank. *Southern Pacific.* New York: McGraw-Hill, 1952.

Winder, Bayly. *Saudi Arabia in the Nineteenth Century.* London: Macmillan, 1965.

Zamyatin, Yevgeni. *We.* New York: Bantam, 1972.

INDEX

About the Author

In 1966, an editor at *New York* magazine placed the name "Adam Smith" on a lively, irreverent, pseudonymous column, using quotation marks to emphasize that this was not the eighteenth-century economist. The pseudonym masked for only about a year the identity of George J. W. Goodman. Mr. Goodman has had a double career in finance and letters. Born in St. Louis, he was graduated from Harvard magna cum laude. As a Rhodes scholar at Oxford, he wrote a novel instead of a Ph.D. thesis, which was published as *The Bubble Makers.* He went to work on Wall Street, first as a magazine editor, then as a securities analyst and fund manager, and, writing evenings and weekends, published three more novels, one of which, *The Wheeler Dealers,* also became a successful film.

The "Adam Smith" columns brought together the unique combination of financial and literary talent and won an international audience of investment professionals. Mr. Goodman became a co-founder of *New York,* of two more regional magazines, *New West* and *New Jersey Monthly,* and of the financial journal *Institutional Investor.* He has been a member of the Editorial Board of *The New York Times.* Among his corporate directorships are those of a worldwide hotel chain and a major airline.

Paper Money is the fourth "Adam Smith" book. The others are *The Money Game, Supermoney* and *Powers of Mind.*